Cuts Close to the Heart

by

Ezekiel Nieto Benzion

"If I am not for myself, then who will be for me?
And if I am only for myself, then what am I?
And if not now, when?"

Hillel the Elder (1st century BCE)

The Second Tale in a series based on
The Judah Halevi Journals

Original edition published: March 2014
Publisher: Ezekiel Nieto Benzion Publications

This book is dedicated to
the members
of my family who
have overcome great challenges
and are helping others to do the same.

Acknowledgements

Writers spend many hours alone. They can do that only because other people, especially spouses, take on much of the rest of life that might disrupt the creative process. I thank my dearest supporter for bearing up under the strain of the additional work and my obsession with the lives of my characters.

Close friends have read snippets of this work and shared their enthusiastic support. As always, I am grateful that they took the awkward spiral-bound drafts with them everywhere to review and to comment on while they went about their busy lives. And particularly, that they postponed reading all those other books, to read and help me edit mine.

The Tales from the Judah Halevi Journals

You Shall Know Our Names (2013)
Cuts Close to My Heart (Spring, 2014)
Claims of Family (coming Summer, 2014)

Contact the author at EzekielNBenzion@gmail.com for updates on the series as the tales unfold.

Foreword

The tale of how the journals of my ancestor, Doctor Judah Halevi Nieto, were given to me by my grandfather, Reuben Nieto Benzion, is described in detail in the first book in this series called *You Shall Know Our Names*. Readers of that book learned that my family preserved the journals, maps and diagrams of the doctor, a self-taught engineer as well as a well-regarded surgeon, for more than 200 years—while Europe was roiled by multiple wars and the Jewish communities swallowed up in waves of genocidal disasters.

The journals however were not diaries per se. Judah Halevi had a brilliant mind interested in diverse subjects ranging from medicine to physics, music, philosophy and religious studies. The journals are notebooks that record his experiments, his readings and his correspondence with other men of learning.

We know from his drawings that he worked on the various mechanical devices that became critical in the story that follows. He also recalled his medical adventures. So, for example, he recorded the incident of the malady that occurred aboard ship. He also described in detail the surgical procedure of adult male circumcision—needed for ritual conversions, for resolution of medical issues and for other symbolic purposes.

However, he did not tell us everything about his life. For example, he chose to not tell us directly how much he was involved in efforts to thwart Napoleon's spies who sought to disrupt the flow of information among the allies. He also revealed very few details about his other activities that many today would call vigilantism. If his journals allude to any of these efforts, names are disguised, places identified only with a single letter and dates are vague. And he did not reveal how his early hopes for a life filled with love, family and good works were raised and then dashed as his secret work took him from London back to Gibraltar and later into hiding.

But others have written about the same times and places described in Judah Halevi's journals. I have had the privilege to study many of those documents. So while the first book in the series was developed largely from Judah Halevi's own notes, this second book has its genesis in other places.

The story told here was recalled largely by Samuel Wharton, who became the Earl of Aylesford after his father's death in 1828. At the distance of more than twenty years from the events, when the wars with Napoleon had begun to recede into history, the Earl told the story of his first experiments with Judah Nieto and the adventures that grew to involve his entire family. Some of what he recounts—the parts that he had not witnessed himself— he had learned from his brother, Ariel Wharton, who became Viscount Embry when his elder brother was elevated to the earldom. The journals are held by the Aylesford Trust in the former country home of the family.

The Baron von Tedesco left journals as well. They are now in the custody of the Central Synagogue Council of Austria. By reading the Baron's journals, it was possible to confirm dates and places and to learn how the communication links between the allies were created and maintained. And in the journals of both the Baron and the Earl, Judah Halevi has an honored place. Referred to sometimes as J.H. or as J.N., it is clear that the doctor was admired for his courage, his intellect and his determination to wrest some iota of justice from a callous world.

What we do not have are any written documents from Ezekiel Benzion, a key figure—almost mythical in power— in all the drama in the series of journals. The nagid (leader) of the nokmim (the avengers) of Bohemia, Ezekiel was the man to whom Judah Halevi had the greatest allegiance. But, as was his style, Ezekiel had no wish to leave evidence and no need to explain why he did what he did. "Words can be tools used to distort history. Let our deeds speak to the ages," he was supposed to have proclaimed and so that is all we have—the deeds done on his orders and the stories about them—to which I hope I have done justice.

So I remind my readers that these books are fictionalized accounts of cryptic notes written in codes in Judah Halevi's journals, but supported by documents dispersed throughout Europe and by the remnants of physical evidence that have been spared the devastation wrought by hate and war. I wanted to make these people come alive again—recognizing that their decisions about what was right and just might seem harsh to our modern sensibilities but honoring their strength to face terrible odds to seek retribution and justice in the world in which they lived.

May these words do justice to their memory.

Ezekiel Nieto Benzion
New York, NY

One

London, 1804

Lady Elizabeth Wharton bounced on her toes, craning to see over the shoulders of the men crowded at the railing, as the handler put the grays through their paces. She grabbed her tall brother's sleeve, "Samuel, what do you think of them?"

One sharp look from her brother reminded her that his name was properly "Embry" in public and "Samuel" only amongst family, but her enthusiasm could not be quelled so easily. She began again, "Embry, the gray horses are beautiful, are they not? I just love, love, love them."

Samuel Wharton, the Viscount Embry, now smiled down at his petite sister with the bouncing curls that were no longer pinned back as her excitement bubbled up with her eager words. "Eliza, you must calm yourself. It is not done to let others know your interest. They are pretty, I agree, but I don't like that the left leans on his foreleg. I am suspicious of an injury on that side. I await Rettick's report. Meanwhile, let's take a look at the bays in the barn."

He turned, offering his right arm to his sister, using his other hand to grasp the silver-topped cane that he needed to support his left leg. He began walking to the barns, limping heavily but holding himself stiffly erect.

Elizabeth tried not to let her disappointment show. She just wished Embry would not be so overbearing. The grays were beautiful. She could see herself in her lady's cart parading them through the park with everyone admiring the horses and her driving skill as she handled them. In contrast, the bays looked, well, just ordinary.

This was to be her eighteenth birthday gift from her brother. While she appreciated Embry's generosity, she wished he did not insist on making all the decisions in her life. Just once couldn't she decide what she wanted?

At these times she missed her father, the Earl of Aylesford, most of all. She knew that he at least would care about her opinion. She also knew, if she was truly honest with herself, that she could wrap him about her little finger. But he was away somewhere—"in His Majesty's service," her mother proclaimed—and Embry was now the head of the family—cautious and domineering Embry. She sighed in frustration.

She had to admit though that Embry knew horseflesh. He was known for his carriage racing stable and his daring as a whip in a sport in which his damaged leg was only a minor hindrance.

He had spent many hours teaching both her and her twin brother Ariel to handle carriage pairs. She had become quite the expert horsewoman under Embry's tutelage, although, as he always reminded her, with a tendency to be overconfident. Ariel, on the other hand, was a steady driver, with a calm that allowed him to succeed in racing when others lost focus in their excitement.

She looked sideways at her older brother as they walked towards the stock barns. He was the image of their handsome father with the same auburn hair glinting copper in the sun and the same Wharton patrician profile. His eyes were his best feature, green with gold flecks, fringed with dark, thick, long lashes and emphasized by gracefully arched brows.

His expression however was often just as it was now—jaws clenched and lips firmly tightened against pain. His strong personality and self-assurance made it easy for others to forget just how much energy it took him to get through each day, hampered as he was by his damaged leg. Elizabeth immediately felt guilty over her unkind thoughts. She sighed in resignation.

Rettick, the head of Embry's stable, approached. Embry asked, "Well, what did you discover about the breeder? Is it the McFarlan stable?"

"Your eye is accurate as always, milord. McFarlan brought the grays over just last week. The groom has been rather closed mouth about the training schedule. Seems no one has seen them pacing since last season. At that time, they placed in several meets. Given McFarlan's reputation, I believe your suspicions might be well-founded. Something happened between last season and this'n."

Embry frowned. "And the bays are from the Tremaine farm? I've seen the trainer handling them and I like the way they respond. Tremaine always has quality cattle—but the best is that he spends time on training. Eliza, the bays are most likely the better of the pairs."

They had approached the barns. While Embry went to speak with the trainer, Elizabeth took another look at the bays. They were handsome, she had to admit. With her brother's guidance, she had learned much about working with horses. She watched the stable boys groom the bays and noted how they responded with affection and yet still seemed spirited.

"So, Elizabeth, are these your favorites?" Ariel, her twin brother, was putting his sketch pad away in his shoulder satchel as he approached. "Nice color they are. They will look well with your hair and your green riding dress."

"Ariel, my dear, I think that is the very best reason to buy them. I might dress them up in ribbons and feathers to match my outfits!" she said with a pronounced lisp and a toss of her head.

Ariel laughed out loud as he put his arm around his twin's waist. He knew that she was acting "missish," mimicking one of the young ladies in the ton whose looks he had praised. He readily admitted that the beautiful young woman was not too sharp about the world outside the modiste's shop. Definitely not up to Elizabeth's standards—Elizabeth whose curiosity and interests knew few bounds of protocol—to his brother Embry's chagrin and Ariel's admiration.

She was now smiling back at Ariel with affection. The twins were stunners as a matched set themselves—both had light brown curly hair with dramatic blond and gold streaks, almond-shaped green eyes, and slender builds. There was a delicate look to their appearances making them appear younger than their almost eighteen years.

Their father, the Earl, always said that Elizabeth was cherubic until she spoke up. Then she emerged as a strong individual with definite opinions, setting the other family members to laughing out loud or shaking their heads in consternation. Her spirit showed in her quick wit, her high energy and her vibrant personality. She found it hard to be quiet and discreet.

Ariel by contrast was thoughtful, letting his siblings take center stage. His calm demeanor and friendly gaze charmed others into confiding in him, struck by his sympathetic air. His was a quiet disposition, deep and reflective and often underestimated. Although willing to stay in the background, the family knew that he missed very little. When he spoke, everyone attended to him, aware that he could get to the heart of the matter with a few pointed words. And often, when he did, he was very funny.

Embry approached the twins. "I have two other pairs I want to see plus a brood mare."

Ariel groaned in mock anguish and rolled his eyes at Elizabeth.

"I note your enthusiasm, Ariel. Why don't you both go to the tea room and wait for me there? The auction starts at four of the clock and I want to be there at the start."

Embry turned and walked slowly back down the stable row, leaning heavily on his cane. Halfway down, he stopped when a tall dark-haired man approached and bowed to him. Bowing in return, Embry drew closer to the man so that they could speak privately. He shook his head a few times then walked on with the stranger, listening intently to him.

"Come, Eliza," Ariel said, "let's do take tea. I want to show you some sketches I made while in the paddock."

After ordering refreshments, he took the sketch book from his shoulder bag and flipped to some quick drawings of the horses and grooms he had been observing. He stopped when he heard someone behind him clear his throat.

"Pardon me. Do I have the honor of speaking with Sir Ariel Wharton?" a blond-haired young man bowed to them. "I am Mr. Philip Bonner. I believe we met at the Academy gallery opening Wednesday last."

Ariel rose. "Mr. Bonner, forgive me. I was indeed at the gallery opening. We might have been introduced but it was such a crush, I don't remember anything very clearly—except the art, of course. Allow me to present my sister, Lady Elizabeth. Would you like to join us for tea?"

"No, thank ye, but I would have a seat if you please. I have been walking the stables and saw your brother looking at some handsome pairs. Is he considering any in particular?"

Ariel shrugged his shoulders. "I am not the one to ask. But Lady Elizabeth has been tutored by our brother Embry. She would know where his interests lie."

As Elizabeth looked at the blond young man's beautiful blue eyes, her words tripped out, "Yes, Mr. Bonner, Embry is seeking a pair for my cart. 'tis to be a birthday gift for me."

"Viscount Embry is well known for his stable. Is he looking at the grays?"

"I believe so. Aren't they glorious? But he is thinking that the bays from Tremaine's stable might be more appropriate. He believes they have been well trained."

They all looked up when they heard the tapping of Embry's cane. As he approached, he said sternly, "Lady Elizabeth, Sir Ariel, we need to go to the ring. Excuse me, sir. We must move on." Embry made a bow to the young Mr. Bonner then gestured impatiently with his right hand. "I am sorry to be so abrupt but it is time."

Mr. Bonner bowed in response before turning away. After he had disappeared into the throng, Elizabeth fumed, "Samuel, you were so rude to him. Lud, I cannot stand when you forge into conversations, pushing everyone out of your way. We were just chatting about the horses."

Embry looked down his nose at his sister. "Let me ask you, Elizabeth, just how much information did you share with young Mr. Bonner about our interests? I wager that you will see that your conversation costs us dearly at ringside. I noticed him trailing me around the stables earlier."

At the auction ring, the Whartons occupied a center position that permitted the auctioneer to notice any subtle finger or hand motion from the Viscount. Embry cautioned the twins to keep their hands and voices down as the bidding commenced. Rettick sat one row behind him with the list of horses on offer, which the two men reviewed, speaking in whispers.

The first few horses that went up on auction garnered final bids that were lower than expected. The auctioneer's frustration showed as the owners stomped their feet in disappointment at the prices their stock was fetching.

When a handsome black mare came up next, the auctioneer announced the lineage then asked for ten pounds to start the bidding. The ring was silent. "Eight pounds, ten shillings?" he asked. "Eight?"

Embry moved his right hand, raising one finger. "I have eight. Do I have eight-ten? I now have eight-ten. Nine?" Embry sat still. "I have nine. Do I have nine-ten?" Embry did not move. "I have nine-ten. Do I have ten?" Embry sat motionless.

"Ten. Do I hear ten-ten? I have ten-ten. Do I have eleven pounds? Eleven? Is it all over at ten pounds, ten shillings? Calling it at ten-ten?" Embry moved his finger. "I have eleven. Do I have eleven-ten? Is it all over at eleven pounds? Calling it at eleven pounds? Done."

Elizabeth looked at Embry. "But why did you wait so long?"

"Sssh," he hissed. Rettick leaned over and spoke in Embry's ear. Embry nodded, pointing to an item on the list.

The bays came up next. The bidding started at twenty pounds for the pair. Embry sat still, waiting to see the interest in the bays. The price rose slowly to twenty-six then slowed. Embry nodded at the auctioneer and his bid of twenty-seven pounds was accepted. As the final call was made, there was a sudden bid of twenty-eight from the back.

Rettick looked back at the bidder then whispered to Embry who raised his hand to bid an aggressive thirty. An answering bid of thirty-one came promptly from the rear. Embry nodded thirty-two at the auctioneer's look. Thirty-three was the offer from the rear. Thirty-four from Embry. Thirty-five came again from the rear. The auctioneer jumped to forty pounds. Embry nodded. There was a pause from the back. The auctioneer closed the bid at forty.

Elizabeth grabbed Embry's sleeve. "How wonderful! Thank you, dear brother."

Embry looked at her harshly. "That was dear, Eliza. They should have gone for thirty but I had competition from Bonner's sire in the back. Your tea conversation cost us dearly as I had thought it would."

The grays came out later in the auction. They made a wonderful impression as they were led around the ring, encouraging some lively bidding. Rettick whispered in Embry's ear once again. The bidding rose to thirty pounds then began to slow. Embry raised a finger to signal his bid.

"I have thirty-one. Thirty-two?" the auctioneer announced. A bid came from the rear. Embry signaled a higher bid.

The auctioneer nodded, "Thirty-three. I have thirty-three. Do I have thirty-four?" The bid came from the rear again. Embry signaled his response. "I have thirty-five now."

Elizabeth grabbed his sleeve and hissed, "What are you doing? You already bought the bays."

He pulled his arm away, looking daggers at her.

"Forty from the rear. Do I have forty-five?"

Embry nodded his bid. "I have forty-five. Do I have fifty?"

There was a murmur rising from the onlookers for whom the auction was becoming more interesting by each bid. The auctioneer slowed his pace to allow the bidders to consider their next moves. "Do I have fifty?" A nod came from the rear again. "Do I have fifty-five?"

Embry signaled a bid.

"I have fifty-five." There was a pause again in the bidding. People were looking at Embry and his competitor. This was getting very interesting indeed.

"Sixty!"came from the rear.

The auctioneer turned to Embry, "Sixty-five to you, sir?"

Embry shook his head slightly.

"Sixty-two, ten, sir?"

Embry nodded.

"I have sixty-two pounds, ten shillings. Any offers at sixty-five? No? I am calling it at sixty-two, ten," he looked at the bidder in the rear of the ring. "Sixty-five, sir? If they were charming at sixty, they are still charming at sixty-five."

The men around the ring chortled. The auctioneer nodded with a smile towards the rear of the audience. "Very good, sir. I have sixty-five. To you then, sir?" He looked at Embry, who shrugged his shoulders and shook his head. "No, are we done at sixty-five? All done to the buyer in the rear row at sixty-five pounds."

There was a smattering of applause among the interested onlookers who had enjoyed the drama. Embry smiled down at his hands folded on the silver handle of his cane. He looked past the twins to the tall dark-haired stranger now sitting several seats to their right. The stranger smiled at Embry, then stood up and left.

Rettick leaned over, "Well done, sir. Serves Bonner right for pushing you on the bays."

Embry settled with the auction agent and sent Rettick to see to the bays and the black mare. He and the twins headed out to his curricle where his spirited black horses were held by his groom. Embry climbed into the carriage, carefully positioning his weak left leg before taking up the reins. Elizabeth sat next to him and Ariel was in the back seat when the groom released the pair then jumped on the rear step as the carriage began moving past.

Embry guided the horses sedately through the crowds leaving the auction barn then flicked the reins urging them into a jaunty trot as the road opened ahead. Elizabeth watched him as his face grew younger right before her eyes. His lips were curled in a smile, his eyes were shining.

"If the road is clear, let's give them some exercise. What say you, Eliza?" He grinned at her.

"Yes, Samuel, let's do it," she cheered.

He flicked his whip and the horses began to canter down the north road to London. Embry laughed out loud as the wind whipped his hair back.

The streets grew more crowded nearer the city, so Embry was forced to slow the horses to navigate through the throngs. He called back to Ariel and his groom, "I will stop at the workshop. It is a few blocks west but it will put us out of the way of the crowd. I need to see if Larkin has finished his project."

Elizabeth groaned. "Samuel, we will be late for dinner and Maman will be furious. Must you?"

He grinned, "Yes, I must. Maman is never really furious. I will apologize for it and she will sigh and kiss us all and call us 'her dears.'"

The workshop was Embry's other passion. He spent hours each day designing what Elizabeth referred to as his "toys"—intricate mechanical objects that spun and whirred and clicked. Because of the casting and smoothing they required, with the accompanying heat, oily messes and noise, their father had purchased a small shop in a stone building located in a working-class neighborhood for Embry to use to build his creations.

Over time, Embry had assembled a small crew of elderly blacksmiths and tinkers and young apprentices to build the devices from his plans. The foreman was Mr. Larkin, a curmudgeonly clockmaker whose small hands with thin fingers were perfect to build the models Embry wanted. Despite his seemingly gruff exterior, the twins adored Larkin and he reciprocated their affection. His relationship to Embry however was inexplicable to Elizabeth. Larkin seemed to absolutely worship her brother.

Now as Embry pulled up in the workshop's yard, the quiet was very noticeable. Missing were the usual chimes of hammers on metal and the grinding sounds of machinery. Except for the jingle of the horses' harness as they shook their heads, there was a stillness that made Elizabeth grow cold.

Embry set the brake and listened intently for a moment. Then he issued orders in a lowered voice. "Elizabeth, take the reins and hold the horses. Ariel, stay here. Roberts, help me down and hand me my pistol."

"Pistol? Embry, do you think something is amiss?" Elizabeth wanted to hear that her intuition was wrong.

The horses jerked the carriage forward. "Hush, Eliza, and keep the horses under control."

Embry limped to the door of the workshop with his pistol held steady in his right hand. He used the cane in his left hand to push the door open slowly as he peered into the dark space beyond. He waited for his eyes to adjust to the dimness inside before opening the door a bit more.

The workshop was a shambles of metal parts and tools scattered about, shelves emptied and furniture and machinery upturned. His desk had been shattered open with his papers and drawings strewn everywhere.

"Larkin?" he called softly into the gloom.

A groan greeted him. He moved to the right side of the room. There a dark form was lying face down on the ground.

"Mr. Larkin, it's me, Embry. Can you hear me?" The answer was another groan. Embry called back to the groom, "Find a lamp or a torch. I need to see what has happened to him."

Roberts felt around in the dimness until he found a lamp that could be lit. He brought it closer to Embry who was kneeling by Larkin on the floor. There was a pool of blood all around the prostrate body.

Embry lowered the lamp and cursed. "His hands…his poor hands." The outstretched hands were bloody pulpy masses of flesh and bone.

There was the sound of a gasp. Embry whirled, raising his pistol. Ariel was slumped against the door, his face a white mask of horror.

"Good God, Ariel, I almost shot you. Go back to the carriage, blast you." Ariel did not—could not—move.

"Roberts, run to the tavern down the street and see if anyone knows a surgeon. In the meantime, Ariel," Embry shook his brother roughly by the shoulders then slapped him. Ariel's head jerked and his eyes moved from the body on the floor to his brother's face. "Ariel, listen to me. I need you to go home with Elizabeth. Tell Morris to get Dr. Calderon. The doctor must come back here to see if he can help. Ask Sherlock to order a spare room made up for Larkin and get the staff prepared to attend to a wounded man. We will need to move him to the House until we can figure out the next steps."

Ariel shuddered. "Embry, who could have done this? And why?"

Embry stopped the questions. "Not now, Ariel. Go!" he ordered as he pushed Ariel towards the door.

Ariel disappeared from sight as he ran back to the carriage. Embry heard the sound of the wheels as Elizabeth urged the horses forward. He bent down to put his head close to Larkin's.

"Stay with us, old man. Stay with us. Help is coming. Stay with us." He stroked the back of the man's head and his hand came away bloody. He touched the back of the man's neck, relieved to feel warmth. "Stay with *me,* my dear friend."

The dark work room was soon lit by several lamps as the men from the tavern converged on the scene with the local surgeon. No strangers to fighting and brawling among themselves, they were angered that someone from outside had dared to do this to one of their own. And to someone in the young lord's employ added to their fury. They knew that Embry paid his workers—their neighbors and friends—good wages and treated them with respect for their knowledge and their loyalty. In return, they felt protective of Embry's little workshop that had provided some with jobs and their sons with training that would help them feed their families.

Within an hour, Morris, Embry's manservant, appeared with Dr. Calderon in the doctor's carriage. The doctor examined

Larkin then conferred with the local surgeon. He approached Embry.

"The old man has been badly beaten about the head. His throat is marked as well—I dare say from being choked—and his hands have been viciously crushed. To be direct, he was tortured. His wounds are not fatal but I am not sure what use he will ever have of his hands. I am also concerned about the blows to the head. He is not conscious enough for us to check his speech and vision but I have concerns about a full recovery. This was a dastardly act indeed."

"Can he be moved?" Embry asked. "He cannot stay here—on the floor in a cold workroom."

"You've answered your own question then," the doctor said brusquely. "He will have to be moved carefully after we cushion his hands the best we can. The lads here have offered to build a stretcher and my carriage is outside so we can lay him across the seats. I will take him to your home, I presume?"

Embry nodded and turned back to Morris. He motioned him to a corner of the workroom and plucked a small white calling card from his jacket pocket. "Morris, I need you to go to the address on this card and give a message to the man whose name is here—to no one else but him. The message is 'There is no time left. A clock was taken.' Go now and tell no one else. Here is money to take a hackney cab. Go quickly."

Two

Elizabeth kept turning her head this way and that to see herself from all angles in the looking glass as Hannah, her maid, finished the elaborate coiffure. She was experimenting with different styles that might look well at the balls this season. The loose curls at the sides allowed her natural blonde and red-gold streaks to gleam through the light brown of the rest of her hair. The coiffure was delightful but it did not raise her spirits. She put her head in her hands and stared somberly at her reflection.

Yesterday she had been happy, thinking ahead to her birthday, the new bays for her lady's cart and her entry into the season. Now she couldn't get the attack at the workshop out of her mind.

The silence in the house emphasized how serious it had been. The staff moved up and down the stairs quietly, bringing linen, basins of water, and supplies to the doctors tending the patient in the back guest room on the third floor. She hadn't seen her brothers since last night and her mother only briefly as she monitored the staff's preparations with Mrs. Patton, the housekeeper.

There was a knock on her bedchamber door. Ariel walked in, dressed for dinner in a dark green jacket and ivory shirt and cravat. He sat on the bed and looked at Elizabeth's reflection in the mirror. She gazed back at him and sighed.

Ariel appeared gray and very sad. Elizabeth knew that he had seen Larkin lying bloodied on the floor of the workroom. Her twin had a sensitive soul. It would be hard for him to get that image out of his mind.

She and Ariel had often visited the workroom because they could count on finding Embry there if he was not at home, and, truth be told, they wanted to see Larkin as well. Despite his gruff manner, he knew how to interest them. As younger children, they had played games of hide and seek with the old man. Larkin hid peppermint drops in a new place at each visit and the twins would be busy seeking them out as Embry and Larkin conferred. Larkin always feigned shock when the cache was discovered and they popped the sweet treats into their mouths.

"I needs be more devious. They are getting too sly, they are, milord. What are you feeding them? Methinks some magical brain food."

In recent years, he left them finely wrought gifts—a tiny treasure box for Elizabeth and a cunningly crafted pen holder for Ariel—built from the scraps left from Embry's projects and crafted with all the skill honed by his many years of work.

Elizabeth now spoke to Ariel's reflection in the mirror. "How is he?"

"He is awake but he cannot speak yet. Oh Eliza, there are tears that run from his eyes every time the doctor works on his hands. I don't think it is only pain. I think he grieves for what he might lose. You know how proud he is of his skill and what he can craft."

Elizabeth felt her eyes glisten. "Poor, poor Mr. Larkin. Was it a robbery? Everyone on the road knows that there is no money kept there."

"But there is a strongbox. Someone new to the area might have thought that there were valuables hidden within. I heard Embry say that it had been wrenched open."

Suddenly, there was another tap on the door. When Elizabeth said, "Come in," a footman appeared with a silver tray. There was an ivory envelope on it addressed to her.

She took it eagerly, thanking the servant who bowed and left. She turned the heavy vellum envelope over to admire the ducal seal that closed it. "It came! An invitation to Lady Daphne's come-out! I was so hoping that I would be invited. My first real ball!"

Ariel looked stunned. "Elizabeth, how can you think about a ball today with Mr. Larkin lying so grievously wounded? Don't you have a care for him?"

"I do feel terrible for him, I do, Ariel, but this ball is weeks away. How will it serve Mr. Larkin if I stay at home? I want to go…I must go. All my friends are going," she exclaimed to Ariel's image in the mirror. "It wouldn't be fair if I couldn't go. I so long to dance."

Ariel responded slowly, "I understand, Eliza, but you must be prepared for Samuel to say 'no.' Now is not the time to be dancing and celebrating."

"He must let me. Maman will understand. She was a young girl once too. Oh, how I wish dear Papa was here so Samuel would just be my big brother and not head of the family. That was trial enough." Elizabeth shook her shoulders in defiance. "I will find a way. I will not be kept from it."

She stood, fluffing out the skirts of her figured silk gown as if she could shake away her tension. She and Ariel descended the stairs of the Aylesford family's London townhouse as the clock struck the time for the evening meal. As they went, they passed the portraits of their Aylesford ancestors and stopped as they often did at the portrait of their parents.

Their father, Lord William Wharton, the Earl of Aylesford, resplendent in evening attire, stood behind the chair on which their mother sat. Papa's green eyes glowed in his regal face with its aquiline nose and high cheekbones. His gaze was fixed on the beautiful, delicate woman in the chair.

The Countess seemed to be basking in a warm light—her rich golden brown hair was arranged in curls with pearls woven throughout and her almond shaped brown eyes rested warmly on the viewer. Around her throat hung her favorite pearl and ruby necklace giving a rosy tint to her white skin. Her lovely lips, slightly smiling, expressed her happiness.

What Elizabeth loved best were her mother's hands, so delicate like the rest of her petite person. One rested in her lap holding a small ivory-covered book. The other rested in her husband's hand.

That simple contact and the warmth of his gaze on her—so rare in formal portraits—signified the strength of their bond. Even close to thirty years of marriage had not dimmed the intensity of their affection and their total confidence in each other.

Everyone who saw them together knew it. It was evident in the looks they shared, the way they seemed to always know where the other was, even in a crowded room, and the way they sought each other out, as soon as propriety permitted, to stand side by side and to share whispers and touches.

But for years they had been rarely together. Maman seemed diminished now that Papa was away "in the service of His Majesty," as she termed it. She seldom went into society, spending more and more time in the small library that Papa had prepared for her near her bedchamber. To see her mother, Elizabeth had to visit her there, interrupting the reading and writing the Countess spent her days on.

The Countess' withdrawal into herself cast a pall upon the rest of the house. Behind it all was a tension that seemed to deepen the longer the Earl was absent. No one would ask but everyone worried, "Will he return? When? Is he safe? Is he in danger?"

"I miss him so much," Elizabeth whispered to Ariel.

He smiled, patting her arm. "Of course you do. You are his princess…his precious princess. And of course, you cannot always get your way with Samuel."

He paused at another portrait nearer the bottom of the stairs. Three children were painted against the gardens of Aylesford Manor—the family's country seat. A youth with the Earl's auburn hair and handsome green-gold eyes stood behind a garden bench on which two younger children, clearly twins, one boy and one girl, were playing with a white and black spaniel puppy. The two children shared the same fair skin, almond-shaped green eyes, and light brown hair streaked with blond and red highlights. They were enchanted with the puppy while their older brother was looking at them, clearly enchanted with his siblings. There was a lovely soft smile on his face.

"I love this picture of all of us," Ariel said.

Elizabeth glanced at the portrait then quickly looked away. "It is too difficult for me," she said. "That was only three months before...."

"His accident."

"Yes, he was so different then. So carefree and eager for adventure. The best older brother...always laughing and always patient with us," Elizabeth remembered.

Ariel reminded her, "But, Eliza, that was more than ten years ago. He was only seventeen then. Accident or no, he would have become a different person with our father away and having to be the head of the family or perhaps with a family of his own by now. And we were different too, not even eight years old with nary a care in the world. We know now that life is not that simple...." He walked on past the portrait and down the stairs.

The Countess stood waiting for them at the door to the dining room. When Elizabeth turned to her with a sigh, the Countess tucked her arm around her daughter's waist and kissed her on the cheek. "My dearest child, be strong. There is much good in our lives. Let us not think on what we do not have but instead on what we have." She reached up and patted Ariel on the cheek.

They entered the dining room together. Outsiders looking in would not have noticed anything amiss. The table was covered with luxurious white linens that were densely embellished with elaborate white embroidery. The gleaming silver place settings, embossed with the Countess' family crest—the rose of Sharon—glittered in the candlelight from the large golden chandelier above the table. The large centerpiece was a silver ship laden with fruits, nuts and flowers—symbolic of the Aylesford family fortunes built on its fleets as well as on its land grants in England and in the former and present colonies.

But the family members gathered in the room knew what was missing. No one would sit at the head of the table. The empty place reminded them of the man who was still far away, serving his King but leaving his family to mourn his absence.

Samuel Wharton, the Viscount Embry, was already standing at the table. He looked very handsome in a dark wine-colored jacket, with an elaborate cravat tied over a high white collar and a fitted waistcoat embroidered with silver. His auburn hair glimmered dark copper in the light but weariness clouded his eyes. Elizabeth knew he had spent last night by Larkin's bedside.

"You are looking lovely this evening, Lady Eliza," he said politely, bowing slightly. "Your hair is especially beautifully dressed tonight."

She threw him a grateful glance, dropping a slight curtsey in response. "Brother, how does Mr. Larkin? Is he awake? Ariel said he observed tears."

"He is awake and in pain. I suspect though that he is distressed by more than bodily pain. Knowing Larkin, he feels he has let me down by not being able to stop the attack in the workshop. He thinks he should have withstood the beating and not betrayed anything to the thugs."

Ariel walked to stand by Embry across the table from his sister. In passing, he laid a hand on his older brother's shoulder. Embry, although functioning at the head of the family, refused to sit in his father's chair at the end of the table.

"Eliza," the Countess said quietly, "join me in lighting the Sabbath candles."

Elizabeth moved close to her mother, and, like the Countess, draped a lace mantilla over her head. Her mother lit the heavy silver candles then moved her hands around the flickering flames three times before bringing them up to cover her eyes. Elizabeth performed the same gestures. Together the two women intoned the blessing over the candles—"Praised are you, our Lord, our God, Ruler of the Universe, who has commanded us to light the Sabbath candles."

The Countess lifted her hands and her sons bowed their heads. "May God bless you as He blessed Ephraim and Manasseh," she said, facing her sons. Turning towards Elizabeth, she placed her hands on Elizabeth's bowed head, "May God bless you as He blessed Sarah, Rebecca and Rachel." She spread her arms to encompass both sides of the table which put her directly facing the empty chair at the table's head. "May the Lord bless you and keep you. May the Lord cause His spirit to shine upon you and be gracious unto you. May the Lord turn his Spirit unto you and grant you peace." They all whispered a quiet "Amen."

The tension in the room increased as the silence deepened. They thought of their father. It was his blessing, the one he recited in English to them every Friday evening when he was present. The Earl would have next recited the last verses of the Book of Proverbs in honor of the Countess, his wife, "A woman of valor, who can find? Her worth is far above rubies. The heart of her husband trusts in her and nothing shall he lack. She renders him good and not evil all the days of her life...." The silence emphasized his absence.

Suddenly, starting slowly and quietly, Ariel began singing the same verse in Hebrew, his beautiful tenor voice gathering strength as he went on. Elizabeth felt tears gather in her eyes as her throat clenched making it hard to swallow.

Ariel then raised his head, looking at his mother as he sang the final verses. "Charm is deceitful and beauty is vain, but a God-fearing woman is much to be praised....Wherever people gather, her deeds speak her praise."

Tears stood in the Countess' eyes as she smiled at her youngest son, "Thank you, my dear. You honor me and you bring your father closer to us all."

The Countess next turned to her eldest son, the head of the family in the Earl's absence. "Samuel, please say the blessings."

Embry paused for a moment, inhaled audibly then leaned forward to grasp the ornate silver ceremonial wine goblet, using his left hand on the table to balance his weight. Erect once again, he raised the goblet and chanted the blessing over the wine. Next, the footman picked up the silver ewer and poured water from it over Embry's hands and into the matching basin he held lower down. As Embry dried his hands on the linen towel draped over the footman's arm, he intoned the blessing over the washing of hands. He removed the embroidered cloth that covered the twin golden loaves of bread, lifted them and chanted the blessing, "Blessed are You, Our Lord our God, who blesses the fruit of the earth." He broke off a piece of one loaf and passed the bread on to the others around the table. They each ate a piece in silence.

Footmen moved to the table to draw the chairs. Embry placed his hands on the arms of his chair, taking his seat slowly and carefully. The footman behind him assisted him in bringing the chair closer.

As the first course was served, the Countess announced, "We can be content this Shabbat. The Admiralty sent a messenger this afternoon with word that the Earl is in good health in service to His Majesty."

"Was he able to tell you *where* Papa is in service to His Majesty?" Ariel asked.

"And *when* he might be home?" Elizabeth added, completing Ariel's words. The Countess slowly shook her head.

Viscount Embry spoke up firmly. "No, he wouldn't tell even if he knew. It is unsafe for that information to be known and discussed. The Earl will be home when his work is done. We must respect and honor his work by remembering that our personal wishes are unimportant when the nation is at risk."

"Good Lord, we're his family. Whom would we tell? Why would we tell? And why is it always Papa? There are others who can share the diplomatic burden. Hasn't he done enough—been away long enough? Haven't we suffered enough?" Ariel's voice was rising."This never ends. Where is the rest of the world? Is it only us battling Napoleon? And is it to be only Papa who spends years trying to keep the allies together, trying to get the resources organized? Why do we need to be the conscience of the world?" He threw himself back in his chair in anger.

Once again, Elizabeth thought, the arguments that consumed them were rising to the surface. She pushed the food around on her plate.

Embry looked at his younger brother as if he was gazing down from a lofty height. He had assumed this air now that he was not only the older brother but also the official head of the family. "Do you really think our sacrifices have been so great, Ariel? Come, look around you—at this table, at this home. There are others who have suffered much more." His voice caught and Elizabeth glanced at his face, surprised to see him struggle for control. "There are thousands of families this evening who are without fathers and brothers and sons—many of whom will never return. How many of them are able to sit down to a feast in a home such as ours? Are we really suffering? Our father is likely sitting at a table in an embassy or palace somewhere with diplomats or princes, discussing how to protect our countries from Bonaparte.

"And you know why it is always Aylesford to whom the Crown turns. Who else has such extensive experience in many countries? Who else can rely on contacts throughout Europe and the colonies to get information? That is one of the benefits of being the head of the Aylesford shipping dynasty—in addition to the luxury and wealth we enjoy."

"Samuel, you make it sound like Papa is on some grand tour. I miss him and I want him back so our lives can resume as they were. We are all living in wait—not going anywhere, not doing anything—waiting until he returns to rejoin the world. It is not fair," Elizabeth fumed.

"And what are you missing, Lady Eliza?" Embry moved his intense gaze now to his sister's face. He looks so much like Papa with his red hair, green eyes and handsome face, Elizabeth thought, but without Papa's softness in his eyes. He looks like a perfect handsome lord—carved in marble. "Some girlish outing? Another trip to the modiste, perhaps, or tea at Gunther's? What big event in your life is being delayed because Papa is away doing important work? Think on it. What have you missed? Others have endured much. What has touched you?"

Elizabeth bristled at the rebuke. "The war is not my fault. Papa being away is not my fault. What happened to Mr. Larkin is not my fault. How does my staying here and doing nothing help anyone? I was hoping to go to Lady Daphne's come-out. Now you probably will not let me. If Papa was here, he and Maman would be invited too so I would be chaperoned!"

Even to her own ears, she sounded petulant and selfish. She thought again of the old man upstairs and swallowed hard. The table went silent as everyone stopped eating and looked down at their plates to avoid each other's eyes.

Embry said coldly. "Ariel and I received invitations today as well."

"Why did not you say so? Oh, how could you be so horrid, Samuel? Leaving me all sixes and sevens and you knowing that the invitations had arrived and that you and Ariel can be my chaperones so it will be proper…."

"Eliza, you astound me. After all this, you want to go? Did you not hear me? You, Ariel and I were invited. The Countess, our mother, was not invited! Even if nothing had happened last night, would you want to go when you know that by not inviting Maman, in Aylesford's absence, our family has been insulted? It never crossed my mind that I would accept when my mother is not deemed worthy to be included as well. Ariel, would you accept such an invitation?" Embry turned his gaze to his brother whose eyes were still fixed on his plate, though his hands on the table were clenched tightly into fists. "Do not tell me that you do not understand the insult."

Ariel now looked at Elizabeth across the table, "I would not accept for myself. But I understand how much Elizabeth wants to be included in the same delights as her friends. She deserves them as much as they do. It is not her fault that Maman…." He looked down again.

"Is a Jewess?" Embry retorted, his face rigid with anger. "That we are all Jews, born of a Jewish mother and raised as Jews, though we pretend to be oh-so English and members of the ton. Was Elizabeth presented to the Queen? No. Would you have been accepted to Eton? Most likely not so we avoided that humiliation by hiring the best private tutors for you as Papa did for me, pretending it was our choice all along.

"We are tolerated because of Father and his family and his wealth and connections. They do not dare be obvious in their feelings but, when they can, they make sure we know we are not one of them."

"Samuel, you are so unfair," Elizabeth retorted as her hands curled in her lap. "Lady Daphne is not like that—nor is her brother Piers to Ariel. We have been invited after all—even you who is known to prefer horses and workshops to people and parties. I have many friends. I have been to their homes and they have been here. You are living in the Middle Ages thinking that they are whispering about us and deliberately excluding us. We are just like them…in most ways at least."

"Oh really? Are the invitations coming as quickly now that you are entering the marriage mart?" Embry asked, raising his eyebrows. "Are you invited to dance with their sons? Be introduced to their cousins? Have parents approached Maman with discussions about putting their sons in your path? I think not, Elizabeth. But fear not, you *will* be invited to meet the poor relations, the titles needing ready cash. The ton thinks that we are willing to pay great dowries to buy our way into 'respectability' and they are willing to hold their noses to ensure they can live their dissolute lives off dirty Hebrew gold." The lights in the chandelier seemed to grow dimmer as Embry's anger grew hotter.

"Are you saying that Papa married Maman just to get her wealth?" Elizabeth gasped. She turned her eyes to her mother, horrified that her brother would imply this in the Countess' presence.

The Countess smiled gently at her daughter. "No, my dear. Samuel knows the truth. The Earl and I married for love. We were thrown together by chance—my father's banking interests and your father's ships were important partners but, as soon as we met, we knew there was something special between us. But we knew also that what Samuel is saying is true. The Aylesford family was none too pleased, as you know, but had to accept it because your father was an only son and would be Earl and there were entailed properties.

"We knew the ton tittered behind their fans. Despite the great wealth of the Earl's family, many in society assumed my dowry was the real attraction. They could not believe that the Earl could love someone like me. There was intense pressure for me to accept the Earl's faith. I did not want to…I love my people and we both knew it would never really change the opinions of others. I would be a Jewess still, not accepted by many in my family for marrying a Christian and mocked by his peers for the same reason.

"However, I am no longer hurt by the exclusion. My family is all I need and I have true friends among the ton and in my community. But, Eliza, I understand what you wish for. I would wish to protect you from any pain that society can mete out but I know I cannot. I have faith in your strength, my dear, to face what you must."

The Countess then tapped her fingers on the table. "But enough of this! This is not a suitable discussion for Shabbat. Your father is doing the work of His Majesty. When the war ends, all of us will be safer and we will be able to resume our lives. Now Elizabeth, tell me about the literary circle."

Elizabeth sighed, still pushing her food about the plate. "We met at Miss Beaufort's home and discussed Byron's latest work...."

Ariel looked up, a smile playing around his lips, "For how many minutes before you began to gossip about the duel between Captain Hastings and Lady Whitford's husband?"

Elizabeth laughed at her twin, "Hmmm—we did mention the poem once or twice before someone began to whisper what she had heard...."

Embry snorted but it was a sound softened with humor, "Ah, yes, when a group of young damsels start talking about Byron, one could wager that the discussion moves to recent love scandals by the time the teacups are filled."

Even Elizabeth had to chuckle at the accuracy of her brother's picture.

Three

"Elizabeth, do you see him?" her friend, Sarah Mendoza, whispered as she held the curtain open a few inches. They were in the women's balcony of the synagogue, overlooking the main sanctuary where the men were conducting the Shabbat morning service. Tradition dictated that women were hidden from view so as not to distract the men from their prayers but the rule was very often ignored when something interesting was happening.

"Yes, Sarah," Elizabeth whispered back. "David is there, next to your father in the second row."

"Oh, I know. Doesn't that dark blue coat look well on him?" Sarah sighed. "It is the finest wool from Scotland, newly arrived at Papa's warehouse. But I did not mean David. I meant the other gentleman, the very tall one, with dark curly hair next to Lord Embry in the third pew. He is wearing a dark green coat. Now that they are standing, you can see how tall he is. Taller even than your brother. Who is he? Do you know?"

Elizabeth looked again. She recognized the stranger from the horse auction, the one who spoken with Embry in the stables and then had nodded at her brother before leaving. From the tiny opening in the curtain, she could see his profile with high cheekbones, a long thin nose with a high arch, and firm chin. Then he turned to speak to Embry.

Elizabeth's breath stopped as she saw his full face. From here, it seemed the face should be embossed on coins, the skin a golden tone, brows finely arched and the lips full. As he talked to Embry, Elizabeth thought his countenance was absolutely regal.

She whispered back, "No, I have not been introduced to him but it seems that Embry knows him."

"Sssh—young ladies," the Countess leaned over to them. "Ariel is called to chant the Haftarah."

Elizabeth watched as her twin walked to stand beside the Rabbi, then chanted the opening prayers before launching into the Haftarah—the reading from the Prophets. His voice rose and fell and held a tremolo as defined by ancient notations and chanted in congregations across the world on the same Shabbat. Ariel's tenor voice was lovely. Pure and liquid and seemingly effortless, it never failed to enchant the listeners. He had studied long and hard to read the Hebrew text flawlessly—a challenge he set for himself at least once a year since the year of his bar mitzvah at the age of thirteen.

After he closed with the final blessings, there was a pause as he walked back to his seat. When he passed other members of the congregation, the men clapped him on his shoulder and congratulated him with "Yasher Koach"—"More power to you." Ariel inclined his head in thanks. Once he reached his seat, he looked up at the women's balcony to where his mother and sister were peeking through the curtains. A proud smile bloomed on his face. Elizabeth let the curtain fall back into place.

But then she heard a beautiful baritone voice begin to chant the final prayers of the service. There was an exotic tone to the melodies. She parted the curtain again. The tall dark stranger was now at the lectern, obviously having been honored by being asked to lead this part of the service. He sang with the fluency of knowledge and experience.

The women's balcony grew still as the melodies flowed up to them. Time stopped. Elizabeth was thrilled by the voice, then she chuckled to herself as she realized that she had held her breath as she listened.

After services, Elizabeth and the Countess stood with Sarah until they were joined by their cousin, David DaCosta, and Ariel in the courtyard in front of the synagogue. Embry emerged slowly from the building using his cane to assist his damaged left leg. The tall dark-haired stranger walked at his side.

Embry introduced each member of the group. "Countess, may I have the honor to introduce Baron Isaac von Tedesco from Vienna? My mother, the Countess of Aylesford. My brother, the Honorable Ariel Wharton, and my sister, Lady Elizabeth Wharton. Our friend, Miss Sarah Mendoza, and her betrothed, our cousin, Mister David DaCosta."

His guest bowed to each in turn and Elizabeth curtseyed when she was introduced. As she rose, she looked up at the tall stranger.

Her first thought was that he was the handsomest man she had ever seen. His curly black hair and his golden skin were dramatically different from the paler men around him. His eyes were entrancing—light brown with golden highlights, they glowed with life. His lower lip was full under an almost sweetly bowed upper lip and when he smiled, he showed very white teeth. She noted that his clothes were impeccably tailored of the finest wools but nothing was overstated. He was tall and lean with wide shoulders, tapered waist and long legs.

Then the Baron from Austria spoke—with a very proper English accent. "It is a great pleasure to meet you all this Shabbat. Lord Embry has kindly invited me to join you for dinner. I hope that will not be an inconvenience, Countess Aylesford."

"No, of course not, Baron von Tedesco. It is a blessing to have guests at a Shabbat table. Will you join us in our carriage home? It is not according to tradition, but we do use it because of Embry's leg and because our home is a distance from here."

Sarah and David said good-bye as they spotted her father and brother exiting the synagogue. They began to stroll to the Mendoza home in the neighborhood where most of the congregation lived within walking distance of the synagogue. At the same time, the Aylesford party walked around the block to meet their carriage out of sight so as not to disturb the sensibilities of the other congregants.

At dinner, the guest was invited to chant the blessing over the wine and bread. He raised his glass and began to sing in that smooth baritone with an exotic chant that made the familiar words seem fresh to the listeners. Elizabeth once again felt breathless and stared at their guest until his eyes connected with hers. She cast her eyes down but felt a blush rising in her cheeks.

Ariel gazed at the guest with appreciative awe. After their muttered "Amens" and the sharing of the bread, he asked, as the soup was served, "Baron, those melodies are from the Sephardic tradition, are they not? I thought Embry had said you were from Vienna. Would not the Viennese style be different from the Spanish style?"

The Baron nodded. "Yes, but my mother's family, the Nietos, was in Spain for many generations. Our family records show there were members of her family at the Spanish court as advisors and physicians to many monarchs. When Ferdinand and Isabella in their great wisdom expelled our people in 1492, my ancestors dispersed towards the east and around the Mediterranean. We have relatives from both sides of my family now in Italy, France, and throughout the lands under the Hapsburgs and even under the Ottomans. Now even in the Americas. My paternal great-grandfather came from Italy to settle in Vienna, sent there by his father to expand the family business. The Viennese branch of the family became the von Tedescos.

"I have traveled throughout Europe—from cousin to cousin as it were—being educated, learning our traditions and our businesses. We Tedescos are proud of our traditions and our family and remember that they are what define us. We are not defined by where we reside for we have had to live in many places over the generations and know that we might have to move to many more in the generations to come. So even though we are in Vienna now, we are not Viennese, deep down in our souls. Although, we can act the part of being Viennese when we must," he laughed a full-throated manly laugh. Elizabeth was transfixed.

The Countess asked: "You are then part of the Nieto banking family? I know of them because my family, the DaCostas, are bankers and originally from Spain as well."

The Baron nodded his head, "Yes, the Nieto banks are part of the Tedesco family businesses now. I however worked at the core Tedesco business which is fur-trading. My brother, Joseph, is the banker. The banks came later to fund the expeditions needed to find new sources of furs—in the Americas as well as in Russia.

"Now I have the privilege of serving the Emperor. My work requires me to travel frequently but I try to connect with Hebrew communities every Shabbat wherever I am. And, as you know, there are communities of our brethren everywhere one travels."

Ariel asked again in awe, "You've been to America and to Russia?"

"Yes, to both places. The northern Americas are rich in furs and in other natural resources. England lost great opportunities for wealth when she lost the American colonies. It is a vast unexplored and open land—nothing anyone in Europe could understand unless perhaps one explores the wide stretches of the Russian tundra. The vastness of the American wilderness rivals the size of the oceans. It is hard to explain what it is like to travel a land that has not been disturbed by cities or settlements or even been seen by any white men."

"But what about the savages?" Elizabeth asked, her voice breathless with admiration. This man not only looked exotic but he led an exotic life.

"The savages, as you call them, Lady Elizabeth, are not what you think. First, there are many different tribes among them so they are not all alike. They are cultured in many ways—just in ways that are different from ours—and they have a relationship to the land and to its creatures that we have long lost in generations of imposing our will on nature. There are ways of trading with the natives with great respect on both sides but I fear that most Europeans have no patience to understand them. In some ways, I feel more comfortable with them than with people in the finest drawing rooms in London or Vienna."

"Whatever can you mean by that?" Ariel exclaimed.

"They are in some ways like our people. Remember, the ancient Israelites were living within their own lands and abiding by their own traditions before they were expelled by invaders who had no respect for them. They were forced to wander, trying to survive in foreign civilizations. The American savages are being treated the same way. The Europeans, and now their descendents, these new Americans, invade their lands then move them out as they will—never trying to understand the traditions of the natives or to work with them or to leave them in peace in their own lands."

"But when you trade with them, are you not also taking advantage of them?" Elizabeth asked.

Embry looked sharply at his sister but the Baron took the question calmly. "Lady Elizabeth, I try very hard not to take advantage. I try to trade fairly with them. I enter their lands after obtaining permission from their elders which they grant because we give them fair value for their pelts. We trade tools, medicines, seeds, fine cloths and valuable goods, not useless trinkets and poisonous alcohol. We provide teachers and doctors when the tribe requests them. That is why we get the best of their pelts and my men can travel freely through their territories.

"The two years I spent in the Americas were the most exciting and most rewarding of my life—so far. I learned much about the peoples and their ways, but even more about myself and my values."

"How do you and Embry know each other?" asked Ariel. "You've been around the world but Embry never leaves his horses and his workshop." Ariel smiled at his older brother who glowered back.

"Embry and I share some scientific interests," Tedesco responded smoothly. "In my travels, I have met with men who are working on mechanical devices. I have heard you call them 'toys,' but I believe that some will have interesting and important uses. As I met these men, I sent notes home to my family. My cousin, Philippe, in Calais, has similar interests and shared some information with Lord Embry at the meeting of the Mechanical Society in London last year. Since then, the Viscount and I have been corresponding. He invited me to contact him when next I was in London."

"You speak English so beautifully, Baron," commented the Countess, "with hardly an accent. I would not know you from any well-educated Englishman. I would guess that you speak several languages with travel so important in your life."

"You flatter me, my lady. However, I think that no member of the ton would believe me one of them, given the color of my skin," Tedesco declared with a tight chuckle. "My travels have indeed helped me gain fluency in many languages. I seem to have a special ear which makes it easier for me to learn the accents, much as I can learn music easily. I find it an important talent to move through the cities of Europe, able to understand what others are saying in their native tongue—both to me and about me. It helps to know what others really think—not to be lulled by appearances. It serves me well even in the salons of Vienna."

"But you are accepted there, are you not? You are a Baron of Austria. Surely that means you are accepted as one of the ton or whatever it is called in Vienna," Elizabeth asked.

The Baron shook his head slowly. "I am a Baron because the past Emperor and the current Emperor were beholden to my family's wealth to underwrite their wars and to fund their empire. We were honored for what we could do for them. We are even more valuable now that the Emperor fears Napoleon. However, I do not delude myself that my title means acceptance—maybe toleration at best. I understand that people do not like feeling they are under an obligation—jealousy and rage often follow closely."

Embry looked at Elizabeth with a tight smile but there was no amusement in his eyes. "My dear sister would argue that we are long past such resentments. She believes that some, perhaps not all but some, of the ton are much more accepting of us this age."

Elizabeth blushed as the Baron looked at her with raised eyebrows. "I would wish it were so," he said softly. "I would spare you the pain were you to learn it was not."

He looked down at his plate. His eyelashes were long and thick against his high cheek bones. Then he looked up, raising his goblet. "Let us talk of something more joyous. Have you here in remote London heard of the new symphony by von Beethoven? It is the talk of Vienna."

Ariel spoke up, "I have heard of this von Beethoven. I even heard a performance of one of his pieces at the Royal Academy. I would be interested in studying anything by von Beethoven if I could get the music."

"So you play as well as sing?"

Ariel nodded, "Music is my passion."

"Almost as much as drawing, dancing, fencing, and—blondes…." Elizabeth added. "My twin brother is a man of many passions."

"Elizabeth, remember your manners in front of a guest," the Countess admonished but with a smile on her face.

The Baron smiled, "I think that is wonderful—to have many interests both of the mind and the body. I too share many of those passions. I study music when I can and have taken to traveling with a guitar I picked up in Spain. It is easier than trying to travel with a pianoforte," he laughed, "and I can practice lute and harp music transcribed for it. I study fencing as well and have taken my turn in the boxing circle. One grows dull without the physical arts to stretch one's muscles."

Elizabeth slid her eyes to her older brother, wondering if he was hurt by the evidence of robust health in the Baron. The Baron noticed her gaze. He turned to Embry, adding without losing a beat, "I've been told, Lord Embry, that you are a master of the cart races and your stable is well-known."

Embry nodded, "My riding days are over but yes, I find I can compete quite well with my hands and my head in the carriage races. Do you race, Baron?"

"Sometimes unintentionally," he laughed, "such as when I found my trail crossed by a stampede of buffalo in the northern American plains. My horse was spooked. He bolted and it was many miles before I was able to control him by turning into the tundra. I did win that race, however. As you see, I am here to tell the story."

There was laughter all around. Elizabeth was pleased to see even Embry laughed. The Countess was smiling happily when she asked Ariel to lead the grace after meals. Ariel started off the prayer slowly but soon, the others joined in. With the lighter mood around the table, the tempo became more upbeat as the group started to tap the table in rhythm to the chant.

"I have not felt such joy at this table for a long period," Elizabeth thought. She could see Ariel watching the Baron avidly. "Ariel seems to have a new hero. I pray he doesn't follow him to the Americas to chase after buffalo."

After the meal, Embry and the Baron went upstairs together. Were they were going to see Larkin? Elizabeth wondered. What interest could the Baron have in one of Embry's workmen? Perhaps Embry was taking him to the room off his bedchamber which was filled with drawings for those mechanical things he designed and in which the Baron had declared an interest.

Since the day was mild, she decided to go into the garden. She strolled around the flower beds then to the farther section near the benches and the fountain, where she sat in the warm sunlight.

Was this exotic new friend really interested in scientific inventions just like Embry? Somehow Elizabeth could not picture the elegant Baron bent over a workbench or looking over the shoulders of a workman building small mechanical devices. Instead, she thought of him charging through deep woods in America with a native guide by his side—the Baron dressed in deerskins with fringes. Or fighting duels in fog-wreathed fields outside of Vienna. Or riding to baying hounds over lush green English fields. Or perhaps boxing in the London sporting clubs she had heard about. What did men wear while boxing? Or rather, not wear? They surely did not wear their cravats or jackets. Shirts? Perhaps not. How much was the golden color of his skin natural or a result of exposure to the sun in exotic climes? Her cheeks flushed with her thoughts.

"Lady Elizabeth?"

She started with her surprise. The Baron had approached her from the house while she was distracted by her thoughts of him half undressed, covered with sweat and blood in a boxing ring. She looked down at her hands, wishing her blushes were less noticeable on her fair skin.

"I beg pardon. I did not mean to startle you. Lord Embry asks you to join him in the library. I offered to find you for him since I noted that his leg was giving him some pain. The injury must have been a grievous one."

"It was, Baron. My brother was a well-known horseman in his youth and was thrown in a hunt ten years ago when he was but seventeen. His horse landed on him, crushing his left leg. A local doctor treated him until a specialist from London arrived. That doctor determined that the bones had been shattered in too many places to mend properly.

"The leg cannot support him well. I fear the damp London weather makes the pain worse. He needs to use the cane always but sometimes, even with it, it is difficult for him to move around. Since then, he has turned his interests to more studious ones but feels grievously that he is so limited. He cannot serve in the military and he is bitter at times that others are doing what he wishes he could do."

The Baron offered her his hand as she rose from the bench and they began to walk back to the house.

"There are many ways to serve," the Baron said softly. "Your brother's fine mind, for example, can solve many important problems."

"Tell me, Baron, did my brother tell you about yesterday—when Mr. Larkin was attacked in the workshop?"

"Yes, he did. I know it weighs on him and I hope it gave him some solace to talk about it. I think that you should be aware that those 'toys' as you call them might be very interesting to many people. I caution you not speak of them and of what happened yesterday to anyone outside these walls."

Elizabeth repeated slowly in surprise. "Those little mechanical things? They are important?"

The Baron nodded, but added nothing more.

She continued, "What can Embry do now? Clearly, he cannot work there anymore. It might not be safe. How can he know who might be dangerous and who might be in danger?"

"From the destruction he described, I think that the thugs have taken what they were after or else discovered that it was not there. The danger at the workroom probably has passed. We will need to think about where such danger might now lurk."

Elizabeth looked up quickly, noticing the use of the plural "we." The Baron seemed to know much more about what the incident meant—much more than a new acquaintance would.

She was about to ask more questions when the Baron smiled, saying, "Lady Elizabeth, I have heard that you are quite a whip yourself according to your brother. Since Lord Embry is considered to have the best stable of pacers in London and be quite a marvel in the cart, you must be very good indeed."

How neatly he changed the subject. She followed him onto the neutral topic.

"Oh, yes, Embry is still horse-mad but now it is for curricle racing. If he takes you out in his phaeton or curricle, beware. He takes on all challengers. That is the only time he seems to come alive now and be like the brother I remember worshipping when I was little. Most of the time he lays down rules and more rules and never bends...." I sound like a petulant child, Elizabeth reflected, suddenly aware of her tone.

But the Baron smiled down from his height. "Hmm—I must speak in defense of older brothers. I am an older brother as well—with two brothers and four younger sisters! The duty of older brothers, I believe, is to plague younger sisters. I wonder what my sisters really think of me. I try to scowl and growl as much as I can. Perhaps, Embry can teach me better ways to torment them." He laughed at the thought.

So he thinks that I am just like his silly younger sisters then, Elizabeth thought unhappily.

They entered the house through the French doors into the drawing room. The Baron bowed to Elizabeth as she walked through the room to the library across the hall while he turned back to the garden. She found her brother at his desk with a book opened in front of him.

"Samuel, the Baron told me you wished to speak to me."

"Elizabeth, pray be seated. I will get to the point direct. I know you desire to go to Lady Daphne's come-out party. I have no love for the ton and no wish to let them get away with the cut to our mother. But I am now convinced that there will be no peace in this house until you are able to see for yourself the truth of what goes on in society. Therefore, I will accept the invitation and act as your escort for the evening if you still wish to go. Ariel will accept as well. You will be well chaperoned so no one can look askance at you on that account."

Elizabeth ran up to her brother and hugged him where he sat. He harrumphed but put his hand on her curls, patting her awkwardly.

"Thank you, thank you, for being so willing to put yourself out for me. You do love me, do you not, Samuel?"

"I do, my dear sister, but I do fear for you as well. Mind, there is one condition. No waltzing—country dances only."

"Oh no! I so want to waltz. It is the coming thing and it is so much talked about. Please do not put that stricture on me."

"No waltzes, Eliza. I insist. We must be above reproof, so we must observe all the rules. For your first ball, waltzing would be beyond the bounds. Believe me in this, sister."

Elizabeth slowly nodded her acceptance then smiled back at her handsome brother.

"Bosh, Samuel. You worry needlessly. I will not waltz, if you insist. All will be well. You will see. It will be a marvelous evening."

As she closed the door to the library, she looked back. Embry had put his head in his hands and closed his eyes over the book on the desk.

Four

The evening of the Lady Daphne's ball was indeed marvelous —at least in Elizabeth's eyes. She was wearing a new dress. It was white with beautiful gold embroidery at the flounced hem and around the neckline.

The neckline had been the source of many battles at the modiste's. Elizabeth, like her mother, was petite in all ways except, unlike her mother, in her bosom. She was blessed with assets which could easily turn the head of any man who saw her. The question was how much should be on display.

Mme. Clermond had lowered the neckline to the latest fashion but the Countess had insisted it be raised to a more modest level. The final result exposed Elizabeth's beautiful white skin to the beginning of the swell of her breasts and left her shoulders on display. Her curls with their natural streaks of gold and red were piled up on her head with a few dangling artfully around her hairline. From her pretty small ears, pearl drop earrings swung and a gold and pearl choker festooned her neck.

Ariel stood next to her, splendid in formal evening attire with a waistcoat of gold embroidery on white satin cloth. Embry stood on her other side, wearing stark black and white evening dress cut to perfection. His cane had a head of graven gold topped with a large ruby.

At their turn, when the major domo announced their names, Elizabeth felt very proud as she curtseyed next to her handsome brothers who bowed to the Duke and Duchess of Hastley.

Lady Daphne greeted her with a purr and a kiss. "I am so glad you are here, dear Lady Elizabeth."

Elizabeth thought her ladyship's eyes were fixed on her hair and she was pleased. Lady Daphne's medium brown tresses were so ordinary in comparison.

Lord Piers Hastley, Lady Daphne's always friendly brother, greeted Elizabeth with a bow then shook Ariel's hand heartedly. "Glad you are here, Wharton. At last, someone for me to talk with!"

Elizabeth moved into the ballroom, which was elegantly decorated with greenery and glittering with candles. She joined a group of young women whom she knew from various tea parties and girlish celebrations over the years. Embry followed slowly, finding a place near a wall where he could lean while keeping an eye on his siblings and on the entrance to the ballroom.

Ariel stood next to him. "I wonder, Samuel, if some men will introduce me to their sisters so I can ask them to dance. I will dance with Elizabeth of course but a chap cannot only dance with his sister all night, you know."

"Ariel, rest assured many mothers and some brothers and some fathers even will introduce you to their female relations. You are an Aylesford after all and expected to be an heir to part of the DaCosta fortune as well. Whatever else they might think of us, they do respect our wealth. And you will be a Viscount some day or perhaps even an Earl. You, my dear brother, are highly desirable to the ton, as I am, even with my crushed leg."

As if on cue, two gentlemen approached them.

"My Lord Embry," said the first. "Allow me to introduce myself—Lord Sherburne. I met you at the horse show in Avon last season. This is my dear friend, Sir William Bonner. I believe he bid against you on some grays at the auction several weeks back. I hope you do not hold it against him." Lord Sherburne chuckled. "We would be honored to introduce our families to you, if you please."

Embry nodded, "The grays, oh yes! I recall now. I thought that the price was outpacing their talent, so I withdrew at the last."

Lord Sherburne paused for a moment, narrowing his eyes at Embry, then turned and waved towards two matrons, two young girls and two young men, all of whom advanced on Embry and Ariel. Embry introduced Ariel. He signaled to Elizabeth to join them. "Allow me to introduce my sister, Lady Elizabeth."

One of the young men was Mr. Peter Bonner. Elizabeth was once again struck by his blond good looks and beautiful blue eyes. He bowed to Elizabeth then asked her for the courtesy of the first dance. The second young man, who was introduced as Sir Laurence Sherburne, asked Elizabeth for the second dance. Ariel asked the youngest woman, Lady Eleanor Sherburne, for the first dance.

Embry bowed again to the older of the young women, Miss Sylvie Bonner. He smiled ruefully, "Alas, Miss Bonner, I cannot dance but I would be delighted to join you in conversation and refreshment during the first interval."

"I accept, Lord Embry. Conversation is often more enjoyable than dancing."

Bows and curtsies all around ended the brief conversations as the families moved apart waiting for the orchestra to begin.

Elizabeth turned to her older brother, "See, Samuel, there was no unease. I have been asked to dance. Ariel's offer has been accepted. And Miss Sylvie Bonner seems eager to spend time conversing with you."

"Yes, Eliza, the evening seems indeed to be starting well."

The orchestra signaled the first dance—a quadrille. Peter Bonner approached Elizabeth, bowed and led her to the middle of the dance floor. Embry noticed that Ariel had done the same to the young Lady Eleanor, joining the set of his sister and her partner. He sighed as pain required him to adjust his weight to ease his leg.

He suddenly spotted Baron von Tedesco heading towards him. The Baron was dressed in elegantly tailored evening wear with a vivid blue heraldic sash draped from shoulder to waist over his waistcoat. Pinned to his sash was a large jeweled honor gleaming with rubies and sapphires. An elaborate diamond pin glittered in his ornately-tied cravat and large rings adorned his hands.

Embry bowed his head as Tedesco joined him against the wall. Without looking directly at the Baron, Embry said in a low voice, "So I see you were invited after all."

The Baron, not turning his head from the dancers in the center of the ballroom, responded in a similarly low tone. "The Duke understood that it was important I be invited. Is our friend here?"

"Yes, Sir William is over there at the table opposite the entrance. I have invited Miss Bonner to spend some time conversing. Mayhap you can invite her to dance. I doubt her father would object to you, with your Viennese title, charm, and all your sparkles."

The Baron looked ahead but a slight smile played around his lips. "You think perhaps I am glittering too much this evening. I did want to be noticed by the Väter and the Mütter."

"I wager they are totting up the value of the jewels right now. *They* at least are appreciated."

"I see Lady Elizabeth and Sir Ariel are dancing. So the evening is beginning as a success."

Embry looked at his companion, "But, Baron, you see that is Bonner's pup she is with. And Ariel has the honor of dancing with Sherburne's youngest."

"Caution, my dear Viscount. Do not make assumptions without reason—just as one decries the assumptions that others make about us. You doubt that the personal beauty of the twins has been noticed by everyone in this room? Are you so sure that there might not be some who have an interest in Lady Elizabeth and Sir Ariel for their own selves?"

"For themselves or for their fortunes? Baron, please remember, they are dear to me. I do not wish to see them harmed."

The Baron nodded then bowed to Embry. "I understand and I honor your concerns. I however must make my rounds of the matrons in the room in order to be introduced to the eligible young women." He smiled then took a deep breath, setting his shoulders as if to enter battle before beginning a slow stroll around the perimeter of the ballroom.

Embry smiled as he observed Tedesco's handshaking with the fathers and brothers and his bowing over the hands of the mothers and of the eligible young women as he went. The Baron stopped at the table of the Bonner family. From his distance Embry could not hear the words but he and the Baron had discussed the topics that would be introduced.

"Good evening, Sir William," the Baron began. "May I be introduced to your family?"

Sir William bowed. His wife and daughter had risen as well.

"Sir, you have the advantage of me. Have we met before?"

"I apologize, Sir William. I thought you might remember me. I am Baron von Tedesco from Vienna."

"I have never been to Vienna, Baron, so perhaps you are mistaken that we are acquainted."

"We did not meet in Vienna. Rather, I think it was in Calais or Marseilles, Sir William. I am not quite certain since I travel so frequently. Yes—I recall—I am certain it was in France earlier this year. Perhaps you were arranging for some goods to be shipped or perhaps to arrive?"

Sir William stood still, the smile on his face frozen in place. He stammered, "Baron, sir, it is not possible. I have not been to France for years—definitely not since Bonaparte has stirred up the mobs." The little rotund man's face had reddened and he endeavored to change the subject. "I do however wish to make my family known to you. Allow me to present my wife, Lady Bonner, and my eldest daughter, Miss Sylvie Bonner? I saw you speaking with Viscount Embry. Are you familiar with the family?"

"Not familiar, my dear sir, although I have the honor of their acquaintance. I share some interests with the Viscount. Lady Bonner, a delight. With your permission, my lady, may I ask Miss Bonner for the next dance if she is not otherwise engaged?"

Lady and Sir Bonner exchanged glances before Lady Bonner inclined her head to give her permission. The Baron turned to their daughter, "May I have the next dance, Miss Bonner?" The young woman nodded and made a curtsy.

"Thank you, Miss Bonner. Good evening, Lady Bonner. Good evening, Sir William." Then Baron set off to continue his slow turn around the room.

Meanwhile, Elizabeth was floating with happiness. Her first ball and she was partnered with the handsome Sir Peter Bonner! And he was graceful as well! In fact, Elizabeth needed to pay careful attention to the patterns of the dance to not hamper the graceful turns and spins of her partner. Ariel passed her in the patterns, smiling happily. Music and movement together—it was natural for her brother to look joyous.

In one turn, Elizabeth faced towards Embry who was still leaning against the wall. "Oh bother, couldn't he look happier? He looks like he has been ordered on guard and is dreading every minute. No one is ever going to approach him with a face like that."

She caught his eye and smiled at him. He nodded back but there was no answering smile on his face. "So be it!" she thought. "You can be a misery all by yourself."

Elizabeth moved on with the pattern of the dance. Now, for a brief pass, she was partnered with her brother. "Ariel, isn't this wonderful?" she exclaimed. Her twin laughed out loud in response.

As she faced Sir Peter once again, Elizabeth caught a glimpse of the Baron over Peter's shoulder. He was near the entrance of the ballroom, speaking to a small group of men but facing her. She smiled at him. His eyebrows rose, a soft smile curled his lips and he nodded slightly in her direction.

"Now there is a gallant who knows how to act at a ball. I wish he could teach Embry how to be a better older brother."

The dance came to an end. Young Mr. Bonner escorted Elizabeth to her brother Ariel. "Lady Elizabeth," Peter Bonner asked, "would you be so kind as to let me partner you in the fourth set if you are still free? "

"I would be honored, Mr. Bonner," Elizabeth curtseyed then put her hand on Ariel's arm as they walked towards Embry. But wait, Embry was moving away from the wall toward the Bonner table. Ariel and Elizabeth turned instead to follow other young people to the refreshment salon.

"Miss Bonner, am I still welcomed to join you?" Embry bowed to the young woman whose recent dancing partner had brought her back to the table.

She invited him to sit down to converse with her and her parents. Resting his hands on the head of his jeweled cane, Embry inquired, "Sir William and Lady Charlotte, I am so glad to spend some time with you. Are you lately come to town?"

"Miss Bonner and I came to town four weeks ago, Lord Embry. We had some shopping to do for the season. Sir

William joined us just a few days ago after traveling on business." Lady Charlotte fluttered her fan as she spoke.

"Just a few days ago, Sir William? I hope the recent squalls did not delay your travels."

"Not at all, Lord Embry. I was able to avoid the worst of them by crossing…by journeying via the interior route rather than going along the coastal road."

Lady Charlotte stared blankly at her husband. Sir William continued, not looking at his wife, "And you, Lord Embry? Were you in town earlier than the horse auction a few weeks ago?"

"Why yes. I have been in town for some months now. I have had some projects to oversee—I have an interest in mechanical design—and then I did want to attend the auction as well."

"So you did not travel with the Baron? I thought you might have spent time with him in foreign parts—a recent trip to France perhaps?"

"The Baron von Tedesco? I do not know him well at all. We have some shared interests in the new sciences and we have corresponded but I have only recently met him. What made you think we knew each other well?"

"I just assumed that you were well acquainted through some family connections perhaps."

"Really? How fascinating? He is from Vienna, yet you assumed we knew each other as family? How ever did you figure? Perhaps he sent some furs on one of the Aylesford ships, but, given the size of the fleet, I would never know that. An interesting person, although he is in trade, don't you know? The fur trade. Travels the world and meets all types of people with all types of interests. And he has a prodigious memory for faces and facts. The stories he can tell about what he has observed as he traveled are quite amazing." He paused, watching as different emotions flickered across Sir William's countenance. Then Embry turned slightly as he smiled and continued, "But, begging your pardon, Miss Bonner, I have not taken advantage of our time to make acquaintance. Pray, how did you spend your weeks with Lady Bonner once you arrived in town?"

Miss Sylvie began to describe the various shops she visited and the tea parties she attended as Lord Embry nodded his head and let his thoughts wander. How boring this pretty young woman was. How shallow her life. He glanced over her head a few times to watch Ariel and Elizabeth as they spoke to their friends. He envied them their innocent enjoyment of the pleasures offered by the social whirl.

The orchestra struck a chord to signal the next dance. Embry rose as the Baron approached the table. "Thank you for the pleasure," Embry bowed to the young woman and then to Sir William and Lady Bonner and finally to the Baron before making his slow way back to the far wall.

As the pairs assembled for the next dance, the Baron placed Miss Bonner and himself in the same set as Elizabeth and her new partner, Lord Piers Hastley. Elizabeth was sure the Baron's eyes were on her every time she passed him but, when she glanced his way, she found him always deeply attentive to his partner.

He seemed to be enjoying his conversation with Miss Sylvie Bonner, whom Elizabeth looked at with a critical eye. Sylvie was middling in height, average in figure with dark brown hair and brown eyes. Nothing to distinguish her except for the fine dress and the au courant style of her hair and jewels. She was definitely "the tip." The low cut of her gown proved it.

Elizabeth inwardly sighed, "If only Maman would be more like Lady Bonner, I would be turning heads as well. Piers is such a nice boy but definitely not as polished as Mr. Bonner." Only two more dances until she would be his partner again.

She observed the Baron as he danced with great ease, seeming to find the complex patterns instinctive. As he passed her, Elizabeth heard him speaking in a low rich tone with Miss Sylvie. In French, was it? His partner seemed entranced. Elizabeth instantly regretted her years of fussing about learning the language, finally convincing the Countess to dismiss the mademoiselle hired to instruct her.

After the second dance with Peter Bonner, Elizabeth floated up to Embry who was still leaning against the wall. "You are glowing, dear sister," he said. "Do not overheat yourself or you will contract la grippe and the season will be over for you."

"Samuel, I declare you can see dark at noon. I am not overheated. If I glow, it is because it is wonderful to be dancing and meeting nice people and…."

"Lady Elizabeth," the Baron's rich baritone was suddenly in her ear. "Before any other gentleman offers, may I have the supper dance?"

Elizabeth turned to look up into his twinkling amber eyes. "It would be my distinct honor," he said, "to lead you in to supper after the set."

She thought quickly. Her hopes had been on Peter Bonner but the Baron had been the center of the discussion among the young ladies. They all wanted to know everything about the handsome, tall, dark stranger. Would not being escorted by him make her rise in their esteem? It would be good for Mr. Bonner to see that other men were interested in her—older, distinguished men who glittered with honors and jewels.

"I would be honored to dance the supper set with you, Baron," she responded with a smile.

But lo, the supper dance was announced as a waltz. Elizabeth turned to the Baron. "Embry forbade me to dance a waltz," she grumbled.

The Baron smiled at Elizabeth. "Let me have a word with Lord Embry."

The Baron approached Embry. "Embry, would you feel more at ease, since it is I introducing Elizabeth to the waltz?"

Embry shook his head as he responded. "Baron, this is not Vienna. If Elizabeth dances the waltz here, there will be talk. The waltz is not yet accepted by everyone. Many consider it too intimate, especially for a young woman. The ton looks for such to talk about. I will not have my sister the on dit of the town."

The Baron smiled, "Ah, Embry, but the waltz is becoming very Viennese and so am I—very Viennese tonight among all these English. Surely the ton would forgive a Viennese when the dance that is rapidly becoming the fashion in his city is being played? And, as I understand it, I am considered by many to be a member of the family already—a relation, a distant one, perhaps, but somehow connected to you....am I not?"

Embry was still stern. "We walk on thin ice here, Baron. I cannot gamble with her reputation."

The Baron countered, "Tell me, Embry, what will be different if she forgoes the waltz? Will she be welcomed in places that have not yet opened their doors to her? Remember, if she has spirit and courage, she will prevail. By building a fence around her, you might force her to bolt it to be free. Rather, let her have some freedom while being guided safely through the hazards."

Embry regarded the Baron seriously. "You would do as well for your sisters?"

The Baron smiled, "I have waltzed with the eldest already...in public at the Palace."

Embry considered this. "I will give you permission to waltz with Elizabeth. I will ask Ariel to do the same. She will then have the dance, hopefully without the danger."

The Baron returned to Elizabeth who stood twisting her fingers tightly together. "Dear Lady Elizabeth, may I have the honor of the supper dance? Lord Embry has given me permission to ask you."

"Oh yes, Baron, I am honored to accept your offer," Elizabeth looked up at the tall Baron, so handsome with a smile on his lips and laughter in his eyes. Her heart stopped for a moment then she felt her blush rising. Oh yes, the other girls will indeed be jealous when he leads me out.

When the orchestra began the waltz, the Baron bowed to Elizabeth and led her to the side of the floor nearest Embry. When the Viscount nodded at them, it was clear to the assembly that Embry had given his permission. The Baron put his hand on Elizabeth's waist and grasped her small hand in his large one.

Elizabeth looked at their hands. How elegant his hand was with long graceful fingers and sparking rings decorating them. She stretched to reach her left hand up to his shoulder—and looked straight ahead—at the glittering honor on his sash.

When she hesitated, he said kindly, "My lady, perhaps it would be more comfortable if you place your hand on my upper arm. It might make the difference in our heights less of a strain as we dance."

Elizabeth moved her hand to his arm and felt the muscles flex as he firmly placed his hand on her waist. How strong he is, she thought and, then, oh my, I am beginning to blush yet again.

Once the music began, she had no time to blush. The Baron began to glide into the waltz and Elizabeth felt herself sailing through the turns of the dance. "I am flying," she thought. "My feet feel as if they were off the ground." As they turned, she could feel his muscles moving under the superfine of his evening coat.

He smiled at her, "Now breathe, Lady Elizabeth, breathe. This is glorious fun. That's better. Now wait for the changes."

She felt a shock of warmth as his thighs moved against hers as on the count of three, he spun her in a new pattern. They moved closer to the center of the floor.

"We must show the English how a Viennese waltzes," he laughed, spinning her in a graceful but wider circle before pulling her closer again.

She stumbled for a brief second but she felt his hand tighten at her waist to hold her steady. "His hand fits so nearly around," she thought. "He is daring them to watch us. Oh my, he is wonderful!" Her body tingled with delicious warmth.

As the dance ended, the Baron held his arm out so that Elizabeth could place her hand lightly on it. "It is now my great pleasure to walk you in to supper," he declared.

Ariel appeared at her side with Lady Eleanor and Mr. Peter Bonner and a Miss Winter. "Baron von Tedesco, we thought to have a table all together. Would you join us with Elizabeth or are you engaged to join Lord Embry?"

"We would be delighted to join you. Lord Embry, I wager, will be fine on his own."

The young Laurence Sherburne approached with a young woman on his arm. "May we join your table, Baron?"

"Of course, Sir Laurence. It would be our pleasure to get to know you and your companion."

As they entered the supper room, Elizabeth saw Embry seated at a table with Sir William and Lady Bonner and Miss Bonner. Everyone seemed to be smiling and convivial including her usually dour brother. "My," she thought, "I wonder if there is some warmth growing there."

The Baron seemed perfectly at ease among his juniors around the table. He told a few stories of his adventures in America after Elizabeth made mention of them to the others. He deflected further inquiries then by asking the younger people about their own travels.

Peter Bonner exclaimed, "Travel? I wish. It is the devil to travel with Boney running loose in Europe. My mother cannot sleep whenever my father needs to be away. Lud, she would be devastated if I mentioned that I wanted to do the tour."

The Baron arched his brows. "Yes, it can be risky to travel unless one has protection and knows people. Does Sir William travel with any diplomatic shields?"

"No I 'spect not—at least I do not know. He travels for business, I believe. We do not discuss such things at home. But, Baron, you travel all the time. How can you manage it? Do you travel mostly for the Emperor?"

"Sometimes, Mr. Bonner. Other times, I am on mine own business. I however have been traveling for years, since I was younger than you, and by now, I have contacts everywhere I go. I also have friends and family in many cities who are interested in my safety."

"But isn't it disloyal to do business with the enemy?" Sir Laurence Sherburne interjected. "Or are there no enemies where business is concerned? And perhaps your business acquaintances have secret ways to keep their close friends safe?"

Ariel grew still, staring at Sir Laurence with narrowed eyes. Disloyalty? Secret ways? Was he intentionally being insulting?

"My dear Sir Laurence," the Baron responded quizzically with a tilted head, "I wonder at the direction of your remark. I am sure you could not mean that I might put business ahead of my loyalties. That would indeed be an insult, sir, that might need redress. However, I will assume you are merely ardent in your interest for your King against his enemies. But do remember, dear sir, that the Emperor of Austria stands with His Majesty and I stand with my Emperor.

"But, on the subject of business, I have met many an Englishman on my travels through Europe. I assumed they were, as I was, concerned about their interests and the people who serve them. I know that there are families whose survival depends on their ability to earn through their employ in my enterprises. The wars disrupt the lives of those who have been loyal to me and my family—those who have fewer options than I. I travel to assist them how ever I can. Sometimes I am able to keep them working by keeping the trade moving and sometimes I aid them directly when I cannot. But secret ways? I do not understand what you mean, sir." Ariel noticed that the Baron smiled with his lips but there was no warmth in his eyes.

"Oh, I mean, people who speak the same language amongst themselves only, who look out for each other, who know ways around obstacles for gold. Shared blood, don't you know? They trust only those who are in their secret society. They are found everywhere, I hear. They change countries as the seasons change, moving from place to place to take advantage of opportunities they share only with each other."

Elizabeth asked with some sharpness. "Sir Laurence," she said, "are you questioning the loyalty of some people because they are newer come to this country? Exactly how many generations does it take to be considered truly loyal?"

The smile had now left the Baron's face as he listened. His voice became softer but Elizabeth heard an undercurrent of danger in his tone.

He said quietly, "Lady Elizabeth, in times of trouble, some look for enemies to blame. A secret society, you claim, Sir Laurence? How intriguing. And if it is so secret, you must explain how you seem to know so much about it, Sir Laurence.

"But I remind you young people of European history. Sometimes countries changed while people stayed in place. Sometimes monarchies changed as empires expanded and fell. Even some English kings had roots in other parts of Europe. As for length of time in one country or another, Mr. Bonner, tell us how long your family has been English. I would wager that not too long ago, Bonner was Bonheur, was it not?"

Mr. Bonner stared at the Baron, his face flushing. "Well, yes, my grandfather had told me that some generations back we had come from France as Bonheurs. I am told it was long ago. But how did you guess?"

The Baron seemed thoughtful. "I really do not remember. Perhaps someone in France told me. Or mayhap I met one of your family there. Perhaps I was charmed by the fluency of your sister's French—I think she speaks as a proper mam'selle. Your family's story is really not an unusual one. In fact, I believe there are many in this room whose forebears are newer come to England.

"So, Sir Laurence, which generation of the many families in this room do you think became truly English? The second one in this country? The third? The one that spoke English first as a babe or the one willing to place his life on the line for his king? Is it just time or is it really action that determines one's true loyalty?"

Sir Laurence began to stammer a reply when a footman approached with sweetmeats for the table. The Baron waved him to serve. "Let us move onto more festive topics. Mr. Bonner, do you share the same interests as Sir Ariel? Tell me about some of the times you have spent together as friends."

Peter looked at Ariel quickly, blushed again then looked back at the Baron. "We are not close, Baron. We have met at some occasions…a few times."

Ariel looked down at his plate. It was true. These young men were really not his friends in any true sense of the word.

"Ah," the Baron nodded, "then perhaps this is a good time to get to really know each other. Mr. Bonner, do you have an interest in the physical arts? Perhaps fencing? I myself am very fond of swordsmanship and look to attend some English masters to compare their styles to the Italians and the Austrians. Can you recommend some venues I might attend?"

The Baron led the conversation to sports and then on to music, seemingly very calm and very much at ease, but Ariel watched his eyes. They were as hard as amber.

Five

The next morning, Sarah Mendoza called at Aylesford House. When Elizabeth greeted her, Sarah excitedly probed for information about the Baron. "Oh Eliza, there has been much talk about the Baron since those Shabbat services. Everyone asked me, as if, as your friend, I would know all about him. I tried to tell them that I do not think that even Lord Embry knew much about him, that the Baron was but a recent acquaintance, but they turned a deaf ear and kept asking me to tell more."

Elizabeth responded thoughtfully, "How interesting. Now that I think on it, while I spent time with him and we sat together at supper, I actually learned very little more last night. He turned most questions back to the asker and seemed to want to know more than he wanted to reveal. And he never seemed bothered even when some seemed almost rude...."

Sarah interrupted with a laugh, "Now tell me the most important fact about the Baron. How is he as a dancer?"

"Oh yes, that is the most important," Elizabeth giggled. "I waltzed with him! It felt like skating! Embry thought that I should not waltz so soon in the season but he gave in to the Baron."

"But the Baron is Viennese. Of course he would want to waltz. It was only one waltz with the Baron so people know there was no special warmth between you," Sarah responded.

Elizabeth thought that must be the truth. He waltzed with me as Ariel did, as a brother. But there was warmth between them. Well, *she* felt the warmth even if *he* was waltzing with her as with a sister.

The young women heard the front door knocker. It was an early time for most callers outside their most intimate circle. When Sherlock, the butler, answered the door, the Baron's unmistakable baritone asked after Lord Embry. Sarah smiled at

Elizabeth with a significant look in her eyes. However, Sherlock led the visitors right past the morning room into Embry's study.

As the butler passed back, Elizabeth called to him. "Sherlock, I heard some callers have come for Lord Embry. Can you tell me who they are?" Elizabeth knew she could count on Sherlock to relay any news he came across.

The butler reported, "Baron von Tedesco, Lady Elizabeth, and another gentleman, a Mr. Lopes, his name is. Somewhat shorter and darker than the Baron, he is, but definitely not in the same class—his coat was not well-tailored at all." Sherlock sniffed as he tried to place Mr. Lopes somewhere in the sartorial ranks.

"A footman, perhaps," Elizabeth suggested.

"I think not, Lady Elizabeth. He went in with the Baron. They then all went upstairs together."

Elizabeth thought about the wounded man in the back guest room on the upper floor.

Sarah whispered, "Ah, the Baron grows ever more mysterious, does he not?"

The friends would have indeed startled by the conversation in the guest room. Mr. Lopes bent over the patient to ask him questions about the attack.

Larkin could not speak but he could nod or shake his head. One man or two? Did he recognize them? Did he see their faces? Were they tall, short, English, foreign? Did they ask about a clock? Did they ask about papers for a clock?

The Baron and Embry watched as Larkin signaled his responses. There had been two men, with mufflers around their faces, unfamiliar voices, foreign accents, asking about papers for a clock, asking if he knew where the design papers were. Then they put his hands on the table and hammered upon them asking over and over again, where were the instructions?

Then Larkin made the error of looking at Embry's desk. One attacker quickly ransacked it while the other held him down. When they couldn't find what they wanted, the second man started choking him, all the while asking where the papers were. His vision went black—and then there were flashes of light. That was all he could remember. Slow tears worked their way down his grizzled cheeks.

Embry moved to the head of the bed. He whispered, "Larkin, do not be distressed. You did the best you could. Nothing in the workroom was worth your pain. The outcome could have been even worse. I am so grateful that you are still with me."

The men left the exhausted Larkin in the care of the silent attendant. When they were seated in Embry's study, the Baron and Mr. Lopes, introduced as an aide to the Baron for various tasks as needed, compared notes on what Larkin had been able to remember.

The Baron started, "We know they wanted the instructions for the clock. And now we know they are likely foreign agents."

Lopes added, "And they are trained to get answers to questions, not just to pilfer what they can."

Embry agreed, "They seem to have had some clear information about the workshop and what goes on there."

The Baron leaned forward, "However, without the instructions, the clock is not useful. We can assume they will be looking in other likely locations for the papers such as your study or your bedroom or the library—so we need to put a watch in this house. You must be very cautious and ensure the members of your household are cautious as well. With your permission, I have some gentlemen I would like to place here as footmen, grooms and the like." Embry nodded his agreement.

The Baron turned to Mr. Lopes. "It was good that Hastley hired you as a footman at the ball last night. Were you able to find out anything about Bonner?"

"Well, sir, the footmen talk a great deal about the families what they know. It came about that I shared some time with the footman to Mr. Bonner. Mr. Bonner travels quite a bit, but not for business, at least not for any business that brings money home to the household. There are quite a few gentlemen what call at the Bonners' but the master is never at home for them. Tradesmen they are, with bills what needs to be paid. Friends of the footman, some of them be, willing to tell him their grievances over a pint.

" The footman says that Mr. Bonner is away from home many a time or lying low t'other times. The help think he got a lady-bird somewhere what is taking all his money and time but none of my lads trailing him found that to be true."

"Where does he travel when he is gone?" asked Embry.

Mr. Lopes replied, "None swear to know for truth, but, since he is gone for weeks at a time with only his manservant, they in the downstairs think he is gone to foreign parts."

The Baron looked down at the toe of his well-shod foot, flexing it back and forth as he considered. "That confirms some of what I observed. He mentioned squalls on his way to London to Lord Embry and we know that the weather was bad on the Channel but nothing like squalls towards the City recently. He also was concerned about whether I had indeed seen him in France. I thought to increase his concern by insisting I had."

Mr. Lopes looked at Embry, "That is why the Baron asked me to set a picket on the Bonner house—to watch what Mr. Bonner does next, now that he might think the wind is up. I've got quite a few pairs of eyes on the watch now." He added, "Bonner has paper spread all over the town. I know some what holds his notes. Seems to like to gamble but doesn't do it well, 'specially when he is foxed. He dabbles in some expensive hobbies—don't you know—and fancies himself a racing man."

Embry smiled at the Baron. "The Baron asked me to put pressure on him so at the auction, I bid up the price on some horses much higher than they were worth. He had no idea of their true value or he would have had the laugh by letting me have them."

The Baron considered the information gathered so far. "Bonner needs an influx of cash and might not put too fine a point on how it comes in. Philippe has had the watch on Bonner in Calais. Bonner appears several days before our ships arrive in port. Sometimes one day ahead and other times a week ahead. Up to now, Philippe has been able to confuse them by having an erratic schedule and several ships loading and unloading close together. If they could break the clock's code, they would be able to know our schedules more exactly, causing us more trouble. "

"And Sherburne—what about him? It seems he is thick with Bonner or Bonner with him. Which one is the leader?" Embry asked.

"Sherburne served as a naval officer during the American war and now spends much time connecting with his old friends in the Admiralty. Your father suspects that when he gets wind of some naval plans at the Admiralty, he dispatches Bonner to get information to and from Calais and from there deeper into the interior of France."

"Mr. Lopes, can you follow Mr. Bonner if he travels again?"

"Aye, I can try. It should get easier as he goes. Once a man does not honor his debts, there is naught in his life that will remain a secret for long. Others will be eager to get paid for telling all they know."

The Baron interjected, "That might take too long. We could be watching him for weeks. We need to speed up the process of uncovering the identities of those who are behind the attack on Larkin. We know they didn't find what they needed. At your good advice, the protocols have never been written down. The worst would have been if they had found out what they needed to decipher the code. Every message we sent would be clear to them from that point on."

Embry looked at the Baron thoughtfully. "We could do more than wait for them to strike again. Since we know they have yet to find what they are after, what if we set a trail of crumbs leading them to what we want them to find?"

"Ah, we could indeed. We know we have something they are in desperate need of. The clock is not useful until they have the instructions for its use or find someone who knows how it works. We need to drop some hints about where the papers are and see who shows up to claim them."

Embry nodded, adding, "If we allow them to obtain the instructions, we could send some codes that tell them what we want them to think to divert them or to confuse them."

The Baron was thoughtful now, "And yet we need to have some way to keep the information flowing to our allies. If we disrupt our own network, we are left without any way to pass messages."

"Let me think on it," Embry steepled his fingers—a clue that his mind was churning with ideas. "I will find a way to mislead our enemies while keeping our friends safe. At the same time, I worry about Elizabeth and Ariel. I permitted them to go to the ball on your suggestion that it would do little good to shelter them. Now they have struck relationships with the very families we are concerned about."

The Baron stared steadily at Embry while saying slowly, "I think that might be a great help. It gives you all a reason to be in closer contact with both families without it seeming out of the way."

"Baron, I told you I would not put them into danger. I especially would not want Elizabeth to be hurt."

"I have great faith in Lady Elizabeth, Embry. She has a sharp mind and a strong spirit. I think your concern will be best served by placing her where she can learn the truths about her friends sooner rather than later and where there are other eyes to keep watch that she comes to no real danger."

Embry sighed as the Baron stood, signaling the end of the conversation. "This afternoon, I will be sending two men here. You can place one of them in service to the twins. He should stay close to them at all times. The second will be in service to you. He will be able to assist you in your workshop and in any travels you need to undertake. I leave London for a fortnight, perhaps more. Do you have any messages for your father?"

"Yes, my mother has written a note that is enclosed with mine. Mine has the news he expects. How useful it remains is questionable. Please tell him how much he is missed and express love from the twins. Also, tell him I am proud to be his son." They shook hands. Embry rang for Sherlock.

"Embry," the Baron turned back as if with an afterthought, "I wish to take my leave of the rest of your family."

"Sherlock, please ask Sir Ariel and the Countess to join Lady Elizabeth in the morning room to say good-bye to the Baron."

The Baron entered the sunlit morning room as the family gathered near the windows that overlooked the front garden. His tall erect posture emphasized the elegance of his appearance. He bowed to the ladies after being introduced to Sarah again and he shook hands with Ariel.

"I have come to bid you adieu for a few weeks. My business calls me to the Continent. I want to thank you, Countess Aylesford, for your hospitality. Lady Elizabeth and Sir Ariel, I am honored to have had a chance to spend more time getting to know you both. I carry with me the warmth of your friendships which I will share with mutual friends abroad. Auf Wiederschauen—until we meet again." He kissed the Countess' hand and bowed. Then he turned and left with Mr. Lopes by his side.

Elizabeth let out her breath not realizing until that moment she had been holding it again. She felt inexpressibly sad to see the Baron leave.

Sarah turned to her with glowing eyes, "Oh my, he is breath-taking, Elizabeth. So princely! So elegant!"

The Countess smiled at the young women. "Yes, the Baron is everything a gentleman should be. And I tell you, children, that he is a man one instinctively knows can be counted on if one is in need."

Ariel looked out of the window, watching the Baron talk with Mr. Lopes at the gate before Lopes headed off down the road on foot and the Baron climbed into his rented carriage. As the carriage pulled away, Ariel wondered, "There is something about the Baron. He seems to be very well acquainted with all of us as if...as if he knows us better than he should."

Six

Elizabeth was sitting with her mother in the Countess' reading room later that same day when Sherlock appeared at the open door.

"Sherlock, I am glad you have come," the Countess said. "Please have tea served in the drawing room. And ask Lord Embry and Sir Ariel to join Lady Elizabeth and me. Do you know where they are? "

"Sir Ariel is visiting Mr. Larkin upstairs. Lord Embry is in his study. That is why I am here. Lord Embry has two men with him that he wishes to introduce to you, my lady."

"We will come down to the drawing room directly. Wait for my ring for tea service."

"Maman, I will fetch Ariel. That way, I can visit Mr. Larkin as well."

Elizabeth walked up the stairs to the third floor. As she turned into the guestroom hallway, she heard violin music wafting from the room where Larkin was recovering.

When she knocked on the door, the music stopped. Ariel called, "Come in." When she entered, she found Larkin sitting up in bed and Ariel by his side holding his instrument.

"Mr. Larkin, how are you? " Elizabeth asked walking closer to the bed. A small smile appeared on the old man's face. He raised one bandaged hand, gesturing toward Ariel. "I see. Ariel has been entertaining you by scraping away on his viol. I hope he has hit more right notes than wrong."

Ariel responded with a dry "Ha, ha, very droll, Lady Elizabeth. I wanted to practice and Mr. Larkin has been kind enough to listen. I am quite proficient, am I not, Mr. Larkin? Lady Elizabeth wants to belittle me but I am hardened to her taunts. You are quite spared, Mr. Larkin, that she has not brought her flute. The crows join into the ruckus when she plays. It quite brings on the headache."

Elizabeth smiled at his exaggeration then asked the patient, "How are your hands, Mr. Larkin? Is Dr. Calderon pleased with your progress?"

Larkin's hands were bandaged but, on both, the thumbs and forefingers were in splints as well. Now he looked at Ariel to answer on his behalf.

Ariel paused, considering how frank to be in front of the patient. "Dr. Calderon is quite sure to save the thumbs and forefingers on each hand. He has them both set as you see. He also thinks to save the middle finger but is not sure of the rest. He must watch for infection because in that case...." Larkin nodded at Ariel to go on, "in that case, he might have to amputate. He thinks though that Larkin will be able to regain much mobility with the fingers that remain healthy, does he not, Mr. Larkin?"

The old man nodded at Ariel but Elizabeth noticed he had swallowed hard and his eyes were glistening. She added, "That is good. We always said that Mr. Larkin was the best even with one hand tied behind him. He will prove us right yet." Larkin turned his gaze on Elizabeth with hope lighting his eyes.

"And now, brother, the Countess would like us to join her in the drawing room. Apparently Embry has some gentlemen to introduce to us."

When the twins arrived in the drawing room, Embry was standing with the two new men. One was already dressed in Aylesford livery of dark blue with white and gold trim. He was tall, with blond hair and brown eyes, and he carried himself with an erect military bearing. The second man was shorter and very slender. He had deep brown curly hair and olive skin and, when he looked up from his bow, startlingly blue eyes behind wire-framed spectacles.

Embry introduced them. "These men have come to us especially recommended by the Baron. I have told them about what has recently occurred at the workshop. Lieutenant Commander Robert Parker," he indicated the blond footman, "is to join our household in the guise of a footman with special duties to Sir Ariel and Lady Elizabeth when they are out on calls and duties for the safety of the whole house when they are at home. His experience is quite extensive with several years in the Navy. We are to take his advice on the safety of our persons and our home."

Parker bowed to the twins and the Countess and murmured, "It is a pleasure to be of service, Mum."

Embry gestured toward the second gentleman. "Mr. Judah Nieto will assist me in my work here and in the workshop. He has scientific knowledge having studied at the University of Bologna and he has worked with the Baron on special assignments. He also will advise me on ways to improve our general safety."

Mr. Nieto bowed and said, "I am honored to serve our family, Countess Aylesford."

His voice had a very slight accent that Elizabeth could not quite place. As his gaze went from one to another member of the family, his polite smile did not touch his eyes which seemed to focus intently on each of them in turn. She had the impression that those eyes missed little as they scanned the room and its inhabitants.

Embry then announced, "Oh, there is another new member of our household. Parker, please bring him in."

A few minutes later, the family heard the click of claws on the marble floor of the hall. Parker re-entered the room with a large brown brindled dog with a square head and sad eyes in a black-masked face. The dog stood quietly by Parker's side but his serious gaze traveled from person to person.

Embry said formally, "Allow me to introduce Sir Beowulf, an aristocrat among English mastiffs. He is a gift from the Baron. Parker will help him become familiar with each of you. I believe you will find him very gentle and quiet with the members of his family, but I have it on good authority that he does not like strangers."

"Embry, my dear," the Countess squeaked, "are you sure it is a dog? It looks big enough to be harnessed to a cart."

Embry laughed, "I did think he might serve as Elizabeth's team for her carriage. What say you, Eliza, to trotting through the park with Beowulf in the traces?"

Elizabeth shook her head but kept her eyes on the dog. Ariel looked at his mother, "Maman, did you know of this?"

The Countess looked doubtfully at the large dog. "The Baron feels that after the incident at the workshop we need to have more care about security here. I thought locking doors and windows was sufficient but I do think having Beowulf on guard might make me feel more comfortable at night."

"I have been assured that he has been well-trained." Embry turned to the new footman."Parker, pray introduce the family to Sir Beowulf."

Parker took Beowulf slowly around the family group. "This is my lady, Countess Aylesford. Countess, could you let Beowulf sniff your hand and perhaps hear your voice?"

The Countess held out her hand tentatively while saying, "Nice doggy. Nice Beowulf."

Parker moved on to Ariel, "Sir Ariel, pray let the dog become familiar with your scent and voice."

Ariel bent down slowly and allowed Beowulf to sniff his open palm. He crooned, "Beowulf, welcome to the family" while patting the dog on his square head.

Elizabeth knelt down as the dog was led to her. She held out both hands to the dog to sniff then scratched him behind his ears, "I am glad to meet you, Sir Beowulf. Welcome to our family. Such a handsome addition and better behaved than my brother Ariel, I am sure. He is not quite as well trained as you are."

Ariel snorted and the dog looked up, suddenly very alert. Parker moved his hand as a signal and the dog stood quietly again at his side.

"He is very well trained," Parker reassured them."He has been taught to attack people he does not recognize unless his family indicates friendship. He also is quite alert, as you see, to sudden noises. He will guard the house particularly well during the night once he becomes familiar with the regular household sounds. I will teach each of you how to command him so that you become more comfortable in his presence."

The Countess looked up at Embry with a smile, "I wonder who will need more training—Beowulf or us? Now, shall I order tea?"

As Parker left the room with Beowulf to show him around his new home and to introduce him to the regular staff, Embry turned to Mr. Nieto, "Mr. Nieto, please stay and join us for tea."

Nieto responded, "Thank you, my lord." He chose to sit on a bench slightly outside of the family's intimate circle.

Ariel had to turn to face him to ask, "Mr. Nieto, Lord Embry mentioned you had studied at the University of Bologna. Are you Bolognese, then?"

Mr. Nieto answered slowly as if he was measuring each word, "No, Sir Ariel, I am from Gibraltar. My family has been there for several generations. Gibraltar, as you know, is ruled by England but I knew I would not be allowed to attend university in this country. I chose Bologna to study science. I also studied medicine and surgery in Alexandria."

"Mr. Nieto is being modest," Embry interrupted. "Not only is he a well-regarded surgeon who has served the allies' forces, he has also studied the mechanical arts and has made some breakthroughs in the field."

Elizabeth spoke up, "Mr. Nieto, I had guessed that English was not your native tongue. I detected an accent but could not quite place it."

The Countess whispered, "Elizabeth, please do not pry. That is rude."

Ariel rolled his eyes and clucked his tongue at his sister.

But Mr. Nieto sat straighter in his seat, looking very seriously at Elizabeth, "Lady Elizabeth, I thought I was doing quite well. Because of Gibraltar's history and its location, most everyone speaks several languages almost from birth so perhaps we have an accent in every one of them. It is hard to tell which language is one's true native tongue. I spoke Ladino and Spanish at home and learned English, Italian and French at school. I have learned Latin but do not speak it of course. Recently I have been studying German for the scientific work I am interested in. And of course, I know Hebrew for religious purposes."

Elizabeth gazed at the very serious man with the very blue eyes. "That is an impressive array of tongues and studies. What do you do for pleasure?"

The Countess put a hand on Elizabeth's arm, "Mr. Nieto, pray forgive Lady Elizabeth's inquiries. We have not been able to teach her to be less inquisitive."

Mr. Nieto turned to the Countess. "I think, Countess, that curiosity is an excellent attribute. It leads us to ask important questions and to seek answers to them."

He turned back to Elizabeth, "Lady Elizabeth, I am not sure that I have ever separated my life into spheres of duty and pleasure as if those are totally distinct parts. Most of what I do is of interest to me and therefore I find most of it pleasant."

"Perhaps you might not feel that way if you saw what happened to Mr. Larkin," Elizabeth snapped. "He is suffering from his sense of duty and I am sure he did not find it pleasant in the slightest."

"Elizabeth, you forget yourself. Your responses are quite inappropriate. I beg Mr. Nieto not to take offence," Embry glowered at his sister.

Elizabeth felt a blush rising on her neck. She looked down at her hands clutching the tea cup.

"Lord Embry, there is no offence to be taken," Mr. Nieto responded quietly."Lady Elizabeth obviously cares for Mr. Larkin and feels deeply for his injuries. Her concern shows a kind nature. Lady Elizabeth, it is true that terrible and unjust actions can be done to people we care about. There should be a balance to the world so that people who cause those terrible and unjust actions do not go unpunished. I only meant that when I spend my time on work that assists people in whom I have interests, and, in some cases, redresses wrongs that are done to others, I find meaning in my life. It is that meaning that encourages me to go on."

There was silence in the room as they gazed at the slender man with the serious brilliant blue eyes behind the severe spectacles. His words seemed to have dimmed the sunny light in the room by reminding them that the world could become ominously dark very quickly.

To break the serious mood, the Countess cleared her throat, then stood up suddenly. The men rose in response. "Well, now I will ask Sherlock to show you to your room, Mr. Nieto. I welcome you to our home and extend our hospitality to you. I am sure you will be of great assistance to Lord Embry."

Seven

The next morning, battle lines were drawn across the breakfast table. The twins had come down to find Mr. Nieto, Embry and the Countess already at table. They seemed to be in the midst of a serious discussion which halted while the twins filled their plates from the breakfast buffet and taken their seats.

An unusual silence prevailed until Embry introduced a new topic. "Maman and I have been discussing how we should celebrate your eighteenth birthdays. We thought of having a supper party of family and close friends with some musical entertainment. What say you about that?"

Ariel looked at his sister quickly before responding to Embry, "For me, that would be quite fine. I could invite my cousins to join me in a concert. I will be able to show off my gift—the fine pianoforte that you and Maman have ordered."

There was a pause. And then the first volley was fired.

"A musicale? Why not a ball? Other young ladies have birthday balls. Surely we can do the same. I had my heart set on it. Do you consider it too dear to have a ball, Samuel? Maman, why can't I have a ball?" Elizabeth demanded, looking at her mother and her older brother and back again as she made her appeal.

The Countess put her hand over Elizabeth's clenched fist. "My child, with your father not here, it would seem inappropriate to have an elaborate event. A quieter affair with close friends and family would be more suitable."

"But we are not in mourning, Maman. Papa could come back for such a special occasion if he really wanted to. We turn eighteen but once. It is not fair, just not fair." She threw her fork onto the table and wrung her hands.

Mr. Nieto spoke up in the tense silence that followed. "Lord Embry, I will get started on the drawings, if it pleases you."

Embry nodded his agreement. The slender man stood, bowed to the others and left the room.

"Eliza, just once think of other people. How embarrassing that Mr. Nieto had to witness your petulant outburst. Consider how hard it would be for Maman to host an event when the Earl is away. It would seem…well…unseemly for her to do so," Embry started calmly.

Elizabeth looked at her older brother with contempt. "I know that it might be disruptive to your life, my dear Lord Viscount Embry, since you are so focused on your models and toys. Are we not staffed to the hilt with people to cook, clean and arrange for a party? Or did we suddenly become poor? There seems to be plenty of money for your interests—your stables and your workshop. I see that there are ample funds for some things but not for what I want. Why cannot I have what my friends have? I am not asking for more—just the same."

"Eliza," Ariel cautioned. "Please do not overset yourself on this. It is of no moment."

However, the fuses had been lit on both sides and it was too late to halt the accelerating battle. Embry smacked his hand on the table and glared at his sister. "Elizabeth, when will you understand? We are not the same. Society does not consider us the same.

"Whom do you plan to invite to this rout? The entire ton? Oh, if the Earl was here, perhaps a large part would come. They dare not insult the Aylesford family. But, with the Earl away, what do you think will be said about such a ball? Do you not see? There will be sniggers and whispers about us trying hard to be just like everyone else. It will be a wonderful opportunity for society to demonstrate how they disdain us."

Elizabeth stood up and faced her brother. "Samuel, you live your life waiting for insults. It is not like that anymore. We are accepted. We are English, just like the others. But you remain suspicious of everyone when they have been nothing but welcoming and friendly. You were not always thus. Do you now have a crippled mind as well as a crippled body?"

Ariel gasped, "Eliza, stop it!"

She could not stop now. The anger was feeding on itself, growing hotter and beyond control. "I refuse to live like you, as if I was ashamed of whom I am. I refuse to have you force me to be less than my friends, to have less than they have, to live less than they do. If I cannot have a ball, I do not want any birthday celebration at all. A musicale will be seen as a defeat, as our admission that we are undeserving of the same pleasures as everyone else." She was white with fury as she ran from the room.

When she was out of Embry's sight, the tears came. She did not like to cry in front of him. She felt that it fed his power to see her thus weakened. Blinded by tears, she ran down the hall towards the stairway to the upper floors and collided right into Mr. Nieto who had just exited the library. At the same moment, she heard the rapid patter of claws on the marble and the snorting breaths of a beast. She felt Mr. Nieto grab her as he tumbled forward, carrying her down beneath him to the floor.

Her head hit the marble. "Incredible!" she thought in a brief moment of clarity. "One really does see stars."

Then there was only blackness. Gradually she heard sounds as if from a great distance followed by a very calm male voice close to her ear. As her vision cleared slowly from black to foggy gray to light, she saw Mr. Nieto sitting on the floor by her side with Beowulf facing him, growling menacingly. Ariel was running towards her while she heard Parker approaching from the other direction. When Parker whistled quietly, Beowulf calmly went to his side.

"Eliza, are you all right?" Ariel asked as he took her hand. "Can you move? Can you rise? Does anything hurt?"

The Countess arrived at her side next, "Oh, my dear child, are you hurt?"

Embry stood at the dining room entrance leaning on his cane, peering down at them all.

Parker apologized, "The running down the hallway put him on alert…I am sorry…Lady Elizabeth…."

Mr. Nieto was gazing at her steadily. "Lady Elizabeth," he said softly. "Can you hear me? Can you see me clearly?" She nodded. "If you permit me, I would like to check to see if you have any injuries."

She nodded again. His hands moved down her legs gently but firmly. His long-fingered hands looked slender and delicate, but she could feel their strength through the layers of petticoats and fabric. She looked up at his face as he worked. His gaze was abstracted as he considered what his hands revealed. She in turn was captivated by his long eyelashes and incredibly blue eyes.

He knelt down at her feet to feel her ankles and nodded with a slight smile. "I think your legs are fine. Can you show me that you can raise your arms? Good, good. Now make fists and rotate your hands. Very good. Can you turn your head? This way? Away from me? Very good. Let me help you up slowly." He looked at Ariel. "Would you assist Lady Elizabeth on that side? Hold her under the arm and I will do the same here. Now rise slowly if you please." Elizabeth folded her legs under her and rose clumsily but firmly up to a standing position. "Now take a step."

"Oh my," she gasped. "It cannot believe where I hurt."

Nieto smiled, "We forget that we humans have a tail bone until we land on it. I fear you will remember for some days to come. It will turn all sorts of interesting colors as well."

Elizabeth blushed as she laughed weakly.

"Countess Aylesford," Nieto turned to speak with Elizabeth's mother, "it would be beneficial if Lady Elizabeth could have a cold compress for the area that is hurting. Twenty minutes on and then twenty minutes off for the rest of the day."

Elizabeth said with great dignity, "Sir, are you suggesting that I sit on a throne of ice all day?"

Nieto looked taken aback.

"Now I can believe that Lady Elizabeth will recover," Ariel sputtered with laughter. "Her sense of humor has returned."

Elizabeth smiled to show she had meant her comment in jest but then inhaled sharply as she took another step. "Perhaps my sense of humor has returned prematurely."

Embry was still silently peering at her from his position at the entrance to the dining room. Elizabeth's smile faded as she looked in that direction.

The Countess took her side as Nieto moved away. "My dear, let us call Hannah to help me get you up to your room. Can you walk upstairs? Thank you, Mr. Nieto, for your care. I think we should send for a doctor to attend Lady Elizabeth."

"But, Countess," Nieto replied with quiet dignity, "*I* am a doctor and, at this time, I think Lady Elizabeth only requires close watching. May I suggest that she spend the next few hours in the library with Lord Embry and me? I would be able to watch her. When she fell, she hit her head as well as her...well, she is likely to endure headaches as the day wears on. I would want to know if the pain increases or if she seems very sleepy or if there are any worrisome changes to her vision or any other behaviors. If you allow, I will ask the Cook to make a tisane with some pain medication that will make her more comfortable. And the ice 'throne' as you call it," he smiled for the first time, "is indeed the best treatment at this time."

So Elizabeth was soon ensconced in the library seated in a comfortable armchair with ice packed into an oilcloth bag placed against her lower back. Her feet were raised slightly on a small stool to alleviate the strain on her back, while she sipped a hot brew with a strong herbal flavor.

Mr. Nieto worked at a large table at one end of the room using rulers and a compass to diagram some mechanical device. Embry looked through books and documents on his desk. Elizabeth avoided looking at him while he avoided speaking with her.

When she sighed, Nieto turned towards her quickly. "Lady Elizabeth, are you in pain?" he asked. She shook her head then winced from the motion. He studied her for a moment then asked, "How is your headache? Has it grown worse?"

"It is easing. Whatever is in this awful drink seems to be helping me."

He kept looking at her intently then suggested, "Would you like a book to read? Perhaps it will help pass the time. I noticed *The Sentimental Journey* by Sterne on the shelf here. Have you read it yet?" He plucked down the volume and brought it to her. "I've read it and found it quite entertaining," he said in a serious tone that seemed to belie his words.

After he opened the book and placed it in her lap, he stood close, looking over her shoulder at the engraved frontispiece. She was very aware of his quiet nearness. When she looked up, the blue eyes were still studying her.

She looked down again. "Thank you. I will try it on your recommendation."

He continued to stand near her, unintentionally distracting her, making it hard for her to remember even the first paragraph. She read it over several times trying to ignore his presence but none of the words made any sense. She sighed again.

He asked, "I wonder, Lady Elizabeth, is it hard for you to read it? Is the print clear? Is your vision changed from what it was?"

Now when she looked up, she found concern in those very blue eyes. "The print is perfectly clear, Mr. Nieto. I just feel a bit distracted and quite embarrassed about all of this." She gestured to her chair and the stool on which her feet were propped.

He smiled, "All of us have tripped and fallen one time or another. Sometimes the more adventurous we are, the more we trip and fall. It is the getting up again that is important and tells more about who we are and how strong we are."

She smiled back then looked down again at the book in her hand. Why did she feel like weeping now?

Nieto went back to the diagrams on the table. The silence in the library was broken only by the sounds of pages turning on Embry's desk, the clock ticking on the mantle and the whisper of pencil moving across paper as Nieto worked. He looked up periodically to glance at Elizabeth. She knew he was watching his patient to observe changes in her awareness or any increase in her pain. She smiled at him when he looked at her to let him know she was fine while she tried to focus on the book.

Embry made his way over to Nieto, examining the diagram on the table. He asked, "How small can we make it?"

"Small enough."

"We need to cast it and polish it quickly. We will need five within a few days."

"How many men do you have?"

Embry sighed. "With Larkin there, it would have been three. Without him, the two who remain are limited. They need close supervision."

"Do you know a jeweler you can trust?"

"The Countess does. I will ask her." Embry turned and left the library, making sure the door remained open for the sake of propriety.

Elizabeth cleared her throat. "Mr. Nieto?"

He moved closer to her.

She continued, "I fear my behavior at breakfast upset you. I apologize. I sometimes find it hard to remain calm with my brother Lord Embry. Our father refers to us as flint and steel."

He looked at her for a few seconds before answering. "I was concerned rather that my presence was embarrassing to the family. Some discussions should be private. And, as you see, I have plenty of work to do."

"Is society in Gibraltar similar to the society here?"

"I am not sure, Lady Elizabeth. I did not spend much time in society. What is it that you wish to know?"

"Embry mentioned that your family is important in its community and you know the Baron and he is acquainted with the Emperor and seems to spend much time at the Court. Are there occasions when the leaders of society in Gibraltar and the leaders of your community—of the Hebrew community—spend time together—at balls and concerts and such?"

"Ah, I see now. My family lived a life apart from any society except those interested in following my father and the teachings of the man he called 'the Great Rabbi.' And when I left my home, I deliberately choose not to spend much time in society, Lady Elizabeth, unless it furthered my goals. There is nothing that I seek or desire among the aristocracy here or in Gibraltar or in Austria. My goals and wishes reside in different places and spheres. So, I am not the person to ask about society and its ways."

"What then are your goals and wishes, Mr. Nieto?"

He became very still, looking at her with his serious intense blue gaze shielded behind his austere spectacles. She saw that he was choosing his words very carefully.

"My wish is, Lady Elizabeth, for balance in this world," he said finally. "My goal is to help that be achieved."

Eight

Elizabeth spent a few more hours in the library, gradually getting engrossed in the book Nieto had selected. When a simple lunch was served there, Embry, Nieto and Elizabeth ate quietly with little conversation. There was still a frigid silence between brother and sister and Nieto seemed lost in some thoughts of his own. However, he kept a watchful gaze on Elizabeth. She felt that he missed very little of what she did or said but made no further comment to her about her accident or her injury.

Embry visited the Countess in her sitting room for tea. A few minutes later, the sounds of the violin drifted down from upstairs. Nieto looked towards the ceiling of the room, listening intently.

"That is my brother, Sir Ariel," Elizabeth explained. "He can spend hours playing the violin or the pianoforte."

"That is Mozart," he said. "Your brother is challenging himself. It is a difficult piece."

Elizabeth looked at him in surprise, "So you are musical as well?"

Nieto shrugged, "I play when I can and sometimes when I need to think."

"What do you play?" she asked.

"I play the guitar mostly," he smiled at the memory that gave him pleasure. "I can travel with it easily so I can play whenever I have a few minutes."

"Did you bring an instrument with you?"

"Yes, I brought a guitar that I bought in Italy."

"You must tell, Ariel. He would love to have someone to concertize with."

He nodded but said nothing more as he rolled out another diagram and reviewed it critically.

At that moment, Embry re-entered the library. "Elizabeth, Maman has an errand tomorrow morning that she would like you and Ariel to accompany her on. That is, if you are well enough to travel."

"Of course, I will go. If I sit doing nothing much longer, I will die of boredom. What is this mysterious errand, Embry?"

"Maman asked me to let it be a surprise so you will have to wait to find out. But I do have a surprise to tell you now. It seems that Maman was persuaded by your tantrum at breakfast this morning. We will have a ball—a smallish ball—to celebrate your birthday. We will invite our family and friends but both you and Ariel can submit a list of your especial friends to be included. We will hold it in about a month, a few days later than your birthday. The family supper party will be on your actual birthday so that Ariel will still have a musical evening."

A wide smile lit up Elizabeth's face. "Embry, thank you, thank you. I am so pleased…it will be wonderful…."

"Eliza, let me forestall your effusive thanks. I am very reluctant to do this but Maman, though concerned about appearances, felt strongly that it was unfair to deny you this amusement just because the Earl must be away in…."

"In His Majesty's service. I know, I know, but I cannot help that and it would be so sad for me to not celebrate on my eighteenth birthday. Oh, I must thank Maman. Mr. Nieto, do I have your permission to go upstairs now? I want to start on the planning with the Countess."

Nieto said with all seriousness, "It seems that the pain has diminished quite suddenly with this news. I caution you to not exert yourself and to let me know if you feel worse or different." His blue eyes twinkled a bit. "But I think visiting the Countess to discuss a ball can only speed your recovery."

Elizabeth started up from her seat then winced. "I see that I cannot help but be cautious. My body reminds me to move carefully and slowly."

After she left the room, Embry walked over to the new diagram that Nieto had unrolled. "Do you think we are ready to build a model?"

Nieto examined the diagram and said thoughtfully. "I would suggest that we start with a full-sized version. There is only the difference in the cost of materials which is not the major hurdle, I think, in this case. And it would save time in testing and readjustments to work full-scale. Are you willing to try it?"

Embry nodded, "Very willing. I rather not let any more time go by."

Nieto nodded his agreement. "Then let me get started on the measurements and then I would like to confer with Larkin about the metals and the tolerances."

Nine

The next morning, the Countess and the twins set off in the carriage with Parker accompanying them as groom. Elizabeth was giddy with excitement, wondering what the surprise might be. Ariel, as was his style, sat quietly watching the path the carriage took to see if he could guess before his sister.

The Countess smiled as she watched them. She had seen this difference in them often and loved that each was an individual. How boring if they had been the same in both appearance and mind? But then, how relaxing it might have been as well—not to constantly be taken aback by their different reactions to the same events or people.

The carriage stopped in front of an elegant shop. Elizabeth looked at the discreet sign:

N. Goldsmid and Son
Jewelers in Gold, Gems and Pearls
Designers of Original Pieces
since 1762

"A jeweler, Maman? For us? Is this the surprise?"

The Countess nodded, "Come in. Mr. Goldsmid will be waiting for us. There are some objects I want your opinions on."

When they rang the bell, the formally-attired gentleman who answered bowed elegantly. "Good day, Countess Aylesford. We are honored to welcome you once again to Goldsmid and Son."

"Good day, Mr. Goldsmid. Lady Elizabeth and Sir Ariel, this is Mr. James Goldsmid. Mr. Goldsmid, how is your father? Well, I hope."

"I am honored to meet you, Lady Elizabeth and Sir Ariel. My father is quite well, thank you. I trust the Earl is in good health and the Viscount Embry as well. Pray have a seat in here."

With Parker standing attentive guard at the front of the shop, Mr. Goldsmid ushered the Whartons into a private room furnished with a finely-carved table and several plush chairs. In the far wall was an opening fitted with a small sliding door. Elizabeth found it difficult to sit still as her excitement grew. In contrast, Ariel sat quietly, waiting expectantly.

The Countess began, "Your father, Mr. Nathan Goldsmid, is crafting some pieces in honor of the twins' eighteenth birthdays. He had sent word that the pieces were ready for us to see today."

Mr. Goldsmid nodded, reaching for the bell pull. A few seconds later, the door in the far wall slid open and a tray lined in black velvet was revealed. The jeweler placed the tray in front of the Countess.

Displayed on the black velvet were two gold pocket watches—clearly one was meant for a man and a smaller, more delicate one for a woman. An etching of a sailing ship with the Aylesford griffon on the prow decorated the man's watch. Tiny gems adorned the tips of the masts and a crown on the griffon's head. The sails were inlaid with ivory and the flags with lapis lazuli. The woman's watch was inset with a circle of beautiful seashells carved from ivory and coral. A seahorse crowned with diamonds, its tail delicately curled around a flower, floated in the center. The precision of the carvings was breath-taking.

"Are you pleased with the work, Countess Aylesford?" Mr. Goldsmith asked, a smile indicating his expectations.

"Very pleased, indeed," the Countess responded. She picked up the man's watch and turned to Ariel. "This is a gift from your father and me," she said softly. "The ship of course is one of the Aylesford fleet and represents an important part of your heritage." She pressed a tiny button on the side of the watch releasing the lock on the cover. "And this represents the other part of your heritage."

The cover opened to display the clock face but the Countess turned the watch so Ariel could see the inside of the cover. An open Torah scroll was etched into the center with Hebrew words inscribed on the parchment: *"Deut 16:20: "Justice, Justice shall you pursue."* Etched into the cover as well were tiny symbols: a singing dove, a harp, a ram's horn, a tambourine.

"The musical instruments of the Bible…we thought they represented you.". She laid the watch in Ariel's hand and he studied it with awe.

The Countess turned to her daughter and held out the lady's watch. "The shells and the seahorse symbolize the oceans the Aylesford ships travel. They also represent your spirit of adventure." She opened the watch to show Elizabeth the inside of the cover. The same Torah scroll with the same words was in the center. Around the Torah were a tiny book, a dove of peace, a pomegranate, an olive tree and a pair of lit candles."These express my wishes for you—for beauty, peace, a happy home, the blessings of children...."

Elizabeth had a catch in her voice as she took the small watch from her mother. "Thank you, Maman, it is exquisite. I wish I could thank Papa in person."

Mr. Goldsmith cleared his throat. "We still have some work to do on the pieces to calibrate the watches and to finish the inscriptions. We did want you to see them as completed so far to approve the design of the cover."

"They are beautiful, are they not, children? I know Mr. Nathan Goldsmid will complete the work in the same high quality. Let us look at chains and fobs for Ariel. And Elizabeth, you can select a pin to hold your watch."

The jeweler raised his hand to the bell pull and two more trays slid through the open hatch. Ariel held on to the watch as his mother selected a gold chain for him and a fob of ruby, diamonds and gold to hang from it. Elizabeth looked at the pins and clips presented to her and selected a pin in the shape of a dove with emeralds as the leaves on the olive branch in its beak.

The Countess nodded at the final choices then stood up. The jeweler rose immediately. "Mr. Goldsmid, we will want the watches by Wednesday next."

The jeweler bowed. "They will be delivered to your home on that date, my lady. I assure you that the work will be completed to the exacting details of your requirements."

The Countess swept out of the room. "Come, children, we need to get home to begin arrangements for the birthday celebrations."

However, the Countess' plans were to be disrupted. When the carriage pulled up at the front of the house, the front door was ajar and Embry's curricle stood out front, a stunned expression on the young groom holding the reins.

A footman rushed to their carriage to hold the horses. As the Countess and the twins descended, Parker leapt from the back of the carriage and ran up to the front door.

Sherlock appeared at the entrance, looking ashen. "Parker…my lord's study…Beowulf…."

Parker raced through the door, disappearing down the hall.

Ariel and Elizabeth looked at each other then together ran up the front steps into the house. The Countess climbed the steps more slowly, dread draining her face of its usual vivacity. "Sherlock, what happened? The Viscount?"

Sherlock shook his head, "My lord is fine. His study….don't go there, wait….."

But the Countess did not hesitate. She followed the twins down the hall towards the open study door.

At first, they could only saw Embry's back blocking the view into the room. Elizabeth looked around her older brother and spotted a man flat on his back on the floor with Beowulf standing on him, growling menacingly into his face. There was blood on the stranger's neck and on his wrist. When he tried to move, the dog's growl grew louder and the beast opened its mouth and snapped his teeth close to the man's neck. The intruder lay still again.

Mr. Nieto was positioned at the man's feet while Parker stood alongside the man, holding onto Beowulf's collar. A breeze entering the room through the opened window riffled the papers strewn around the desk and on the floor. Nieto, turning his back to the intruder on the floor, exchanged words with Parker that no one else could hear.

Parker then whispered a command to Beowulf who moved off the invader but stayed near his head, growling into his face. Parker grabbed the man's arms and twisted them, forcing him to turn over. He tied the intruder's hands together behind him, kneeling on the man's back to keep him still and to draw the ropes more tightly. Finally Parker jerked him to a standing position, pushing him towards the door.

The twins and Embry moved away as the two men approached. Elizabeth looked straight into the stranger's face. His eyes were dilated with terror.

Parker snarled, "Move it, you miscreant. Don't say a word and keep looking down at the ground." The growling Beowulf pushed against the man's legs, forcing the prisoner to march out the study door.

Embry started to follow them. Nieto walked quickly ahead of him, turned back and put his hand firmly on the Viscount's chest, gently pushing him back. "No, it's not for you…you do not belong there…I insist… sir…Lord Embry, sir. In this you will obey me."

Elizabeth looked at her brother's face. His eyes were wide with shock while his jaws were clenched so tightly, his lips had lost all color.

Embry sputtered, "How dare you? This is my home. That man invaded my home."

"I dare because the Baron has asked me to do this. Do you trust the Baron? Then you must trust me and I say this is not for you."

Embry stared into Nieto's piercing blue eyes. Then the Viscount's stiff posture changed, relaxing just a hair, as if some pressure had been released and he could now think more calmly. He finally nodded slowly.

The doctor swept from the room. Elizabeth could hear Beowulf still growling and the sound of a man stumbling and being pushed up the servants' back stairs. A door from the back of the third floor, the section that led to the servant's hall, slammed shut. Something banged into furniture. Then all became ominously quiet.

Ariel and Elizabeth stood still, looking at each other. Embry stared at the doorway through which Nieto had exited. His face was still drained of color.

It was the Countess who moved first, holding her hem up while she skirted around the papers on the floor to reach the open window. She closed it with a definitive slam.

"Sherlock," she ordered brusquely, "have this room straightened. Put all the papers in a pile on the desk for Lord Embry to go through later. Order lunch to be served in the morning room. Tell Rettick to oversee the horses and carriages. Sherlock! Did you hear me?"

Sherlock shook himself from his trance, "Yes, my lady." He left the room to give the staff the orders.

"Now, Elizabeth, Ariel, we will go to the drawing room until lunch is set. Now, please," she ordered, pushing the twins out of the room. Embry walked slowly behind them.

As they entered the hall, they heard from far overhead a shriek that was abruptly cut off and what sounded like furniture being dragged. The Countess stopped momentarily to look up the empty staircase, then straightened her back and continued down the hallway.

Once inside in the drawing room, with the door closed, the group assembled around the hearth. The Countess turned to Embry. "Tell me what happened," she ordered.

"Maman, there is little to tell. Nieto and I had gone to the workshop to discuss a design with the workmen there. After that, we headed home. When we arrived, the door flew open and Sherlock was yelling that there was an intruder and that Beowulf had taken him down. Nieto ran to my study—I followed. When I got there, the dog was atop the invader and Nieto was standing nearby. The rest you know."

"Who is he?" the Countess asked.

"I don't know who he is but the Baron expected something like this after the workshop had been ransacked and Larkin had been attacked. That is why Parker and Nieto are here and why Beowulf has been brought in to patrol."

Elizabeth broke in, "What was he looking for? Is this intruder one of the men who hurt Mr. Larkin? What is it that they think we have? "

Embry looked at his mother first then at his sister, shaking his head. "I cannot explain."

"You mean you will not explain," Elizabeth demanded.

The Countess looked at Elizabeth, "Elizabeth, Samuel means what he said. He cannot explain. There are reasons and you must trust him."

"Trust? We must trust Embry and he must trust the Baron who says he must trust Nieto. You are all hiding something from me so I cannot trust any of you. Ariel, do you know?" Ariel shook his head. "Now I don't believe you, either."

"Elizabeth, trust me…," her twin began.

"Don't say that!" she yelled.

Embry turned to her, "Elizabeth, Ariel knows nothing. I cannot explain. That is final."

There was another crash somewhere above their heads. A loud cry was heard. Elizabeth turned a whitened face to her mother. "Something horrible is going on…."

A sudden knock on the door caused everyone to gasp. Sherlock walked in and stammered when he saw their white faces and eyes wide with anxiety. He cleared his throat and, with great effort to remain calm, announced, "Luncheon is served, my lady."

No one could eat although they went through the motions of selecting food from the offered dishes, nodding to the servant who filled their glasses and pushing food around their plates. They were all very conscious of the silence that hovered above stairs now.

A few minutes later, Rettick appeared at the morning room door with his cap in his hands. "Milord, excuse me for a moment. I need a word with you, sir." Embry followed Rettick out into the hallway, closing the door behind him. He did not return to finish his meal.

Ten

When the bell sounded at the usual time for the evening meal, Elizabeth met Ariel in the gallery outside the family bedrooms. They headed downstairs to the dining room. The door of the library opened. Nieto emerged with Embry. They both looked at the twins, nodding a good evening.

The Countess was in the dining room already and greeted each of them as they took their places. They began to eat but there was no conversation until the Countess tried to start one. "Ariel, have you given some thought to the music for the family at the birthday celebration?"

Ariel was startled from his absent-minded eating by the direct question. "I have not thought much on it yet. I guess a piece by Mozart…on the pianoforte. I wonder if Cousin Frederick might be willing to play the violin? Perhaps we could try a duet," he added doubtfully.

"Mr. Nieto," Elizabeth said, a sharp tone to creeping into her voice. "Perhaps you would be willing to help out in this as you have helped us in so many other ways. You do play the guitar, you said. Perhaps you might entertain us with something from your mysterious past."

Nieto looked at her with his usual serious expression but did not respond to her direct question. Instead he turned to Ariel. "Sir Ariel, perhaps I could look over the music you have. I have done some transcriptions of pieces and might be able to take a part in a duet or trio. Have you any Hummel? He wrote some pretty songs that might work up nicely."

Ariel poked at his food with his fork as he tilted his head in thought. "Perhaps," he answered. "After dinner we can go through my sheets. Cousins Frederick and David both have some musical interests. We could visit them tomorrow and ask them if they might be interested in joining us. Elizabeth, would you play....?"

"No," she said curtly. "I will not." The Countess glanced at her, surprised at her tone but said nothing.

The silence thickened around them. Embry remained silent, lost in thought.

Perhaps because the family members all seemed so lost in their anxiety and shock, for the first time, Nieto initiated a conversation. He turned to the Countess, asking politely, "My lady, would you enjoy it if I played some Ladino songs at the musicale? I know some love songs and lullabies."

"I would love to hear some of the old songs again. Do you know Los Aminantes?" the Countess asked eagerly. "My abuela sang that at our family gatherings."

Elizabeth looked at the Countess and Mr. Nieto in disbelief. She threw her fork on the table and declared, "How can we all sit here as if nothing unusual has happened in this house? Am I going mad? We are all pretending that everything is normal. Who are these people who hurt Larkin and now invaded our home? What do they want? And...and...," now she looked directly at Nieto, "what happened upstairs?" She ended on a strangled whisper. "Who are you, Mr. Nieto, to speak to my brother, Viscount Embry, as you did?"

Nieto put his fork and knife down carefully, placing them precisely back into their proper positions. He seemed to consider for a few seconds before turning to Elizabeth and speaking very carefully, "Lady Elizabeth, I am in myself of no moment. The man you saw however was quite significant in that he assisted us in understanding some threats to others that can now be averted. His presence here must be forgotten totally by you and by your household. Rest assured that he is no longer a threat to you or your family. "

"Where is he now?"

"Gone…he is gone. That is all you need to know." He picked up his wine glass and looked at Elizabeth over its rim. "And he will not return."

The rest of the dinner was eaten in silence. At the end of the meal, Nieto went to his room and returned with his guitar to join the family in the formal parlor. He sat with Ariel on the piano bench to review some music. When they selected a piece to try, Nieto began picking out the melodic line on the guitar while Ariel explored some chords on the pianoforte. While they rehearsed, Elizabeth sought to speak with Embry. She found him in his study.

"Samuel," she said, leaning over his desk where he pretended to look at the stack of papers now piled in a messy heap. "Help me understand. I never knew anyone who could speak to you like Mr. Nieto did—to give you orders in your own home—and to have you obey him. I am frightened because there is something here that is not right. What is the hold that Mr. Nieto has over you?"

Embry shook his head. "Elizabeth, you misconstrue. Nieto has no hold over me except perhaps that of gratitude. I cannot explain but I understand more clearly how much I will owe him. I must do anything he asks. It is to my great shame that I cannot do more than just obey at this time."

Elizabeth sat down in shock in the chair across from the desk. "Oh, Samuel," she whispered, "what have you become entangled in?"

Eleven

A week later, with the resilience of youth, Elizabeth found that the unresolved questions about the break-in at Aylesford House only very occasionally intruded on her thoughts. Most of her attention focused on the plans for the birthday celebrations.

Ariel's new pianoforte gleamed in its place in the formal parlor and in the evenings he was happily practicing for the musicale with his cousins Frederick and David. When Nieto could join them, they explored some quartets.

The family party was but a week away and the invitations for the ball to occur in a month's time had already been sent out days ago. The guest list for that grand occasion was half family and family friends and half the acquaintances of the twins from the ton and their required chaperones so that the number of invitees to the 'small ball' had swelled to one hundred and twenty guests.

Acceptances to the ball started to arrive within days—from the family and the family friends. Ariel quietly went through the mail, trying to shield his sister from an awareness of the low number of acceptances from their friends.

In the meantime, the Countess spent time with caterers, decorators, and agencies that provided extra serving help by the day. Beowulf had to be leashed as the steady stream of hired helpers going in and out of the house put him on high alert and his ferocious appearance frightened the new employees.

Mr. Larkin, recovered enough that he was no longer bedridden, returned to his home. He occasionally appeared at the workshop to oversee what the other men did. Dr. Calderon reported that the danger of gangrene had passed and that his thumbs and forefingers were mending nicely. The other fingers were of little use, paralyzed by the damage done to them. But, as

Elizabeth had said, Mr. Larkin's skills with limited fingers were still outstanding and he now spent most of his time teaching the young apprentices who were eager to learn his craft and to be hired as skilled workers by the Viscount.

Embry and Nieto also spent part of each day together at the workshop. There were times however when Embry returned home without Mr. Nieto or when Mr. Nieto failed to appear at dinner at all. No comments were made about his absence by the Viscount or by Parker.

The clutter of diagrams in the study seemed to disappear overnight leaving the room neat and well organized. Elizabeth glancing through the doors almost did not recognize it. Embry usually spread more paper around. She attributed the new orderliness to the influence of the serious Mr. Nieto.

The day before the birthday musicale proved to be a fine spring day. Embry, in a gesture of good will, said that he would be glad to accompany Elizabeth if she wished to take the bays out for some exercise.

After Rettick had the stable hands bring the small lady's cart around to the front with the bays in the traces, Elizabeth took up the reins under her brother's watchful eyes, touched the whip to the horses' flanks and set them off slowly out of the gate. They turned up the avenue towards the park. Embry quietly made some corrections to her handling as they went and she took the comments in good spirits. The beauty of the day seemed to lift her mood, making her willing to be cordial even to her older brother.

When Elizabeth flicked the whip and loosened the reins, the bays began a spritely trot. The fine day had brought out many groups of people who were strolling along the walking paths that meandered through wooded groves, near ponds and then looped back closer to the carriage path. There were rumors among the girls in her set about romantic trysts that often took place where the pathways entered small copses of trees.

She was about to tease Embry about his knowledge of such places when she noticed a man walking briskly in the same direction as they. The blue coat and slight but erect build looked familiar. She was not certain, however, until, as they drew nearer, she saw the sun glinting off his spectacles as his head swerved to look at the other walkers on the path.

"Mr. Nieto," she said to Embry, pointing with her chin towards the figure, her hands occupied with the reins. She began to slow the horses. "I don't believe I ever met him outside our house, come to think. I wonder what he does when he is out on his own."

Embry grabbed the reins, signaling to the horses that they should pick up the pace.

"Embry, surely we should acknowledge him," she turned in surprise to her brother who kept his eyes straight ahead, "or at least offer him a ride since he is going in our direction...."

Embry kept his face forward, his expression neutral. "Elizabeth, look away. Do not acknowledge him. Do as I say—now...no questions. Do not look back in his direction—stay looking forward."

As they passed, Elizabeth noticed that Nieto was headed towards a copse as the path diverged from the carriage way. He did not seem to see them. Instead, he appeared deep in thought. The carriage path veered away and he was gone from her sight.

Embry handed the reins back to his sister as they continued their drive around the park, stopping occasionally to talk across the path to their acquaintances in other carriages. When they approached the area known as The Long Meadow, Embry suggested that Elizabeth step up the pace. She needed no further urging. They sped down the open path for a half-mile.

The park was filling with other carriages and riders out to enjoy the day so they had to slow down as they made their circuit around the fountain and headed back up the path. After they passed the spot where they had previously seen Mr. Nieto, Elizabeth heard the sound of horses approaching their carriage from behind.

"Halloo, Lord Embry, Lady Elizabeth."

She slowed the cart to allow the riders to catch up. Sir Laurence Sherburne and Mr. Peter Bonner approached on horseback, looking flushed and a bit tousled from their exertions and the light breeze of the afternoon. The two young men doffed their riding hats at Embry and Elizabeth.

Mr. Bonner said cheerfully, "Good day, Lord Embry, Lady Elizabeth. Beautiful day, 'tisn't it? A great day for running a stretch. The bays are looking fine, Lady Elizabeth. Oh, by the bye, Lord Embry, my parents, my sister and I will be delighted to attend the birthday ball. I believe our acceptances should arrive in the mail today."

Sir Laurence added, trying to catch his breath, "Our acceptances are also being sent. We are honored to have been invited."

Embry replied, "We are glad of your attendance, however late the acknowledgement."

The young men looked taken aback for a moment, then they doffed their hats again before cantering off.

"Really, Embry, did you have to scold them?" Elizabeth turned to her brother.

"I did not scold," he responded firmly. "You know very well that there is no mistaking my comments as scolding. I just indicated that I had noticed their tardiness in responding to the invitations. I wanted them to be aware that I noted it."

When they returned home, the Countess and Ariel were sitting in the family parlor. On the table were two beautifully wrapped boxes. Ariel pointed to them and said, "These arrived from Goldsmid's while you were out. I told Maman that I wanted to wait until you returned, Eliza, to open them."

The Countess rose and presented each twin with a box. When they were seated side by side to open their gifts, Embry smiled as he watched them, thinking how they still looked like a matched set with the sun glinting off the beautiful streaks in their hair as they bent over their work. Elizabeth lifted her watch from the black velvet box. It dangled from the dove pin with the light sparkling off the emeralds on the olive branch.

"Maman, it is beautiful. I love, love, love it! I must write to Papa at once to thank him for this lovely gift."

Ariel sat quietly admiring his watch as it lay in the box. When he looked up, his eyes were glistening. "I will treasure this, Maman. It represents all the things I love. It is perfect."

At dinner that evening, when the twins appeared wearing their new watches with pride, Elizabeth looked around the dining room and asked in surprise, "Where is Mr. Nieto?"

Embry responded, "I assume he stayed late at the workshop. He is very diligent about his work. He has a few projects that he is completing for me and he mentioned that he needed to supervise the work this afternoon. We will not wait dinner for him but I have instructed Cook to keep something warm for when he finally arrives."

Elizabeth was startled. They had seen Mr. Nieto in the park that very afternoon, so clearly he was not diligently supervising the men in the workshop. She wondered that Embry did not recall that fact himself. For this time, though, she held her tongue. She did not wish to disturb the peaceful mood of the evening by contradicting him once again.

During the meal, the Countess reviewed the preparations for the birthday musicale evening as well as the responses for the ball. All their family and dearest friends had sent back acceptances and, in the day's morning mail, a note had arrived from the Baron. He would be delighted to attend both events since his business permitted him to return to London just in time. He was honored to accept the invitation to stay with them for a few weeks.

Both of the twins were pleased but surprised. Embry took the news with no reaction. Elizabeth remarked, "Samuel, you seem not surprised. Did you know of the Baron's plans?"

"Not directly, but Mr. Nieto had received word last week that the Baron would be returning to London just before the musicale so, of course, I extended invitations to him."

"Maman, what about the ball? Have we received responses from the other guests?" Elizabeth asked her mother. "We met Sir Laurence Sherburne and Mr. Peter Bonner in the park today and they said they and their families were coming. Their responses are expected today."

Ariel shifted in his seat before looking at his sister. "Eliza, there have been no responses yet from other than our family and family friends. Perhaps it is just a busy season and there might be other parties at the same time making it harder for them to plan."

Embry sat quietly for a few seconds then said softly, "That might be it, Ariel. Responses might come more slowly this time of the season. I will ask around to see what else might be occurring the same night."

Elizabeth looked sharply at her older brother, throwing her concern about not disturbing the happy mood to the wind. "I wager you are feeling pleased, Samuel. It is just as you said, isn't it? You do not believe that the responses will be coming at all. You believe that we are being cut by the ton and you feel vindicated, don't you?"

Embry shook his head, "Not pleased at all." He said nothing else.

Nieto did not appear later that evening nor was he seen at breakfast the next morning. Ariel entered with a concerned look on his face as he dropped into his seat. "Mr. Nieto was to come with me to Frederick's house. We were planning to rehearse for the musicale. But when I asked Sherlock, he said that no one had seen him since mid-morning yesterday. Maybe he will meet me there?"

He looked at Embry seeking a response, but his brother seemed to have not heard his question. Instead, Embry drank his morning coffee, rang the bell and asked Sherlock to have his curricle readied for his use immediately after breakfast. Then he raised the paper, appearing engrossed in the news of the day.

The Countess announced that since she and Elizabeth were headed off for final fittings for their ball gowns at Mme. Clermond's shop, she would have the carriage drop Ariel at Frederick's home on their way.

Ariel objected. It was a beautiful day, so he had thought to walk the short distance across the square and up the few additional streets.

At this, Embry finally lowered the paper, "Ariel, Parker is to be with you when you are out of the house. He cannot be with both you and Elizabeth if you are not traveling together. You will go with Maman and Eliza."

Ariel asked calmly but firmly, "Why do we need protection, Samuel? I know that someone was looking for something at your workshop and in your study and presumably the two events are connected but why would I be in danger? I don't know what they are seeking. I have nothing and know nothing of special importance to a gang of thugs."

"Since we do not know who they are, we cannot presume to know what they want. I know that both the Baron and Mr. Nieto feel that we should remain cautious and I respect their judgment in these situations."

"What situations are these?" Elizabeth joined in. "If we are to limit ourselves, shouldn't we know why?"

Embry gave no answers as he raised his paper once again.

Twelve

That evening, the night of the birthday musicale, the house glowed with fresh flowers and candles. Chairs had been arranged in the formal drawing room so that the guests would be comfortable during the performance. All day, Cook and her helpers had been turning out beautiful desserts and savories and now the aromas of the meats and vegetables for the meal drifted throughout the lower floors.

Elizabeth was in her room letting Hannah finish her coiffeur before she pinned her watch on the shoulder of her dress. She heard Ariel practicing some chords and scales on the pianoforte.

A carriage rattled in the courtyard. Shortly after, there was a rap on the front door. She opened her pocket watch. It was seven—too early for even the closest family members to arrive for the party scheduled for eight. She heard Sherlock at the door, a few mumbled words and then Embry's cane tapping towards the front of the house. More mumbles and the carriage started to move out the gates and down the street.

A few minutes later, Embry appeared in her room in elegant evening dress, looking very handsome. He closed the door firmly behind him. "Eliza, you look lovely and the watch looks beautiful. I wondered if you wanted me to take the gift for Ariel to hide it downstairs so he doesn't see it before time?"

"That is a wonderful idea, Samuel. Let me get it."

She handed Embry the wrapped package containing several Beethoven scores in a beautiful embossed leather portfolio. Surprisingly, Embry did not leave immediately but instead sat down on her bed and smiled at her. She frowned and thought, "I cannot remember the last occasion he spent time with me like this."

Her brother cleared his throat."Eliza, I know that we are sometimes at odds. It seems that we each have a talent to infuriate the other. I am newly come to the role of head of the family and perhaps hold the reins too tightly. Be assured I am always thinking of your and Ariel's welfare. I did want to tell you how proud I am of you. You have become a beautiful young woman with many good qualities—not excepting your strength of character. I know I speak for Father as well and realize how much you must feel his absence and wish he were here. I miss him too," he sighed, looking at his hands atop the cane resting between his legs.

When the handsome Viscount smiled at her, she suddenly recognized the sadness in his eyes. Elizabeth blinked back tears. At that moment, she thought, "I never thought of how burdened he is by all his responsibilities. He has lost some of his own life in assuming his new role."

She recalled his life in the years before their father had left to travel in his Majesty's service. The air reverberated with the clattering sounds of horses and carriages and the shouts from his friends after a win at the track or in a carriage race. There seemed to be young men everywhere about the house—in the stables, the parlor, the dining room, reliving the races and laughing about the spills endured and the challenges overcome. Elizabeth and Ariel thought they were all wonderful—exciting, handsome, full of life.

She also remembered the sounds of Embry and his friends late at night staggering upstairs with Morris' help, singing some ribald songs that were quickly hushed by whispered cautions. Ariel and she would laugh about the noise in the hallways and at Embry's ashen face in the morning, as he tried to hide the lingering effects of his nights out from his parents, who smiled behind their morning cups of coffee.

The Earl had looked at his eldest son and said simply, "Samuel, you are an intelligent man so I assume you see the connection between too much indulgence last night and the resulting ill effects today. Am I correct that the lesson has been learned? I need not say more, I wager."

Now Embry stood awkwardly using his cane for support and patted Elizabeth on the shoulder. "I will be stopping by to speak with Ariel after I secret this package somewhere he will not see it. You should be down in a half hour to greet early arrivals." He kissed her on the crown of her head and walked out, closing the bedroom door behind him.

When Elizabeth went downstairs at a quarter to eight, she found the Baron waiting with her mother and brothers. Once again she was impressed by how dramatically handsome the tall Austrian was. She felt her heart beat more rapidly as he turned to look at her, a warm expression lighting his amber eyes.

"Baron? When did you arrive? I would have been down earlier to welcome you if I had known you were here."

"I only just arrived, Lady Elizabeth. About seven, I think. I am pleased that my business allowed me to come back to London to be here this evening. Lord Embry and the Countess have graciously invited me to be a guest in this house."

The Countess smiled at her daughter. "Eliza, that green dress is lovely on you. And I love how you pinned the watch. It is perfect."

A sudden loud crash resounded overhead causing all conversation to cease. The members of the family pondered over the source of the sound. We are all here, they each thought, but the crash seemed to come from the guest room wing above.

Parker appeared, quickly descending the stairs in his footman's formal evening uniform. "Pardon me, Mum," he said, bowing towards the Countess, "I had to put Beowulf into the back guest room. He was beginning to get excited about the noises and the carriages." He motioned to the front door where the sounds of arriving carriages were clear. "He did not want to be locked away so it was a bit of a rough go to get him confined. I am afraid he knocked some books off a shelf."

At that moment, there was a knock at the door. Everyone assumed their places to greet the arrivals once Sherlock ceremoniously flung the doors open. The guests included Sarah Mendoza and her parents; her betrothed, their cousin David DaCosta and his parents; the Countess' brother Emmanuel and his wife Paulina. The Wharton side was represented by the Earl's cousin, John, and his wife Sybil, and their three children, Frederick, Beatrice and Claire. Cousin Frederick Wharton was a few months' older than the twins and Ariel's closest friend.

Great-Aunt Jeannette Wharton, the spinster sister of their grandfather, the late Earl, lived with John Wharton and his family and had arrived with them. Dear Aunt Jeannette was famous for her elaborate costumes and her inadvertent and sometimes embarrassing discourtesies and well-loved for her bewildered concern when she was made aware of them.

This evening, true to form, when she approached the Baron, offering him her hand, she burbled, "Oh, Baron von Tedesco, I have heard all about you. You have made quite an impression on the ladies. They speak of little else. You really do cut quite a handsome figure, as they said. Is it true you were hunting buffalo with the wild savages in America? Did you really wear fringed leather pantaloons and feathers in your hair and go bare-chested?"

Elizabeth and Ariel tried to hide their grins while the Countess smiled behind her fan and rolled her eyes at them.

The Baron chuckled good-naturedly, "No, dear Lady Jeannette. The real tale is that the buffalo hunted me and I rode away as fast as I could. At the time, I believe I was wearing proper riding attire. But I do believe that at least one part of the story is true. I did wear a feather—in my hat!"

With all the guests assembled, Sherlock announced that the evening meal was served. The Baron had the honor of leading the Countess in. Embry led Aunt Jeannette, followed by Elizabeth and Ariel and the rest of the guests.

Aunt Jeannette started the conversation during dinner by recalling the first time she had seen the beautiful twins. The Earl had brought out his newborn son swaddled in soft blankets, the serious-faced infant studying his proud Papa with solemn eyes. At the same time, Embry emerged holding another bundle that emitted a hearty wail.

Aunt Jeannette recalled looking down into the scrunched-up red and angry features of tiny Elizabeth, already loudly bawling her opinion. "I knew then that she was going to be a trial while Ariel would be the thoughtful considerate type—good as gold," she recalled.

"Thank you, dear Aunt," Elizabeth spoke up. "So everyone knew from birth who was the good child and who was destined to be a trouble-maker. I hope I did not disappoint the family and that I lived up to my reputation of being a harridan."

"Better a harridan, Eliza, than being a boring good child," Ariel laughed. "Not exactly what any boy wants to be called. My reputation was ruined at an early age. What young beauty will want to walk out with the boring good son," he sighed dramatically, looking forlornly down the table at his aunt.

Great-Aunt Jeannette was bewildered. "Oh dear," she fluttered, "I did not mean to offend by calling you a good child. Imagine that. Being a good child is an insult? Oh dear me...."

Embry broke in, "Dear Aunt, do not be distressed. Ariel appeared to be good, but that only misled us in not noticing his tricks. The good child switched salt and sugar in Cook's bins when he was eight and we of course only discovered it after soup was served. No one could look more innocent as we tried to learn how the mistake was made. Of course, we all assumed it had been Elizabeth."

The guests laughed while Ariel had the good grace to blush. Then Elizabeth chimed up, "And what about the time that Father found his claret watered. It seems that Ariel and Frederick had been playing 'gentlemen at the club' when they suddenly realized that Papa might notice the drop in the level in the decanter. But more than that, he noticed the change in their composure…and how sick they were afterwards." At this, both Ariel and Frederick bowed their heads in exaggerated embarrassment.

The Baron smiled at Ariel. "So Ariel, you now have a turn to tell an amusing story about Lady Elizabeth. Did she indeed live up to her early reputation?"

Ariel smiled wickedly at his sister before saying slowly, "Well, let me see. Which story shall I tell? The one when Elizabeth took Embry's ….no, not that one. I know! The one when she dressed up in my clothes as a ….perhaps not, that might mean Maman will need to confine her to quarters for a long time…."

Elizabeth looked alarmed as the company egged Ariel on to tell all. He grinned at Elizabeth but kept her secrets.

After the meal, the family and guests moved into the formal parlor for the musical portion of the evening. Ariel went to his new instrument while Frederick tuned his violin. Just as the two young men paused before beginning, a thud was heard from upstairs. All the guests looked at the ceiling at the same time as if they would be able to see clear through the painted plaster to discern what was happening several floors above. Parker signaled that he would check into the source of the noise and quietly left his post by the door as Ariel and Frederick began to play.

When the two young men bowed to the applause of their guests, the Countess turned to the Baron. "Mr. Nieto had promised to play guitar and sing some Ladino songs. I am so sorry that he is not here this evening. I thought you too would enjoy hearing the songs from our Spanish heritage."

"My lady," the Baron responded, "I would be pleased to play my guitar and sing for your guests. I know some Sephardic songs. Please excuse me while I fetch my instrument."

Ariel launched into some piano études while the guests waited for the Baron to return. He played with concentration and joy, entrancing the audience as the music filled the room.

When the Baron returned, he seated himself next to the piano. While he tuned the strings on his beautiful guitar, Ariel took a seat next to his mother who enfolded his arm in hers, patting his hand affectionately.

The Baron smiled at the Countess as he began an intricate melody on the guitar. As he added chords to the melodic line, he began to sing softly, his strong voice clearly articulating the medieval Hebrew-Spanish blend that was Ladino and sliding over the glissandi that made the melodies so exotic. The Mendozas and the DaCostas looked at each other with smiles of remembrance of the melodies of their grandparents while the Whartons were charmed by the handsome Baron with the amber eyes and the silken voice.

The Baron next launched into a joyous up-tempo folk song that coaxed the audience to clap in rhythm. At the end of the second piece, he strummed a flourish and made an exaggerated bow to the enthusiastic applause. His eyes were focused above their head on the rear door through which Parker had just returned. Parker nodded at the Baron.

Embry twisted slightly in his chair. When he noticed Parker had come back, the Viscount relaxed with a quiet sigh.

The doors opened with a flourish as Sherlock supervised the footmen who were wheeling in a large trolley laden with a beautiful cake lavishly decorated with candied fruits and a coffee trolley. A third footman entered with a tray of crystal flutes filled with champagne as Embry ushered the twins to the head of the room.

After everyone had been served champagne, Embry lifted his glass in a toast, "My parents and I thank all our dear family who have come to celebrate this wonderful occasion. The Earl wished he could be here. He is very proud of the twins and the wonderful, kind, and talented young people they have become. Let us drink to their good health!"

As dessert was served around, the twins opened their gifts. Ariel was thrilled with the leather portfolio for his music with the Beethoven compositions tucked inside. Elizabeth opened a thin box that held the gift from Ariel—a gossamer silk shawl in a deep green. "Oh, Ariel, this is lovely. Thank you so much, dear brother."

There was yet another box for each twin from the Baron. Elizabeth took out a beautiful red fox fur muff. "Oh my," she cooed, as she slid her hand over the silky fur. Ariel's gift was a pair of soft black leather gloves with deep cuffs of black fur. When both twins thanked the Baron profusely, he responded with a smile, "May you wear them always in good health and on happy occasions."

The evening had been filled with good cheer and affectionate banter from those who had gathered to celebrate with the twins. Periodically someone had sighed and mentioned how much the absent Earl would have enjoyed this evening. Finally, as the clock chimed midnight, the guests began to depart as their carriages moved up in a queue to the front door.

When the house fell silent after the final guest had left, Elizabeth and Ariel took their leave of the Baron, and hugged first their mother and then Embry, thanking them both for a wonderful evening and for their generosity. They made their tired way up the stairs. The Countess soon followed them, as the Baron and Embry repaired to the library for brandies and cigars.

Thirteen

What a warm and comfortable feeling, Elizabeth mused, as she lay in bed that night, to be with the members of her family who openly expressed their love and affection for each other—even for Aunt Jeannette, who so often uttered unintentionally barbed comments. No one seemed willing or interested in stirring up animosity or being offended. Nice people, she yawned sleepily. And the Baron, she smiled, so elegant, so handsome.

What a beautiful gift—a stunning red-fox muff. None of her friends had anything so exotic. And he'll be at the birthday ball so she will waltz with him again. She began to drift off.

She could not recall what woke her, but she lay in bed with her heart pounding. There had been some sound—a bang perhaps, or a thump. She got up to look out of the window. There was no wind or storm that might have rustled tree branches against the house. She sat on the edge of her bed for a few minutes to think and to listen closely to hear if the sound was repeated.

She thought she heard a few creaks from overhead and perhaps...perhaps footsteps? Then there was the sound of claws tapping on the floor close by. Beowulf, she thought, making his rounds throughout the house at night.

A sudden soft rap on her door caused her to gasp. She took a few steps to her bedroom door then whispered, "Who's there?"

"It's me," the reassuringly familiar voice of her twin whispered back. Ariel, in his green robe, stood outside her room, holding a small candle-lamp in his hand, his hair tousled from sleep. Beowulf stood by his side. "I wasn't sure – but did you hear something from upstairs?"

Elizabeth nodded. "The Baron is in one of the guest rooms. Maybe he is having a restless night?"

Ariel looked at her thoughtfully. "But he is in the suite in the west gallery. I thought it came from overhead—the back guest room. Since Mr. Larkin is back home, that room is empty."

They considered this for a few seconds then both looked down at the large mastiff. Beowulf stared back with his soulful eyes. "It cannot be another intruder. Beowulf would not be calmly standing here," Ariel said. "I am going upstairs to see if anything fell down." He smiled weakly at Elizabeth, "Since my bedroom is right underneath, I don't want water from an overturned pitcher dripping upon my head all night."

"I am coming with you. I wouldn't be able to sleep while you thudded around upstairs anyway," Elizabeth said firmly, grabbing her robe. "Lead on, brother."

Ariel crossed the south gallery and started up the steps with Beowulf calmly climbing beside him. Elizabeth followed behind, lifting the long skirts of her nightgown and robe to avoid tripping. At the head of the stairs, they saw pale light leaking out from under the door to the back guest room. They looked at each other and silently agreed to creep down the hall towards the light.

When they reached the door, Ariel put his ear to it to listen. He raised his eyebrows toward Elizabeth and shrugged his shoulders. He pushed carefully and the door opened slowly. He peeked around the door then stopped.

Elizabeth reached over and yanked on his sleeve. He motioned to her to stop while his head was still in the room. He pulled back, whispering, "There is someone in the bed."

"Can you tell who it is?"

Ariel shook his head then opened the door wider to enter. Beowulf sidled in past him, as if used to visiting the room. Elizabeth grabbed the back of Ariel's robe to follow.

They cautiously approached the bed set against the wall farthest away from the door. Ariel held his lantern away from the sleeping figure's face so as not to awaken him but to let enough light shine to illuminate the face.

Elizabeth gasped in a whisper, "Mr. Nieto!?"

They both peered down at Nieto, the covers drawn to his chin. His eyes were swollen shut and there were bruises on his cheeks only slightly hidden by the stubble of his beard. Deep furrows appeared on his forehead and between his brows—highlighting tension that was apparent even as he slept deeply. He turned his head back and forth, moaning through clenched jaws as beads of sweat appeared on his forehead. One of his arms flailed wildly, hitting the small table next to the bed. A loud thud resounded through the room.

"You should not be in here," the Baron's voice startled them, coming from close by, its rich baritone in a hushed whisper.

The twins turned quickly. The Baron was holding a filled goblet in his hand.

Elizabeth saw first the broad expanse of golden chest with curly black hair revealed by the robe wrapped about the tall man's frame. Only then did she notice the stern expression on the tall man's face.

She stared back at the Baron with a defiant glare. "Why shouldn't we be here, Baron? This is our home after all and we have never been locked out of any rooms before. We have as much right to be here as you...."

She was cut off by the sound of more thrashing from the bed. Nieto emitted another moan of pain.

When she turned back to the bed, she saw that the covers had been kicked aside revealing Nieto's bare leg and part of his chest and arm—his heavily bandaged chest and arm. It took a few moments for her to realize that she was seeing half his naked body—and just that quickly she had noted that it was a lean but muscled body at that.

The Baron pushed past them to reach the bed. He bent over Nieto—putting an arm behind his thrashing head to raise him slightly. He lifted the goblet to his lips. "Drink, Judah, drink. It will help with the pain," he whispered.

Nieto's eyes fluttered open as he struggled to avoid the goblet. The Baron sternly repeated the order to drink until finally, the doctor sipped from the glass. His body began to still as the Baron guided his head back down to the pillow, then rearranged the bedclothes to cover him.

The Baron turned back to the twins who had stood stock still, watching from the middle of the room. "I must stay here until Doctor Calderon's man returns with more laudanum. If you wish, wait for me in the south gallery and we will talk." The twins stood still for a moment to consider this and then, as one, turned to retreat out of the room.

Ten minutes later, the Baron joined them. He ran his hands through his thick dark hair slowly as if he was stalling to consider what he should say. "Elizabeth, Ariel, I trust that you will understand that everything I say must be held as secrets. I will tell you what I can share. Nieto was attacked yesterday by people we believe are part of a dangerous gang seeking information to sell to our enemies. We suspect the same people are behind the attack on Mr. Larkin as well as the invasion of Embry's study. We cannot go to the authorities because our important work here must remain secret."

"But why did they attack Nieto?" Elizabeth asked.

"I can only say that they believed him to be in possession of something that would help their cause. Indeed, they took some papers from him before beating him senseless."

"Were the papers important? Would they help our enemies?" Ariel asked.

"We hope that they think they have gotten important information for their cause. That was our plan."

Elizabeth gasped, "We … our plan? Who are the 'we' and the 'our'? And you say that …it was planned. Nieto was deliberately sent out to be beaten?"

The Baron shook his head, "I cannot go into details. It was planned that the papers be stolen. I did not believe it would go as far as bodily harm."

"You sent him out to be robbed, then?"

The Baron smiled grimly, "I never ordered Judah Nieto to do this. He himself determined the plan and then executed it. This is not the first time he has suffered the results of his own strategies but Dr. Calderon assures us that this will not be the last time either. His injuries are deep but not fatal.

"He does however need time to heal. That must happen in secret. As you saw, like many doctors, Judah cannot abide being a patient himself. He hates to feel helpless and to have people fuss over him. I know that your rest has been disturbed already and the night might pass slowly but you must return to your beds. I beg you on your honor that all that you have seen and been told this evening will not be shared with anyone."

Elizabeth asked, "Does Embry know? Does my mother?"

The Baron looked at them intently. "Yes, they know. But no one must know outside this house. Do I have your word?"

The twins nodded silently. The Baron then saw them to their rooms and turned back down the darkened hallway. From the safety of their bedrooms, they could hear the tap-tap-tapping of Beowulf's claws as the mastiff made his rounds.

Fourteen

When the twins came down to breakfast the next morning, the Baron was already at the table. He and Embry had been talking but the conversation halted abruptly when the twins arrived. The Countess followed them in, holding a sheaf of papers.

When all were seated, the uncomfortable silence continued. The Countess rustled the sheets in her hand, while signaling the footmen to withdraw.

When they had left, she spoke. "There is so much left to do for the ball," she sighed. "Cook will need additional kitchen staff and Sherlock will need more footmen to attend the guests."

The Baron looked up from buttering his toast. "Countess, perhaps I can be of assistance. When I travel to London, I have need to hire staff myself. Mr. Stein, my man of business, uses the services of a reputable agency to find them. I can have him make the arrangements for you if you think that it would suit."

"Embry, would that be acceptable?" the Countess looked at her eldest son eagerly. "It would be such a help."

Embry nodded, "I have faith in the Baron's judgment in this as well as in all else." He looked significantly at Ariel and Elizabeth. The twins wondered if the comment was a signal that it was safe to broach the topic on their minds.

The Baron took the initiative. "I fear the twins' sleep was disturbed last night. I explained a bit about Mr. Nieto's injuries and the importance of keeping it a secret within the house as he recovers. They know that all of us are aware of his condition."

The Countess sighed with relief. "I do find it so unpleasant to dissemble so I am glad that you both know. It is, as the Baron has said, important that others do not learn about Mr. Nieto's condition. Obviously the household staff has been told that he is quite ill and that they are not to go into the room for a few days. Parker and Dr. Calderon's man are attending him until he can get up and about."

Ariel asked, "Can I visit? I know that Mr. Nieto enjoys music and I can play for him if he might find it soothing."

"And I can read to him. He told me he had enjoyed Sterne's novel. Perhaps I could bring him other books as well?"

"That is very thoughtful of you both," the Baron responded. "It will be a few days yet before Dr. Calderon permits visitors. Currently Mr. Nieto is sedated to avoid the pain of his injuries and to keep him from arguing with us about his care. As skilled a surgeon as he is, he makes a truculent patient. When Doctor Calderon says it is proper, then perhaps you can attempt to entertain the invalid."

It was a full five days before Dr. Calderon gave permission for the patient to have visitors. When Ariel and Elizabeth went up together to see if Ariel could entertain the doctor with some violin music, they found Nieto sitting in a chair, looking very pale but alert. His left arm was in a sling across his chest and the outlines of bandages were visible under his loose shirt. His face, still marked by fading bruises, was drawn and thin, making his piercing blue eyes more dramatic than ever. He smiled wanly when Ariel offered to play.

Elizabeth sat in the other chair in the room while Ariel played some folk songs on the violin. Nieto closed his eyes, took a deep breath and listened, leaning his head back against the chair. From where she sat, Elizabeth was able to study his profile. She had not noticed before the fine sculpture of his head, the planes of his cheeks and his strong jaw. Even his ears were beautifully formed—small and close to his head. His thick curly hair, longer than was now fashionable, was a very rich dark brown.

She wondered now why she had never seen how handsome he was. She thought, "Perhaps one cannot see other men when the Baron is around. His golden glory puts others in the shadow. I wonder how old Judah is…Judah…what a beautiful name. I wonder about his story…."

As Ariel ended the cycle of songs, the door opened, admitting Dr. Calderon, who was pleased with his patient's progress."I am glad that Mr. Nieto is able to have visitors. Now I need to examine my patient and attend to his bandages. I wonder, Lady Elizabeth, if you could ask Cook to send up more substantial food for Mr. Nieto. He is ready for something more appetizing than broth and dry toast. Mind, nothing heavy or highly seasoned. Perhaps an omelet and a baked apple."

"How sad," Nieto sighed but with a gentle smile on his face, "that an omelet and a baked apple sounds like a meal fit for a king. I thank you both for your visit. It was kind of you. I cannot get up to see you out, I am afraid, but I believe soon…."

While Nieto recuperated upstairs, the preparations for the ball continued apace all over the house. Mr. Stein, the Baron's man of business, was a dignified gray-haired and bespectacled gentleman who spoke excellent English with a slight Austrian accent and looked every bit like a government minister. Before meeting with the Countess and Embry, he accompanied the Baron to Mr. Nieto's sick room and was closeted there for half an hour. When he left the house, he had lists of staff to hire and extra furniture and serving dishes to rent.

By the next day, Mr. Stein's efficiency was made manifest. More skilled kitchen and well-trained household help started to arrive along with porters carting rented tables and chairs and linens and serving dishes.

Almost everyone in the house was kept very busy. Sherlock and Cook were training the new employees. The Countess reviewed menus and seating plans, conferred with staff and spoke with decorators about creating a spring garden fantasy throughout the public rooms. Ariel and the Baron spent afternoons going out to listen to musicians to select an orchestra for the evening.

But, for most of the day, each day, Elizabeth felt in the way as the hustle and bustle in the house reached a crescendo. She did spend time with Embry practicing her driving skills but he was also very involved in projects in his workshop. In fact, he often visited Nieto, carrying drawings for new designs up the stairs to the sickroom.

She also wandered up to the back guest room to see if she could amuse the patient, now that Ariel was busy with the Baron. Dr. Calderon's attendant sat in the room while she read out loud from a popular novel of the day. At other times, Mr. Nieto read to her. She sat enthralled as his quiet clear voice took on the speech patterns of the people in the story. He stopped periodically to ask what she thought about the characters and their motivations. He listened to her opinions thoughtfully but challenged her if she became flippant.

One afternoon, he stopped after just a few pages. "Lady Elizabeth, you are troubled and distracted by something. Can I help?"

She shook her head. "No, there is nothing…" but her hands betrayed her by continuing to twist handfuls of her skirt's soft muslin into tight wrinkles.

When she lifted her eyes, she found Mr. Nieto's gaze on her face. His intense blue eyes looked sympathetic. Something had opened between them, inviting her to share her concerns.

"Mr. Nieto, did you ever want something so much because you thought it would make you really happy, and you worked hard to get it and when you finally were going to get it, you realized that it wasn't what you thought it was…that it wasn't going to make you happy at all? And then you just couldn't stop it?"

A few seconds passed before he responded, "Lady Elizabeth, is it the birthday ball of which you are thinking?"

She nodded. "I wanted it so much. Ariel did not care overmuch but I wanted to have everything that my friends were having. But now I find that so many of the people I thought were friends are not at all. Only half the people we invited have accepted. The others have not even sent regrets. They have not responded at all. They as good as cut us. I have brought this humiliation on my family. I see the effort that my mother is making and the expenses that Embry is paying to create this wonderful evening but all I wish now is that I could make it stop.

"Embry was right after all. This ball is very wrong. I am mortified that my family has been treated so badly by so many—and the ton is watching it being done. I have held my dearest ones up to ridicule."

Nieto turned in his seat so that he could look her fully in the face. "Lady Elizabeth, I understand the pain you feel. But if it is a comfort, consider that you have in fact discovered something very important. You have found that there are things that are truly valuable—rare and precious and genuine— and other things that appear valuable but are merely colorful baubles that break easily once you grab them. Likewise, there are people who are true and genuine and caring in your life and then there are others who appear to be caring and exciting but are merely brittle images with no substance to them. There are values that can be divided the same way—those that are enduring and precious and others that are of the moment, ephemeral and shallow and easy to discard."

He unexpectedly touched her hand. "Sometimes, one learns these things only after a great tragedy—after much pain and heartbreaking grief. Some people never learn this so they spend their lives chasing after the shiny but fake baubles, never seeing the true gems in their lives. You understand my meaning?"

She nodded.

He went on, "It is a sign of your true and genuine soul that you can sense now the difference between true values and false ones. It often takes a lifetime to understand this. You have had a rare gift because you are learning all this when you are young and still surrounded by people who love and care for you."

"Mr. Nieto, I am so ashamed. I cannot bear the thought of the ball, of having to look happy when I feel angry at the way my family is being treated. There must be a way to stop it now."

He smiled. "Stop it? Some people would be very happy to learn they have so much power over you that, if they do not attend, you consider it not worth having the ball at all. And what would you be saying to those who want to come to celebrate with you? That they are not as important to you as those who wish you ill?

"It is perhaps more appropriate that those who are eager to celebrate with you have a wonderful time that evening and that you have a wonderful time with those who should be valued in your life. After all, our teachers tell us that God created the earth for us to find joy and pleasure."

Elizabeth was surprised. "So that is what you would do, Mr. Nieto? Defy the naysayers by having a wonderful time with true friends?"

The smile left Nieto's face. "I wish, Lady Elizabeth, that I had had a chance to do just that. My experiences have not lent themselves to turning the tables quite that neatly. And alas, I find that my nature does not let me rebound as quickly as I suspect you will. In my case, the lessons were harder to learn and my responses had to be harsher as well. You are blessed that you are surrounded by so many who wish you well and who will protect you from harm. Those who wished me well suffered for it."

Elizabeth had no response to those somber words but looked into the blue eyes that held such depths of feeling. Nieto blinked twice and gave a sudden shake of his head as if returning to the present. "I fear I am becoming fatigued, Lady Elizabeth. When I do, I tend to become melancholic."

The attendant rose, saying, "Lady Elizabeth, Dr. Calderon ordered me to bring Mr. Nieto back to bed if he became fatigued. Pray excuse us. It is past time for him to rest."

Elizabeth touched Mr. Nieto's hand as she rose. "I should not have stayed so long. I presumed on your kindness, prattling on about my girlish worries. Rest well, Mr. Nieto."

Fifteen

Elizabeth found Embry in his study bent over papers. She suspected that the pile contained the bills for the ball she now dreaded. He looked up and smiled at her as she entered.

"Samuel, may I have a word with you?" He motioned her to the seat opposite the desk. She slumped into the chair and sighed. "I wish to apologize."

He said nothing so she went on. "I wanted this ball so much and kept at you so long that, against your better judgment, you finally agreed to it. I now realize how right you were. I have brought embarrassment to the family and," she waved at the papers, "needless work and expense. I fear we will need to go through with it nevertheless but I am so sorry."

Embry steepled his hands and rested his chin on them. He thought for a few seconds then smiled again. "Eliza, it is very honorable that you come to me with these thoughts. Yes, I was against the whole idea but I have found myself rethinking my own position as well.

"Consider what has happened in this household in the last few weeks. Maman is so busy with all the arrangements that she spends her days downstairs with the staff, the agencies, the merchants and with us, instead of being secreted in her library upstairs. Ariel is delighted. Every day he goes about town with the Baron, listening to and discussing music with someone who is knowledgeable and interested and has so much to share about adventure, travel and life. Cook is enjoying every minute—though of course she complains of all the extra work—dusting off her old recipes and pulling out the pots and pans she has had no occasion to use in many a day. Sherlock is playing general, organizing his troops for the big engagement. It has been a long time since this house has been so lively and so happy."

"But what about the insults from the ton? Those who have not even responded to the invitations—who are smirking at us and talking about us? Do those not bother you?"

"Eliza, yes, I am angry but I have chosen to celebrate with those who wish us well. Those who do not—and there might be many—would not think well of us even if they deigned to come. They would be here to sneer at what they see. The only difference is that we now know who they are and that makes us so much wiser. And," he laughed with real glee, "they will miss the most wonderful evening of the season. Their loss indeed."

"Mr. Nieto said the same."

"I know. I spoke with him about this."

"You spoke with Mr. Nieto, Samuel? I would not have thought that you would share your intimate thoughts with a member of your staff."

"You must think me an abominable snob then. I have been working with Mr. Nieto these past weeks on some special projects. I have learned to listen to him. He is very wise about the ways of the world.. I would say that with the Earl and the Baron, Mr. Nieto is one of the few men I truly admire. Oh, and there is Mr. Larkin of course." Embry smiled at his sister once again.

"And the expense?" She eyed the papers on the desk. "Isn't this dear? And wasteful?"

Embry laughed yet again, causing Elizabeth to smile back at him. "Mr. Nieto reminded me that we are meant to be joyous and to take pleasure in the world. Too often, I fear, I see only the darkest side of things. As a wise sister once said, I can see dark at noon.

"There will be times we must use our resources to avert disaster or to meet challenges but we should not miss the times we have to celebrate. Besides spending on the ball makes me feel easier about spending more on my stable. And, for each person who does not attend, I am going to donate to charity so they will be doing good for others by trying to do ill to us."

Elizabeth sat silently so long that Embry began to turn back to his pile of papers. Finally she whispered, "Samuel?"

"Hmmm?"

"You are quite wonderful, you know. I am fortunate to have you as my big brother."

He looked up in surprise, then a wide smile lit his face. "I am also fortunate to have you as my baby sister—or rather, my sister who is now a young lady." He laughed, "How long do you think this truce will last?"

Elizabeth laughed in return, "Until tea time, perhaps, if we are very fortunate."

Suddenly, the library door was flung open. Ariel loped in with the Baron close behind. He threw himself in a dramatic heap onto the sofa nearest the fireplace and put his booted feet up on the low table in front of it, announcing, "I believe even I have had my fill of music and musicians this day."

The Baron chuckled, "Well, all of our hard work ended with success! We have found a wonderful small orchestra with a gifted young violinist just arrived from Italy."

"Samuel, you should have seen it. The Baron was chatting away in Italian—charming everyone and learning their life stories. The violinist has agreed to give me music lessons as well after the ball. If that meets with your approval, that is." He clasped his hands making a silent appeal to his brother. Embry nodded then pointed to Ariel's feet on the table. Ariel dropped them to the floor with a loud thud as he added, "By the way, Mr. Larkin just arrived with a large wrapped package and asked to see Mr. Nieto. I thought it would be all right for Parker to take him upstairs. I guessed they needed to discuss a project from the workshop."

"Hmmm—I would assume so," Embry stood, grabbing his cane lying against the desk. "I will go up to see what it is about. Baron, perhaps you might join me?"

When the two men left the library together, Ariel stretched his hands over his head, put his feet back on the table and sighed happily. ."This has been a great treat—going around London with the Baron and listening to music all day. Imagine, Elizabeth, the Baron spoke in German and French and Italian. He was so charming. Everyone was eager to audition for him and to discuss the latest dance music. The ball will be absolutely wonderful! Thank you for prodding Embry into it."

"Ariel, don't you care that some of the ton are not coming and are not even sending responses? Don't you feel embarrassed about that?"

"Bah…I do not care a fig for those…those foppish fools and missish chits. I have no time to even consider them. It will be a wonderful evening for those fortunate to be there."

"Well, Bonner and Sherburne will be coming at least. They have sent their responses and compliments."

Ariel cocked his head at his sister. "I do wonder about that. Some of their friends have refused the invitations. I did not think they would be willing to go contrary to others in their set. After all, we are not really close. Oh well, perhaps it is your beauty, dear Eliza, that has enticed them to throw over the bounds of the ton and come to dance…or perhaps their sisters are swooning for me and must come to quench their romantic thirst."

He threw himself back on the sofa in a swoon with his arm over his eyes. However, he was able to see enough to dodge the book that Elizabeth picked up from Embry's desk and chucked at him.

Sixteen

The evening of the ball was indeed memorable—but in ways no one in the household could have predicted.

The first surprise occurred when Ariel, frustrated with his cravat, went to seek Morris, Embry's valet, for help. He entered Embry's bedroom but finding it empty, he headed into the dressing room. There he stopped short in shock.

Embry was seated on a bench facing the door with his shirt on but with his evening trousers down past his knees. A man was kneeling between his legs with his head down doing something with his hands. Embry was leaning back with his head up, bracing his body with his arms against the bench. His eyes were closed and his jaws were clenched as if to prevent sounds or cries from escaping.

Without realizing it, Ariel uttered a gasp. Embry opened his eyes to see his brother standing at the door of the room—his face ashen, shaking his head in disbelief. The man at his feet raised his head, looked first at Embry's face, saw his look of distress then glanced over his shoulder at the doorway. It was Nieto—on his knees with his hands on Embry…doing something that Ariel could not see clearly but he could guess….

"Ariel," Embry said breathlessly, "stay a moment…wait." But Ariel had turned and rushed out.

Nieto asked, still kneeling, "Shall I go get him?"

Embry shook his head, "No…not yet…please continue…I have waited too long for this. We do not have much time. We might be interrupted again."

Ariel had run blindly back to his bedchamber. There he paced up and down, wondering what he should do next, twisting the cravat tightly in his hands as he went. He knew exactly what he had stumbled upon. He had heard the jokes and sneers that boys make about those types of men. He had even known some boys at school....

His mind went over everything he had heard Embry say about Nieto and every time he had seen the men together. Is this why Embry seemed to value Nieto so highly? Did it explain why Nieto, just one of his brother's many employees, seemed to have special privileges? Ariel felt his chest tighten until he thought he would not be able to draw another breath.

There was a knock on the door followed by the Baron's voice, "Ariel, may I speak with you?" Without waiting for a response, the Baron opened the door. He went up to Ariel and put both hands on his shoulders. "Ariel, calm down. We need to talk." He pulled the now-sodden cravat from Ariel's fists and looked at it with amusement. "I think this will not be used tonight."

"This is no time for a joke."

"Ariel, I can imagine what you think you just saw. But I am here to take you back to Embry's room to clear up your confusion. Come with me—now."

"I cannot face him. I cannot believe...I need time to think about this...."

"No, Ariel, you must come with me now."

The Baron took Ariel by the arm, forcing him back to Embry's rooms. They entered the bedchamber where his brother stood, waiting for him. Embry opened his arms and walked towards Ariel with a concerned look on his face. "Ariel, I must explain."

Ariel shook his head "no." He was not ready to talk about this. He saw Nieto standing in the corner of the room, watching them quietly. He felt a surge of anger. How dare this man come into their lives and suddenly change everything—enticing his brother down that path?

His brother stood in front of him, smiled warily and said, "Ariel, look at me. Am I different in any way?"

Ariel looked at his brother in disbelief. He seemed so normal, so himself—so tall and handsome and straight. How can he be so normal after being discovered in such a compromising position?

Then he saw what was not there. "How did this happen?" Ariel asked in shock.

His brother was standing with both hands outstretched towards him—both hands because he was not holding a cane.

Embry smiled broadly. "A surprise…a wonderful surprise—almost a miracle and I have Mr. Nieto and Mr. Larkin to thank for this. They have been working on an articulated brace for leg injuries and I am proud to be wearing the first. Here—feel this."

He placed Ariel's hand on his waist and carried it down to his thigh. Ariel could feel what seemed to be a leather belt and a metal piece extending down the leg under the fabric of the trouser. "It has joints at the hip and knee so it can flex but when I stand, I can force it to lock in place giving me more support. I can walk some distance with it with only a slight limp since my leg can bend for each step. But I can now hold my weight without a cane. I am practicing to walk stairs and I fear I will never be able to dance but when I walk and when I stand, I can have both hands free. Of course, I will never wear evening knee breeches again but that is no loss. I never liked those things anyway." He clapped both hands on Ariel's shoulders, grinning with joy.

"Oh, Embry, I can't believe…I thought…oh my God, what I thought…."

Embry patted Ariel on the cheek. "Oh, my dear brother, I realized when I saw your face what it must have seemed to you. Someday it might be funny but now I am sorry for your confusion and distress." He lowered his voice to a conspiratorial whisper, "Now this is to be a surprise for Maman and Elizabeth.

So put on a blank face now and don't drop a hint until I am safely downstairs."

The rest of the family had assembled outside the formal rooms on the first floor where the partitions had been drawn back to expand the space down the entire length of the house. The Countess was resplendent in a shimmering copper-colored silk. Elizabeth sparkled in a pure white gown with hundreds of crystal beads decorating the neckline and sleeve cuffs. The dress revealed her white shoulders and beautiful long neck. There were more crystals glimmering through the curls crowning her head. Pearl and diamond pendants swung from her ears.

Next to her, Ariel stood in full evening dress with an intricately-tied freshly ironed cravat held in place with a sapphire pin, courtesy of Morris' skills. The Baron stood behind the family, towering over them, once again dressed in court finery including jeweled medals on his chest sash, diamond pins in his cravat and glittering rings on his fingers.

They were waiting for the curtain to go up on the evening's celebration when the Countess turned to the Baron, asking worriedly, "Where is Lord Embry? Have you seen Lord Embry this evening?"

"Countess, I believe he is approaching now."

Embry came slowly towards them dressed in evening attire but with trousers, not the short breeches with hose that the other men wore. The Countess frowned in puzzlement. Embry was always proper in his dress.

Then she gasped, "Your cane? Samuel, where is your cane?"

Elizabeth swung around and her eyes widened. Her brother was still limping but the Countess was correct. *He was walking without a cane!*

He smiled at them. "The cane is resting in my study, Maman, and I am walking without it for the first time in ten years. A dramatic entrance, what?"

There was a clamor for explanations finally summed up by Embry. "Mr. Nieto has had a long interest in applying mechanical design to the bone injuries that he saw on the battlefield. I was his benefactor for funds to try his design on condition that I be his first model. A good partnership, I think. Since my workshop finished building this prototype, I have been practicing with it there and only had it brought home a few days ago. I can use it for part of the evening before I get fatigued. I will need to resort to my cane then but I believe the day will come when I can store that blasted thing away forever."

"Where is Mr. Nieto? I must thank him," the Countess was almost sobbing with gratitude. "Oh, where is he?"

The Baron spoke up. "Mr. Nieto will join us later. His energy has not quite returned in full so he thought to come down a few hours into the party. He begs your pardon that he cannot attend the whole evening."

The clock chimed the hour and at that signal, carriages began arriving at the grand entrance. The orchestra started to play soft music as the guests were announced and made welcomed. Sir William Bonner and his family were among the first to arrive, followed soon after by Lord and Lady Sherburne and their young adult children.

Once the ballroom was properly filled with enough people, laughing and talking in small groups, the orchestra signaled the start of the dancing. Elizabeth was partnered in this first set by her brother, Ariel, as the honorees of the evening. The onlookers admired the twins as they charmingly demonstrated their skill and grace. Others soon joined them on the floor as the ball formally began.

The ball was indeed all that Elizabeth could have wished. Those who were present were having a wonderful time. The music was splendid, the food superb, the serving staff, even the newly-hired ones, were well trained. All her dances were promised. And the Baron had requested the honor of a waltz.

Ariel was delighted as well, partnering the pretty sisters of his friends and a few newer friends of Elizabeth to whom he was introduced by their chaperones.

When the guests were on their way to the supper room, Ariel took the opportunity to fetch a book from the library. One of the young women, a lovely blonde with whom he had just danced, had mentioned that she longed to read the latest popular book of poetry but alas—all the copies seemed to have been purchased already from the book vendors. It was his chance to be a hero in her pretty blue eyes.

On his way, Ariel passed by a door to the terrace. He halted at the sight of the rotund Sir William facing a pale-looking Nieto. Ariel had not been aware that Nieto had come downstairs and he definitely could not think what Sir William might have to say to him. He was sure the two had never met before . He moved behind the open door, peering through the gap between the door and the wall to see what was happening.

The red-faced man poked his finger repeatedly into Nieto's chest to underscore his displeasure. Nieto flinched at each touch, recalling to Ariel's memory the thick bandages that the doctor had worn for days across that very part of his torso. Ariel could hear nothing that was being said until the very angry Sir William raised his voice.

"I've made it clear that we will not be strung along on this. You need to turn over the next one to me here—this evening. That is the only reason I am at this…gaudy display of … wealth by the mongrel offspring of a once lofty aristocratic house now polluted by Hebrew blood. Or perhaps you want your friend, the Viscount, to know about the goods you have taken from his home and pawned to the Shylocks in Cheapside. It is really too droll—one Jew stealing from another Jew to pay off a third. You people are truly a deceitful tribe."

Nieto stood shamefaced as he said something quietly to Sir William, who nodded in turn. "Ah, good, so you finally see how it will play. I'll wait here. You have but a few minutes."

The blue-eyed man turned and started to advance on the very terrace door behind which Ariel was hiding. Ariel stepped back deeper into the shadows in hopes of remaining hidden. Nieto crossed the threshold, passing right by Ariel before continuing down the hall to the library.

He disappeared into the room. A few seconds later, Nieto emerged holding a small pamphlet. Moving swiftly back up the hall towards the terrace where Sir William waited, the doctor turned his head slightly. His eyes caught Ariel's. The blue eyes widened but his footsteps never faltered. Walking right past Ariel's hiding spot again, he returned to the terrace.

The doctor said in an undertone that carried in phrases to the hidden young man, "... written on the margin of the middle page ... will be sent tomorrow...copy what you need immediately ...leave ...this is the end...I will be caught."

Sir William emitted a sharp snort then spoke loudly again. "You are caught, you greasy Jew. We've got you by the ballocks. If you do not continue to do what we ask, we will be glad to turn you over to the Admiralty as a spy. They will believe Lord Sherburne's word about your crimes. So you are trapped either way—hang as a spy by the Admiralty or be whipped like a dog by us. We will contact you about next week's delivery. But it is not as if you don't earn something for yourself in all this—enough to keep you from being beaten by those who hold paper for your gambling debts." Sir William threw a small handful of coins onto the stone floor of the terrace. He laughed as the coins chimed and skittered across the flagstones. Nieto bent, methodically picking up each of the scattered coins as Sir William swept through the door and down the hall to re-enter the ballroom.

Ariel leaned against the wall, thinking. He did not wish to misunderstand once again what he had observed. He heard Nieto's footsteps approach and waited as the man drew closer. He will surely explain, Ariel thought. He will help me understand.

Nieto walked through the door, passing Ariel for a third time but once again he did not stop. Instead, he continued down the hall as the music floating from the public rooms signaled that dancing would soon recommence.

Ariel was shocked into stillness. I know he saw me. He must be so ashamed he cannot face me. I must find Embry. I must let him know what Nieto is doing. I must tell him that Nieto is…what? Stealing? Selling secrets to Sir William? Could that be really true? What secrets did Nieto find that Sir William would want?

As Ariel re-entered the ballroom, he saw the Baron approach the Countess and bow. His mother smiled and stood to take his arm. How happy she seemed as the Baron led her to the dance floor. It is not right, Ariel thought wildly—not right for his mother to be gazing so rapturously up into the handsome Austrian's face.

Peter Bonner was now leading Elizabeth to the floor. Sir William's son! If his sister only knew the contempt in the father's voice and the disgusting ridicule he had lavished on her family. Ariel felt panic rising like bile in his throat. His world was being invaded on all fronts.

Ariel scanned the room and spotted his brother seated talking to Miss Sylvie Bonner. Sir William's daughter! He walked over, inhaled a calming breath and bowed to the young woman. "Excuse me, Miss Bonner. Lord Embry, may I have a word?"

Embry glanced at Ariel's face, raised his eyebrows in concern and made his excuses. He stood slowly as his new brace unfolded from the seated position. He nodded in the direction of the library. "Come this way, Ariel." He walked slowly and deliberately, still with a pronounced limp.

When they were in the library, Embry turned to face his younger brother. "What is it, Ariel? You look devastated."

"I…I am not sure…I can't believe…it is so wrong."

"Tell me what this is about. Start to finish. What has happened?"

Ariel took a deep breath and described the interaction between Nieto and Sir William on the terrace. He finished with, "I know Mr. Nieto saw me. But he did not acknowledge me or try to explain or …."

Embry looked at his brother intently. "I want you to forget that incident. Do not confront Nieto. Definitely do not approach Bonner or his son in any way. I will consult with the Baron on what to do next."

"Do not approach his son? Peter? Who is now dancing with Eliza? Do you think he is involved in something bad or dangerous?"

He received no answer. Instead, Embry repeated, "Ariel, you need to remain silent about this. Go back to the ballroom. Please ask Parker to come here." Embry leaned his head on his arm braced against the mantle of the fireplace. He looked haggard.

"Samuel, I have another concern. I do not like to see Maman waltzing with the Baron. It seems so…so …disloyal…."

Embry raised his head. "I know, Ariel, that it might seem…disloyal. But have faith in Maman and in the Baron that nothing untoward will happen. We have all missed the Earl but Maman I think suffers the most. She is very much alone. She lost many connections to family and friends when she married and she has depended on Papa to fill the spaces left empty. We all know that he has been far away for a long time."

"I never considered her loneliness. I guess I thought that older people could exist more on their own."

Embry took his brother by his shoulders and peered down into his eyes. "Ariel, Ariel, you take too much on your shoulders. Go back to the ball and have a wonderful time. We are celebrating your birthday and you should be happy. You can rest assured that I will take care of everything else."

Ariel returned to the ballroom through a secondary door. He stood watching the dancers spinning past him. Footmen, many unknown to him since they had been hired just for the evening, stood around the room, at the ready to bring refreshments or to pick up empty glasses. He spotted Parker standing at the main door so he approached the blond man and delivered Embry's message.

Parker did not move for a few seconds as he peered over Ariel's head into the crowd of dancers. Ariel followed his gaze over his shoulder and saw the Baron pass by with the Countess who was laughing up at him. Ariel's heart thudded—his mother looked so beautiful and vibrant in the Baron's arms.

At that moment, the Baron looked right past him to Parker. A signal seemed to pass between the two men. Only then did Parker bow to Ariel and leave the room, heading down the hallway to the library to fulfill Embry's request.

Sudden awareness hit Ariel like a blow. He felt icy fear crawl up his spine. "My family is in thrall to the Baron. He has control over all of us. He has captured the affections of my mother, my sister and me. Embry—strong and definitive Embry—does not make a move until he consults the Baron. The man has installed his own people in our home—Parker and Nieto, even Beowulf, are first loyal to him. Mr. Stein, his man-of-business, arranged for all the staff this evening and spent our money to do it. How many footmen here are really the Baron's spies in disguise? We are surrounded by his influence and power. We are even dancing to the tunes played by the orchestra he selected for us!"

He had to think. He left the ballroom and walked back to the library. It was deserted. Ariel was not sure what he had hoped to see but the empty room increased his tension. He thought of Nieto leaving the library with a pamphlet in his hand, then giving the book to Sir William. He again saw the image of the doctor scrounging for gold coins on the terrace. He shivered with disgust. He was still standing at the library's doorway trying to decide whether to enter or leave when he heard footsteps behind him.

He whirled. Nieto was approaching, heading toward the ballroom. The doctor slowed down as he was about to pass.

Ariel stepped into his path. "Sir, we need to talk."

Nieto stopped and stood very still. At first, Ariel wondered if he was going to say anything at all. There was a coiled strength in his stance that made Ariel feel that any second now Nieto might strike him. Then there was a subtle change. The coiled spring seemed to relax. "Sir Ariel, we have nothing to discuss. I wish to pass and enter the ballroom. If you think you need to speak with someone, speak with the Baron."

Ariel grabbed the other man by his lapels. "I do not wish to speak with the Baron. I am speaking to you, sir. You have been a guest in this house, nursed back to health at our expense and you work for my brother. You are in our debt and you will not pass, sir, without an explanation to me at this time."

Was that a smile tickling Nieto's mouth? Ariel felt a shock of surprise. "You laugh, sir?"

Nieto took Ariel's arms by the wrists, pulling the younger man's hands off his coat. "Sir Ariel, do you wish to call me out? Shall we meet at dawn? Pistols or swords? Please speak with the Baron first. Then if you still want to meet me at dawn, the Baron and Parker are my seconds. Let me add, sir, I commend you for your outrage."

He deliberately moved Ariel out of his way as if he were a piece of furniture then continued towards the ballroom.

Through the doors, Ariel could hear the music ending. The interval would begin soon. He needed to speak with his twin, his sister Elizabeth.

However, when he entered the ballroom, he found Elizabeth glowing amid a throng of young men and women. There was much laughing among them. He recognized Lady Daphne Hastley, her brother Lord Piers, Peter Bonner, Sir Laurence Sherburne and his sister. As he approached, they opened a space to welcome him into their circle.

Piers, a jolly good-natured young man, hailed him, "Glad to finally see you, Wharton. You've been gone so long we thought you had already turned nineteen!"

Elizabeth added, "We were just speaking of a trip to Vauxhall—maybe Saturday evening next. We thought we could go as a group. Perhaps we could ask the Baron and Mr. Nieto to go with us for propriety's sake."

Ariel shook his head at his sister. "I don't think Lord Embry would permit it—especially having Mr. Nieto as a chaperone. He would not consider that man an appropriate companion."

Elizabeth's surprise was so clear that the other young people quieted down, looking back and forth between brother and sister. This might prove interesting.

Lady Daphne interrupted with a giggle, "I am not sure of the other gentleman but imagine telling my Mama that the Baron von Tedesco will be my chaperone for Vauxhall. She will not believe that. And perhaps it would not be altogether proper—having such a handsome aristocrat—a foreign one, no less—in charge of one's virtue. I wonder if the rules of propriety are the same in Vienna."

She fluttered her fan, trying to look provocative. Ariel regarded her in astonishment. He had thought her charming before this evening. Now he wondered, what does she have in her head under all that elaborately-dressed hair?

Laurence Sherburne sniggered. "He…an aristocrat? Hah! He had to go all the way to Vienna to clean off the stink of trade on his boots. I wonder just how much it costs to buy a baronetcy in Vienna. I am sure it is cheaper there than in London. You know those people love bargains above all else. Tedesco and Nieto—they do have the strangest names."

Peter Bonner grinned at him but scolded, "Hush, Sherburne, remember your manners. We are surrounded by many here and one might take offence."

"Why should I worry? You saw how the Spanish one, the doctor, cringed and whimpered. Have you known any of them to fight back like a man? They just pay others to do the work for them. But only if it is a real bargain!"

"I say," Lord Piers blurted out. "You are being damned rude, don't you know. I beg your pardon, ladies, for my language but Sherburne, Bonner, you are guests here. It's bad form to be saying such things about friends of the hosts."

Ariel waved his hand and interrupted, "Lord Piers, they are not being rude. Are you, Bonner? Sherburne? You are just being honest, isn't that true? Finally, you are being honest, but yet not quite totally honest, not truly. You say "them" and "they" and "those people"— but you don't say who those people are." He raised his voice, "Bonner, Sherburne, who are they? Say it! Say it!" He swung his arms wide. "Tell everyone here whom you mean—whom you despise." The conversations around them had hushed. "Who are the cowards who love bargains? Whose hands are dirty with trade or usury? Do you mean the Jews? The Hebrews? The Israelites? The Christ-killers? The mongrels? Say it, damn you, or did you just remember that my name is Ariel DaCosta Wharton? Oh yes, DaCosta is one of those very strange names *they* all have."

Elizabeth stared at him in horror, her face so white that he could see the blue veins under her skin. "Oh Ariel, Ariel," she gasped. "Oh my...oh my…I don't know….I cannot believe….oh, what have you done?"

They were marooned on a vast sea of silence. All around them, people had stopped talking in mid-sentence to stare at the circle of young people.

Suddenly a voice boomed out in the room. "Sir William, Lord Sherburne, would you see to your children? I believe it is past their bedtimes. You know how badly children behave when they are over-fatigued. They begin to say the first foolish things that come into their heads." It was Embry—every bit the Viscount, standing straight and tall as the heir to the Earl of Aylesford should. "My footmen will send for your carriages now. Sirs, it is well past the time for your departure."

Parker stepped forward with another footman and they stood rigidly behind Bonner and Sherburne. Their very closeness caused the young men to start moving forward. Embry approached the group, now with his cane swinging loosely and threateningly in his hand. "If you are not gone quietly within two minutes, I will instruct my men to have you thrown out. But only after I give you both a thrashing."

"You would not dare, Embry," seethed Lord Sherburne who came up behind him. "Your behavior cannot be borne."

"His behavior? Lord Sherburne," a cool voice in a resonant baritone with a slight Austrian accent interrupted. "I think you are misinformed. The insolence was your son's. Whatever else he thinks, he has accepted this man's hospitality and paid it back in insult. Surely not the behavior of a gentleman. You would be wise to teach him better manners once home."

Lord Hastley now stood next to the Baron and looked scornfully at Sherburne. He turned to Embry, announcing in a loud clear voice. "Viscount Embry, I commend you on this wonderful evening. We are all grateful for the important work your father has done for the Crown. We are privileged to share this celebration with your brother and sister. And Sir Ariel, you have my respect. It is important that a man stand up for his family and his friends. You have shown that you are indeed your father's son and he will be very proud of you. My dear Countess, may I have the honor of the next dance?" Lord Hastley bowed and, at the Countess' nod, he led her onto the dance floor.

Within minutes, the Sherburne and Bonner families were gone. The rest of the guests still stood around, speaking in subdued whispers. At a gesture from the Baron, the orchestra signaled the start of a graceful waltz. Mr. Nieto suddenly appeared and approached Elizabeth.

"May I have the honor of this waltz, Lady Elizabeth?" he bowed.

"I cannot," she stammered. "I fear I might collapse."

"No, you will not," he whispered firmly. "You will not let them win. You are proud, you are strong and you are in the right. You will not let them defeat you."

He placed his hand around her waist and waited for her to place her hand on his shoulder. He looked at her without a smile but with warmth in his very blue eyes. When the music began, he swung her into the first turn. She felt stiff for a few steps then began to let the dance carry her into the smooth glide.

She looked at him, just a head taller than she, with the lights of the room glinting off his spectacles and soft dark-brown curls falling on his forehead. He was slender but there was no mistaking the strength of his body. She felt it as his muscles moved under her hands and as he guided her through the waltz's circles. In his arms, she did feel stronger and she did feel proud.

As they danced, she whispered to him, "How do you bear it?" He cocked his head in a quizzical pose. "How can you bear all that they say about us?"

"That assumes what they say is the truth of us. Do you believe that?"

She shook her head. "No, I do not think we are any different than they are."

"Ah, but I believe we are. Not better perhaps, but different, and the question is really, are you proud of the differences or ashamed of them?"

She thought about his question as they continued to dance. She also thought how well they were suited as dancers. She felt comfortable in his arms, not doll-like as she had with the Baron.

As the waltz ended, the Countess thanked courtly Lord Hastley and approached Ariel who was standing at the edge of the room, seemingly watching the dancers but with eyes that were focused on an undefined distance.

She put her hands on either side of his face and peered affectionately at him, "My dearest child, Ariel DaCosta Wharton, you made me so proud. Ariel—the lion of God."

Embry appeared behind her, smiling over her shoulder at his younger brother, "So the cub roared tonight, Maman. Truly there is no mistaking that he has grown into a lion."

The Countess kissed Ariel on each cheek before returning to circulate among the guests who remained.

Ariel looked at Embry in a worried and distracted way. "Samuel, Mr. Nieto is dancing with Elizabeth."

"Yes, I know. Ariel, have faith. She is safe with him."

Ariel shook his head. "I do not understand. I told you what I saw. He was with Sir William and Sir William was forcing him to do something under threat. And then Sir William threw money at him and Nieto actually groveled on the floor for it. It was demeaning. How could he do that?"

Embry asked, "Ariel, think over what the Sherburne pup said about Nieto and a fight."

Ariel responded, "You mean that Nieto cringed and whimpered and refused to fight?"

"Hmmm, yes, and think, Ariel, how would he know that? How would he ever know that?" Embry's gaze locked with Ariel's as he watched a dawning awareness appear on the younger man's face.

When the waltz stopped, Nieto bowed to Elizabeth. She smiled as she curtseyed, "Mr. Nieto, you waltz beautifully. Almost as well as the Baron."

He smiled back, "The Baron insists that every man in his service dance the waltz almost as well as he does to be in his good favor."

They had reached the end of the room. When Elizabeth sat down on a sofa, Nieto asked if she wanted a refreshment. A ratafia, perhaps? She shook her head 'no' and instead asked if he would be kind enough to sit with her for a few minutes.

"Mr. Nieto, I wish to ask you some questions. You said we are different from the others. What do you mean?"

"Lady Elizabeth, think on it. You more than many here could describe how we differ. In what ways are the Wharton and the DaCosta sides of your own family different?"

"The DaCostas came from the continent a few generations ago. The Whartons have been English for hundreds of years."

"Are the privileges for the DaCostas the same as those enjoyed by the Whartons? Do you live the same type of lives? Mark the times of your lives with the same ceremonies? "

"I begin to see what you mean. But those are not important differences. We are the same basically—we are human, male and female. We want the same things—families, comfort, happiness, peace."

"In that I agree. But I do not hold that the differences are trivial. Our history shows that the world has not thought the differences trivial except for brief moments in time. I believe we are different – and we have a different role to play in the great world. We Hebrews are told to repair the world in partnership with God and one way to do that is to insure that differences can be respected—if not by the force of law, then by the force of righteousness and, if not even that, by fear of retribution."

"Mr. Nieto, what happened to you in the park that day? Were you using the force of righteousness as you call it to earn respect?"

Nieto looked down at his hands in his lap. There was another silence then he sighed. "That day, I had another part to play—one that was quite difficult for me but which I understood was needed. I cannot say more. Someday we might be able to talk of it. Lady Elizabeth, I will go get you some refreshments now." He stood, bowed and disappeared into the crowd of people near the buffet tables.

Seventeen

It was late or rather, early the next morning. The rooms recently echoing with music and conversation were now silent. All the guests had left and the family stood around for a few moments looking at the remains of the ball as servants moved through the rooms, clearing dishes and resetting the furniture.

Embry ushered everyone into the informal parlor and asked Sherlock to offer sherry to the ladies and brandy to all the gentlemen. The Countess and Elizabeth sat together on a sofa and Embry and the Baron took chairs opposite. Ariel stood pacing behind the sofa while Nieto watched him from a spot near the door. After everyone was served, Embry stood to offer a toast.

"To our twins. We owe to them an unexpectedly exciting occasion. And a special salute to the young lion who roared this evening."

Everyone turned to Ariel and raised their glasses. Ariel drank his brandy down in one gulp. He handed the glass back to Sherlock and motioned for a refill. Embry raised his eyebrows but said nothing. The second glassful followed the first and Ariel signaled for a third. Sherlock looked at Embry who nodded, signaling it was to be the last.

Everyone watched Ariel down the third. They felt the tension and recognized that there would be a confrontation of some sort. They did not have long to wait.

Ariel swayed on his feet and looked at his family around the room, one by one as if making certain that they were all in attendance. "What a damned bloody horror this evening was. I feared that I had entered bedlam. Every way I looked, I saw something I did not understand, that I could not believe, that I could not abide. How can you sit here—all of you—pretending that we are all fine, just like we were? That it was a wonderful night—a splendid occasion? Didn't you see the masks come off tonight? There is no one—no one—I can believe in anymore—no friends, no family, no…anyone. Whom can I trust? Whom can I trust?"

He brought his hands to his face and hid his eyes. His hands started to move up and down convulsively as if he was trying to rub images from his vision. Embry walked towards him.

"Don't come any closer, brother," Ariel brought his hands down in fists. He looked haunted. "Don't you have to confer with the Baron first to know what to do next?"

The Countess turned in her seat and said in a strained whisper, "Ariel, you know not what you are saying. It is fatigue and the brandy—you are unused to the brandy."

"No, Maman, I am unused to seeing my family as puppets controlled by the Baron. Haven't any of you noticed the strings? Oh, they are fine and silken—but there are strings nevertheless. Even you, Maman. You are being controlled by him. The Baron has put his own men in this house to watch our every step, to decide what we do and what we think, where we go, and with whom we speak. From the moment I saw him with Embry at the auction, he has been the real head of this family. I did not see it all until tonight when I saw you in his arms, Maman—in *his* arms instead of Papa's."

The Countess' face went white. She whispered, "Ariel, how dare you?"

The Baron stood and walked toward Ariel. Ariel put his hand out in a defensive gesture. "No, Baron, I do not want you near me. I fear you. When you are near, I no longer can think for myself. I am going to my room. Yes—I am going to my room now. Sherlock, another brandy. Do not look at Embry for permission. Ask the Baron if you may pour one for me. He is the master here."

In silence, Sherlock filled the glass once again and Ariel lurched through the door, spilling the drink as he went. They heard his steps up the stone stairs followed a few seconds later by the tapping of Beowulf's claws.

Elizabeth began weeping. Her mother put her arms around her, hugging her close. "There, there, my dearest. It will all be better in the morning....you'll see...we are all over-tired and our nerves have suffered some shocks...."

No one noticed Nieto as he quietly left the room and headed up the stairs.

Beowulf was lying by the door to Ariel's room. He raised his head as Nieto approached but made no sound.

Nieto did not bother knocking on the door. He quietly opened it and went inside, closing it softly behind him. There was a smell of rich liquor in the air and while there was no lamp lit, the fading moonlight brightened the room enough for him to make out the figure of the young man lying face down across the bed, still fully clothed.

Without permission, he approached. Before he could say anything, he heard Ariel mutter, "Get out! How dare you come in here? Get out."

Nieto paused and righted the glass rolling on its side on the bedside table, but he did not move away from the bed. Ariel lifted his head and turned towards Nieto.

He sneered, "You disgust me. How could you go down on your knees before that man? Just like a disgusting dirty Jew." He drew out each word as if to wring as much disdain as possible from them.

"Ariel...."

"I am Sir Ariel to you, Nieto. Remember your place. You work for my brother. You are not my equal."

Ariel turned to face Nieto, raising himself on one elbow. His face was pale and his hair curled into his eyes. He sat up, looking around. "I want something to drink. Nieto, get me more brandy. I order you to do it now."

"Sir Ariel, who are you really angry with? Me? The Baron? Your family? William Bonner? His son, Peter? Who are you really angry with?"

Ariel swayed where he sat. "Of course I am angry at you and the Baron and my mother and Embry. Who else is there? Oh, foolish Eliza. I am angry at her too. I hate Sherburne and Bonner and all the others. I hate them all. I am not angry at them—they are what they are—despicable Jew-haters, they are as they have always been. But I had not admitted the truth to myself...."

Nieto went closer, putting his hands on Ariel's cheeks, holding him still. He forced the younger man's face up and peered intently at him. "But who angers you the most, Ariel?"

Ariel grabbed at his arms, trying to force them down. He couldn't. Nieto held him still. They both stayed silent, frozen in place, facing each other. Tears started down Ariel's cheeks, running around Nieto's hands as he held him still, dripping off his chin and onto his wrinkled shirt front.

Ariel gasped in a small voice, "I could only stand there and…and…use words. Why did I not realize what they were really like? How could I have been so blind? And foolish….I think…what a fool I have been, living a life that was a lie…thinking that I fit in…just like Piers….instead they all hated me. How they must have laughed every time I turned my back."

Nieto handed Ariel a handkerchief from his pocket. He sat down on the bed next to the younger man and put his arm around his shoulder. Ariel shuddered and leaned against the older man. "I feel everything has crumbled into a pile of lies…."

"My dear child," Nieto said softly. "You remind me of my younger brother, Aaron. Such a gentle soul. Quiet and tender. A brilliant scholar. My father was so proud when he was accepted to study with the Great Rabbi of Prague. He would become a great leader of our people—like my great-grandfather, who was the first of our family in Gibraltar.

"Aaron saw only beauty in people and in the world. We used to argue all the time about that. I thought that he was foolish to have those beliefs. How could someone go about so innocently when all I saw was the pain and suffering around me? He used to tell me that it was a choice you make—to see the good or the bad and that we must always try to see the good."

"'He used to tell you?' And something horrible happened. He is gone." Ariel stated it as facts.

"Not gone, Ariel—that sounds so innocent. He was murdered." Nieto's face was cold and still. "There was trouble in Prague. There were gangs attacking and beating Jews in the streets. It had always been a concern but Aaron, innocent sweet Aaron, he did not take precautions. He could not believe that the people he saw every day—the people he greeted, the young men he saw on the street, were anything but good. When he was found, the bones in his legs and arms had been shattered. All his ribs, even his pelvis had been crushed. He had been kicked and stomped to death. But for some reason, they had left his beautiful face alone.

"I had been in Vienna at a medical conference and word was sent to me. When I was able to see him, days later, he looked so cold and small but still peaceful. It was hard to believe that his death was violent until I looked at the rest of his body. I knew from those injuries that he had felt each and every one. There was no blessed unconsciousness until the very end. So he knew as he was dying that the world he had so fervently believed in did not really exist. How terrible that realization must have been as he slid towards death. Perhaps that hurt more than any physical pain.

"I could not bring his body back to Gibraltar. It would have been many days since his death and it is not our way to leave a body unburied for so long. He is buried in a grave in the old Jewish cemetery of Prague. Alone, far from our family."

"Oh God, how horrible you must have felt."

"Yes, I felt hatred for his murderers and the authorities who had let such violence go on year after year. But most of all I was angry with myself. I should have protected him, I thought. I should not have been focused on my own life, my own goals. After all, I was his big brother.

"But instead I had been away for years—busy with my medical studies in Alexandria and he was left to learn the truth about the world on his own. When I saw his body, I swore that I would avenge his murder. I would seek justice for him and for the others who were innocent and who have suffered—especially those who suffered for no other reason than that they were Jews. It has consumed my life."

"Did you find who killed him? Did you punish them?"

"Ah, Ariel, would it were that simple. No, I could not find the people who killed my brother. The Jews all along that street were too scared to tell me. And of course the goyim protect each other. No policeman would make an effort to find the murderer of a Jew. No government official cared and the aristocrats who ruled the city—they care little even for the poor Christians they rule. Do you think they would do anything for the oppressed Jews among them? So I am left seeking justice for Aaron by seeking justice for others whenever I can. There are always others who suffer. The pain never stops."

Ariel looked at him with fear in his eyes. "Have you killed to get justice?"

Nieto nodded.

"Do you regret that you have killed?"

Nieto slowly shook his head and said in a low voice, "No, I do not regret but I do not forget, either."

"Does it give you peace?"

Nieto shook his head again."No, never peace—but I must do what I can to repair the world. Evil must be punished so the scales of justice can be balanced.

"Each time, I try to think of the people who have been saved because there is one less evil animal in the world. Anger gives me strength to keep on. I just need to keep thinking about Aaron and how all his love of peace was stomped to death before he himself could slide beyond his grief in learning that truth about the world."

"But, Mr. Nieto...."

"I can be Judah to you, Ariel."

"But Judah, is it right to take justice into your own hands? Shouldn't the judge and jury be the ones to decide?"

"What judge? What jury? Ariel, do you know why your family left Spain?" Ariel hesitated then shook his head. "No one has ever told you how just the Spaniards were to your mother's people—her ancestors who had been bankers and ministers in the royal court for generations? Regardless of their years of service, they were expelled from their homes for being Jews. They had to try to find safe havens elsewhere.

"We are Jews, Ariel. We do not often get justice from the courts of the Gentiles, although the Baron has made it his life's work. He moves in the aristocratic and powerful circles of many countries and sometimes he can shame and intimidate the rulers into doing justice. He has that power and that presence. He tries to force them to do the right and just thing.

"I help him by applying pressure from behind. Since I do not have his influence and his patience, I move around in the dark, hidden from view when necessary, to make sure that justice will be done—however it needs to be brought about."

"Judah, why did you let Sir William abuse you so? You groveled at his feet for coins."

"It was a part I needed to play. He needed to believe in the information I was handing over. I had to appear unwilling.

It is all part of a complex piece of work we are doing for your King so that he and his court might be willing to return the favor when we seek justice for our people who suffer."

Ariel looked down and was silent. In a small voice, he said, "I want to make justice too, Judah. I need to do something…not just go on feeling like a victim. I can be stronger than that."

"Ariel, my friend, it is a terrible burden—one that can never ever be put down once you take it up. You will cut yourself off from much that is precious in life. Once you head down that path, your life can never be lived in the open. You must think about it very carefully. You must reflect on it for a very long time.

"See what your life brings you in the next few years before you make such a dreadful decision. You will know if it is your path in life at some point in the future. You must be sure of it. And if it is your path, you will always be able to connect with those of us who are doing the hard work to find justice."

"How, Judah? Years from now, how would I ever find you?"

"Ah, you have not seen the whole truth yet, Ariel. Just ask your brother. Lord Embry will know." At the young man's astonished look, Nieto nodded and repeated, "Samuel will know."

Eighteen

The house remained quiet until well past noon the next day. Not that anyone was sleeping the day away. Elizabeth had finally fallen asleep after exhausting her tears. She wept for her brother who had seemed so tragically shattered. She also wept for the loss of her innocence. She awoke from troubling dreams that she dimly remembered—vague images of being in the center of a throng of demonic figures who were pointing and sneering at her—but whose voices she could not hear and whose faces she did not recognize. She lay in bed, refusing to get up to face anyone else in the household.

The Countess sat at her desk in her dressing gown. She tried to write to the Earl but kept tearing up sheets of paper to begin yet again. How could she explain the pain she had seen in her children's eyes? And how could she trouble him with this news while he could do nothing across the wide distances that separated them?

She felt guilty as well. The Earl and she had thought that money and position would protect their children. They had hoped the world was changing fast enough that the old hatreds were dissolving into new acceptance. Their hopes had instead left the children unarmed in the face of such hate.

But how do you explain to children the unwarranted hatred of others? How can you prepare them for the feeling of being separated from the rest of the world? How do you protect them from a life distrusting others? To be wary of love? Even of friendship?

She thought about Samuel, her eldest son, who put on protective armor each day to face the world. It was not just his physical injury which tormented him. She knew where the bitter stoniness had entered his life. He had experienced the truth about society at a younger age and had been changed forever by it. Was that the way all her children had to live?

At the same moment, Embry sat at the desk in his study, drumming his fingers against an opened book. He kept reviewing the scene in the parlor after the ball and the harsh look on Ariel's face. He felt the heat of anger rise in his chest and he pounded his fist against his weakened left leg. If only he was able-bodied, he would have had the relief of physically challenging the bastards. Ah, he knew, they were boys and it would never be countenanced that a man attacked boys for a matter of family honor.

But the fathers! That would be different. He would have to think how to punish the fathers for the sins of the sons. But it wasn't only the sins of their children. The ancient hatred had been learned at their father's knees.

There was a quiet knock on the door. Embry raised his head as the door opened to reveal the Baron and Nieto.

"We're here to discuss some next steps," the Baron said. They closed the door and spoke quietly. When the Baron and Nieto left, Embry went to seek his mother.

It was teatime before the family finally met that day. The Baron and Nieto were not present. Elizabeth once again sat on the sofa next to her mother. Ariel sat at the other end of the room facing away, looking out through the window at the garden in the rainy mist of the early afternoon. The Countess served tea and Sherlock passed the cake tray around. No one had any appetite for a sweet.

Finally, Embry put down his tea cup and cleared his throat. "Ariel," he called to his brother who shrugged his shoulders in response but kept looking out the window, "and Elizabeth, Maman and I have been speaking and we have come to a decision. The Baron is going to meet with Lord Hastley at the Admiralty to discuss the details but we are thinking you should journey to visit the Earl."

Ariel's head whipped around, his eyes wide with surprise. Elizabeth jolted erect in her seat. "What? When? Where?" she blurted as Ariel rose to stand behind the sofa, bracing his arms on the back of the furniture.

"Father is heading towards a location where it is possible for him to have guests in safety. It has been almost three years since you have seen him and Maman and I believe that it is important that you have time together. There has been much to distress you recently. It would be good for you to be in his calm presence again. And we know how much he has missed you both."

"But what about you, Samuel? And you, Maman?" Elizabeth clenched her hands together. "You miss him grievously as well. Won't you come too? We could all be together—a complete family once again."

Embry shook his head. "It is not possible for all of us to go at once. It might raise some questions .... I also have some business I must attend to here—for the Earl. The Countess must stay also for ...for appearance's sake.

"There is something else I must say. We will need to be mindful about keeping this a secret. The Earl's location is not to be known in order for him to continue his work. So you will not know any details in advance. You are just to be ready to go when the plans are prepared. You will need to be discreet and to be trustful."

Elizabeth was flustered. "Samuel, you know how much I wish to see Papa. But really, this secrecy is a bit much. How do we make arrangements when we do not know where we are going or when we are leaving?"

Embry put his hand up. "Eliza, those are the conditions. You will need to trust me. Arrangements will be made by others and you will be guided by people who will protect you. You must rely on them and do what they say. Those are the conditions. You must agree or you must stay here."

Ariel spoke up. "Who are the people on whom we must rely?"

"You know two of them already. Mr. Nieto and Parker. Others you will meet along the way."

When the Baron returned for dinner that evening, Nieto was not with him. No one mentioned his name or remarked on his absence. The conversation swirled about the latest opera and the concerts held at Court. Even Embry made an effort to keep the conversation light and fluid. He pretended interest in news about the latest scandal—something everyone in the family knew he usually could not abide.

There was no further mention of an impending trip for several more days. Hannah and the footman who served Ariel as manservant went over the twins' wardrobes, cleaning and pressing garments, mending tears and tightening loose buttons.

This trip is different, Elizabeth reflected, from any she had taken before. There is no rushing about shops to buy new dresses or bonnets. It was clear that there was to be no sign outside the house that a journey was in the offing.

It was the darkest part of a moonless night when the light tapping of Beowulf walking the floor woke Elizabeth. She heard a quiet knock then the door opened. The Countess entered and said in a whisper that was clear in the silence of the house, "Elizabeth, it is time for you to get ready to leave." She was in her dressing gown with her soft brown hair in a braid down her back. "Please get up and dressed for a carriage journey."

The Countess moved to the dressing room where Hannah slept to awaken the maid. "One trunk, Hannah, and one grip. Be sure to pack some waterproofs and warm coats."

Elizabeth sat up, watching her mother selecting clothes for her. She shook her head to clear it. "What time is it? Where are we going?" The Countess brought a traveling dress, undergarments and short walking boots to the bedside. "Eliza, now is not the time for questions. You must get up and dress."

The Countess began riffling through the pins, combs and ornaments on Elizabeth's dressing table, setting some aside in neat piles. She looked over at Elizabeth, "Just remember, my dear, you will be seeing your father in a few weeks. Just remember that and follow the directions of the men who will lead you to him."

She went back to the dressing room to check with Hannah who would be traveling with Elizabeth. The trunk was already half-packed and Hannah paused in the packing to assist Elizabeth to dress. The Countess pinned the pocket watch carefully to Elizabeth's dress, handling the precious object with great care.

A few minutes later, there was another soft rap on the door. Ariel called through it, "Maman, I am ready. Morris is finishing my packing. I am going downstairs for something to eat. Is Eliza ready?"

"Ariel, go to the kitchen. We will be down directly."

When Elizabeth and the Countess reached the kitchen a quarter-hour later, Embry was there with Ariel and Parker, who had stirred the kitchen fire into life and put a kettle on. There was bread and cheese on the table. Parker was in the pantry, filling a basket with foodstuffs that he wrapped in linen towels—cheese, preserved fruits, bread, smoked fish, and a few bottles of cider. Evidently he was experienced in packing for sudden trips.

When the kettle had boiled, the Countess deftly put a towel over her hand to safely lift the steaming kettle from the flame and poured the water into the teapot. She began to slice the bread and cheese and put the plates in front of her children. "Eat, my dears. It might be several hours before you have a chance for a meal."

Embry sat at the kitchen table as his mother bustled around the kitchen in efficient, measured and practiced actions that none of the children had ever observed before. When she returned to the table with steaming cups of tea, her smile was tremulous. "Cook will be very angry at the disarray in her kitchen," she sighed. "I fear she will think there were burglars in the night."

She finally sat down and gazed at her children, fighting for a cheerful demeanor. "There are things I need you to take with you. First, be sure you have your pocket watches with you at all times. Your father took enormous care in their design. It will do his heart good to finally see them. Secondly, I am giving you my Bible and my prayer book. They are my good luck talismans. They belonged to my grandmother whom I loved dearly. I need to know that they are with you, providing you with comfort and protection." She handed Elizabeth the ivory covered book that she knew so well from the portrait of her parents. The Countess put another small white leather book into Ariel's hands.

Embry spoke up at last. "I want to give you some things as well." He left the room, returning soon with two wooden boxes and a cane ornamented with a large beveled blue glass stone on its handle. He put the boxes on the table and opened the first one. Two small pistols were nestled inside.

Ariel looked at them in disbelief. "What are we to do with these? Have duels at dawn?"

Embry winced. "Ariel, do not now tell me that you have forgotten everything I have taught you, that those mornings in the fields at Aylesford Manor were ill-spent. If you forgot how to use these, Parker will show you again. And Elizabeth, you will learn as well and probably become a better shot than Ariel."

He opened the second, smaller box. In it were two enameled-covered pens. "Some of my more practical toys," he said with pride. He picked up one and held it in front of him. A thin stiletto blade suddenly shot out of the quill point. Elizabeth gasped. Embry leaned the point against the table and pressed on the button concealed in its handle. The point quickly retracted back into the enamel case. "You will carry these with you at all times. Parker will show you how they can be used most effectively." Ariel gazed at his brother with wide eyes as he absorbed the meaning behind the word "effectively."

Embry next lifted the cane. He smiled as he looked at it. "I need these less often these days. But this one I am especially fond of." He grabbed the ornamental globe and, with a click, it separated from the body of the cane, coming away with a long thin sword blade. He hefted the weapon skillfully.

Ariel's tension would not let him stay seated any longer. "You must tell us, Embry, why you are sending us on this trip thus armed. This seems more than a visit of children to their father. Treat us as adults. You must if there is danger in our path."

"We are at war, Ariel, as you know. And you will cross over some routes on your way, where the French threat is quite present. You are children of a wealthy man known to be in service to the Crown. There will be dangers from some quarters and, while we are trusting in others to keep you safe, you must be able to protect yourself, if need be.

"In line with that, you will travel with documents that provide you both with new names and identities." He passed some papers to each of the twins. "You are John Allingham traveling with his twin sister, Emily Allingham. Those names, as you no doubt recognize, are from grandmama's family so there are records of Allinghams in Herefordshire for generations. The family histories documented in those papers have enough truths in them that they will pass as real. On your travels this morning, you will need to memorize the facts about your past. Then the papers will be burned."

"Where is Mr. Nieto? If he is to be our guide...." Ariel asked.

"I do not know. He will be with you when you need him. Right now, you will go out the back door into the mews. The carriage is being readied. We need to say our good-byes."

There was a choking gasp from the Countess but she quickly stifled her reaction. They all rose together. The Countess put her arms around her youngest son, "May the Lord lead you to your destination in health and peace and bring you home in peace." She kissed Ariel on both cheeks then turned to Elizabeth to bless her with the same prayer. She kissed Elizabeth then whispered, "Please tell your father that I think of him always and pray for him always and love him always." Her tears had started so she fled the room.

Embry's eyes followed her then he turned back to his brother and sister. "I wish I could go with you. But it is a sign of our faith in you both that you are going alone. You will hear news as you travel that may surprise you but it is imperative that you keep your identities secret. You are too valuable as prizes to our enemies. Try not to draw attention. When you see Father, you will understand. I too send my love with you both." Ariel and Elizabeth stood stunned as tears flowed down their older brother's cheeks. He nodded at Parker before turning away.

Parker held out their wraps and scarves. They picked up the boxes, books and cane and followed him. He ushered them quietly and quickly through the dark garden into the mews.

A carriage and horses they had never seen before were waiting there. A dark bearded man was in position as driver and an outrider dressed in dark anonymous cloaks was mounted on a horse. Both men were unfamiliar to the twins. The one familiar element was Beowulf sitting quietly next to the driver.

Ariel turned to Parker with a questioning look on his face. Parker smiled, "Beowulf was first trained to guard postal carriages. See how comfortable he feels, back in his element."

Their boxes had already been packed into the wagon. Parker handed them up into the coach with the remaining parcels and the basket of foodstuffs then followed them in. Hannah was already seated inside, looking terrified. Elizabeth sat next to her and took her hand, squeezing it with a reassurance she herself did not feel but needing to help the little maid feel calmer.

The carriage pulled out of the mews at a slow pace and kept moving very slowly through the streets of London. Elizabeth raised her eyebrows at Parker sitting next to Ariel.

He responded, understanding her silent question, "We will move slowly to keep the noise down while we are in town. In that way, no one will remark on it. The people in the townhouses will think that it is the refuse wagon making its rounds and turn over in their beds to go back to sleep."

The darkness outside and the silence inside gradually became soothing. Elizabeth found herself dozing, leaning against Hannah who was already snoring quietly.

When the carriage began moving more rapidly, she awoke suddenly. Parting the curtain and glancing out, she saw that it was early dawn and the houses were more spread out. They had left the city. She tried to catch some signpost to guess their destination but saw none. She assumed that Parker would not answer any questions.

Looking over to the opposite seat, she saw her brother asleep with his head leaning against the curtained window. Parker sat still—fully awake and attentive to any changes in the pace of the horses and in any sounds from outside He smiled at Elizabeth then looked out of the window. Elizabeth, confident that all was under Parker's control, felt drowsiness overtaking her once again.

It seemed just a few seconds later when she felt the carriage stop. Ariel, awakened by the sudden halt, pulled his window curtain aside. It was full morning and they had stopped in the courtyard of a small public house.

Parker turned to them. "We can now take some time to visit the necessary, to stretch our legs and to have some hot food. Remember, you are John and Emily Allingham and I am your manservant. Hannah, it is Miss Emily and Master John to you and your name is Betty. Can you remember?"

The confused maidservant nodded. She was a quick study, Elizabeth knew, and she would follow orders to the letter even if she did not understand why.

The Allingham party entered the public room, after passing through a small courtyard where two men were talking quietly and having some food. Both men were dressed in the well-worn dusty cloaks and hats of traveling merchants and, against the chill of the early morning, they still had their scarves wrapped high on their necks as they huddled over their bowls of hot porridge and their tankards of ale. The men nodded cursorily at the new arrivals then resumed their conversation.

Parker ordered breakfast for the party. When the food was served, Hannah and Parker sat at a table separate from the twins, preserving the only separation of masters and servants possible in the single public room. As befitted the early hour, all were quiet as they ate the simple food and then took turns using the privy. Before the young travelers had finished their meal, they heard the sound of horses leaving the inn's small courtyard and moving up the road.

Now that they were the only guests and the publican had vanished into the kitchen, Ariel motioned to Parker who came and bowed to his young master.

"Yes, Master John," Parker said softly.

"Tell me, Parker, where are we headed?"

Parker responded in a clear voice, "Master John, surely you jest. You told me that we are headed to Portsmouth. Have you changed directions since setting out this morning?"

Ariel sighed. "You are insolent, Parker. Beware! I might sack you."

Parker bowed with a grin and went back to his food.

The travelers resumed their journey, the carriage now moving at a rapid pace. For a few miles, Ariel swore he could smell sea air but that sensation diminished over time. The sun was rising behind them, so he knew they were now headed west. A crossroads lay up ahead, marked by a stone pillar at one corner and a thicket of tall shrubs and young trees diagonally across the road.

As they approached the stone pillar, two horsemen emerged from the thicket. Parker ordered the carriage to halt. He drew his pistol as he ordered the carriage to hand. He descended slowly from the carriage, the weapon pointed towards the two strangers. Ariel, watching from a corner of his window, recognized the two merchants from the inn's courtyard earlier that morning.

One rider dismounted and Parker surprised the twins by pocketing his pistol and immediately mounting the riderless horse. Without a word, the stranger climbed into the coach, sat down next to Ariel, and tapped the carriage roof authoritatively, signaling it to resume. Then he removed his hat and the scarf revealing a face covered with brown stubble of several days' growth and marked by a wide scar that extended from his left eye down to his jaw. Elizabeth's eyes were drawn to the very angry-looking wound so it took a few seconds for her to notice the piercing blue eyes.

"Mr. Nieto?" Elizabeth gasped.

"Yes, Lady Elizabeth," he smiled. "It is my turn to provide you with some companionship on this journey but you must forgive my informal dress."

"You have been injured, sir," Ariel said pointing to the scar.

"Oh this," the doctor chuckled, slowly peeling the scar away from his face, wincing a bit as it caught a few whiskers. "The old foppish French fashion of wearing face patches advanced the manufacture of good adhesives. Now I can use them to affix scars and wrinkles to provide disguises. I have found that a pronounced scar stays in the mind of the observer—making other facial characteristics nigh invisible."

"And your spectacles, sir? You are not wearing them now," Elizabeth said. "Another disguise?"

He bowed his head. "Yes, although at least useful for some magnification when needed."

There were a few minutes of silence before Ariel spoke again. "Where have you been, Mr. Nieto? How did you know where we were?"

Nieto turned to each of them, searching their faces. "I have been pleased to see the successful end of the work of several weeks. I think it is time to tell you some of what has transpired. Yesterday, Mr. William Bonner was taken in Calais by British agents just after he passed on to French spies some coded messages he believed were to be sent from the Admiralty. The messages had to do with the English actions planned against the French navy currently in the ports of Marseilles and Nice.

"Bonner had earlier passed on the protocols that would enable the French to decipher the information. The protocols work with an intricate mechanism hidden in a set of clocks that transcribed the code back into English. Mr. Bonner had worked for weeks to obtain one of the clocks, the protocols for their use and the weekly coded dispatches that used the code."

Silence followed this as Elizabeth and Ariel stared first at Nieto and then looked at each other. Ariel asked, "Embry is involved somehow. The break-in at Embry's workshop and at the House?"

Nieto nodded. "We knew from Mr. Larkin what they were looking for and we made sure they got it when and how we wanted them to so that we could uncover the whole network."

"I don't understand," Elizabeth wrung her hands in confusion. "Embry is working with spies in his workshop?"

"No, Elizabeth," Ariel turned to her. "Embry is working for the Admiralty on ways to use his mechanical devices for coding information. Am I right, Mr. Nieto?" He looked back at Nieto, who nodded.

"Yes, very good, Sir Ariel. Lord Embry has worked out ways to have the mechanicals make codes harder to decipher. To break the codes in any reasonable amount of time, one would need the mechanical device, the instructions or protocols for it and, of course, the messages. By keeping those various elements separate, it was harder to break the coding scheme. Embry designed the machines, but Larkin built them. Larkin didn't know how they would be used because Embry had the protocol in his head and would test them alone at night. Embry of course never wrote any actual coded messages, so he didn't have any information about naval operations. Once the clocks were delivered to the senders and the receivers, the protocols had to be explained to more people and perhaps written down and that made the whole process more vulnerable to our enemies."

"How did anyone ever find out?" Elizabeth asked.

"The Baron's cousin, Philippe, had received a clock and the protocols in Calais. When he went to London last winter for the Mechanical Society meeting, he heard questions from one member of the society that led him to suspect that some people had an idea of what the system was. Embry was being asked an unusual amount of questions about mechanical interpretation of codes. Philippe contacted the Baron and he in turn made contact with Embry."

"And you? Where did you fit?"she asked.

Nieto smiled ruefully, "We needed to find out who was involved in the plot to steal the clocks and the protocols. I became the weak link connecting the pieces of the coding scheme. I spent many days and nights in London behaving in such ways that my terrible dissipation and gambling debts became well-known to those watching for ways to break into the circle of secrecy surrounding your brother's work.. They thought me vulnerable to threats and blackmail. I became the target of intense intimidation to pass on the protocols and the coded messages which they assumed I would have access to since I worked for your brother. The French spies had no idea that Embry did not know any real naval information. They just assumed he would be privy to such news with the Earl so high in the Admiralty's command."

"But why didn't you just falsify the protocols so the codes wouldn't work," Ariel posed thoughtfully.

"Ah, very good," Nieto responded. "Let me pose it back to you. How would it help us if the French spies kept thinking they were deciphering our coded messages?"

"We would be able to send them false messages that misled them away from what we really were doing," Ariel sat up excitedly. "We would then be able to predict what they would do or where they would go since we were really directing them through our false secret messages."

Nieto nodded. "Sir Ariel, you might have an aptitude for espionage." His blue eyes were lit with amusement.

"But," Elizabeth added, "we would not be able to use the system to pass on the right information any longer to our friends since everything we would send could be read by our enemies."

"So the answer would be?" Nieto prompted.

"The answer would be to…have a new system that they were not yet aware of? Side by side with the old system and to keep using the old system as long as possible," Elizabeth replied thoughtfully.

"As Larkin warned me, you twins are very clever."

"But the arrests would signal that we know that the codes have been broken," Ariel added.

"Yes, but it happened after the last codes were passed with very critical information that the French would find difficult to ignore. With the drama of the arrests in the papers in the next few days, the French would have to assume that the messages were important. At the very least, they would need to wonder if they were true or not. If they made the wrong decision, their naval campaign might be at great risk."

"And at the same time, there would be a new system in place to send real information to our allies," Elizabeth said slowly.

Ariel added, with awareness growing on his face. "So, Mr. Nieto, you had to be intimidated and beaten to make it appear you were finally caving in to their will. They would believe then in the information because they had to force you to hand it over. And somehow Peter Bonner and Laurence Sherburne knew this. They were involved in this scheme?"

Nieto said coldly, "Yes, that was my role. As just a foreign employee in Embry's household, I had no politically connected allies they would fear. I appeared to be a derelict who could not control his gambling and drinking, who would steal from his employer for more money to wager. I was seen in gambling dens and out late at taverns, too drunk to realize what I said. But even then I could not give in too readily to being a traitor. I had to be forced into it by physical intimidation.

"Whoever headed up this ring sent some thugs to meet me in the park at an appointed hour. I saw you and Embry pass that way that day, Lady Elizabeth, in your cart. But Bonner the younger and the Sherburne heir were there also and enjoyed joining in and kicking a person already lying half-conscious. Made them think they were real men. When the thugs emptied my pockets, they of course found the protocols that they had forced me to bring. The beating was not really necessary. It was just some extra amusement for them."

"They could have killed you," Elizabeth looked at him thinking about his long recovery.

"That was unlikely. The Baron had sent some men to follow me. They rode into the fray as if by accident and everyone scattered. We do this very carefully," he said calmly.

"The Baron," Ariel said in a flat undertone. "So he is involved in this scheme as well?" Nieto nodded. "And next? What is the next part of this plot?"

"I must disappear so this trip became a way for me to leave England before anyone had a chance to investigate who I really am and what I might be doing. But now, you need to study the lives of John and Emily Allingham so we can burn the documents. I have a new identity as well. I am a doctor, a friend of your family, traveling home to Italy by way of Gibraltar, our destination. My name is now Mordecai Halevi."

"Gibraltar?" the twins said in unison. "So that's where we will meet Papa?"

Nieto did not answer the question. But he smiled as he motioned that they should begin their study of the documents describing the lives of the Allingham twins of Herefordshire.

Elizabeth and Ariel bent their heads over the papers. As Embry had promised, many facts related to the Earl's family on his mother's side so the blur between family lore and their new identities made the stories seem natural.

When they thought they had it all by memory, Nieto asked them questions trying to trick them into errors. They were flawless. When he congratulated them on their mastery, both twins beamed with pride that Mr. Judah Nieto was pleased with them.

Nineteen

The carriage finally stopped on a side road between an open field of winter wheat and a treed boundary lane. Nieto informed them that it was the only chance that afternoon to have something to eat and to relieve themselves. He motioned that the young women should go into the wooded area for privacy. Elizabeth and Hannah stared at him with their mouths open.

He persisted, "We will even turn our backs so your privacy is assured. There will be no time or place to stop for a meal anywhere and, since this road is not well-traveled, we will be noticed if we try to go into a village inn or ask to use a farmer's privy."

There was nothing else but to follow the instructions. Despite the promise of privacy, Elizabeth felt herself growing beet-red with embarrassment as she fumbled with her skirts and petticoats. She grumbled that of course Mr. Nieto would not think this a crude and difficult situation. It was not fair that the men had such an easier time what with their fewer layers of clothing and the more efficient placement of their body parts.

It was even more humiliating that Parker had some linen towels and water for them to wash their hands when they returned to the carriage, thus reminding everyone of what they were about in the woods. As Parker opened the basket of foodstuffs to offer everyone bread, cheese and some fruit, Nieto introduced the two additional men who were in their party. The coachman was an Englishman called Gilbert, and the outrider, a small, swarthy, bearded Spaniard called Jose.

Nieto asked Ariel, "Would you wish to ride outside with me for a while? The day is proving quite fine. Parker can go back into the carriage."

Ariel eagerly mounted Parker's horse as Jose handed his reins to Nieto, who mounted the Spaniard's. Jose climbed up on the rear step of the coach and the party headed off down the country lane. They had to go more slowly due to the poor conditions of the road, but, by not stopping for a meal, they were able to put some distance behind them. The two riders spoke little but rode companionably side by side.

As the sun started to set, Parker stuck his head out of the carriage window and called out, "Follow the path off on the right at the next turn."

Nieto nodded, waving a hand to show he understood. The path at the turning was even narrower but soon the smell of a wood fire alerted them that there was a house up ahead. When Nieto signaled a stop, Parker left the carriage and walked up the path and out of sight. A few minutes later, he came back into view, waving them on.

The house was a thatched-roofed crofter's cottage with a small gravel court and a well in front and some outbuildings and a kitchen garden in the back. Incongruously there was an elegant carriage with four bay horses in the front court. Parker was speaking quietly with a young man, a young woman and her maid. The young man had an English mastiff on a leash. The strangers were of similar stature and coloring to the Wharton twins. An onlooker glancing quickly at the group would find it hard to distinguish Elizabeth and Ariel from the young people now waiting at the cottage.

Beowulf jumped down from his seat to investigate the other dog, approaching with raised hackles and a menacing growl. When Parker whistled a command, Beowulf sat but kept his eyes trained on the twin mastiff. While Jose unpacked the luggage, Elizabeth, Ariel and Hannah dismounted from the carriage.

The new young people passed them without a greeting and took their places in the Allingham ride as Jose loaded new luggage. The second mastiff jumped to the seat beside Gilbert. A new outrider appeared from the back of the cottage leading another horse to join the group. The Allingham carriage turned and headed back the way it had just traveled down the country lane. Elizabeth and Ariel watched in stunned silence as their doubles disappeared from view. All of this was accomplished within minutes in a well-coordinated sequence with no words exchanged.

Now a young blond woman, holding a young child on her hip, appeared at the door of the cottage, smiling and waving at them. Parker went up to her and kissed her warmly on both cheeks then stroked the child's blond curls, before taking the toddler into his arms. When he turned back to the group, the family resemblance was clear. Elizabeth knew immediately that this young woman with the brown eyes, tall stature and good-humored smile must be Parker's sister.

When Nieto approached, the young woman threw her arms around him in an affectionate greeting. He returned the greeting with a smile, his eyes glowing with such happiness that Elizabeth felt her face unexpectedly flush at the sight.

After Nieto had taken the baby into his arms to kiss and cuddle him, Parker made the introductions. "My sister Belinda and my little nephew, Thomas. Emily and John Allingham, my employer's friends." Belinda pantomimed that they were invited into the cottage.

The main room was small but immaculate with a glowing fire and the enticing smells of home-cooking. Belinda placed a steaming vegetable stew, a meat pie and a pitcher of cider on the table. The young woman motioned that they be seated and proceeded to fill bowls and to offer fresh biscuits with butter and honey around.

Nieto smiled across the table at the little boy in Parker's lap. "Ah, he is handsome, Belinda. And I see he is growing hale and hearty." Belinda glowed with pride at the doctor's compliments but still did not utter a word in response.

When she returned to the cooking alcove to bring another course of food to the table, Parker explained to the twins, "Belinda does not speak but she is not deaf. Feel free to talk naturally around her. As you will learn, she can make herself understood by hand motions and pantomime or she can write on her slate."

The travelers however were initially in no mood for conversation themselves. The food was hearty and hot and everyone focused on eating. Elizabeth was amazed how hungry she had become by just sitting in a carriage all day

Gradually, as their energy levels returned, the conversation picked up. Parker was eating with one hand while holding his little nephew with his other, occasionally sharing small choice tidbits with the quiet little boy in his lap. It was a man very different from the very reticent but efficient footman-bodyguard who sat across from them now, talking and whispering to the toddler.

"Is this where you grew up, Parker?" Ariel asked.

"Nay, Belinda and I, along with our older brother John, grew up thirty miles away in a small village. Our father was the local publican. Mother had died a few years after Belinda was born. For a variety of reasons, each of us sought to leave that tiny village. My brother John was the first one to leave. He joined the navy. I followed him three years later after Belinda found a position in service to a local landlord."

"And Belinda's husband?" Ariel inquired.

Parker said quietly, "Belinda has no husband. The father cared naught for the babe he made on her and she has learned to care naught for him. The only good he did was to deed this cottage and a few acres to her for the care of the child as long as she remains out of his sight and out of his life. His wife would not appreciate meeting her and his bastard so she lives at this distance from all she knew before."

Belinda came in, her face flushed—by the heat in the kitchen or by overhearing her brother, Elizabeth wondered—and picked up the little boy to take him out of the room for changing. When she returned, she held Thomas dressed in warm nightclothes in one arm and an old guitar in her other. She handed the instrument to Nieto with a pleading look on her face, gesturing in turn to the other guests and to the child.

Parker grinned at the twins, "Did you understand that request—or perhaps better, that command?"

Elizabeth responded with a smile, "I think Mr. Nieto has been ordered to play for us."

Nieto smiled then grimaced at Ariel after strumming the guitar. "I think I will need some time to get this box in tune before I can make any pleasant sound on it."

He concentrated on the tuning of the strings for a few minutes and, after a few more tentative strums, began playing a plaintive folk melody. The music filled the small room, accompanied only by the crackling of the fire. The little boy was transfixed by the sound, staring at Nieto's hands as they moved over the strings and the frets.

Jose, who had eaten voraciously and in silence, spoke up for the first time. "That was Spanish, was it not? Played in my honor, no doubt." He grinned so happily that the twins laughed.

Nieto announced, "Now that I paid my respects to the Señor's homeland, it is time to play a tune in honor of the British navy." He began a gay sailor chantey with Parker supplying the lyrics in a passable singing voice. The chorus was a simple one so soon all were able to join in. Belinda bounced her son to the beat which set him off giggling so hard that everyone laughed. He in turn basked in the happy attention.

Nieto then threw a significant look around the room, looked at the child, and began a soft lullaby. Belinda began to rock the child in her arms. Near the end of the song, she slowly walked to the back bedroom where the child's small bed stood.

When the last chords of the lullaby faded, Nieto leaned across the table and whispered. "We will need to follow little Thomas to rest. The ladies will be in the bedroom with Belinda and all of the men will make do with the floor in this room. Get your coats and all the carriage blankets to warm you. We will arrange a picket during the night. I will take first watch. Parker will have second. Jose will take the third. Beowulf will be on watch also so we will be secure."

Ariel spoke up, "And me….am I to do nothing? I am not a child…I need to do something."

Nieto looked at him, thoughtfully, "Perhaps you can sit watch with Parker during the darkest part of the night. Parker, what think you?"

Parker assured him, "I will wake you when it is time."

The women retreated to the small room that served as Belinda's bedroom. Elizabeth and Hannah snuggled together in the small bed while Belinda put an extra blanket on the floor for herself. The child was in his cot in the far corner.

In the main room, the men assembled a sleeping area near the fireplace with the travel blankets and coats they had—assuming that their communal body heat would be sufficient to keep them warm. Ariel lay between Parker and Jose on the floor. It was the hardest bed of his life and he thought, as he tried to find a comfortable spot, he would never be able to sleep.

He watched Nieto bring Beowulf to lay down outside the women's sleeping area before assuming his own watch position by the one window at the front of the cottage where he had a view of the lane. A pistol lay in his lap as he sat on a bench by the window. When Ariel noticed the doctor also had a knife in its sheath wedged into the waist of his trousers, the young man was reminded that danger could be lurking in the dark beyond this friendly room.

It seemed only a few seconds later when he was being shaken awake by Parker who whispered, "Quiet. Go to the bedchamber. Wake the women and take these." He handed Ariel one of Embry's small pistols and a stiletto pen. "Everyone must remain very quiet. And whatever you do, do not leave that room unless Nieto or I tell you to do so."

Jose was already up and standing against the wall by the door frame, with a pistol in his hand. Nieto was nowhere to be seen. Parker sent Ariel toward the back room with a push and a hand motion to hurry. He moved to Nieto's former position.

Ariel entered the women's chamber. Belinda had awakened when the door to the room first opened and she picked up the sleeping child. When Ariel shook Elizabeth and Hannah awake, Elizabeth looked at him quizzically but he shook his head to indicate ignorance of what was happening. Putting a finger to his lips, he motioned the girls to silence.

A few minutes later, they heard a crash and the tinkling sound of breaking glass. The smell of burning tar seeped under the door and smoke began to fill the air. There were sounds of scraping and scrabbling and men's voices raised in shouts and curses in the front of the house then closer to them in the main room. A door crashed open. Beowulf was growling and running. A gunshot rang out followed by a scream as a heavy object crashed into something in the front of the cottage.

Suddenly, the door to their room flew open. A man stood there with a pistol which he pointed in turn at Elizabeth and Hannah in the bed then at Belinda in the corner with the now-wailing baby in her arms. The invader turned his attention and his gun back to Elizabeth.

"Where is it?" he snarled. "I've come for the new clock. Where is it? You have but a few seconds before I shoot one of you. The new clock—we know you are carrying it. Where is it?"

Elizabeth shook her head at him. "I know nothing about a clock."

He raised the pistol towards Hannah. "You have only three seconds before I shoot her."

Elizabeth licked her lips. Ariel was standing unnoticed in the darkened corner behind the intruder, hidden behind the opened door. Elizabeth deliberately looked at the chest in the opposite corner. "Over there, on the chest." The man's eyes moved across the room and he stepped in that direction.

Ariel leaped forward onto the man's back, plunging the stiletto blade deeply into the back of his neck. The man roared, twisting violently, throwing Ariel to the ground. He turned towards him with the pistol raised.

Suddenly the pistol dropped as his hands went to his throat. His body was being pulled back, his spine arching from the force.

Ariel scrambled back into the corner of the room and watched in horror as a length of cord around the man's neck was pulled harder and tighter by Nieto standing behind him. As the man tried desperately to pull the cord loose, Nieto drew him closer and tightened the cord more viciously.

What Elizabeth was to remember was the cold calmness on Nieto's face. Beyond the jaw clenched in the effort, his face was impassive. The man's feet was scrabbling against the floor and his hands clawed Nieto's arms and hands—leaving bloody marks. He could get no purchase as Nieto kept the garrote drawn tight. Finally the struggle ceased when the man sagged down to the floor.

Nieto bent over him, quickly running his hands through his pockets, inside his shirt and his trousers, pulling out some papers and coins. He looked through the objects. Next he pulled off the dead man's boots where he found a small knife.

Parker ran in, a bloody sword in his hand. "We have one alive up front trapped by Beowulf but there are two down and now this one."

Nieto asked, "Are you hurt? What about Jose?"

"I have a cut but Jose was shot. Not grievously but he needs your attention."

Nieto turned to the others in the room. His shirt front was open and it and his chest were soaked with blood. Blood was also oozing from the claw marks down his arms and on the back of his hands. "Is anyone here hurt?" They shook their heads "no" but Ariel sitting stunned on the floor in the corner said nothing.

"What did he say? What did he want?" Nieto asked the women.

Elizabeth raised her eyes from the body on the floor. She was surprised that she could put words together in coherent sentences. "He asked about a clock. He thought we had a new clock. I told him I had no idea what he meant but he pointed his pistol at Hannah. I had thought to distract him by looking at the chest. He went towards it and that was when Ariel…."

Nieto now crouched down beside Ariel. The young man shrank away, horrified by the blood splattered all over the doctor.

"Ariel, you did what you were forced to do. There was great danger and you had to use the weapons you were given. You were in the right. Doing nothing would have led to greater tragedy."

Nieto touched Ariel on his arm, leaving a bloodstain on the white cotton of his shirt. Ariel stared at the stain in horror. The doctor pulled the stiletto from the dead man's back and, after wiping it on his already stained shirt, he closed it and tried to hand it back to Ariel. Ariel shuddered, shaking his head "no."

Nieto made no comment, just pocketed the weapon then rose, saying to Parker, "Help me move the body out of the house. I will then attend Jose and see to your wound."

Parker looked at Nieto, "And you? You are covered in blood."

Nieto shook his head, "Not my blood this time but his—from the wound Ariel inflicted. Excepting the scratches on my arms, which are nothing of concern."

The men dragged the body from the room. Soon after, the women heard movements behind the house. In the meantime, Belinda got up and handed the child to Hannah. She left and a few minutes later returned with hot water and cleaning rags. She proceeded to scrub away the bloodstains on the floor. Elizabeth watched in silence as the young woman methodically erased the evidence of the violence they had just witnessed.

Ariel sidled past Belinda to enter the main room. Shards of glass from the broken window glittered in the flickering light of the banked fire. Blackened rushes showed where a torch had landed and set them ablaze before the fire had been doused by one of their men.

He found his boots, pulled them on and went outside. Jose was sitting on a bench with his shirt half off, his shoulder and chest exposed as Nieto examined his wound. The doctor said, "The ball is still in so I will have to cut it out. Ariel, stand behind him and hold his arms tight. Be prepared to lean against him to keep him upright."

Jose demanded through gritted teeth, "What? No rum to deaden the pain? Doctor, that is not the way it is done!"

Nieto growled back, "Shut up, you Spanish turd, and let me work. Now!"

Jose's scream was cut off as his eyes rolled to the top of his head. Ariel leaned against him to keep him upright as Nieto quickly cut the ball out of the shoulder muscle then probed to examine the surrounding tissue. He poured some liquid into the wound—Jose convulsively twisted away in pain—and then he sutured the wound quickly and adeptly without being distracted by the writhing patient beneath his hands. "Parker, see if Belinda has any spirits that we can pour down Jose's throat. He needs a reward for his pain and we need to be spared his complaining."

Nieto slapped Jose sharply, reviving him from his stupor. "Jose, can you walk into the house? I want you to lie down before you fall. Young Ariel here can no longer support you, you lump of lard."

Jose nodded slowly—still in a stupor—but Ariel and Nieto were able to raise him to his feet and help him stumble back inside. Parker assisted them in getting the Spaniard down on the floor and covered with blankets. Parker had found a bottle of brandy. When he lifted the wounded man's head and tipped some in, Jose's eyes opened as he drank thirstily.

Nieto grinned, "That is the best medicine for Jose. Watch how quickly he recovers if there is free liquor available."

Parker handed Ariel the bottle. "Let him have all he wants. Nieto, we have a prisoner to attend to in the cowshed."

The two men disappeared around the back of the house. Soon after, those inside the cottage heard muffled screams and moans, pauses and a resumption of screams and moans. Then, finally, silence prevailed followed by the drawing of water from the well and the sounds of splashing and whispering.

When Parker and Nieto walked back into the cottage, their chests were bare and their hair wet. Nieto stirred the fire to survey the room in the brightened light. As he looked around, he was using the few remaining clean parts of his shirt to dry his body. When he finished, he threw the shirt into the fire.

"I would never wear that again," he muttered quietly, as if speaking only to himself.

The light glanced off his body revealing a network of scars that crisscrossed his chest. Parker saw Ariel's astonished gaze as he was using his own shirt to dry off. He quickly stepped nearer Nieto into Ariel's line of sight. "Here, use my shirt until you get to your luggage."

Nieto looked over his shoulder in surprise until he saw Ariel staring. Without a word, he put Parker's damp shirt on. Parker slipped on a loose workman's shirt he drew from his bag.

The brandy bottle had run dry but the drink had done its job. Jose was snoring loudly as Parker and Nieto began to set the room to rights.

Nieto explained as Ariel joined them to help. "I heard some noises near the side of the house so I went around the other way to discover the source of the sound and to attack from the rear if necessary. There were four of them. One threw a stone at the window followed by a small torch. They were hoping the smoke would force us out the front so they could capture or slay us. Then they could look through the house for a new coding clock. I was able to cut one down, Parker took another, while Beowulf—bless him—terrorized the third and kept him pinned to the ground. But one was able to get past by shooting Jose then running into house. You know the rest."

Ariel was stunned. "So the pistol was not loaded? I knifed a man who could not shoot anyone."

Nieto responded sternly, "You did not know that and you saw he was also armed with a knife. You did what was necessary."

"And the fourth man?"

Nieto bent to pick up some shards, "He is dead as well."

Ariel stopped what he was doing to say harshly, "You tortured him. I heard it. You took your surgical kit and you tortured him." It was a statement— not a question.

Nieto said quietly, "There was no choice, Ariel. I had thought to distract anyone who was following us by the counterfeit twins in the carriage heading off in another direction. That failed. Those men followed us here. We needed to find out all we could about who is behind them and what they know about our plans. We especially needed to know how they learned so quickly that the old coding clocks were no longer important. He was not willing to tell us. I needed to use my skills to make him more willing."

"And did you find out what you needed to know?"

Nieto shook his head, "We found out that he knew little except that he would get a large reward for finding what he called 'a clock.'"

"So the torture got you nothing and yet you killed him."

Nieto did not respond directly. Instead he asked, "What would you have suggested, Ariel? Should we have called the local magistrate to arrest him? Do you fancy staying around here to testify at the hearings? Or perhaps you wish to risk being jailed on some charge yourself for attacking his friend with a knife?

"These men were ready to kill one or all of us to get their prize. Think of the possibilities. It could have been your sister, Parker's sister, the little boy—any or all of them could be dead now. Those bastards were willing to do it for money. What was the right thing to do, Ariel? What was just?"

Parker finished moving the furniture back into place, glancing back as the two men talked together. When Belinda emerged with the baby, she nodded her approval at their work.

Nieto continued, "Ariel, go back to your sister and try to comfort her. Parker and I have some work to do before dawn. Parker, bring a torch from the fire."

The two men left the house again. Ariel returned to the bedroom. Sitting on the bed with Elizabeth and Hannah, he tried to reassure them that they were safe now. But he held back the details of what had been done to insure that safety.

The smell of burning wood began to waft into the cottage followed soon by the smell of burning meat accompanied by a sharp metallic tang. Ariel knew there would be no bodies by morning—only ashes and bones in the refuse pile that would be dumped into the deepest part of the woods.

When Nieto re-entered the cottage with Parker, the smoky smell clinging to both of them, the doctor ordered everyone back to sleep. He cautioned them that they would be traveling long and hard the next day and he could not promise what accommodations would be available for the next night.

Despite the terror, or perhaps because of its enervating effect, Ariel dropped off into a deep sleep. Belinda and the baby and Hannah also fell asleep quickly but Elizabeth felt restless. In all the danger, she had remained passive, cared for by others. She needed to move to ease her tension.

She rose quietly, wrapping a shawl around her before tiptoeing through the main room. She heard the sound of men sleeping—Jose snoring with his mouth wide open, Ariel gently whistling in sleep. Parker, lying between them, stirred and slowly raised his head. He watched her open the door slowly and go into the courtyard. He thought about the young woman and the doctor meeting together outside.

Nieto was sitting on a bench, fully awake and ever watchful. As Elizabeth approached, he rose, looking at her as if he had expected this. "Ah, you cannot sleep, Lady Elizabeth."

She nodded, "I cannot lie still anymore. I can still hear and see what happened. I keep thinking, I could have been killed or Ariel or the little boy or Belinda. How quickly my life would have been over before I have really lived."

"Sit for a while, Lady Elizabeth," Nieto patted the empty seat next to him. "The quiet of the night might soothe you. I look at the stars and think how big the heavens are and how small our part in the universe. Somehow it makes my concerns shrink in size."

She sat down and he sat back down next to her. They both looked up at the stars. She said quietly, "It is beautiful here—so still and clear. I forget, after months in London, how big the sky is in the country."

He asked, “And even bigger when you are on the ocean.”

"I have never been at sea."

“How ironic that is for a member of the Aylesford family with its fleet of merchant ships. Out on the ocean with no land in sight, the sky is immense, especially at night when it is hard to see where the ocean ends and the sky begins. I have found in that vast space that I feel closer to God—perhaps because I feel unfettered by others and by society and more open to Him all alone facing the heavens. Or perhaps it is my own yearning that makes me think that is possible."

“Do you think God understands the things you do?”

He shrugged his shoulders, “I have not yet found an answer to that. In each case—one at a time—my path seems clear, so clear to me. But when I add all of the separate actions together, I do not know. God will decide. I can only see one page at a time in the book of my life. I cannot turn back nor can I look ahead.”

The leaves rustled in a passing breeze. She shivered.

“You're cold, Lady Elizabeth. Perhaps you should go back inside.”

“Let me stay here, with you, for a little bit longer,” she begged. “I need time to clear my mind from all that has happened.”

“It takes longer than a few minutes to clear such thoughts away," he sighed. “Here, take my coat. I would not be much of a doctor if you catch a chill sitting here with me.” He draped his coat over her shoulders. She smelled his scent in the warm wool.

“Mr. Nieto,” she whispered. “Would it be wrong if I leaned my head on your shoulder?”

“If you would be comforted, not wrong, but only if you call me Judah since we are alone here.”

He drew her closer, putting his arm around her shoulders, gently pushing her head down to rest on his shoulder. He began humming the lullaby he played earlier in the evening when they were joyous together around the table. She felt the melody rumbling in his chest.

Looking up, she saw his profile framed by the night sky. He looked confident and strong as he gazed up at the heavens. He projected such confidence while, as she was learning, he held so much turmoil inside. How can he live that way?

He must have felt her gaze on him because he suddenly looked down into her eyes. Her breath caught in her throat. The intense blue eyes looked like midnight blue in the half-light. "Judah," she murmured and stretched up to him.

He did not move as she drew closer. His lips were half-open while he seemed to be considering what his next move should be. She reached her hand to his cheek, felt the stubble on his unshaven face and kissed him. His lips were surprisingly soft and warm. She did not pull away while she waited for him.

He put a hand to the back of her head and pulled her closer. He pressed his lips hard against hers and his tongue entered and touched hers. She quivered and inhaled as she felt him react. He tightened his arms around her to hold her firmly against his chest. He kissed her again, harder and deeper, causing an exciting sensation to pulse through her body.

She put her hands in his thick soft hair, whispering, "Judah, love me."

He paused suddenly at her words, shuddered slightly, then pulled her hands down from his hair and placed them in her lap. He held her face in his hands, gazing seriously and sadly at her. "I cannot, Eliza. It is not proper at this time." Despite the denial in his words, she thrilled at how he had said her name. "I have been entrusted with your safety. I cannot take advantage of you in this place."

"How are you taking advantage, Judah? I kissed you."

"But on this night and in this place, you have suffered a great shock. It is natural for you to want to be comforted, but you might not see the impropriety and risks in it."

"Judah, do you think me so addle-pated that I do not know what I want to do? I wanted to kiss you. In fact, I think I have wanted to since you knocked me down."

He did not smile at her attempt to lighten his seriousness. "No, Eliza," how sweet that sounded to her, "you are the least addle-pated girl I know. But you cannot be sure of your feelings after such a day."

"I am sure."

"You cannot be. You are a mere eighteen years old and I am old enough to be... old enough to be Embry."

She laughed. "You are not my brother."

He refused to smile. "Eliza, you are too young to know your mind. Last week you were in love with the Baron—I could see how he charmed you—and today perhaps you think you are in love with me. I might seem exotic and exciting but that is not the truth of my life. I am foreign, I am poor and I am totally dependent on the Baron and others for support. I have no future that can provide for a family. I cannot live in the open, freely as other men can because I am covered in blood. The stain of my deeds clings to me wherever I go.

"Your future is bright. You will have an important role in your world. I will be gone from your life in a week or two." She was shaking her head 'no.' He tightened his hold on her, keeping her at arm's length, saying firmly. "You must go back inside and rest. You cannot stay outside with me."

"You said you see one page at a time in the book of your life. How can you tell what your future will be? Or mine? Perhaps there will be a time when you can settle down and live an open life."

He shook his head. "That life is closed to me. The gates have been locked. I am meant to wander to do my work and find peace in nights like this—with a sky like that. I fear that I can find no peace among people and society." He was looking up at the stars again.

"And you, Judah? What will you do when you send me away?"

"I will sit here and think. I must think for both of us."

She handed him his coat and wrapped her shawl tightly around her once again. Before she reached the door of the cottage, it opened, revealing Parker. He looked at Elizabeth then at Nieto. She passed him quickly without a word and he closed the door behind her. He walked over to sit beside Nieto who was still staring at the sky.

"I think it dangerous for you to be alone with her, Judah. I thought to interrupt before anything went too far."

"Yes, Robbie, I know. She reminds me of how much I have lost. She is too much in my thoughts. It would not do for me to be distracted that way."

Parker looked at his friend's profile as Nieto stared at the sky. "You are not alone, Judah, on the path you have taken. There are others who travel with you and some who wish to join you. Perhaps you can find some comfort in that."

Nieto shook his head, "All I ever wanted was to learn to heal those who have been injured, do good for my community and live quietly with my family. I wanted a wife to love and children whom I could raise to be good and to see my future extended in the lives they would build. Somehow, by each step I took, my path diverged further from the one I had dreamt of. And my choices have sealed that dream world off from me…and I cannot see how to ever get back…."

"But, Judah, there could be other paths that might lead to destinations that hold some peace and happiness for you. You must have hope that you will find some happiness."

Nieto sighed, still looking at the sky. "Perhaps…I just cannot see it yet."

The next morning, Elizabeth and Hannah woke to the smell of eggs frying. When they left the little room, they found all the men gathered around the table except for Parker who was helping serve since Belinda was busy with the child. With great surprise, Elizabeth realized she was hungry and she noticed she was not alone. Everyone was devouring the hot breakfast that was laid out before them as if it was a normal morning after a normal night.

Within the hour, they were saying farewell to Belinda and thanking her for her hospitality. Ariel pressed a few coins into her hands. "For the little boy," he said.

When Nieto said his good-byes, Elizabeth watched with a lump in her throat as Belinda put her hand to his cheek and kissed him. The young mother ran her hand down his shoulder and his arm then gripped his hand. He returned the gestures of affection until he finally pulled himself away to help Jose mount the first horse as the smaller man cradled his bandaged shoulder.

Parker's leave-taking was difficult to watch as well, reminding the twins that they too had left dear family members behind. The blond man wrapped his arms tightly around his sister and the child and rocked them back and forth. Then , as Nieto drove the coach slowly down the lane, Parker leaned out the window to watch his sister until the curve in the path finally hid the cottage from their sight. He sat back against the squabs, his jaws clenched tightly to control his emotions.

All stayed quiet for awhile then Elizabeth said, "Your sister was very generous to put us up in her small house. It required much work to cook for us. She had a young child to tend as well."

Parker replied, "That is kind of you to say, but she would do anything Nieto asked."

Elizabeth tried to sound unemotional. "There are feelings between them clearly."

Parker said bitterly, "Yes, there are feelings. My sister was attacked by the master of the house in which she worked as a maid. The bastard knew she would never be able to scream. He beat her and raped her and left her to face her shame alone. I wanted to kill the man but Nieto said that would not really help Belinda. He made it clear that justice for my sister had to include financial security for the child. The cottage and the land that surrounds it are part of that security."

"But surely justice should also include punishment for the evil he has done. He should not be able to just pay his way out of his wrongdoing." Elizabeth declared.

"Oh, he was punished. He is unable to harm another woman in that way ever again. Nieto used precision in surgery to guarantee that."

Twenty

When the carriage stopped for another picnic lunch, Nieto, Parker and Jose went off to the side to confer. After some discussion over a map, Parker mounted one of the horses and set out ahead of the coach.

Nieto approached the twins, "Parker will find lodging for us tonight. We cannot push on much longer without a good rest. We need to find a larger town which on one hand provides cover for us but on the other hand provides cover for anyone who might be interested in us. You must use your aliases now."

They arrived in the old cathedral town as the sun was setting. Parker was waiting on horseback to greet them as they entered through the east gate from the post road. He led them through the town center to a working class neighborhood of small stone houses and shops. An old coach house stood at the intersection of two streets.

The hostler was expecting them and, once the luggage was unloaded, took the carriage away to a stable yard where the horses would be fed and watered. Meanwhile, the innkeeper and his wife were waiting to greet them in the tap room.

Parker explained quietly to Nieto within the twins' hearing. "I've taken the entire inn. This is the single entrance except for the back kitchen door. Mr. and Mrs. George are the owners. I served with their son Michael and he will be coming at night from his home nearby to sit watch with us."

Jose surprised them all by suddenly stepping forward quickly to be first to enter. He hallooed boldly to the Georges, introducing first Emily and John Allingham, and Emily's maid, Betty. Then, pointing to himself, he declared, "I am Mordecai Halevi at your service. This," he pointed to Nieto, "is my manservant, Rodrigo."

Nieto looked stunned for a moment then made an overly dramatic bow. Jose had made him suffer through this type of play-acting before. Perhaps this time, the swarthy little man might help them disguise who they were even more effectively.

Parker turned away so as not to laugh while Jose as Mordecai Halevi berated his manservant, Rodrigo, with a continuous stream of curses and complaints. Rodrigo was not quick enough, did not handle the baggage with care, and made too much noise as he went up and down the stairs. In the meantime, Mrs. George showed Elizabeth and Hannah to the upstairs back room that would be theirs. The room was small but spotless.

Mrs. George apologized for its size. "I had offered the front room to Robbie Parker for you ladies as more suitable. It is more spacious and brighter with a large window overlooking the courtyard and the street. Howsoever, he insisted that the men take the front room because the noise of the street might disturb your rest."

Elizabeth, gazing out of the small window of this back room that overlooked the walled garden, understood that Parker had made his choice because the front room most likely offered a better view of the street below. She assured the kind woman that the back room was lovely and indeed quiet and just perfect for their needs.

By the time Elizabeth returned to the taproom with Hannah, Mr. George was filling tankards of ale for each man. The innkeeper offered her some sweet cider but she asked for ale instead. She was done with feeling like a fragile porcelain figurine. To emphasize the point, she sat down with the men at the table, sliding onto the bench next to Parker and across from her brother and Jose. The Spaniard smiled broadly at Elizabeth and winked at Ariel as Nieto stomped downstairs after dragging the baggage into the bedchambers.

When the doctor headed for the table, "Halevi" signaled to him. "Remember your place, my man," Jose ordered, pointing to the small table in the corner of the room. Then he told Mr. George to bring a tankard to his manservant, Rodrigo, adding, "I am a kind master—better than that lazy cur deserves."

Nieto hesitated for a moment, his bright blue eyes staring at Jose with annoyance. He suddenly smiled broadly as he marched to the corner table.

Parker leaned closer to Jose to whisper, "I think that you will pay for your joke tonight, Halevi."

Jose shrugged nonchalantly, taking a noisy swallow from his tankard. He said loudly in a voice he tried to make sound aristocratic, "One cannot get good help these days. First these Spanish servants are slow to learn—quite dimwitted they are—and then they become quite insolent from time to time. A good caning every now and then reminds that Spanish lout of his place." The little swarthy man beamed with his cleverness, looking so self-satisfied with turning the tables that Elizabeth almost choked in an effort not to laugh out loud.

A few minutes later, Jose smacked the table with his empty tankard. He bellowed, "Rodrigo, fetch another ale for me—now!"

Nieto got up slowly, bowing obsequiously, "Si, Señor Halevi." As he picked up the tankard, somehow it accidentally tipped over Jose's head so that the few drops remaining in it fell on the little man's face. "Begging your pardon, Señor."

Nieto next ambled over to the innkeeper, where he, the image of a slow-moving servant, waited with his hands in his pockets and his back to the table, whistling a Spanish melody while Mr. George filled the tankard from the tap. Nieto then seemed to have great difficulty balancing the full tankard and the plate of pickles and eggs the innkeeper had handed him, needing several trips to manage the task. Finally, when he had everything on the table, he asked humbly, "Have you any other requests, Señor?"

"Yes, that you crawl back into your cave, you slow-moving worthless excuse for a man," Jose yelled, waving his hand in dismissal, clearly enjoying giving orders in his role as the master. He lifted his tankard with a cackle of glee and swallowed long and hard, downing several full gulps. His self-satisfied grin dimmed after the third long swallow. A few seconds later, the full reaction set in.

Jose spit a mouthful of ale onto the floor, coughing up as much as possible. "Holy God of Abraham, what did you put in this, you poxy son of a whore?"

Elizabeth said with great dignity, "Mr. Halevi, you forget yourself. There is a lady present."

A large belch, like a deep croak of an enormous bull frog, erupted from Jose's throat before he clamped a hand to his mouth and ran from the table to the privy in the back of the inn.

Parker laughed out loud. "Oh, Rodrigo, what did you do to the little Señor?"

"Syrup of ipecac," Nieto called from the servants' corner table, managing to look innocent and mirthful at the same time, "induces violent vomiting. Useful in some cases of poisoning. I just gave him the dose I would use on a man twice as large."

Ariel was shaking with suppressed laughter, tears running down his face. However, when he glanced back at the doctor, he saw Nieto's face change suddenly. It had assumed the cold hard look he had seen before. The doctor gazed out the front window with his pistol at the ready. Before Ariel turned to follow Nieto's gaze, he heard loud footsteps on the gravel outside approaching the door.

Just then Beowulf on guard in the front yard growled loudly. There was a human growl equally loud in response, "Whose hell-hound is this? Take care of this cur or he will be gutted in an instant."

Beowulf's growl changed suddenly to a yelp. Parker ran out the door, whistling the "stand down" signal.

Mr. George beamed as he wiped the bar calmly. He announced proudly, "That be our son, Michael!"

Parker walked back in, accompanied by his friend Michael, a big burly man holding a very quiet Beowulf in his arms.

"Halevi, you have a patient," Parker pointed to Beowulf.

"Halevi is heaving his guts up outside, but I, Rodrigo, will attend this patient," Nieto stood up, tucked the pistol into his trousers and walked over to the big man.

Parker made the introductions. "Ignore this nonsense, Michael. It was a joke started before you arrived. Michael George, my former bos'n, taught me all I know about running a deck crew. My friend, Mordecai Halevi." Michael put the big dog down on the floor then extended a large calloused hand to Nieto.

Nieto kneeled down to inspect his patient. "What happened?" He asked over his shoulder.

"That beast ran to me with those jaws of hell flapping open. I kicked at his mouth and hit him in the head instead. Went down like a sack of rocks."

Ariel crouched down next to Nieto and watched the doctor run his hands over the dog's head and body. "Ouch," Nieto remarked, as he felt the lump on the side of the animal's head. "That's a mean bump and you almost took out his eye. I would not want to be around when he wakes and notices that you are still here, but I find no broken bones. His eyes are responsive so we'll see what'll be when he wakes." He placed Ariel's hands on the dog's injury and showed him how to test the eyes by lifting the lids and watching the pupils.

The back door was flung open with a crash. Jose reappeared, less swarthy than usual, his legs wobbly and his face covered with a sheen of sweat. He glared at Nieto, "You son of a whore…I've been puking my innards out. You almost killed me."

Nieto stood and pointed to the dog, lying immobile on the floor. "You can join Beowulf in my surgery. Lie down, and I'll check you for fleas, Señor."

Mr. George came over with more tankards of ale while his wife brought out a cauldron of steaming beef stew. She looked at Nieto and Jose one at a time, "You have gotten me spun around. Who are you? And who are you? I am confused over who be the master and who be the servant." She shrugged, turning her full attention to the most important man in the room. "Now, Mikey, have a seat with Robbie here and have a good jaw over old times whilst you tuck into the stew."

In response, the big man picked her up, spun her around and kissed her on both cheeks with loud smacking sounds.

"There's a good lad," she whipped at his head with her dishcloth. Mr. George patted his son on the back and, with his aid, pushed several tables together so they all could eat as one group. Jose however was still groaning on the floor with his head on Beowulf's side.

As they introduced Emily, John and Betty to Michael, Mrs. George ladled big bowls of stew for each person. Ariel eyed his filled bowl with some trepidation. How was he ever going to eat all that? Not finishing it, he assumed, would be taken as an insult by Mrs. George. From the look on his sister's face, Elizabeth was worried about the same thing. How different this meal was from the elegant dinners at home!

Nieto, as always, bypassed the meat and selected some bread and cheese. He whispered to the twins, "Don't worry. Jose will join us soon and finish all your bowls." He then raised his voice and asked, "So Michael, tell me about Parker as a young sailor. How long did it take him to stop leaning on the rails?"

"Well," Michael said thoughtfully between large spoonfuls of the hearty fare, "more than some but less than most. Good sailor, our Robbie was, but a bit shocked by the life aboard ship, as I recall. Needed to teach him about giving as good as he got so he warn't pushed around. But he was a thin lad then—not like he is now. With the blond hair and fair skin, he looked a bit fairylike and had a hard time out on the deck in the sun but the tars took to him over time. A few long nights ashore where he showed he could hold his own and they respected him—they did. And them that didn't learned to be wary of his fists. Good boxer for such a light weight."

"Enough, Mikey," Parker warned, his face flushing, "or I will tell some tales your Mum should not hear."

Mr. George beamed proudly, "I bet my Mikey was a wild one, right, Robbie? Learned to be a real man at sea and rose high in the ranks. Now he has a wife and two bonnie boys. Made me a proud grand-dad, he did."

Parker looked surprised. "A wife, Mikey? Never thought you would be shackled, back here on shore. And two little'uns. That's grand. No more sailing?"

"I still sail, on merchant ships now out of Falmouth. In fact, I am leaving in two days' time on a merchant ship bound for Gibraltar. Hate that it takes me away from my boys and my Sweet Sue for six months or more but then I stay home as long as I can until I needs to earn again. The family life, 'tis truly grand, Robbie. Never thought of it until it happened to me but it gives a center to your life. Like a lodestar."

"Sweet Sue? Not Sue Buxton from Falmouth? The bar maid you kept calling Buxom Sue? "

"The very same. Went out from shore calling her 'Sweet Buxom Sue' and came back from the Indies to call her 'wife.' 'tis terrible strange but true. First son came quickly too, almost afore the parson," he winked.

As his mother came by to pick up the bowls, she smacked the back of his head.

"Yow, Mam, what's that fer?"

"Telling such stories about your own. Better keep yer yap shut and in front of a gentlewoman too," she nodded towards Elizabeth.

Mr. George scolded from the bar, "Now, Mother, there's no never-mind. They's grown people and Robbie and Mikey knows each other like brothers. Leave him be. 'tis no harm now that they's wed and the second bairn came good and proper."

Elizabeth was delighted. It was family life she had never seen before. She marveled at the slaps, gibes, give and take and the honest acceptance of the realities of their lives. She glanced at Ariel who was similarly enthralled, his mouth slightly open with a happy grin.

"And Robbie—what about you?" Michael asked over yet another serving of stew and ale. "Are you sailing still?"

"Still in the service but seconded to other duties in the Admiralty," Parker explained.

"So you are one of the toffs now? Should I be honored that you are sitting with a crewman then instead of in the officer's mess? So is there a wife? Babes? Or just babes in some ports—with no wives?" Michael jibed.

"No wife—no babes. Just more careful than some," Parker smiled back.

They were interrupted by two terrible groans. Nieto announced, "My patients awake."

Beowulf snorted, jerked himself up then shook his body as if shedding water. Jose's head hit the floor when the dog moved, and, after another groan, he sat up, sniffing wildly. "Dinner? Is that stew I smell? I could eat a horse."

Nieto reached over, took Ariel's bowl and added Elizabeth's leftovers to it. "Señor," he called, "I saved some dinner for you."

Jose eagerly went to the table to take the bowl but then hesitated. Dare he take any food or drink from Nieto's hand?

"It's fine, Señor. And delicious. Don't you agree, Miss Emily? Master John?" The twins nodded seriously so Jose felt reassured and ate with relish.

When the stew pot was empty, Mrs. George returned with the pudding—custardy, creamy and smelling of raisins and rum. Ariel felt almost desperate now, once again concerned that he would have to choose between insulting the cook or dying from over-indulgence. Mrs. George filled the pudding bowls generously then poured clotted cream on top. "Now eat –don't be shy. I've made my Mikey's favorite pud tonight."

Nieto tapped his spoon quietly on the table to catch Ariel's eye. He lifted a spoon to his mouth and tasted the pudding, rolling his eyes with delight. The next spoonful never quite made it to his mouth. It slid to the floor and the slurping sounds from under the table indicated a happy Beowulf was enjoying dessert. Ariel followed suit with strategically spaced drops of pudding. They were scraping their bowls clean when a beaming Mrs. George came back to retrieve the empty dishes.

After dinner, the party made plans for the watches during the night. Mikey would stay near the back door. Jose would spell him after four hours. Nieto and Parker would split the watches downstairs using Beowulf as another pair of ears. Ariel insisted that he be given a turn as well so Nieto told him to go to sleep first and then awaken when Parker took over in the early morning.

The house grew quiet quickly. Ariel lying in the bed he would be rotating with Nieto thought he would drift off to sleep immediately but found that he could not lie still. He pulled on his trousers and boots and left the room.

Ariel found Nieto sitting by the front window in the dark room hidden by the window frame from any onlookers who might be watching from outside. The doctor smiled at the younger man. "It seems that you and Lady Elizabeth take turns with sleeplessness."

"Too many thoughts in my head. They are buzzing about, making me feel jumpy. I could not lie still anymore. Besides, I spent all day napping in the carriage."

Nieto agreed. "Thoughts do buzz at times. It is often best not to fight them. Instead just let them gradually extinguish or perhaps, you will just adapt to the sound so you don't hear it anymore."

"How do you stay up through the hours? You seem never to sleep."

"I've never needed much sleep and there were years when I got practically none. When I treated soldiers on the battlefield, it seemed that there was no time for sleep or just time enough for a cat nap. Sleep is the worst time for me. I am cursed with bad dreams so, if I can, I try not sleep more than absolutely necessary and only when I can no longer stay awake."

"But what do you think about alone in the dark? To keep yourself awake?"

"You might be the only one who will truly understand. I think about playing music. I think through the compositions in my head and hear each note as I imagine playing it on the guitar. Sometimes I even transpose music. I take a piano piece and think through how it might be played on a guitar. It keeps me awake and pushes away the thoughts that buzz.

"And then I watch the night. Some people think night is just the absence of daylight but it's a world unto itself—with its own colors and sounds and creatures. And it changes. Each hour it seems to be created anew. During the day, we cannot see such subtleties. There is so much else going on to distract us."

"You spend so much time alone, Judah. Do you ever get time to go home to be with friends or with your family?"

"I will be seeing friends when we get to Gibraltar and there are friends in ports and cities throughout Europe. I see them when I can. But I actually have very few friends—real friends, that is. People, like Parker and me, who travel a great deal have difficulty finding and keeping friends, so the friends I have are those I spend time with…like Parker, the Baron, Jose. Yes, Jose," Nieto smiled as Ariel shook his head, "despite the rough ways we might express our affection. It's the way of men not to be direct."

"And family? Judah, you did not mention family."

"My father does not approve of what I do—and it is a deep schism. I live a life he cannot support and thus, he has ordered the rest of the family to cut me out of their lives. First I lost a brother and then, because I sought to avenge his murder, I lost the rest of my family."

"You have no family of your own then—no wife or children either?"

Nieto looked at the young man and thought about his twin sister. The message should be delivered again. "What kind of husband or father could I be, Ariel? I do not stay in one place long enough to be able to provide for a family. My work is dangerous and would endanger anyone who was connected to me. I told you that my work can be a terrible burden and the worst part of the burden is the solitude. I understand why solitary confinement is a brutal punishment. A solitary life with glimpses of what others enjoy every day is indeed a refined type of torture."

They grew quiet. As the minutes dragged on, Ariel found his eyes were finally getting heavy. Going back upstairs seemed too much of an effort. He yawned deeply. Nieto chuckled and pulled him closer. He pushed Ariel's head against his shoulder to let the younger man sleep as he watched the night change through the window.

He heard Parker and Jose, still groaning theatrically from his wound and his bout with the syrup of ipecac, come down the stairs. It always amazed Nieto how men's bodies could learn to tell time in watch shifts—at sea or on guard. He'd seen it time and again—men would awake on schedule and change shifts without consulting or needing a clock. They would do it even before the watch bells rang to remind them.

Jose went to the back door to relieve Michael and Parker approached Nieto. He smiled at the sleeping Ariel. "Good idea to give him the late watch. It let him get so deeply asleep that he will sleep right through it. I'll get Michael to carry him to bed."

Ariel did sleep through being carried upstairs and being undressed by Nieto then covered by the bed quilt. The doctor slipped out of his trousers and shirt and slid into the bed next to him. Lying on his back, listening to the soft snores of the young man, he thought how much more alone one could feel next to another person—how much harder it was than being truly alone watching the sky.

And how much sadder it felt to spend time with those whose choices still lay ahead of them. It made it all the more evident that you had made your own choices and were now condemned to live with their consequences.

Twenty-One

During the ample breakfast the next morning provided by Mrs. George for her son and secondarily to Parker and his friends who happened to be staying at the inn, they discovered that Michael was going to Falmouth on the same timetable as the rest of them. They made the decision to travel together. He assured them that they were only one day away.

The smell of the sea announced their approach to the port city. The sun was setting when Nieto asked Michael about finding a modest inn that they would be able to commandeer entirely as they had his parents' the night before. He thought for a bit then suggested that they stay at the Sisters'.

"The sisters? A convent? " Nieto asked.

"Nay," Michael laughed, "the sisters, well—they was sisters in tending to the needs of the sailors what came into port—if you get my drift. Don't even know if they are real sisters. And lo, one of the captains ups and marries one sister then he dies and leaves her a big house. Of course, we all thought they would set up as Mother Abbesses theirselves and make more money from the ladies what worked for them. But instead, they announced, no more were they making money on their backs. They opened a nice clean house for seafarers to stay.

"The town folks however will not forgive the way the sisters had earned the money afore they became respectable so they have been spurned. Some of us sailors though try to steer friends there. It is hard enough in this life —no need to keep reminding people of what they once was when they are no longer such."

Parker was nodding his head. "Yes, I remember the stories about the Sisters. Their house was always reputed to be clean and well-run."

"It might serve our needs," Nieto responded. "It will not be a place that one might think to look for our friends, the well-bred Allingham twins. Clean and well-run you say? And not patronized by the locals? It sounds as if it would indeed suit us."

The sisters' inn was unpretentious and neat from the looks of it as they approached. Michael and Parker went in to see what was available for rent and how secure the premises were. As Michael had suggested, there were no other customers so the entire inn was rented by Parker for the night. When Parker returned to the carriage, he seemed confused.

Nieto asked, "Is it bad, Parker? You are looking a bit less sure."

Parker shook his head, "I am not sure what to think. There is just so much of ...everything. You'll see."

The party entered the main room, leaving Jose to see to their luggage. The sisters, Mrs. Trout and Miss Fenton, greeted the visitors, dressed for the occasion in the elaborate fashions of an earlier era. Their full-skirted gowns had tight waists and low-cut bodices that displayed their more awesome qualities.

They greeted their guests enthusiastically in some strange version of a continental accent, "Messieurs et mam'selles, bienvenue to our humble hotel. We will spare no effort so you enjoy your stay."

Their curtseys defied gravity. Nieto fully expected them to tip over from the weight of their exposed décolletages and elaborate hairdos. It was the latter that Elizabeth found enthralling—intricate fantasies of curls arranged high on their heads with artificial flowers and birds stuck hither and yon.

At that moment, the door opened again, with Jose leading a hotel porter carrying the luggage from the carriage. He took in the tableau of the two sisters bent into their deep curtseys.

"How wonderful are your creations, O Lord," he intoned prayerfully as he eagerly approached the women, introducing himself and leaning closer for a better look as he grasped their hands to raise them."Dear ladies, I am Jose Franco at your service. How lovely, lovely you are—clearly the mistresses of this lovely, lovely hotel."

The ladies rose elegantly, beaming at the short swarthy Spaniard who turned to Nieto with a look of excited delight.

Nieto whispered to Parker, "I think, Robbie, we have found the perfect hideout for us. No one would think to look here for the twins and their party. However, we must rein in our companion's enthusiasm. We need all eyes and minds focused on our tasks, not on the ladies of the hotel."

The hotel itself was a fantastical re-creation of the ancien régime. Clearly, the sisters assumed that if gold, mirrors and ornate carvings were the markings of taste, then the more of each, the better the taste. The main room was red—red walls, red draperies, red silks on spindly legged sofas—and gold on moldings, picture frames, table legs, chandeliers and candlesticks. Even the tiny dog that Beowulf was sniffing at warily sported red and gold ribbons. The dark portraits on the walls were of gentlemen and ladies posed stiffly and formally dressed in rich fabrics and yards of lace.

Michael beamed, "I told you the sisters had done well. Isn't it the wonder?"

Ariel slowly spun around, smiling with amusement. He whispered to Elizabeth, "I cannot imagine what could possibly be missing. Everything has been piled in here. What a great place to explore. I would love to sketch the sisters. I feel whisked back to the court of Louie Seize in France without having left merry old England."

They were shown to their rooms. For security reasons, Nieto did not want the twins alone in their own rooms. While Elizabeth had Hannah as a companion, he thought that Ariel would be best partnered with Parker. He was not sure if Jose would stay focused on guard duty, not after he had seen the impression the sisters had made on the Spaniard.

Opening the door to the front bedroom, Nieto announced that he would share the room with Jose, who immediately narrowed his eyes in anger.

"I know what you think," Jose snarled. "You think you must keep an eye on me—you the night owl who never sleeps. You think I might be distracted from my responsibilities. I, Jose Franco, am not so easily distracted."

"That is what I fear," Nieto responded calmly. "You are not easily distracted once you conceive a plan. Remember, Jose, we have serious responsibilities here. There are other 'sisters' awaiting you in any port. You do not have to follow every scent under your nose."

"Oh, but have you noticed, Nieto, there is a very special scent under this bush?"

Nieto smacked the smaller man on the head but Jose did not react. He was staring intently at the painting on the far wall. He walked closer to get a better look, cocking his head right and left and rolling back and forth on his feet as if considering a fine masterpiece in an art gallery.

Nieto was mystified until he walked closer. Now he saw what had enthralled Jose. A partially-clad nymph was lolling on the grassy banks of a river while a well-muscled naked young man knelt between her legs, his face hidden from view by the white drapery of her clothes. There was no doubt what the satyr peering from behind the trees was watching and the effect on him, as his hands were placed lower down on his large swollen protuberance.

It appeared that the sisters' taste in art in the private rooms was a far cry from the formal portraits that lined the main room downstairs. Nieto stood in shock—not at the painting itself but at his sudden realization that perhaps the twins' rooms also....

The answer came immediately. The door banged open and Parker lurched in, trying hard not to laugh too loudly. "Oh, Judah, you must see our room. Ariel is spellbound. I don't know if it is very shocking or just very funny."

Nieto entered the second bedroom to find the young man slowly circling a carving on a table. At first the doctor only saw the figure of a muscled young man, leaning forwards against a tree stump, pushing against it with such force as if to uproot it that his arm muscles bulged with his exertion.

As Nieto moved to stand beside Ariel, he recognized that the tree trunk was not one at all but the lower half of another person's body bent over so that the head and the face were hidden. The musculature implied that it was unlikely female.... Ariel bent closer for a better view.

Nieto put a hand on the young man's shoulder to pull him back. "Ariel, hmmm, perhaps this is not a good idea. We might need to find another hotel."

Ariel turned to him with a wide grin, "Oh no, Mr. Nieto, this is quite a marvelous place. I've heard of, but never been in, those galleries that specialize in showing such things. I have always wanted to see but whom was I to ask to take me? And now, here it is, right in front of me."

Nieto smiled weakly, "This is not usually part of my regular duties but let me know if you have questions."

There was a loud snort behind him. Parker was leaning against the door, "Ariel, yes, definitely ask Nieto if you want the medical explanation. He can give you so many details about the wonders of the human anatomy, the processes that affect it in precisely what ways, the scientific reasons for everything and the medical risks and dangers to terrify you. Or you can ask the men who might actually know by experience." He laughed at Nieto's flush of annoyance.

Ariel suddenly spun around with a start, "But Elizabeth's room?"

The three of them set off to the back bedroom leaving Jose behind to admire the sculpture. They knocked on the door and heard the sounds of giggles cut short and then some scurrying about before a calm "come in" was uttered by Elizabeth.

Nieto walked in first and asked, "Just wanted to find out if everything is fine in this room."

His eyes were quickly scanning the walls and table surfaces for anything that might cause concern. He breathed a sigh of relief that was cut off when Ariel asked, "Elizabeth, tell me what is causing you to blush so red."

Nieto looked at the young woman seated on the plush red sofa. She was indeed looking feverish and so was Hannah by her side.

"Nothing," Elizabeth replied to her brother as her blush deepened. Hannah giggled behind her hands and neither of them could look directly at the men standing in the doorway.

Ariel, knowing his sister well, scolded, "Elizabeth, we have all seen the …umm…art in the other rooms. It is unlikely that this room was set aside for maidenly sensibilities. What is it that causes you and Hannah to blush?"

Elizabeth shook her head but her brother was insistent. "Give it here."

Finally she pulled back the pillow on the sofa and handed Ariel an ornately bound book with gilt-edged pages. Ariel began to open it when Nieto scooped it out of his hands. He took a look at the binding and opened to one page before shutting it firmly. He said, "It is in French. A book about the …erotic…"

Elizabeth giggled, "One does not need to even know French at all. The drawings are very well done and quite easy to understand."

Parker chuckled, "Judah, why not check to see if they are medically accurate or even plausible? Then let us know...."

Ariel reached out his hand, "Can I just take a ....?"

Nieto hugged the book closer. "No...I am responsible for you both. I cannot let you...."

Parker was laughing again. "Oh, Judah, I think this is exactly what is meant by closing the barn door after the horses have escaped. There is no erasing what has been seen. Better to explain it than to hide it. Or might you prefer some time alone with that book yourself?"

"A minute...just give me a quiet minute." Everyone waited as the usually serious and calm Nieto struggled to regain his dignity. He took a deep breath. "I have always believed that knowledge is good in all things...." He was interrupted by another hoot from Parker. "Better that people know the reality to avoid tragic errors....I saw young men in the army who sought to protect themselves from the French pox by doing the most bizarre...."

Parker was now incapacitated by convulsions of laughter. "Judah, I swear that you are digging a deeper and deeper pit. Just tell them that you will answer questions and stop trying to control their lives."

Jose appeared behind Parker. "Has anyone seen Michael recently?"

Parker gasped and looked at Nieto. Both of them quickly left the room and walked rapidly down the hall to the last bedroom.

Suddenly Nieto turned to Parker, "Wait! What are we thinking? Michael is a grown man and not our responsibility. He is free to do what he wants."

Parker smiled back, "Oh, but you forget. I was under his command for months at sea. I just want to pay him back for those times he played tricks on me aboard ship. It would be wonderful to see him on the receiving end for once. So let us see what we can interrupt...."

They pushed open the unlocked door and peered in. The big man was lying on the bed, fully clothed, fast asleep with his hands folded across his chest, looking every bit at peace with himself. Parker sighed, turned and walked back to the room he was to share with Ariel.

Before Nieto could turn away, however, Michael popped open one eye and then the other and grinned widely. He pressed his finger to his lips and winked at Nieto while pulling a thick book from under his pillow. He beckoned Nieto to come closer. It took only one glance at an illustration to get the gist of the contents. When Nieto turned to leave, Michael leaned back against the headboard, happily turning the pages and sighing deeply.

Dinner was served late in the continental style. Nieto stood alone in the sitting room waiting for the others to assemble so they could go to the table together. Most of the party straggled down late, obviously more reluctant than usual to leave the charms of their various rooms. They sat quietly while the first course was passed around by a waiter. The sisters stood off to one side beaming at the full table and asking if there was anything else wanted.

Jose opened his mouth to reply but a stern look from Nieto cut him off. "Perhaps later," Jose said innocently, "you might explain about some of the wonderful objects in the house."

Mrs. Trout smiled at him, "It would be my pleasure, Mr. Franco, to show you all our treasures."

The sisters left the room. Now that they had privacy, Parker started the conversation with a wide-eyed innocent look on his face. "So, I wonder, er...Miss Emily and Master John, if you had any questions about what you saw today. I am sure Mr. Halevi would be glad to answer them."

Ariel turned eagerly to Nieto while Elizabeth blushed and stared down at her plate.

"Parker, consider what you say," Nieto scolded. "It is not done to speak of such things in front of a gently-bred woman."

Ariel interrupted, "It's only my sister, Mr. Nieto, and she is known to ask embarrassing questions herself and to speak her mind."

"But I am not used to treat young women so," Nieto responded.

Jose piped up, "No, he is not. But older women now, he has been known to treat quite…quite…."

"Professionally," Parker added, "Or perhaps we could say 'with consideration'?"

"Aye," Jose laughed, "with consideration for when they's husbands or fathers might come home…." Parker responded with more laughter.

Nieto slapped his hand down hard on the table to put an end to the ribaldry. When he got up suddenly and left the room, Parker and Jose looked at each other with some surprise at the doctor's reaction.

It was a full ten minutes before he returned and the next course was served. The dinner proceeded quietly. Nieto told the twins that tomorrow they would be boarding a ship headed to Gibraltar called "The Ruby Goddess."

Michael raised his head from his intensive focus on his dinner. "That's the one! The one I am hired on. What luck, Robbie! There's boys on her that you know from the Navy. It's a beauty. Owned by the Aylesford fleet and well-fitted and fast. Has to be since we cross some parts where Boney's navy might lurk."

Elizabeth added, "How wonderful. It's one of …."

Nieto interrupted quickly, "Yes, Miss Emily, it's one of the newer ships that cross to Gibraltar. It is widely known that it makes good time and brings goods safely into the Mediterranean ports, right, Michael?"

"Aye, and it is a pleasure to serve on her. One of the few that was built to make the life of the men what work as comfortable as can be. I try to work Aylesford as often as I can because it is a lot easier and safer to oversee deckhands what are pleased with their work and how they be treated—fairly and respectfully as can be. Too often the seamen are treated worse than slaves by the officers on other ships, including lashings for every small misstep. No wonder many often talk openly about overthrowing the old ways as tempers flare...."

The big man stopped abruptly when Parker signaled with a warning look and a nod towards the twins that the conversation was sailing into dangerous waters.

Nieto continued smoothly, "Because we need to get on board early tomorrow, I suggest, Miss Emily, that you go up to supervise your packing with Betty. I asked Miss Fenton to see if she can provide any supplies that you might need. Her maid will assist in mending and laundering the garments that need attention. You might also take advantage of the bathing room. The accommodations on board might not be as spacious."

Elizabeth agreed. It had been days since Hannah had had the opportunity to review their supplies and tend to her wardrobe. And a good soak in a bathing tub would be a real luxury. She had glimpsed into the bathing chamber and found it well-equipped with scented soaps, lotions and thick toweling.

After dinner, while Miss Fenton led Elizabeth upstairs to attend to her wardrobe, Mrs. Trout offered the gentlemen cigars and port. Parker assisted Ariel in the process of preparing a cigar, lighting it and inhaling. Ariel was able to handle a few puffs comfortably, although he had yet to discover what the pleasure was in the nausea he felt. He quietly put the cigar down.

The men relaxed in companionable silence, sipping the fine port and enjoying the cigars. Nieto laid out watch rotation once again then Jose and Michael made their excuses.

Having the second watch, Jose headed off to the back office area, no doubt to spent part of the first watch with Mrs. Trout. Also assigned to the second watch, Michael headed upstairs, murmuring that he wished to read the good book before turning in. He would leave them right after the second watch to get a head start on getting reacquainted with the deck hands and the officers of the Ruby Goddess and to supervise the loading of the vessel.

That left Parker and Nieto sitting with Ariel, who cleared his throat as he turned to Nieto. "I did want to ask you some questions, Mr. Nieto, if I have your permission."

"Do you want me to leave you in privacy?" Parker asked.

"No, Parker, I think I will feel comfortable with you as well. I just wanted to understand, given all the art in this house, all about the…umm…variety. I mean, I talk with my friends and we all talk about…all of us…you know…we think about the parts women have that we don't and we think about …the act …but mostly in the same way. But here, there are so many different ways that the men and women in the pictures …in the books…and then there are the men with the men…there are so many things that are kept secret."

Nieto looked calmly back at Ariel, ignoring the expectant grin on Parker's face. "First, let me tell you, Ariel, that despite Parker's attempts to place me in an embarrassing position in front of your sister, I do welcome your questions. I'd rather that young men ask questions of people who might actually know the truth than to whisper among themselves half-truths and downright myths.

"But know too that many people have different senses of what is right and proper between men and women. They might declare certain types of behaviors as evil or sinful and they might even think that people who do those things deserve terrible punishments. I might tell you that I think something is natural for some people but your father might feel that it is not something he would countenance in his son. However, I can only tell you my beliefs and what I know to be medically true."

Ariel nodded but Parker sighed theatrically at this long introduction. Nieto continued, trying hard not to sound too clinical, understanding Parker's signal. "So back to your question. Our bodies feel pleasure in many ways—you know this from how you feel when you smell something you like or when you touch something that is soft and perhaps when you taste something sweet."

There was another groan from Parker. The sailor finally had to interrupt. "Ariel, you know the places on your own body that are exciting to touch and stroke, don't you?"

Nieto threw a dark look at Parker but Ariel nodded with a smile. He turned back to Nieto, who continued, "Well, yes, there are places on our body where we can feel excitement and pleasure when someone touches us or strokes us there. So over time, men and women have taught each other those ways and passed that knowledge down to other generations. Some people like some ways more than others so it also gives people choices and adds variety to their times together."

"But why then do people think of one way as the only proper way? Why would feeling pleasure in other ways be considered so wrong? Why are those ways sniggered over?"

"There is one way that has been valued and exalted over the others because it is the only way humans can produce new humans. Most people are driven towards that way over all the others. If that was not so, there were be fewer babes in the world. Most religions, including our own, say the other ways are sinful—in order to encourage the one way that produces the next generation for the faith."

"So you are saying that perhaps there is nothing wrong in variety if you do not want or need to have children? If I had a wife and we had all the children we wanted, we could do everything else if we wanted to so as not to make more babes."

"Or you can learn how to lay with each other even the most common way—and use methods that can prevent having more children."

"But then why are these books and art considered so scandalous? One would think that everyone would want to know about this—to learn all the ways to find pleasure and the ways not to beget children or how to make sure they breed offspring. I guess I wonder why so much is laughed at or hidden away or considered lewd."

Nieto paused and said, "Some religions consider the drive between men and women a result of sin but a necessary evil if we are going to continue to have generations of humans. It is a powerful force which can be distracting so perhaps they fear it diverts the faithful from their faith.

" Our faith does not hold it to be so but rather a blessing when performed at the right times. But even our religion has labeled some behaviors praiseworthy and others evil or sinful. When certain behaviors are hidden because they are not accepted, they in turn become secrets and then people start to whisper about them. People become even more intrigued because after all, don't we all relish secret knowledge?

"And there are some behaviors that are not accepted at all by any modern faith. Most people understand that men and women might find pleasure in a variety of positions, but most people would not countenance a man and a man finding pleasure together—even if both are willing and are private about it."

"When I look at those pictures, I find some of them exciting but others not. That is normal? Other men think that too?"

Parker spoke up, "Ariel, like some men like blondes," at this Ariel nodded, "and others like red-headed women, people find some actions exciting and others might not. We are all individuals when you come to think of it. So why do we find it strange that in relations between people there are difference preferences and why should you care about what I might find exciting and why should I be concerned about your desires?"

"I don't think it is quite that simple, Robbie," Nieto disagreed. "There is force and power that can be misused. It is not just a simple choice if one person has no choice at all. The use of force makes a difference."

He paused. Parker looked away, swallowing hard. Ariel remembered Belinda, Parker's sister, and her child.

Nieto continued, "Also each of us must consider the ramifications of our choices. One act between a man and a woman can create a life and that has consequences. An act between two men, if known, can heap ridicule and shame upon them and even subject them to criminal proceedings. Can they live with the scorn of society and the dangers to their lives for doing what they want but what others consider evil?

" Consider why the ladies who run this house are still scorned by society. They did things with men that others might not be willing to do and perhaps with men who had wives who felt betrayed. And they did it for money—not for love or for pleasure. All that is not accepted by our society and they are living with the consequences."

Parker responded with some heat in his voice. "Nieto, spoken very logically. But where is passion? And where is being true to oneself in this lecture? Isn't it more important for a person to be able to comfort and love another than to be over-concerned about what the rest of society thinks? Especially if the other person is of like mind?" He stopped suddenly as he had just remembered there was a third person in the room. He stood up with an exaggerated yawn. "I need to attend to Beowulf before we begin first watch. I want to check that he did not eat that rat the sisters call a dog. I will let him run outside for a bit."

Ariel watched Parker leave the dining room while he continued to swirl the last bit of port in his glass.

"Mr. Nieto..."

"Call me Judah. We are alone now."

"Judah, I would like to ask something but it is perhaps improper."

"Ariel, I will answer it if I can. I truly believe that knowledge is good. I'd rather not hide the truth if I can."

"Then Judah, do you have preferences for some of those ...various...actions in the books? Is it common to have some of those images in your mind all the time?"

Nieto confessed, "What you ask is very personal and I am uncomfortable in telling such things about myself. But this I can say. There is a need for sexual pleasure in our nature that is a powerful drive. It is the force that pulls men and women together—at times almost like a madness. It has nothing to do with marriage although our religions want it so. It has to do with the time of our lives and so for you at your time in your life, yes, it might be all you think of. For me, at times, it becomes all I think of. And Jose, I am quite sure, thinks of little else." Ariel grinned at this. Nieto continued, "And yes, because I am not married and I do not want to make babes yet, some of those ways are better for me to lay with a woman than a way that might create life."

Ariel looked at the glass in his hands again and whispered, "And with a man?"

Nieto felt a jolt and a cold draft down his spine. Was this where the conversation had been going? He thought over the past ten minutes and looked for questions he had misunderstood. "Ariel, there are places and times when men are together only with men. Sometimes they have no choice—like men aboard ship for months at a time. And sometimes it is a time in their lives—boys at schools together who are learning about their lusts and their bodies. And sometimes it is a preference—something calls them to other men instead of women.

"People do not talk much about it because it has for generations been considered more than just a different choice. Many religions decry that type of preference as evil or sinful. Our Torah calls it an abomination." He paused then added, "Interestingly, some societies actually thought of it as a higher form of love because it was between equals, since men had all the power. The Greeks were supposedly of that mind and the Baron claims that some of the American natives believe so.

"I wonder at the very powerful forces brought against such behaviors—almost as if the religions believed that more men might wish to lay with other men if free to do so. There seems to be great fear in their hysteria over it. I believe that men who do those things with other men are not evil but they are in danger. They are often made to pay terribly for their choices."

There was another, even more quiet, whisper, "Have you ever been with a man?"

Nieto hesitated then said very quietly, "I will answer that only if you are willing to tell me the same truth about yourself. It is a dangerous hold to have over someone."

Ariel nodded, saying very softly. "I have, Judah, at school and I have been haunted that I am doomed because of it. It was once with someone who was like that and I knew he wanted me. I was curious. But afterwards when I saw him tormented, I did nothing. I mocked him just like the others did. I was so afraid of what would happen if they knew about me and him. But he never told about me. That was brave, was it not? He was much braver than I was."

Nieto sighed. "Yes, he was very brave to bear the scorn alone and not try to push it on you. For your honesty, I will tell you that a few times when I had spent months in hiding with some of my fellows, there was no way to find release except alone or with each other. We knew that it was not what we wanted or needed for always in our lives. But at that time and in that place, there was tension and fear and the possibility of death was always near. It seemed important to be close to someone who understood and cared for you.

"I was more fortunate than you. We all knew what it was and why it was. It never became a threat to us or among us. We cared for each other and we kept each other safe. We knew that what we had done together would never be discussed or revealed to anyone else."

"Would I be safe with you, Judah?"

The green eyes with gold flecks looked up from under the thick lashes. Nieto knew the real question but, with a sad feeling, he chose to misunderstand what Ariel was asking. "Yes, you are safe with me. I will not tell anyone what we discussed here. You have my promise on that."

Ariel stared at him a long time with something simmering in his eyes. Nieto looked away first. He was not able to bear what the young man was revealing this evening.

He abruptly stood up and gestured to Ariel to do the same. "I have first watch with Parker and you need sleep. Good night, Ariel. Try to rest. I will see you in the morning."

Ariel hesitated then added calmly, "I am grateful, Judah. I do not know if I could ever have asked these questions of anyone else. I am sorry Elizabeth won't have an opportunity to do the same."

"I am hoping she had one this evening. Miss Fenton was very gracious when I asked her to assist Elizabeth by welcoming her to ask questions. I suspected she needed someone to talk to as much as you did."

Ariel went upstairs to the bedchamber he would share with Parker. Nieto checked the locks on the windows and doors on the main floor and set a chair at an angle that afforded him a clear view through the window to the front courtyard. A few minutes later, he saw Parker returning with Beowulf at his side. When Parker entered the front door, Beowulf wagged his tail as he sniffed and licked Nieto's hands.

Parker asked, "Any more surprising questions from young Sir Ariel?"

Nieto nodded, "But I promised not to tell."

"Let me guess," Parker responded. "He asked about being drawn to men."

Nieto stared at him but said nothing.

"And you said, as I have heard you say before, that some men have those feelings and in and of themselves they are not evil feelings but they should be hidden and fought against because of the derision of others."

Again, Nieto did not respond.

"Oh, Judah, you have sentenced him to much pain by telling him to live life in fear, denying who he is. You whom he admires so greatly have told him that he is not to be fully himself. It was kindly meant and perhaps very truthful but...."

"Robbie, what should I have said? He is young yet and perhaps does not know what he really desires. All this might be the curiosity of a sheltered young man. But he is a Wharton and he is destined to be a leader in his community. People will note what he does. Isn't it fair to tell him of the dangers?"

"So he will be another sacrifice to the aristocracy, to the society where each of us must know our place and play our role in the very system that seems to be collapsing under its own weight. Why not tell him to follow his heart and do what is right in his soul? Perhaps he will suffer but at least he will know he has been true to himself.

"Think on it, Judah. What have you done with your own life—you who was destined to be a leader in your community? If you could start over, would you do differently? Would you do what your community expected? Decide to be a rabbi instead of a surgeon? Would you not tried to avenge Aaron, knowing that it would make you a pariah? Didn't you feel compelled to follow your own path, no matter the cost?

"Maybe being true to himself as a leader in his community is a path he could take to do good, to shake his world loose from its old hatreds and beliefs." Parker sighed then shrugged, "I'll take Beowulf to the back door and watch from there."

The house became silent. Nieto, watching through the window, reflected on how many nights he had spent like this—alone, trying to block his thoughts by focusing on intricate puzzles. He thought over Parker's words, wondering about its truths. Was his own path really a choice? Had he ever thought about the implications? Or was it, as Parker had said, a compulsion that could not be opposed? Was it that way for most people? Believing they had choices, but really compelled to follow the one path visible at the moment, spurred on by passion or love or righteous anger or faith? Was it God's will working through man? Was it like the visions and voices that drove the prophets to confront kings and the mobs despite the dangers?

He slowly shook his head. The decisions were made and he had taken this path. There was no benefit in wondering why. He let his mind wander to the music that helped him keep the memories at bay. What piece should he think about tonight? Ah, the Mozart one that he had not finished transposing in his head the night before. That was complex enough to exhaust him.

Twenty-Two

The next morning, the party met at the ample breakfast buffet set out by the sisters. Parker, noting the sunny day with clear skies and a light breeze, pronounced it a good day for sailing. He would be heading dockside earlier than the others to see to their accommodations. At mid-day, the rest of them would board the ship scheduled to set sail early in the afternoon.

Nieto pointed out that they would have some time to purchase any personal supplies needed for the many days at sea. Since he wished to restock his kit with some medicinal herbs, he and Jose could take the twins with them to the market.

Jose and Nieto were not relaxed strollers. They scanned the crowds in the market, alert to anyone who seemed to have an unusual interest in the twins beyond appreciative smiles at their good looks. The shoppers were a mix of local folk and sailors from the ships in the harbor The vendors included traders from many foreign countries displaying exotic wares and merchants from the town hoping to entice the foreign visitors as well as the locals to spend their coins.

It was a great new world for the daughter of an earl. For the first time, Elizabeth observed up close the theatrics between customer and vendor as they haggled over prices and the merits of the wares on offer.

When she admired the quality of a beautifully woven shawl, Nieto drew the soft fabric from her hands, tossed it down in front of the watching weaver and asked his price. When the number was named, Nieto acted astounded, "Really, sir? It is a plain wool scarf—woven with skill, I agree, but still only wool."

The man shrugged then lowered his price a bit. Nieto shook his head, taking Elizabeth by the arm. "Come, my dear," he said loudly. "There are other merchants with other shawls further on. You should not be taken advantage of."

Before they could take a step, the weaver sputtered with anger, looking directly at Elizabeth, "I have the right to make a decent living from the work of my own hands—more right perhaps than those in high places who have others to labor for them. You would not demand that the lord of the manor lower his prices on his harvests to suit you."

He paused, reining in his emotion, looking at Nieto and considering the doctor's simple dress. The weaver said with more civility, "Excuse me, sir, you look to be a hardworking man yourself. I have a family to support. You tell me what you are willing to pay."

Nieto named his price causing the man to shake his head with great vehemence but this time, he recovered quickly to name a price halfway between Nieto's and his first quote. Nieto thought about it then returned with another compromise—a bit higher than his first low offer but still less than the merchant wanted. The doctor turned to Elizabeth and mentioned as if the thought had suddenly struck him, "I just recalled that I have some gifts to buy." He turned back to the merchant, "Good sir, perhaps you can accept my price if I purchase three shawls today."

At this, the merchant finally nodded. He brought out more shawls to choose from—white, ochre, indigo and red—their colors brilliant in the bright sunshine.

Now that the negotiation was over, the merchant and Nieto conferred over the choices as the best of friends. Elizabeth and Nieto selected three pieces and Nieto placed coins in the merchant's hand—slightly more than the agreed-upon price. "The extra is for your children," he smiled. The merchant bowed his head in thanks.

As they walked on, Elizabeth asked, "That was rather tense. The man was quite rude. I expected him to spit at me."

For a moment, Nieto was silent and Elizabeth wondered if he had heard her. Then he said in measured tones, "The weaver knew where you belonged in society by your dress and your speech. He knows he must act the part of an obliging servant to make a living from the people of your class. It is a terrible burden for a man who is proud of his skill and is tired from his long hours of labor to humble himself before others who enjoy wealth and power they did not earn."

"My good fortune is not my fault," Elizabeth responded, angered by a surprising feeling of shame. "I cannot change the fact of it. I am just blessed that it was so."

"Lady Elizabeth, that is the truth that ignites so much rage among those who must work hard to survive. As you said, you did nothing to earn your good fortune and they did nothing to be condemned to lives of desperate struggle. Yet the working classes are expected to pay homage to those born in the right beds.

"The so-called leaders of this country and many others like them throughout Europe are blind to the anger that simmers just outside the gates of their elegant homes. The anger rode the waves across the Atlantic almost three decades ago. It lit fires in France and now embers are being carried with the winds across the Channel to here."

Elizabeth retorted, "Mr. Nieto, you paint a picture that is too dark in color. Those who are wealthy hire those who are poor and provide them with wages to buy what their families need. Families like mine are the ones who can afford to buy the goods of the weaver here. To whom else would he sell his fine work?

"We do much good with our wealth to help those who have less. We hire them to work with us. They live with us and become members of our families. Like Hannah and like Sherlock."

Again there was a pause before Nieto asked in a quiet voice, "Tell me about Sherlock, Lady Elizabeth. What do you know about him?"

"Sherlock? He is a member of our family. He has been with us forever. At least, as long as I have been alive, Sherlock has always been with us. He was not always a butler of course. He started first as an under-footman then rose to be valet to my father. He became our butler about five years ago."

"And?"

"And what?"

"What does he do on his day off? What are his interests? Does he have family? Does he has someone he loves? Do you know old he is? Do you even know his given name?"

Elizabeth's face first drained of all color than a red flush flowed from her neck up to her cheeks. Despite seeing her discomfort, Nieto continued in a more gentle tone, "You know Sherlock after all these years just as a servant in your household, not a free man with his own life and concerns. Can you not see why someone might find that demeaning? To be known only for being useful to the master, much like a good horse or loyal hound could be."

The words of rebuke stung. Elizabeth responded in anger, "If you think us so terrible, why are you working for my brother and the Baron? If you feel such sympathy for all these people who suffer under such oppression from the landowners and the aristocrats, how can you work on the side of the English monarch and the Hapsburg emperor and the others who have inherited power?"

Nieto stopped walking to look at her. "Because, Lady Elizabeth, men to whom I have pledged loyalty have asked me to do so. And they will expect payment from the King and the Emperor for my services. They will ask for concessions for our people who are suffering. I have no other reason to help the monarchs of the allies against the Emperor of the French, who, I remind you, has declared our people free and equal citizens of the lands under his authority."

Silence hung over them as they strolled on. Elizabeth tried to restore the earlier comfortable feeling. She went back to the negotiations with the weaver. "So the weaver did not wish to lower his price to me but he was willing to discuss prices with you because he recognized that you were somehow part of his world." Nieto shrugged. "So tell me, how did you know what to offer?"

"It is rather simple. He will ask for double what he wishes to get and I will offer a third of that. Eventually we will arrive at the real price."

"But why bother? Shouldn't he just tell you the real price at the start and be firm on it?"

Now Nieto chuckled, also eager to lighten the seriousness of the earlier conversation."Well, Lady Elizabeth, what would be the challenge in that? When we bargain, there is always the chance that I might not do it well and he will get an outrageously high price and the glory when he tells about his victory over a tankard with his friends. Or he and I will have a dramatic negotiation that spices up our day and makes us both feel like victors.

"In Alexandria, it is even more extended and more filled with drama. The merchants do not ask a price. They avoid it as a courtesy so one must say, 'If I was to buy a shawl like that, I might consider spending this amount on it.' And then they would respond, "If I was to sell a shawl like that, I might consider setting a price of this amount'…and all this over tiny cups of very sweet coffee."

She laughed. "How I envy your travels and experience. To think, I am going on a ship for the first time and I from a family that owns a fleet."

He smiled, "You are still young and all your adventures lie ahead. You have the spirit to grab onto adventure and to take joy in the challenges that might lie ahead."

Her smile back at him reflected her relief that she could still earn his good opinion. "Mr. Nieto, I want to try my hand at bargaining next. Do you think that any vendor would be willing to listen to me, rather than spit at me?"

He looked ahead. "It would be best if you bargained with a woman and perhaps if you ask more questions in the beginning to show your appreciation of the quality of the goods. See that booth with herbs. I will tell you what I need and you can do the bargaining with the market woman."

Nieto pointed out some of the herbs: willow bark, yarrow, ginger and valerian root. When Elizabeth approached the vendor, she indicated one of the herbs she wanted, asking some questions about its use and its quality. The woman was eager to display the varieties she offered. When asked, the vendor stated a price and Elizabeth responded lower, indicating a willingness to buy more if the price was right. They discussed the prices for a few rounds then Elizabeth nodded. She pointed to more items and, as the woman was wrapping the purchases in twists of paper, she noticed Nieto standing near, watching the negotiations.

The woman smiled at him, saying loudly to Elizabeth, "Your husband is a fine-looking gentleman. Nice of him to come along to help you carry the parcels. I like that he stayed out of women's business. Some men do not believe their women have enough sense to handle money." Elizabeth smiled back, took her parcels and thanked her.

When she rejoined Nieto, she laughed at the slight flush visible beneath his olive skin. "Mr. Nieto, I am insulted that you blush so at someone thinking we are married. Would it be so embarrassing to you to be married to me?"

"No, Lady Elizabeth. On the contrary, the good herb lady might be wondering that such a young woman was the bride of an old man like me. And such a dark-skinned man at that."

"Come now, Mr. Nieto, here in a port, there are many men darkened by the sun. You do not appear exotic where there are people of many nations coming in and out? Perhaps it is I who is the unusual one here."

He glanced at her, at the red and gold streaks in her hair shining brightly among the light brown, her green eyes glowing with the sheer joy of being out and active once again. He smiled but tried to calm the anxious tightening in his chest. It would not do to dwell on her loveliness. That was a path to nowhere.

He changed the topic abruptly. "I wonder where Jose and Sir Ariel have gone. I would not trust that Spaniard to stay out of trouble."

Just at that moment, he spotted them on the other side of the market in an alley off the main square looking through a stand filled with shelves of bottles and large apothecary jars. He suggested to Elizabeth that they hurry along to forestall any trouble into which Jose might lead Ariel. As they drew nearer, Nieto began to recognize the types of wares on display.

He looked around rather desperately. Noticing a woman selling small bottles filled with flowers and oils, he urged Elizabeth to look them over. He walked quickly to join Jose and Ariel.

Jose smiled brightly at Nieto as he approached. "How timely, Nieto, that you arrive just now. For the life of me, I couldn't explain everything here. As I was saying to young Sir Ariel, we need the doctor now. This here yohimbe root for one and this puncture vine for another—which one increases the male power the best? Which one do you recommend for what?" He held up two jars of bark-like chips.

"For you, Jose, neither. Chasteberry for you."

Jose laughed but continued to examine the jars.

Ariel was studying larger jars as the vendor showed him the various kinds of "assurance caps" on offer—there were some made of fine linen, kid intestines and pale calf bladders. The young man called Nieto over.

He whispered, "Would you help me here, Mr. Nieto? I am not sure about the various merits among these and I think it wise to be ready—based on what you said last night."

"I cannot believe I am doing this with your sister only a few yards away. Take three of the kidskin quickly."

The merchant nodded then held up a small jar of ointment. "And the salve that makes everything so smooth, sir?"

"Yes, yes. Quickly, my man."

There was no time for haggling now. Nieto fully expected that their purchase would be the subject of stories in the tavern that evening. He could imagine the scene and the sound of laughter, "And the fastest sale of the day was when a dark-skinned man, all flushed and bothered, hurried a young gentleman. The older man practically threw the coins at me in his embarrassment to get away." Thank God, Ariel had not asked about the carved dildoes on display in the rear of the stall, looking like so many small statues in exotic woods and ivory, lined up in size order.

The owner wrapped the purchase in a paper package and handed it to a very pleased Ariel. The merchant then went over to Jose to continue a whispered conversation about various herbs and ointments. Nieto called over his shoulder, "Franco, five minutes more, then join us down this path. We must get to the ship."

Elizabeth was just having her own purchase wrapped. "I found some lovely scented cream and soaps. I thought Maman might enjoy them. Ariel, what did you purchase?" She was curious about the small paper package in his hands.

"Something Nieto recommended as a health treatment, particularly valuable for young men." Ariel smiled back at Nieto, his eyes brimming with laughter.

The doctor made no comment himself as a flush appeared under his olive skin. He avoided looking at Elizabeth as he hurried his charges towards the ship.

Twenty-Three

The Ruby Goddess glittered in the bright sunshine. With its flags fluttering, men climbing the rigging, calls and whistles from ship to shore and back, it appeared and sounded like a glorious circus. As the ship creaked against its moorings, sea gulls circled the masts, squawking in hopeful anticipation of something edible being tossed overboard.

Despite the numbers of men and the noise level among them, the party was noticed immediately as they approached. The captain greeted them as they arrived on deck. "Master and Miss Allingham, I was told to expect you by your man, Parker. As I had explained to him, I would normally have reserved the stateroom for you but the Earl's family had booked it and they are already on board."

Elizabeth and Ariel were taken aback, but Parker, who had followed the captain, interceded quickly, "It is perfectly understandable that the Earl's family should be so quartered."

The captain continued, "I do however have second cabins on the next deck that I am sure you and your party will find comfortable. My bos'n will see you to the cabins. The Earl's family has requested that you join them for tea in the dining saloon. I think that you will enjoy meeting them for they are about your ages."

Michael George appeared with a welcoming grin on his face to show them to their cabins, which were elegant and new, leaving them all to wonder about the additional luxuries the "Earl's family" was enjoying. The twins' cabin included two spacious bedchambers joined by a small sitting room. Each bedchamber had a dressing room with an alcove for the servant's cot. Parker, assuming the role of Ariel's valet, showed the young man to his chamber. Hannah explored Elizabeth's room then set to work, placing her garments in the storage areas.

Nieto, now reassuming his alias of Mordecai Halevi, would be in a cabin further down the deck. His manservant, Jose in his new position, would bed down in the dressing alcove. Beowulf would stay with his master, Ariel.

Ariel left the cabin to take a walk with Beowulf. He was captivated by his first trip aboard an Aylesford vessel. Now he understood better the power and wealth of his family. All these men were working for his father! Someday this would all be his and Embry's responsibility. He wanted to be worthy of this glorious heritage.

The "all aboard" whistle sounded, the ropes were cast off, and the ship was freed from its berth. The deck hands were moving in a tight choreography of pulling on lines, climbing rigging and adjusting sails. Whistles sounded up and down the vessel signaling the next movement in the nautical dance.

Parker appeared at his side. "Would you like a tour?" he offered. "I could explain the tasks the men are performing to get us underway."

Ariel nodded with enthusiasm and the two men set off, trailed by Beowulf who found the new scents interesting enough to be pausing every few yards to sniff more closely. Another young man with reddish hair and a mastiff on a leash approached.

He bowed when they met. "Mr. John Allingham, I presume," he said clearly to Ariel. "I would like to present myself, Sir Ariel Wharton. May my sister, Lady Elizabeth, and I have the honor of your attendance with your friends at tea in the saloon?" Ariel stammered a gracious acceptance and the young man moved on with his dog by his side.

Ariel turned to Parker, "That was terribly strange—trying to remember whom I am when faced with someone who is so calmly taking my place. But why, Parker, is this still necessary? This is my family's ship. Surely we are safe here."

Parker urged Ariel forward so that their discussion seemed part of the tour. "Nieto is concerned that if you were placed in such an obvious location as the stateroom, anyone who wished you ill would have a clear target. He wishes to be as cautious as possible by letting the others play their roles until we arrive in Gibraltar. He asked the actors to clearly announce their identities as frequently and as naturally as possible."

The tour continued. Parker commented on the fact that Ariel seemed to have gotten his sea legs right away, not evidencing any discomfort with the motion of the ship. It was as if he had been born to it. Ariel beamed at the compliment.

When teatime arrived, the Allinghams and the Whartons gathered in the saloon and were formally introduced to each other. Nieto joined them in the guise of Dr. Mordecai Halevi, a family friend. The conversation remained stilted as the Allinghams and the Whartons maintained their false identities for the benefit of the galley staff who moved in and out of hearing range, serving tea and elegant French pastries to the people posing as the Earl's family and their guests.

Ariel felt he was in a strange drama hearing his past life played by an actor who relayed events and referred to people whom he knew. Elizabeth, he could tell, was feeling the same sense of strange closeness and yet distance from the people who sat across from them.

For their part, the twins relayed as much of their Allingham lives as was needed to fill any gaps in the conversation. Nieto very smoothly tried to take on the burden of keeping the conversation flowing. As Dr. Halevi, he told stories of his holidays spent the past few weeks in London followed by a tour of the counties on the way to the port. The imaginary tales he told made Ariel feel that he was becoming familiar with yet another new person who just happened to look very much like the man he knew as Judah Nieto.

They left the saloon at half past five, arranging to meet in the dining room at eight for dinner. The "Allinghams" walked along the deck, with "Halevi" as their companion and Parker and Beowulf following behind. Ariel proudly pointed out some of the important parts of the ship, using the terms Parker had explained earlier.

Elizabeth was astonished at how quickly and eagerly Ariel was absorbing this new world. She watched the breeze play with his hair and thought she had never seen him look so physically present. She had always thought of him in more ethereal terms—engrossed in music or art—more of a fragile sensitive boy rather than a robust man.

Now, as he turned to ask Parker questions about the work of the men climbing the rigging, and how one learns nautical skills, she began to see the possibility of her brother assuming a leadership position in this world. That meant that she too was growing up—transforming from a young miss to a woman. How had these changes happened so quickly? Was it only a fortnight past that they were reeling from the disastrous ball? How far away it all seemed now?

The breezes across the deck signaled the cooler evening coming on. The Allinghams retreated to their cabin to relax for the few hours before dinner. Parker, fulfilling his role as Ariel's manservant, could keep watch on the twins as they napped.

As Parker assisted Ariel in dressing for dinner, the young man asked more questions about how a man learns seamanship. Parker described his own training, starting as a cabin boy and being promoted several times over ten years to Lieutenant Commander before he was seconded to the Admiralty Office.

But, he pointed out, Ariel's path would be very different. As a son of a fleet owner, he could enter the Royal Merchant Marine Academy for officer training. As part of that training, he would serve in various capacities on merchant ships such as the

Ruby Goddess, rapidly moving up the ranks to captain in short order.

"I would get special treatment?" Ariel inquired with his lip curling in distaste.

Parker laughed, "Do not assume that it will be an easy path. You will be watched very carefully by the crew and officers to see if you were ascending by merit or by influence. No mistake will go unnoticed. You will be proving yourself continually.

"And it would be hard to be accepted as a peer. The crew will be fearful to be themselves around you. As much as you might wish it were not so, your family's influence and power would intimidate those who need Aylesford goodwill to stay employed."

"So it would be best for me to work for another fleet perhaps keeping my family name unknown—to prove myself for a few years without the family connections, as it were."

Parker was impressed. The young man was willing to take a harder, but perhaps more honorable, path to his goal. He offered, "I can arrange a meeting with the first mate after dinner. He can show you how they use the mariner's astrolabe to chart the course. The nautical mapping is interesting too. Mikey also invited us to go down to the lower deck later to hear the chanties sung and see the hornpipe danced." Ariel eagerly agreed to the evening's plans.

Dinner was a reprise of tea. Two footmen in formal dress served the excellent cuisine in the style of the most elegant restaurant in London. The wine was also of the best vintage, meaning that it had likely been smuggled through the embargoes against French goods.

The wonderful meal emphasized Elizabeth's feeling that they were actors in an elegant drama with a small audience to appreciate their performance. What made it even more awkward was that the captain had been included in the party and he added reminiscences and stories about the Aylesford fleet. Both twins were frustrated that they could not ask questions about the events and the people he described. Nieto, as Halevi, once again tried to control the conversation by asking the captain more questions about his experiences sailing through waters where the French fleet was a real threat.

As they left the saloon and the party headed towards their respective quarters, Parker leaned over to Nieto, "Judah, I offered to take Ariel to the first mate to see the navigational instruments and maps and then I thought we could spend some time with the crew—perhaps see the hornpipe danced."

Nieto nodded, "I will ask Jose to take the first watch at the twins' cabin."

Parker grinned, "Jose, responsible for young women? Aren't you putting the fox in charge of the henhouse?"

"Truly, I do not believe that. He is a scamp for sure but responsible when lives are at stake."

Parker laughed out loud, "Oh, of course, he will protect them to his last breath if it came to that. I was just thinking that, up until that moment, he can be quite scandalous. Just think what stories he might tell to entertain the fair maidens."

Nieto looked out at the ocean and the dark sky and sighed. "You are right. I can't put Jose in that role. I will take first watch in the cabin in his place. Take him with you to the hornpipe. It will give him a chance to shake out some of the energy that makes him so explosive."

Parker gave the doctor a searching look. Nieto seemed tense about guarding the women. It was true that Hannah, green from seasickness, would not be an effective chaperone. But this was not some soirée where the maiden aunts and the tyrannical fathers need stand guard to protect their daughters. And he was Judah Nieto, a respected colleague of the Baron's, not some London rakehell.

Nieto watched Parker and Ariel walk to the ladders leading down to the crew's quarters. With his arm around Ariel's shoulder, Parker's blond head leaned toward the brown head of the smaller man. They looked like boon companions and close friends, great intimates and possibly....Nieto tamped down his anxious imaginings...it was unfair of him to make such assumptions.

When the doctor arrived at the twins' staterooms, he found no one in the sitting room. He called, "Lady Elizabeth?" and heard an answer, "Back here!" from the bed chamber.

He opened the door. Also empty. Elizabeth emerged from the dressing room, wringing her hands. "Hannah is in great distress. She cannot keep any food down. Even water troubles her. She is moaning terribly."

As Nieto moved past Elizabeth into the small dressing room, his arm brushed against hers. She felt the warmth of his body through his cloth jacket at the same time he hesitated, looked at her as if to say something, but then continued into the tiny room. A quick examination of the young maid showed that she was indeed in distress. Her dry lips and sunken eyes indicated she was already dehydrated.

Nieto asked if Elizabeth still had the herbs purchased that morning. She nodded.

"Order hot water for a tisane and let me have the ginger."

A young cabin boy responded quickly to her bell. The hot water was ordered. When it arrived, Nieto pared a small piece from the ginger with the knife he wore and used the handle to mash the piece into pulp. He put the ginger into the pot with some sugar and asked the cabin boy to bring it up to the deck with a cup. "I would have Hannah stand up in the fresh air. Help me get her outside."

Elizabeth draped Hannah in one of the newly purchased shawls and with Nieto bearing most of Hannah's slight weight, the three of them descended the stairs to the deck and walked to the aft.

"Hannah, take some deep breaths of the fresh air. It will make you feel fresher. Look out at sea—far away at the end of the sky," Nieto instructed. He looked around and saw a wooden storage box that would serve as a bench. He guided Hannah to the bench to sit. The doctor took the pot and cup from the cabin boy, and ordered a second pot to be brought to the cabin. He coaxed Hannah to sip the spicy sweet brew.

"It will calm the motion sickness. Keep sipping, Hannah. Do you like the taste? I find it quite nice—spicy and sweet and better than most of the concoctions I must force down my patients' throats."

Hannah smiled weakly. She clutched the cup in two hands and dutifully kept sipping.

The breezes on deck were exhilarating. Elizabeth stood to face into them. She thought that her hair must look disgraceful but it felt wonderful to feel the sea air rushing through it. She turned her head side to side and enjoyed how, with some angles, the wind whipped her hair back and, with others, the breezes draped her face with the loose tendrils. She drew in deep breaths, raising her arms as if to catch the fresh air.

She turned to see how Hannah was faring and saw her leaning against Nieto with her head on his shoulder. He was staring intently at Elizabeth—his eyes wide and his lips parted. When Hannah moaned, Nieto bent to encourage her to sip more ginger tea. It was the movement from his fixed stare that made Elizabeth aware of how intent his gaze had been. She flushed with pleasure that she had captured his attention so completely.

Color was returning to Hannah's cheeks. Nieto refilled her cup and asked, "Does your stomach feel more settled now? Ginger is a good herb for seasickness so I had a fresh pot made for you when you finish this one. Gradually you will get what sailors call 'sea legs'—you will get more used to the movement of the ship against the swells of the ocean. I promise, Hannah, this will pass."

The young woman looked at him shyly and gratefully. She shivered in the breeze so he said, "Are you able to get up and return to the cabin? Let me help you." He busied himself in raising her, adjusting her shawl, and tucking her hand under his arm to guide her back to her bed.

Elizabeth thought, he wishes to avoid looking at me. She felt power in her effect on him. As he moved away from her, guiding Hannah down the deck, Elizabeth picked up the teapot and the cup and followed them back to the cabin.

Nieto assisted Hannah in sitting on her cot and left the dressing area and bedchamber so Elizabeth could help the young maid into her nightclothes. Now that the maid felt more comfortable, Elizabeth left Hannah to rest alone. When she returned to the sitting room, she found Nieto standing at the door of the cabin with his arms crossed over his chest, studying the night and the stars. In turn she had a few moments to study his figure and face in profile as she stood in the bed chamber's door.

He was really a fine looking gentleman, as the woman in the market had remarked. Not tall, but with a slender yet masculine build. Slender but strong. She recalled his long slender fingers with the strength to understand the body's secrets and to draw beautiful music from a guitar. For a brief moment, she recalled his hands pulling a cord ever more tightly around a man's neck.

She pushed that image away and studied his profile. His hair was over-long perhaps, curling over his shirt collar and down on his forehead. She again noticed his beautiful ears and the aquiline profile. Even from here, she could see the long lashes. They would be envied by many women. In this light, at this distance, the piercing blueness of his eyes was hidden from her but she recalled the times that her breath caught in her throat at the sight of them.

As she approached him, he shifted his posture, standing erect and tense. He clasped his hands behind his back, as if in facing her he was determined to block any possibility of an errant touch.

"Thank you," she said. "Hannah is quite recovered. I had no idea what to do. It seems that both Ariel and I are spared seasickness. Remarkable, isn't it? We've never been on the sea, and yet somehow the generations of seafarers in our family might have passed down to us a comfort here." She gestured to the expanse of dark ocean.

The wind carried faint sounds from other parts of the ship. A riff of flute, a tenor voice. "Ariel," Elizabeth smiled. "I can tell his voice singing. He has changed so quickly. Today I noticed it. He has discovered some things about who he is and where he wants to go."

Nieto nodded, "He is of an age when changes can happen quickly. It is the time when one is leaving childhood behind and trying to find one's direction in life. A fortunate few find it quickly. Some explore for decades and perhaps are never satisfied. The saddest I think are those who never question or explore but do what others expect of them. I often think they will have much to regret at the end."

Elizabeth reminded him, "I am of the same age, Judah. I believe I have discovered new things about myself as well."

Silence. Another snatch of music on the wind. Elizabeth continued, "Ariel was well pleased with his purchases and grateful for your help in that and in answering his questions. I understand I have you to thank for my interesting discussions with Miss Fenton."

He could hear the chuckle in her voice. The darkness hid his blush."I see there really are no secrets between twins. I wonder why Ariel could not see his way to talk to Embry about such things. An older brother is the logical person to go to for advice."

"Embry?" she snorted. "I cannot see him having such an intimate conversation. Of course he would understand the mechanics of it all and probably be able to diagram it with great precision—to a perfect scale. He pores over bloodlines and such when he breeds horses. But about the other parts of it—feelings, emotions? No, I cannot see Ariel speaking with Embry at all."

"Hmmm—it seems to be the fate of all older brothers to be thought dull and without passion and understanding. The Baron tells me that in his family it is the same. With two younger brothers and four sisters, he feels often more a captain of the regiment than a wise older brother."

Silence again—this time more comfortable. She drew her shawl around her. "We should close the door. The night is growing cool."

Nieto shook his head, "I cannot. It would not be proper. Perhaps, Lady Elizabeth, you should go to bed now. You will be warmer there."

"Not proper, Mr. Nieto? You are like Embry—a man of rules? There is no one here to criticize or to tell a tale. Surely a man and a woman, two good friends, could be in a room together without bringing scandal upon their heads."

His serious expression when he looked at her took her breath away. "It is not a rule, Eliza. It is a defense. I cannot be alone with you. I will not have the strength for that."

She had that much power over him? She was amazed and gratified. She took a step closer. He did not retreat but he held his head back to create more distance.

"Say it again, Judah, please," she said quietly.

"What?" he tilted his head in question.

"Say my name again. It is lovely to hear it on your lips with that beautiful accent—so different but now so familiar."

Silence—this time fraught with tension and then, "Eliza, Eliza, Eliza" slowly and prayerfully. He shifted closer and took her face in his hands. His thumbs traced her lips. "Sweet Eliza, brave Eliza, adventurous Eliza." He delicately touched her lips with his. His hands went to the back of her head and pulled her tight against him. His kiss grew harder and more insistent. "Dear Eliza," he breathed.

Her lips parted and his tongue entered, caressing hers. She wrapped her arms around his neck and let her fingers explore the soft curls at the nape. "Oh, Judah, love me," she murmured, repeating words said once before.

He sighed deeply as he wrapped his arms around her, stroking her back while his tongue became more insistent. She felt giddy with excitement and pleasure—and with the feverish heat spreading down through her body. Being this close and feeling his need was feeding the throbbing inside.

She opened her mouth to him, inviting him to plunge deeper and he eagerly did so. She put her hands on his chest and could feel the pounding of his heart through the thin fabric. So he felt what she felt, she thought. The pounding in her chest was making her breathless.

Through her haze she heard the flute and Ariel's tenor drifting again through the night. How sublime this moment was. She wrapped her arms around his torso under his coat, feeling the heat rising from his body as he left her mouth to kiss her eyes, her cheeks, her ears and down her neck all the while whispering her name slowly—over and over again like an incantation. "Eliza, Eliza, Eliza."

His hands traveled down her body and then drew her hard against him. She felt his arousal with joy in the power she had. She put one hand down and stroked him outside his trousers. He gasped as he kissed her collarbone. She murmured "Miss Fenton's lesson" and she heard him laugh softly before resuming his passionate kissing. His hand traveled up from her buttocks to a breast and he stroked firmly, causing a hot ache to rise. Her heart was pounding and she felt deliciously dizzy. She whispered his name, "Oh, Judah. Dear Judah."

The wind picked up another sound and tossed it towards them—a sigh, a sob, and at first she thought she, in her passion, had made that high-pitched sound.

It was Nieto's sudden pause that alerted her that it had come from elsewhere. He lifted his head, listening intently. There it was again—a shriek, wordless but full of pain. Then barking followed by howling and yelping. The sounds of more pain. An answering howl from somewhere else. And a flute that stopped abruptly.

His eyes widened and his face went cold and pale. "Oh no, oh no, oh dear Lord, what have I done?"

He pushed her deep into the cabin. "Where is Embry's cane? And the pistols?" He was shaking her to hurry. "Elizabeth, where are they?"

She went through to Ariel's room, threw open the dressing area. She handed him the cane and the box with pistols. He gave a pistol to her after loading it. "Can you shoot this?"

She nodded.

"Lock the door behind me and do not open it unless it is Parker, Ariel, Jose or me. Anyone else—shoot first," he shook her again. "Do you hear?"

"Judah, you are scaring me. What has happened?"

He picked up the second pistol, loaded it and pulled out the sword hidden in the cane. "Lock the door, Elizabeth."

He left. She heard him running down the deck. She heard more footsteps and the sound of claws. Parker was yelling, "Judah, where?"

And Nieto's voice, now steely and cold, "I heard the other dog. It must be the stateroom. God forgive me. How could I have let it happen?"

Twenty-Four

Blood was spattered everywhere. Nieto had imagined what he would find but, in a frenzy, he ran from room to room examining each body for any sign of life. He felt for pulses and found none, looked under eyelids for responses and saw none, listened for heartbeats but heard none. Parker stood in the center of the cabin, turning slowly, looking for any evidence or clue that could tell them who had done this. Drawers had been pulled open and books, papers and packages ripped and strewn about.

Nieto stood over the young man's body, the youth chosen because he resembled Ariel Wharton so well. The doctor was staring at the violence of the stab wounds, each still dripping warm red blood. He said tonelessly, "They started with the maid then went on to the woman and then finally to him. I don't know when they killed the dog—it must have been at the end because I heard it howl."

He looked at his hands now covered with the victims' blood. Blood was smeared as well across his face where he had laid his cheek on a bloody chest searching for a heartbeat. "I should have predicted this could happen. It was after all the purpose of my brilliant plan. I could have prevented this. Oh God, forgive me. I made this happen. How was I so blind?"

Parker went over to him. "No, Judah, stop. You couldn't have known."

"Robbie, they wanted the new coding clocks and they assumed that the Earl's family would be carrying them. They thought this was the Earl's family. We had done all we could to make everyone on this ship believe these were the Earl's children. The captain believed it, Michael believed it, the staff moving in and out of the cabins and the dining room believed it. I was busy protecting the Allinghams and left the Whartons unprotected. But nobody would be interested in the Allinghams. We knew the truth but the murderers did not. I should have protected these poor souls as if they were indeed the Earl's family. I let my guard down and they were tortured and slaughtered because I grew careless."

"No, Judah, I won't let you assume...." Parker put his hands on Nieto's shoulder. Nieto pulled them away violently.

"Damn you, Robbie, stop it. Stop trying to protect me. It is my fault, my responsibility, my carelessness, my guilt. I recruited these young people, taught them what they needed to know and do then placed them as decoys because I worried that the Wharton children would be in danger. And I was right...and it cost these poor children their lives."

There was a pounding on the door. Parker opened it to the captain, Michael, Jose and Ariel. The captain looked at the blood and the bodies and moaned, "Oh, sweet Jesus, how could this be? The Earl's children? Dead—all dead?" He stared in horror at Nieto who nodded.

Ariel was white and trembling. Jose grabbed the young man as he bent over and vomited. The Spaniard held his hair back and whispered to him, "That's fine, my lad John. 'tis a horrifying sight. Let the heaves come if they must."

Nieto stood still as his emotions began to drain away, freeing his mind to be distant from the horror, to think methodically again. This had been his way on the battlefield, allowing him to do what he had been trained to do to save whom he could while ignoring the screams and the pleading of those dying men around him, those he could not save.

He turned to the captain. "How well do you know the crew? Are there any new members? People working for you for the first time?"

The Captain glanced over at Michael. "My officers have been with me for more than ten years. Mikey, how about the crew?"

Michael shook his head, "I have worked with the men for years. Robbie, you know many. They's been around from when you was a deck officer in the Navy. Because Aylesford pays the highest, they gets the talent among the Navy's old tars and from other fleets. They's straight lads. And besides, they was with us at the hornpipe or standing watch. If they be gone, they would have been noticed."

Nieto watched the distraught faces of the men around him, looking for any hesitation or second thoughts. The captain seemed to be concerned.

"Captain, a person or several on this ship did this so not all of the men are loyal or long-term. Who are the newest?"

"The only ones are the galley workers. We were to go with our regular mess crew but, at the last, two did not show up. To fill out the crew, the galley master hired two men on the recommendation of a master on another merchant. The galley master has been with me for years. I cannot believe he would be part of something like this."

Of course, Nieto thought, the galley servers would have seen and heard the decoys talking about the Earl and the family over tea and dinner. It would have confirmed their belief that they were the Aylesford twins. Elizabeth and Ariel were well protected because they continued to act their parts as the Allinghams. His decoy strategy had worked beyond his imagining.

"For now, take the galley master to your quarters and stay with him, Captain. No one else is to speak with him and I caution you to keep your conversation to a minimum as well. The rest of the galley crew is to go to quarters with the exception of the two new men. Bring one here and lock him in that room," he pointed to the bedchamber to the left with the bodies of the

Elizabeth decoy and the maid. "The second bring here. I will need rope, shackles and chains. Jose, go back to our cabin and bring me my surgical kit. Parker, take John back to his cabin. His sister will be concerned about his continued absence."

The captain left to find the men while Jose went for the surgical kit.

Ariel shook his head. "No, I will not go. I need to see people punished for this horror. I am not a child. I demand—I order you to let me stay to see this through."

Nieto faced him coldly, "You must not stay. What will be done here is necessary but not decent. You should not be part of it. If necessary, I will put you in chains and lock you in your cabin myself. What happens to me as a result, so be it, but I will not permit you to take part."

"Come," Parker murmured, approaching Ariel with his arms outstretched. "You will be blessed to be spared this sight. Let us not quarrel over this. You must go."

"I refuse," Ariel screamed, pushing Parker back. "I am part of this. It is close to me. Do you understand how close this is to me? It should have been me and Elizabeth slaughtered like this." He waved his arms wildly. "This was meant for the Earl's family! And I must see it avenged."

There was a cold silence in the room. Parker looked at Nieto and shook his head "no." Nieto however nodded slowly. He recognized Ariel's need for vengeance. He had felt the same, viewing the body of his murdered brother. He understood as well that this would be the end of innocence for Ariel. No night would ever be totally peaceful for him again. The best he could hope is that the horror the young man witnessed would cause him to sink early into blessed unconsciousness.

The Captain returned with the equipment Nieto requested. Jose came back with the surgical kit. He whispered to Parker, "I did what I could to calm her, but she is furious about being locked in."

The first man was brought in—dragged between Michael and Jose—already shaking with fear. Nieto stared at him impassively with his brilliant blue eyes. The man's tremors seem to grow more violent as Nieto pointed, saying in a cold voice. "Lock him into the bedchamber with his victims." Michael then left to get the second man.

The second man entered with a defiant tilt to his head, walking under his own power but with his hands tied behind him and forced forward by Michael, who pressed the point of a sword against his back. This man was larger than Nieto and looked at the smaller slender man with a contemptuous grin. He had not seen the tall blond Parker approach behind him.

When Parker put a pistol to his neck, the man collapsed when ordered onto a wooden deck chair. Parker bound him with shackles then asked Michael to leave and not return until he was requested to do so. Parker locked the door then leaned against it, waiting for the next scene in the terrible drama to unfold.

The room grew quiet. Minutes more ticked by but Nieto allowed the silence to thicken around them. The only sound was the soft swoosh of a scalpel against the whetstone as the doctor methodically sharpened the instrument.

Finally, he looked down at the chained man. "Your name, sir?" he asked in a casual tone. There was no response. Nieto asked again, "Your name?" Again there was silence. The doctor examined the scalpel blade carefully and finding it satisfactory, he walked up to the man and pulled his head back by his hair. He placed the tip of the blade by his eye.

"Your name?" he repeated in the same casual voice, his blue eyes boring into the man's brown ones. For a second there was a pause that caused everyone to hold their breaths. Nieto carved a large letter C around one eyebrow. Blood started to run into the prisoner's eye.

"Leonardo," the man finally said in an Italian accent, struggling to control the quaver in his voice.

"That is better, Leonardo," Nieto nodded patting the man on his other cheek. "Now, Nardo, let me explain how we will proceed. I will ask questions and you will give me the information I seek. If I think you are not telling me everything or, God forbid, not telling the truth, I will remove a body part. It might be an eye or a finger or an ear or maybe a ballock. It will depend on my mood and how angry you have made me. After little pieces of you have been removed, I will begin on the larger pieces until—well—until there is no more of you. You can decide if you will live as a whole man or as a horror that frightens small children or just die tonight in great agony. You have free will so you get to choose. Do you understand me, Leonardo? You must say 'yes' or I will not be certain that you are clear on the rules of our game."

"Si," Leonardo responded.

"Ah, buona," Nieto continued smoothly in Italian in response. "Raccontami la tua storia, il mio buon amico Leonardo. Chi ti ha chiesto di essere su questa nave? But, I forget, we must continue in English so everyone here understands your story. So I ask again in English, my dear friend Leonardo, tell me how you came to be on this ship."

Silence followed. Nieto cocked his head and looked Leonardo over thoughtfully. He grabbed the prisoner's hair once again. In fear this time, the man tried to kick out but the shackles held him. Nieto quickly drew the scalpel down from over the left eye, down the side of his nose, across his cheek to the chin—totally undistracted by the ear-piercing screams. The blood cascaded down the bound man's face and ran into his mouth and dripped onto his shirt. "Perhaps you will now begin to tell me your story, my friend. Who asked you to come aboard? And why?"

"I was paid to serve in the galley and to spy on the Earl's children."

Nieto nodded understandingly. The scalpel flashed and another scream shattered the air. Nieto held Leonardo's left ear lobe in his hand and placed it in the man's lap. The blood running from the ear was cascading down the Italian's neck. The prisoner was sobbing—his whole body shaking against the restraints that held him in place. The sharp tang of urine stung the air.

Nieto wiped the scalpel slowly against Leonardo's leg. The prisoner's eyes followed the motion, fixed on the instrument in fear.

In a most reasonable tone, Nieto said, "Let's start again. Who asked you to come aboard? And why?"

Leonardo was gulping for air and through trembling lips responded, "Giovanni asked me to come aboard with him."

"Giovanni?"

Leonardo pointed his chin towards the bedroom. "He told me what to do. He promised me fifty pounds to help him find a clock of some type. That is all I know."

"How do you know Giovanni?"

"We worked together aboard another Aylesford vessel until the war broke out and they did not want anyone who was not English working for them. I was stranded in Falmouth and could not get back home. I had no money and a family to feed back in Firenze. Please understand. I had to do it. I took the job just to earn money and to get closer to home. I have never done anything like this before."

Nieto nodded sympathetically. The scalpel flashed again, this time down the man's shirt front, slicing just through the fabric, not touching the skin. Nevertheless, Leonardo shrieked in fear.

Parker stepped forward and ripped the shirt off the man's body. Nieto walked slowly around the trembling man, running the flat side of the scalpel down the man's neck and back. Each contact of the steel against his skin made Leonardo's whole body shudder.

When Nieto faced Leonardo again, he ran the scalpel's blade down the center of the Italian's chest. The blood was now running freely as the man writhed and moaned.

"Tsk, tsk," Nieto scolded. "You tell me lies. The whip marks on your back tell me that you have been severely punished—either in the military or in prison. You have not told me everything."

"Oh God, I have—I was accused of stealing on the Aylesford ship and they whipped me. I was innocent. They did not believe me—like you do not believe me. I told the truth. I have—I know nothing else."

"You tell the truth? You are innocent? Then tell me what happened to the men who were supposed to report here?"

The question surprised Leonardo. He stared at Nieto. "Who?"

"Nardo, Nardo, you weary me. The regular mess crew—the men you replaced. What did you do to them?"

The Italian began to shake his head. Nieto inserted the scalpel blade behind a trouser button and cut the threads. The button flew off. He did the same to the other side. Parker approached to force the trousers down to the man's knees. His flaccid penis and testicles lay exposed.

"Nardo, my friend, what happened to the crewmen you replaced?" The man's eyes bulged with terror and his body twisted back and forth in a desperate attempt to move away from the scalpel Nieto held right above his scrotum.

"We killed them."

"You need to tell me more. How? Where? When?" The scalpel nicked the scrotum so that blood started oozing.

"At night at a tavern in Falmouth. We were drinking together and left to go back to the rooming house where some of the crew boards when ashore. Giovanni told me we had to take their places on board this ship so we had to be sure they did not show up. Giovanni did one with his knife and I strangled the other. We hid the bodies in a waste pile behind the hospital there."

"So there are two families back in England now needing to be fed—just like your family in Firenze, yes? The families of men you killed for money. That is correct, is it not, Nardo?"

"I guess," he hesitated then realized there was no other answer. "Yes, it is true."

"What should be done to a man who starved children, Leonardo? What is the just punishment for a man like that?"

"I don't know...please...I've told you everything you asked."

"You want my pity now? Are you begging for mercy?"

"Yes, yes. Have pity! Have mercy!"

Nieto leaned closer to the man and said quietly, "I have no pity for a man who is willing to kill for money."

His hands reached down to the Italian's groin. The scream was ungodly but cut off abruptly as Leonardo fainted. Blood was running down his leg into the trousers pooled around his feet.

Suddenly there was a gasp from the far corner. Parker and Jose turned as one. They had forgotten that Ariel was still in the room. The young man's eyes were moving wildly between the bloody scalpel in Nieto's hand and the pool of blood in the Italian's trousers. His skin was greenish-white and his eyes rolled up until only the whites showed.

Jose was able to reach him just before he fell in a heap. The Spaniard pulled him into a corner, left him sitting lopsidedly on the floor, his head lolling to the side.

Nieto said coldly to Jose. "He has been blessed to faint, to not see the end of this. I must now speak with Giovanni."

Jose needed Parker's help to drag the terrified man from the bedchamber. One glance at Leonardo, bloodied from head to belly, appearing dead, slumped in the chair, and Giovanni's eyes started to roll as his knees buckled. Nieto moved a second chair next to the first so that Parker could tie Giovanni next to his partner. A loop of rope was placed around his neck and tied to the chair and around his waist so that any movement greater than a few inches would cut off his air supply.

"Now, Giovanni, it took a while but your friend Nardo here was finally convinced to tell me about your work this evening but I want you to fill in the details. You will cooperate, won't you?" All the while a new scalpel was being stroked against the whetstone. "I am growing weary so I am no longer interested in delicate work. I will need to work faster—in bigger pieces as it were. Do you understand what will happen if I am not pleased with your answers?" The smaller man nodded, his eyes wild. "Tell me what will happen so we both have a clear understanding."

"You will cut me unless I tell you everything."

"Quite well put, Signore Giovanni except I perhaps might have said 'butcher' instead of cut. So let us get started. Who hired you? When and where?"

The words tumbled out in a torrent. "I don't know his name. He said he was English—well, he spoke only in English to me but he did not speak like the English sailors. He was foreign, I am sure. He told me that there would be small devices—like clocks of some type—that were being carried by the children to their father, the Earl, on this ship. He promised me 100 pounds sterling if I brought him one of the clocks. I only needed to find one. I would get another 100 pounds if I found instructions or learned how the clock worked."

"This 'Englishman' who was not really English. Where did you meet him?"

"In Falmouth—two days ago before we sailed."

"Describe him."

"I can't. He was sitting in a corner of a bar—in a dark cloak, with a muffler and hat. I only saw his eyes."

"Tell me about his eyes."

"They were—how you say? They were incrociati occhi–crossed."

"How did he find you?"

"He was given my name by a man I had worked for before."

"Oh, Signore Giovanni, you are wearying me. I must speed this up." Nieto slashed the blade against the man's thigh, cutting through fabric and tissue. The piercing scream was cut off when his body sagged and the rope started to strangle him. In a panic, Giovanni fought to sit upright.

"Now tell me about your employer who sent you to the so-called Englishman."

"He was a noble from my area near Firenze. His family owns much property. His father employed my father as gamekeeper on his estate. Duca di Lucca often sent me on errands. Small things—deliver a package, pick up a portfolio. When the wars started, he sent me on more errands and paid me more. He asked me to go to London to see the man he called 'the Englishman' to learn what to do. I would be paid well, he promised."

"And how did you know what to look for in the workshop in London?" Nieto asked the question casually, examining his scalpel for nicks to the blade.

"It was the same thing—a clock. We found one...." The man stopped as he realized that he had given over more secrets.

Nieto nodded encouragingly, "If you had already found a clock, you thought, 'Why not get another 100 pounds by finding the instructions?' but that stubborn old man was not helpful, was he?"

Giovanni nodded then hesitated and began to shake his head. "It was not my idea. The Englishman told me to do what I needed to find the clock. He told me that they were a stiff-necked people and that they would need to be convinced to give up the clock and the instructions. He said to keep at the old man to get the instructions for the damned clock."

"So you first met the Englishman in London, not in Falmouth," the scalpel flashed and blood flowed from a gash on Giovanni's cheek. The Italian screamed in pain then gagged against the rope around his throat. "You lied to me, Giovanni. That was not wise. So, after London, he sent you to Falmouth where you met your friend, Leonardo." Nieto waved the scalpel at the unconscious man slumped in the next chair, covered in blood. Giovanni slid his eyes over, shuddered and nodded.

"So my Italian friend, tell me about the Englishman's accent? He was not English. You knew it by his pronunciation. So what was he really?"

"Italiano, italiano." The prisoner whispered, his voice rasping in fear.

Nieto did not react but continued, "Now, Giovanni, did the Englishman tell you to kill the Earl's children?"

"He just told me to do what I needed to find the clock."

"Then why there are so many bodies in this cabin?"

"It was Nardo. He said that the only way to find the clock was to threaten them—so they would tell us to spare each other. But they wouldn't even do that. Even when we tortured them, they wouldn't tell us. They kept denying they had the clocks. Just like that old...." He stopped, looked at the scalpel in Nieto's hand and then continued. "They even denied who they were—telling us that they were not the Earl's children—they were…come si dice in inglese? Impostori? And then they just kept pointing to different places in the room as if suddenly a clock would appear. They could have saved their lives but they would not tell us what we needed to know."

Nieto waved the scalpel, tilting his head as deciding if his work of art needed any finishing touches. He leaned closer to ask, "So who did you kill, Giovanni, beside the crewman whose spot you took?"

The scalpel was held right above the Italian's face. "The sister," he whispered hoarsely. "I did the sister."

"Eh qui," Nieto smiled bitterly, slashing across the man's throat. The Italian gurgled and his body sagged against the rope but he could no longer sit up to lessen the stranglehold.

Nieto turned to Parker and Jose. "It's done. Giovanni is dead. And Leonardo," he lifted the larger man's head and slashed his throat, "is dead as well." He stood up and wiped the blade against the cloth of Leonardo's torn shirt. "Get rid of the bodies. I must let the captain know that these were not the Earl's children but have him keep the secret until we get to Gibraltar. That poor decent man is suffering terribly."

Parker and Jose carried the first body out of the room. A few minutes later, they were back for the second man. During this time, Nieto kept his back turned and methodically started to put his surgical instruments away in the kit, first wiping each one carefully with a soft rag moistened with a liquid he poured from a bottle.

When the bodies were gone and the scalpels were locked back in the kit, he turned towards Ariel whose eyes were open in his pale bloodless face. Nieto's face was also transformed. It had the grayish-white pallor of a man close to death. His lips were bluish. The intense blue color of his eyes was grayed and the skin around them looked bruised. "So Ariel, are you feeling avenged? Do you feel peace now?"

Ariel shook his head. Nieto continued in a hollow voice. "I know, my child. Anger makes you believe that shedding blood is the solution. It is often necessary but it is never the solution. It brings no peace and no end to the evil.

"I cannot come closer to comfort you now. There is too much blood on me. You will have questions. Ask them when you are up to it and I will answer them the best I can. When

Parker comes back, he will take you to see your sister and he can help you tell her as much of this as necessary." Ariel nodded.

Nieto opened the door where he waited until Parker and Jose returned. Ariel heard some whispered comments among the men then Parker and Jose reentered the cabin. Jose was carrying a brandy flask and some glasses. He poured a small drink and passed it to Ariel. "Drink, little one. It will restore the blood to your face."

Ariel gulped down the liquid and gagged. Parker grabbed him by the elbows and led him to the railing on the deck. For the first time since he had arrived on board, Ariel bent over the railing, vomiting violently.

Parker put his hand on the young man's head. "When you are ready, we will go to speak with Elizabeth."

Ariel put his trembling hands to his face. "I need some time," he whispered, "I cannot face anyone right now." He took his hands away from his face and stared into Parker's eyes. "How can he do that?"

"Ariel, think on it. Judah just put to death two men who murdered two unarmed and innocent crew members to take their place on board this ship and then tonight tortured and killed unarmed young people they thought were you and your sister. All for money. If there is a scale of guilt, these men were among the most guilty. In putting the knife to them, Judah uncovered details of a plot, even learning who had beaten Larkin. He has a description of one of the leaders and, by getting all that information, other lives might be saved.

"I have seen men to whom torture is a perverse pleasure but Judah suffers when he does this. You saw him. He looks like death himself. He does what he does because he cannot live with the knowledge that men who kill innocents can escape justice. It makes the world too unbalanced for him to exist in it."

"Can he help me explain this to Elizabeth?"

"No, Ariel. You will not see Judah for a while. He needs to mourn—alone. He especially could not face Elizabeth." Parker put his arm around the young man's shoulder. "Come, I will help you explain it to Elizabeth. And then you will need to rest. I will stay with you both until you feel better. Judah has gone to see the captain. He will be arranging for increased guards around you while on board. Later, Jose will attend Judah. The doctor will need to be cared for himself."

When the captain finally understood that the Earl's children were still alive, Nieto requested that additional guards of trusted men be placed around the ship close to their living quarters. The crew would be told that the people known as the Earl's family were grievously ill and were quarantined. Then the crew would learn that the young people had died and their bodies buried at sea.

Next Nieto went to question the galley master to discover who had recommended the Italians as replacements for the missing crewmen. The man's eyes bugged at the bloodstains that covered the doctor. Nieto had forgotten about his appearance but it impressed the master enough that the doctor knew he was being told everything that the man could remember.

Only after these tasks were done did Nieto go back to his cabin. He lay on the bed, still dressed in his bloody shirt and he closed his eyes, breathing slowly to allow the ice inside to thaw. He hated the time when he must release his control on his emotions because, as his feelings returned, the horrors would as well. But he knew it was necessary if he was going to work past the darkness of death to once again walk among the living.

He heard the door open and the clink of glass. Jose leaned over him and said, "Parker told me to help you. Judah, let me change your clothes. I have brought the grappa you like."

Nieto sat up. He lifted his arms passively like a child to let Jose take off his shirt, sponge the blood off his hands and his chest and dress him in a clean garment. Jose poured him a glass of the clear liquor.

The doctor gulped it down then held the glass out for a second and then a third, before lying down again, putting his arm over his eyes. Jose left the cabin, closing the door behind him. He sat on a barrel with his back against the cabin wall. He would check in with Judah every so often but he knew from Parker that at this time the man needed solitude to deal with the horrors of what he had done.

Elizabeth greeted Parker and Ariel with a furious tear-stained face when they entered the Allingham quarters. "How dare I be treated like a badly-behaving child? Locked in my room while I do not know what is taking place just a few yards away. And where is Judah? What happened? I demand to know what happened."

Parker let her continue to rant while he guided her to a seat. He waited until she was out of breath then told her succinctly what they had found in the stateroom. He did not mention any of Judah's actions except to say that the murderers would not harm anyone again.

Stunned, she sat, white with shock. "It would have been Ariel and me if not for Judah's plans."

Parker nodded, "Yes, but Judah is grieving over the deaths of the young man and the young women. He set them up as decoys and feels responsible for that very success."

"I need to see him. He must be kind to himself. His actions saved our lives."

Ariel interrupted, "No, Eliza, you cannot comfort him. I saw his face. All this weighs heavily upon him. He is suffering terribly as it is. I believe he cannot be with anyone now."

"You do not know the truth, Ariel. I must see him. There is a special understanding between us. I can comfort him."

Parker stopped her before she was able to leave. "Nay, Elizabeth, I know him very well—more than you at this time. It will destroy him to have you see him now. Ariel is right. Judah must mourn by himself, away from even those who care for him.

"He will be better tomorrow. Then you may find the time and the words to be of comfort to him. Right now it would be like salt in his wounds. He believes that his feelings for you distracted him from his duty and cost those young people their lives. No one can tell him otherwise. It is a part of his soul to feel thus responsible for others."

Elizabeth saw the conviction on both Parker's and Ariel's faces. "Assure me that he will not feel unloved or abandoned if I do not go to him now."

Parker said, "He will not. I swear it. Try not to overset yourself on this. He truly needs this time alone."

She sank down onto the sofa, weeping in frustration. Ariel wrapped his arms around her, weeping as well as he tried to offer consolation. Parker left the twins alone but stayed outside the cabin on guard until he was relieved by Michael.

He then headed down to the cabin where he knew Nieto would have barricaded himself against the external world. Jose was sitting on a barrel outside the cabin, whittling a stick and softly whistling.

"Has he spoken?" Parker asked.

"Nay, silence since we returned. The only sign of life has been the drop in the level in the bottle."

"I'll take a turn at the watch if you need to stretch or get something to eat or drink."

Jose nodded, sheathing his knife before heading off to the galley for something to quench his terrible thirst. The scenes during the night had made him feel desperately drained.

Parker opened the cabin door. It was totally dark inside so he waited for his eyes to adjust to the dimness. He gradually could make out Judah's shape on the bed, facing the wall. Jose was right. There was no sign of life and now, no sign of grappa in the bottle. He approached more closely.

Nieto's eyes were open, staring at the wall but he made no motion to indicate that he was aware of Parker's presence. His lips were moving but there was no sound. Parker placed his hand on Nieto's shoulder. A shrug indicated that the gesture was not welcomed.

Turning away, Parker left the cabin to take up his watch at the door. As he sat down on the barrel just outside the door, a whistle sounded indicating a change of the watch. Life on the ship was quickening just as he felt the pull of sleep.

Jose was suddenly shaking him—was it a few seconds later? Hours? The sun was already climbing over the horizon and the sky was clear blue. The pink of early light had already gone. "Robbie, come quickly."

"Huh…what?"

"Please, come in. We must help him."

"No…No, he was lying there…quietly…." Parker shook his head to clear his memory. Judah hadn't been asleep. Parker recalled the trance-like state. As he stood up, cold dread was gripping him. Nieto, he knew, was in a very dark place after events like that of the previous night. Parker had always worried that someday the darkness would be too deep for Nieto to continue to live on long enough to let it pass.

He followed Jose back into the cabin then gasped. Blood covered the sheets on which Nieto lay but the doctor was not dead. He was lying on his back with a soft smile on his lips. His eyes were closed as his left hand kept stroking his blood-soaked shirt gently, as if the touching was pleasurable.

Jose was wild with tension, "Who attacked him? How did they get past you?"

Parker shook his head. "No one attacked, Jose. I've seen this before. We should have taken the scalpels away."

Jose blinked in shock. "Judah did this? He did this to himself?"

Parker pointed to the scalpel in Nieto's right hand. He removed it carefully. "I should have remembered to remove the kit. I don't understand it fully but it happens sometimes after great strain. He needs to punish himself or to destroy the numbness, or both. Wild drinking or fighting or this...you've seen the scars."

"I thought that those were scars from fights. I never thought that he would do this to himself."

"It is hard to comprehend but he seems to feel relief afterwards. We just need to just be sure the cuts are not too deep or too severe." The two men leaned over Nieto as Parker slowly lifted the shirt stuck to the skin with wet blood. The even straight slashes were each several inches long but not deep—the blood flow was already slowing. The careful work of a gifted surgeon.

"I'll go get the ship's doctor," Jose said nervously.

Parker shook his head, "I do not want to expose Judah in that way. He would never forgive us. He will be awake soon to treat himself. He has done it before. The blood is slowing so we can wait. I'll take the surgical kit and stow it in Ariel's room."

Arriving at the twins' cabin, Parker found Elizabeth looking for Ariel. "He was here just a half hour ago writing in his journal. I went to dress and when I came out, he was gone. I don't know where he went. Now I am worried."

Parker, trying not to panic, found Michael on the main deck assigning duties to the first crew. "Have you seen the young man, John Allingham? He is missing."

Mikey smiled, "No, he is not missing. He is fine. Look!"

Parker looked up and saw two barefooted figures sitting on the jib rigging. He saw the gold and red glints in the brown hair on the young man who was waving at him. His heart rose to his mouth. "You are telling me that he climbed all the way up there?"

"Aye, like he has done it for years. I sent him up with young Georgie who showed him the ropes and we anchored him with a cable just in case. Having a jolly good time at it. I swear he is in his element—took to it naturally—like he was born to it. I saw his interest and, since Georgie is of his age, I paired them. Thought that young John might trail him today to understand the real work what's done aboard."

Parker nodded, "He reminds me of myself at his age. I remember following you up the rigging my first time—not sure I could trust you not to toss me off."

"Aye—I remember that, although you were more greenish around the gills than that young'un."

Parker looked again at Ariel sitting and talking with young Georgie high above the deck. Yes—just like he was born to it.

Twenty-Five

Nieto made his first appearance at dinner that night. Looking pale and exhausted, he entered the dining saloon just before dinner service commenced and ordered the waiters to taste each of the dishes prior to serving them. He pointed to the place on the platter where the taste should be taken. Only then would he permit the twins to take a portion. He finally sat at the table next to Ariel and across from Elizabeth. Parker tried to keep the conversation light by asking Ariel about his day.

The young man was effusive in his respect for the work of the seamen. "Not only is it hard work but they know so much about the weather and the stars and the tides and the fish. And Georgie—he's the ordinary seaman who showed me the ropes—showed me the square-knotting he is doing and the carvings that Willy does on whale bones. Tonight I am going to sit with the first mate on his watch. He promised to show me more about the navigational devices and the maps."

"Miss Emily, did you know that your brother climbed up the rigging today and was hanging up there like a crack able seaman? For a first time aloft, it was very impressive." Parker prodded Ariel to keep talking.

Elizabeth was not to be dissuaded from trying to involve Nieto in the conversation. "Mr. Halevi, how are you feeling this evening? Parker told me that you were unwell."

Nieto looked up from his plate where he was moving pieces of food around. "I am quite well, Miss Emily."

"Did you see my brother climbing the rigging? I understand that he was quite adept."

"No, Miss Emily, I did not see it."

"Mr. Halevi, my brother was telling me about the newer mechanical devices they have on board for navigation. I thought that you would have an interest in them considering your scientific background. Apparently they are more accurate than the older models and should make travel by ship safer than previously."

"I assumed a modern ship such as this one would have the best equipment."

"I wonder what this ship is carrying to Gibraltar. I mean besides the few of us as passengers. Do you know the cargo?" Elizabeth was determined to get a response.

Nieto stared at her, his face devoid of expression. "I did not think to inquire, Miss Emily. As long as it had room for us, I thought that was sufficient."

She threw her fork down in frustration. "Mr. Halevi, it is considered a requirement in polite society to converse with your dinner companions. I think you very disagreeable this evening for not making any effort at all."

"Pray excuse me, Miss Emily. I fear I have no interesting news to offer."

"Few of us do—except perhaps my brother. It has been a hard day for us all following a hard night, but it is our duty to try to contribute to the ease of the group."

"Miss Emily, those who are conversing need to have polite listeners as well. In that way, I can be of service to our group."

She tossed her head in anger at the pat answer. She tried a new topic next. "Mr. Halevi, would you be willing to play some music for us this evening? It has been long since we have heard you play."

"I fear I must decline, Miss Emily. I am not able to provide entertainment this evening. Pray excuse me."

"I have an idea," Parker inserted in an attempt to break the increasingly tense mood. "Early last night we heard some great chantey singing among the crew. Mikey says that the crew members have been together for a few years and enjoy singing and dancing in the evening. Why don't I arrange for all of us to visit with them again tonight? It is a real treat to see how the men provide their own entertainments and how talented some of them are."

Ariel added, "Oh let's. It was great fun and I learned some chanties and sang along."

Elizabeth brightened, "I heard your voice on the wind last night…." And then she suddenly stopped, remembering the circumstances, the intimate and warm moments before the world had split apart. Her eyes flew back to Nieto as the blush rose to her cheeks. He was gazing at her and his lips trembled for a moment.

Then he clenched his jaw. He said in a monotone, "It would be good for you all to see the singing and dancing. But pray excuse me from attending. I will need to update some notes."

He was pained as her bright eyes dimmed. He again looked down at his plate.

Nieto left as dessert was served. As the others continued to sit at the table, Parker caught up with him at the door of his cabin. "Judah, I must speak with you."

"Robbie, I am not fit company. Pray excuse me."

"If you say that again, pray excuse me while I beat you to a pulp. I am watching you turning away from something very precious and it is tearing me apart."

"Robbie, it is not your concern what I do."

"Oh no, Judah, it is very much my concern. You are very dear to me but not as dear as you are to Elizabeth. One needs only to have eyes to see how much in love with you she is but you seem determined to deny her and to punish yourself. I do not understand how you can do it."

"I cannot do otherwise. I am covered in blood. Can you not see it? I can see nothing else. I can smell its odor on my hands no matter how I scrub. I am so immersed in blood and death I cannot bear to think of touching her…as much as I wish to do so. It is torture but it cannot be otherwise."

"So your solution to the puzzle of loving Elizabeth is to inflict pain on her, to make her feel that she is foolish to love a man who is not perfect, who is human with all the faults that come with the breed. This woman who is bright and courageous and spirited could not possibly know her own mind and understand the complexities and contradictions that are Judah Nieto.

"Do not flatter yourself, Judah. You are like all of us—good and bad mixed together, triumphs and failures, saint and sinner—just like the rest of humanity."

"You cannot ignore what I do and how I live, Robbie. She belongs to another world from the one I exist in. The people in her world are those whose power I fight against. What can I offer her, Robbie? I have no family, no home, no means of support, nothing to offer Lady Elizabeth Wharton."

"You have the only thing she wants and can get nowhere else, Judah. You could give her Judah Halevi Nieto—and, with that, your love and your heart and your strength and your loyalty. That only you have the power to give and this might be the only time you have to offer it. She is brave and strong and defiant when she wants to be.

"Soon we reach land. Once we do, the society that governs how you and she should live will assert its power once again. Think carefully, my friend. Many men go their entire lives without a blessing like this and you have but a few days to secure it."

Parker grabbed Nieto's face in his hands, trying to see if his words had any effect—any effect at all. He sighed and turned to rejoin the rest of the group headed to the crew's deck for the evening.

Nieto entered the cabin with the full intention of recording all the details of the night before—the discovery of the bodies, the facts about the plot that he was able to wring out of the murderers, the connections to other facts previously unearthed and the gaps that needed further investigation. However the music from the lower decks drifted up to him and he could not think to write. He kept on seeing her bright face dim as he had deliberately parried every attempt she made to connect to him.

He pushed his journal away and picked up his guitar. She had wanted him to play for her and he could not, would not, give her that joy. He deliberately set his mind to a complex piece of music, trying to distract himself from his thoughts of her. Even with his head bent over the instrument to block the sounds of the chanties from the lower deck, he heard the soft knock on the cabin's door.

He knew before he opened it that she would be there—brave Eliza who would not give up so easily. She smiled a timid tentative smile.

He asked harshly, "After all this, you are walking the decks alone? How can you be so careless?"

She shook her head, "No, Judah, I asked Parker to bring me here."

He looked down the deck and saw Parker walking away into the night's dimness. "Lady Elizabeth, it is not proper for you to be approaching a man's cabin so publicly alone."

"Mr. Nieto," she replied scornfully, "it was not done publicly but with Parker, your friend, and I do not care for any of your rules. May I come in or will you have me catch my death of cold out here? I will not go away."

He opened the door further so she could enter the cabin. He pushed the chair away from the desk and bade her sit there. He walked back to the door, leaning against it. That put them as far apart as could be managed in the small room.

She looked at the chair but shook her head. Instead she walked up to him as close as she dared without touching and said softly, "Oh, Judah, to think I could have died last night. That it could have been me and Ariel lying bloodied and cold and dead. I can feel the chill to my bones and I cannot get warm. Can you warm me, Judah, please?"

He gasped audibly and pulled her to him, wrapping his arms around her. "Yes, it could have so easily been you. I stood there looking at those innocent young people lying in pools of their own blood because I had allowed myself to become absorbed in my own pleasures. I felt the tragedy but I also felt the relief that it was not Eliza. She was still alive. I was feeling relief looking at their bodies. How despicable of me."

She tilted her head up, "Not despicable, Judah, but human. Can you allow yourself to be human?"

He shuddered, "Eliza, I have done terrible things but I was always able to say, 'they were guilty of terrible crimes.' Last night, I led innocents to death as surely as if I had bound them and opened the doors for their killers and put the weapons in the hands of the murderers and stood by and watched. I cannot forget and I cannot forgive myself. How can I have joy in my life," he rested his tormented gaze on her face, "knowing the great horror of that night?"

Her smile was gentle. "Judah, He who created the heavens and the earth has commanded us to find joy in creation. I remember someone I respected telling me that. Why would we feel love if we were not to celebrate it? Perhaps it is to remind us that goodness is still possible in the world."

The first kiss was sweet and gentle. She felt his tentative reaching past his guilt to touch her with his lips. The next kiss was firm and hot and he pressed her tightly against him. On the third kiss, their tongues touched and she felt the hot tingle through her chest and down through her body. His hands were stroking her back and her buttocks, constantly pulling her closer as if he would not permit the slightest space between them.

She wrapped her arms around his neck and threaded her fingers through his soft hair. She pulled his head away, breaking the kiss and trailed kisses down his cheek and his neck. She opened the first button of his shirt and kissed him right at the top of his chest.

He pulled her head up and did the same to her, trailing kisses down her cheeks and her neck and on her collar bone but stopping at the top of her bodice. She looked at him and smiled and undid more buttons on his shirt. She slipped her arms inside the soft linen and ran her hands over the soft curls on his chest. She opened the shirt and laid her head against his chest. "I want to hear your heart, Judah. It is strong and steady." She ran her hands down his chest and then looked up, with a worried expression. "Who has hurt you this grievously, Judah? These scars? Some of them are fresh…."

"Shh," he whispered, "they are my history, Eliza, not my future." He grabbed her head and kissed her with a passionate insistence. He put his hands on her shoulders and gazed at her with a tender smile. "I want to hear your heart, Eliza. May I?"

She nodded and he put his long graceful fingers to work on the tiny buttons down her bodice. He pulled the muslin down to her waist and kissed the tops of her breasts revealed by her dainty chemise. He looked at her again and she nodded her permission. He pulled the thin straps down her arms so her full breasts were revealed, white skin with pale blue veins and rosy tips. He kissed each nipple and she arched her back with pleasure looking down at his curly head. She ran her fingers through the curls and held his head against her as he licked and suckled making each nipple taut and ever more sensitive.

She was gasping with the sensations radiating from his touch and felt that her knees would buckle any moment. He sensed it, scooped her up and brought her to the bed. She felt the muscles in his arms and reveled in his power—so lean, so slender but so strong.

He pulled her boots off then kicked off his own and lay down beside her. He put his head to her chest and listened to her heart as his hands stroked down the center of her body under the fabric of her clothes. She tugged at his shirt, open but still on and he shrugged it off. She admired the colors of him—the golden tones of his arms against the white of her stomach, the dark brown of his hair and the brilliant blue of his eyes.

He leaned up to kiss her again, whispering softly, "Eliza, Eliza, Eliza, there is so much life in you. I taste it and it gives me hope."

She smiled and kissed him fiercely, her tongue exploring his mouth—not like a shy maiden but honest and direct. He chuckled.

She looked at him, "What?"

He kissed her eyelids, her cheeks, her nose and her mouth. "You are so truly yourself, Eliza. It is wonderful." He bent back down and suckled her breasts making her moan with passion. He loved that sound.

She pushed him gently back so she could put her hands on his chest to tease his nipples. He gasped as they hardened. She put her mouth to them through the soft brown hair and licked and sucked. He moaned softly and she marveled at her power and the response in his body as she saw him arch to press himself against her hands.

She let one hand travel down the line of hair past his navel and to his trousers. She stroked his arousal through the fabric and he moaned again. When she looked at him, his eyes were intensely blue. He licked his lips and smiled but then reached for her arms and pulled her back up to face him. He said between deep breaths, "Eliza, I cannot tell you how much I want to go further but …it would not be proper…."

"Is this another of your rules, Judah Nieto?"

"Yes," he chuckled softly, "but it will serve us both well. You have already made me breathless but right now, Eliza dear,

I wish to just hold you, skin to skin to find peace with you. Would that be sufficient for you?"

"Yes, Judah, it would be quite sufficient—for tonight."

He leaned back against the pillows and pulled her up until her head fitted under his chin. He pulled the blankets up over them then wrapped his arms around her. Her hands stroked his chest and lingered on his nipples playing with their tips and the curls of hair. She could feel his heart thudding under her hands. She sighed with contentment and he chuckled again and held her more tightly. Her breath began to slow as wonderful drowsy warmth spread through her limbs.

Jose opened the door slowly and smiled at the sight. They were both sleeping and, from what he could see, were both naked. He pulled up the barrel again and sat down on it outside the door. "I will give them a little longer together," he thought, "until the cold out here seeps deep into my bones."

A half hour later, he stood up and knocked the barrel over. The loud crash echoed down the deck. He heard the sound of movement and whispers in the cabin.

Jose began to sing a chantey in his loud and unmelodic voice as if too drunk to carry a tune. The whispers in the cabin turned to giggles. He chuckled to himself at the cleverness of his act. As he fumbled at the locked door knob, he heard Judah say, "Just a minute, I'm coming."

Jose yelled, "Take your time, Judah. Go any slower and I will no longer feel the cold. I would have turned to ice!"

The door swung open. Nieto stood there, quite passably put together. Elizabeth was sitting at the desk, calmly looking through papers as if she was searching for something important. Jose noted that her hair was undone but he chuckled silently, saying out loud, "Lady Elizabeth, I am glad I found you. Ariel was quite distraught when he saw you had gone missing."

"Lady Elizabeth," Nieto said with great dignity, "I will walk you back to your cabin now. I would not want your brother to be distraught much longer."

She smiled, rose and walked past Jose, who noticed with a grin that her bodice was buttoned awry. He motioned that fact to Nieto as he went to close the door. Nieto grimaced in concern then turned to walk Elizabeth back to her stateroom.

Twenty-Six

The Ruby Goddess was scheduled to take a wide path around Portugal, especially the city of Lisbon, currently occupied by Bonaparte's forces. The route forced the ship to go farther into the Atlantic and, as it turned out, into the path of storms. Indeed, the ship was soon waylaid by strong winds and pelting rain.

As the seas roughened, members of the Allingham party retreated to their beds to wait out the bad weather, having turned various shades of green. Hannah had been sensitive to the sea movement for days but now Elizabeth joined her in suffering.

Surprisingly, Jose was also in bad shape and he let everyone know it with theatrical groans and strings of colorful curses. Nieto, not seasick himself, spent much time pushing ginger tisanes on the others. Jose threatened him with bodily harm if he insisted that he down more of that mixture.

"I need ale or whisky—not that bloody drink that looks like piss and tastes even worse!" he cursed at Nieto.

As night settled, a greater calamity struck. Violent vomiting and diarrhea were felling many of the crewmen with the result that the healthy were being asked to extend their watches and their work shifts—an exhausting trial with the weather so wretched. Word was spreading that this was the same contagion that had proved fatal to the Wharton party a few days before, since the crew had been told the young people had died from a mysterious illness.

The captain approached Nieto after dinner where he sat with Ariel and Parker over port. "Now our surgeon is gravely ill with this ailment as well, Mr. Halevi. Can you assist us in his place? The disease has traveled quickly through the crew but what is more disturbing is that many of the men seem touched with madness. They are more convinced than ever that they have a deadly disease eating away at their brains."

Nieto followed the captain down to the crew's quarters. The stench was overwhelming as the few healthy men tried, without much success, to keep up with the needs of their sick comrades. Men were vomiting, others were lying in fouled clothes and some were incoherent, muttering and shrieking.

Nieto bent over to examine one of the most grievously stricken men. He was writhing on his cot, screaming, "My head! My head! Make the thudding stop. It is causing my teeth to fall out. Oh, the pounding. It is like a hammer against an anvil. More teeth! I am losing more teeth!"

His mate, clearly frightened, said, "Tis madness for sure, doctor. There is nothing wrong with his teeth, sir. But he keeps complaining about them. I am piling blankets on him but he keeps asking why am I packing him in ice. There is no ice!"

Nieto patted the distraught man on the shoulder. He then asked the captain, "Was fish the last meal served before this started?"

The captain was surprised by the doctor's guess. "Why, yes, the crew had codfish stew just last night—a favorite of most of the men. Others had shepherd's pie made from the remains of the joint served the day before. With the bad weather coming on, the galley master knew both dishes would be easier to serve. They've had such before—with no trouble."

"That fish dish was served only to the crew, correct? You and the officers ate something else at the last meal as well, I am guessing."

"Yes, we had a choice—the fish stew or grilled steak. Now that I think on it, the doctor had the stew—said he was partial to it."

Nieto turned to the healthy mate attending his suffering friend. "And you? Did you have the fish stew?"

The man shook his head. "Nay, I knowed that fish will be served over and over so I takes the chance to eat meat whenever." The sailor looked down at his friend, "But Willy here, he did have the fish stew. Aye, he did."

"That convinces me. This looks like fish poisoning. The contagion is in the fish flesh itself and cooking doesn't kill it. It can happen if the fish is not iced properly—and that could have occurred at the fishmonger's—even before it was laded onboard. The fact that only those who ate the cod are ill indicates that was the likely source. The hallucinations of teeth falling out, the confusion between cold and hot sensations and the headaches are all typical. All cod must be thrown out.

"No one will die of the fish poison. The real dangers are the secondary problems—dehydration, the onset of other diseases due to filth, injuries to those still feeling well who become overly fatigued by working double shifts. We need to keep the sick men drinking fluids and as clean as possible to avoid the other contagions. And as soon as possible, we need to relieve those who are working extended shifts."

The worried captain looked at the dozen men moaning in the bunks. "The weather is giving us trouble as well. I have few well men to spare to assist these down here."

"I will see what I can do with my friends," Nieto responded. "The disease itself is not contagious. It will only affect those who ate the tainted fish, so those who are currently well will be spared. We'll make a plan to handle these sick men while those still able to work attend to the ship and relieve their fellows who are fatigued. Can you send someone to my friends in the dining room? I can use them down here to assist me."

Parker and Ariel joined Nieto to work side by side throughout the night. Nieto had the galley master brewing soup pots of different herbal concoctions to rotate the medicinal benefits. Ariel was assigned the task of continually plying the men with fluids. He moved from man to man, refilling mugs for those well-enough to drink independently. He raised the heads of the more weakened men, urging them to take sips of the hot brews.

Parker cleaned the soiled men, stripping clothes off the dirtiest and wrapping men in spare blankets and sheets. When there was nothing else left to use, he took table linens from the dining rooms.

After a few hours, they heard a loud curse as Jose staggered down the ladder. "This smells like a ripe dung heap. I heard that there were some lads worse off than me. Here to help what I can—if the smell don't kill me first."

Parker pointed to the next soiled man. "He needs to be cleaned and changed."

Jose grumbled, "And me wiping the hairy arses of some mighty big babies. Never thought I would see the day." But the Spaniard, as they all knew he would, rolled up his sleeves and worked steadily and diligently at the worst of the tasks—keeping his humanity safely hidden under his thorny bluster.

Nieto examined each patient repeatedly, checking against complications and choosing among the various herbal brews to match the maladies. Ariel called him over to look at the young cabin boy.

"I cannot get him to drink at all," Ariel said gravely. "He seems too weak to even swallow."

Nieto examined the boy. His skin was papery and dry and his lips were peeling. He was barely conscious. "He is severely dehydrated. Get my kit from over there."

Nieto pulled a glass pipette from his bag and asked Ariel to bring him a mug of the ginger tea. "Blow on it to cool it down," he ordered. "I need you to sit down here and let me put the boy across your lap. Tilt his head up so he does not choke." He draped the young boy across Ariel resting his head against the young man's arm. Putting his finger in the boy's mouth, he made a pouch in his cheek. Filling the pipette with cooled tea, he let it dribble into the cabin boy's mouth. He stroked his throat to encourage swallowing.

Nodding that it was working, he did it again and again, carefully watching to be sure the fluid was being swallowed. Ariel admired his patience and concentration as time and again he dribbled liquids drop by drop down the boy's throat. The minutes ticked by, yet Nieto continued as if fatigue was not possible. Finally the mug was empty.

"Let him rest while I examine the others. I will come back in a few minutes and we will start again." Ariel sat with the young boy in his lap, thinking how very precious life was.

A half hour later, Nieto was back with another mug of tea. He once again started with the pipette and the slow drops of fluid. The cabin boy's eyes began to flutter open and the bewildered boy gradually became alert enough to take a few sips on his own. Ariel sat him up in his bunk, encouraging him to keep sipping.

Gradually the crisis was easing—more and more men were able to drink on their own. Jose and Parker were able to catch up on cleaning and changing the sickest men. Others became strong enough to help their mates. The men in charge of laundry carried the dirty clothes away.

Dawn was breaking and the violence of the storm was abating although the drenching rain was still falling when Allingham party stumbled up the steps. After hours spent in the foul-smelling quarters, they felt exhilarated to breathe fresh air.

Parker tilted his head, letting the rain fall over his face. "Time for a seaman's shower," he announced and called down the stairs for someone to bring up soap. A few of the healthier men came up with the soap and started stripping off their own clothes. Parker pulled his shirt and trousers off and Jose soon followed. Nieto smiled and did the same, ignoring the stares that the scars on his chest caused. After some hesitation, Ariel stripped down as well.

Parker, after soaping up himself, handed Ariel the bar. "Do my back and I'll do yours," he offered.

Nieto was scrubbing Jose's back, laughing out loud. "You are a bear, my Spanish friend. Beware, the Baron might prize you for a pelt," as he slapped Jose's hairy back.

"Real men have hair, Nieto," the Spaniard growled back. "It matches the amount of male power. Didn't you learn that in your studies, doctor?"

They soaped their hair then let the rain cascade over their bodies, carrying suds away down the deck. Ariel looked at these men, whom he didn't know at all one month before. The dark hairy Jose, the tall blond Parker and the olive-toned slender Nieto. He thought, "I have lived a lifetime in such a very few days. I think back to what I knew and believed and worried about a few weeks ago and how little of it remains important to me. I hardly recognize myself."

Then he laughed joyfully, saying out loud, "I feel so happy even though I have spent the last hours amongst piss and shit and vomit. I feel alive in a way I never understood before." He sobered and whispered, "Is it wrong after those others died in our place? I feel somehow I owe them something special but I never knew them. I haven't mourned them. Is that wrong?"

Nieto shook his head, his wet hair flying in dark curls. "It is one of the miracles of life, Ariel, that we can continue on and find joy despite great tragedy. Without that blessing, we would have given up at the first calamity. Without that strength, our people would have been wiped off the face of the earth centuries ago. Find joy…it can be the best revenge."

Parker added quietly, "Doctors must learn to take their own cures." Nieto threw him a sharp look but said nothing.

Jose spoke up again. "Okay, mates, the cold is causing me to shrivel up. I don't fancy it becoming a permanent condition so I will get dressed. Don't let the ladies out. They would be overwhelmed by the sight of all this hardy manhood."

Ariel started as he looked at the other men standing naked around him. "Oh Lord," he thought, "I hope Elizabeth is still abed with the seasickness. This is not a sight for a maiden sister."

Ariel snuck quietly into the cabin after checking that the sitting room was empty. Parker followed close behind him. The two men went to the dressing room and toweled off quickly. As they dressed, Ariel turned to Parker, "I am not sure how to ask this but…."

"Just start…don't worry," Parker said as he drew his clean trousers up.

"Nieto said...on board ship…for months…only men together without women?" Ariel stammered.

Parker turned towards the handsome young man with the beautiful eyes. He responded frankly, "The answer is what you would expect, Ariel. Sometimes yes. Before the wars, captains could put into port when possible to give the men some time to seek release. Places like the sisters' for example are found in every port. But on long voyages over the open ocean, it was not possible and many men found what release they could with each other. For some men, it was just a passing way; for others, it was a preference. It was not discussed or mentioned. If it was, there could be bloody fights so we all kept each other's secrets."

Ariel sat thoughtfully, his trousers not yet buttoned and his shirt still open. He looked intently at Parker, his gaze steady and deep, "And if two men have a preference for each other, they should hide it from everyone else?"

"Yes, Ariel. There are few places in our world where such men can be open about their affection. As Nieto warned, there is great danger for them."

There was a knock on the cabin's door. Parker left the dressing room, walking through the bed chamber to the sitting area to open the door.

Nieto was there, fully dressed with his hair still damp. "I wanted to check on the women," he said. He moved towards the women's chambers but stopped when Parker put his hand on his shoulder.

"Judah, I think that I need to be moved to another post," Parker said softly as he tilted his head towards the men's bed chamber. "I feel that there is an intensity building that will make it difficult for me. He is asking some questions and I cannot miscomprehend the direction…."

"Isn't it better that it be you to answer him?"

"I fear that it will not stop at questions. He is a handsome and nice young man. I might not want it to stop."

Nieto gazed at Parker, slowly nodding, "Ah, I see." He paused for a few seconds then added, "I will take your place. You will have the pleasure of listening to the Spaniard's snores."

Elizabeth was able to raise her head when Nieto entered. He smiled at her, "You are looking quite exhausted, Eliza. It is calming outside so you will feel better soon." He sat on the edge of her bed, holding her hand and stroking her cheek with the other. She kissed his palm then sighed happily.

"I will be here tonight, Eliza. Parker will stay with Jose."

She looked surprised but then a sweet smile bloomed across her face. "I am feeling much better already."

Twenty-Seven

Later that night, when the rain finally stopped completely and the ship once again moved smoothly, Nieto and the twins sat companionably in their cabin's sitting room after dinner. Elizabeth perched on the sofa in her nightdress and robe, with her hair hanging loosely down her back in brown curls, the gold and red strands glinting in the lamplight. The doctor strummed his guitar softly, teaching the young man Ladino melodies that his mother might enjoy once they returned to England. Ariel's beautiful tenor rose with greater confidence as he mastered the foreign words Nieto had written out for him.

Elizabeth reflected that, despite the extraordinary events of the past weeks, this scene was pure and sweet and ordinary. It was an exquisite miniature of a lovely family portrait as an artist might depict it.

Eventually everyone agreed it was time for them to seek their beds. Nieto, laying on the cot in the dressing alcove, listened to Ariel's slow breathing.

He waited a few minutes more to confirm that the young man was sleeping before he got out of bed, wrapped one of Ariel's robes around his naked form and padded his way to Elizabeth's bed chamber. He tapped softly and heard her whisper, "Judah?"

He walked in to find her waiting for him, with her arms out and an expectant smile on her face. He took off the robe and slid naked into the bed beside her.

She giggled, "Mr. Nieto, you do not waste time, do you? You come right to the point!"

He chuckled, "To a point, yes! Do I shock you, Eliza? "

She shook her head, "No, Judah" and she lifted her night dress and drew it off. "Now do I shock you, Judah Halevi?" she challenged as she snuggled against him.

"No, Eliza, but you thrill me in wonderful ways."

He kissed her gently and ran his hands down her back, reveling in the smoothness and warmth of her skin. She intensified the kiss by thrusting her tongue into his mouth and wrapping her arms around his neck. Her wonderful full breasts were soft and warm against his chest as he drew her tightly against him. He kissed her neck, her throat and ran his tongue down to the tips of her breasts to lick and tease the pink nipples.

Waves of heat cascaded down her body following his touch and his mouth. Her back arched as he kept teasing her nipples to be harder and tauter with his tongue. He pulled her buttocks closer and kneaded them. She felt his erection hard against her softer opening already hot and wet and tingling. His mouth ran down her torso to her navel. She felt breathless and her heart pounded so fast and loud that she was sure it might wake the sleeping maid.

He had a soft smile on his lips. "Ah, Eliza," he whispered, "you are wondrously beautiful. Let me pleasure you but still leave you pure. I do not want to take you before you are mine—totally, in the eyes of our families, our communities. I wish that honor for you. Do you understand me?"

She nodded, recognizing that there was so much she did not yet know. She trusted him to be a tender teacher. He would guide her to pleasure with love. She had no fear.

He put his lips to her breasts again while he began stroking her thighs, letting his hand come up between her legs. She found herself stretching against him so that his stroking was harder. His hand landed on her tender center and he began rubbing her there rhythmically.

She felt the hot wetness and heard its sound against his fingers as he stroked her. Excitement rose in her and she shuddered against his touch. Her hands were gripping his back harder as he used his thumb to rub her sensitive bud. Sensation was sweeping her away and she thought that nothing else could happen to make it better. She moaned and wrapped her legs around him.

He sank lower and lower until, in a jolt of pleasurable shock, she felt his lips on her hot center and his tongue teasing it. She moaned louder this time and grabbed his hair holding his head down so that he would not stop. Waves of spasms started deep inside, forcing her hips to move in rhythm with his licking and sucking. His brilliant eyes glowed as he watched her writhe and moan.

"Yes, yes," she groaned in a throaty whisper, her eyes closed so she could focus on the hot waves surging up her body. "Oh Judah, yes, yes." And then her most emphatic "Yes!"—a long shout held back with her clenched jaws and tightened lips. The spasms started to fade even though she arched herself against his hands and his mouth to keep them performing their magic as long as possible.

He had been moaning and breathing in rhythm with her. "Ah, yes, yes, yes!" he sang back to her now, moving up her body so that his lips were tight against her neck as he gasped for breath. He shuddered, his heart pounding against her chest so loud that she thought Hannah might hear it in the dressing room. Then he sighed and smiled at her, methodically and slowly placing kisses on her breasts, her throat, and finally her lips. She tasted the saltiness of her own juices in his kiss and realized that she had never known such intimacy was possible.

She grabbed his face and looked into his eyes, the pupils dilated so that they almost obscured the beautiful blue. "I want to give you pleasure now, Judah Halevi."

He smiled, "You have, my wild Eliza. Watching you, hearing you, I could not help myself." He placed her hand on his organ and she felt the moistness of his discharge.

I have this power over him, she thought, to make him come to his pleasure just by watching me come to mine.

She looked at him seriously. "But Judah, I want to do for you what you did for me."

He kissed her then said, "God willing, Eliza, there will be plenty of times for us to give pleasure to each other." He pulled her back up into his arms and ran his fingers through her hair. He kissed her forehead and her eyes and her nose and then her lips again.

She was thrilled by the honesty of his touch. This wonderful, strong man was showing his desire for her. She held his face in her hands and whispered, "I love you, Judah Halevi." She felt tears slide from his eyes onto her fingers as he smiled at her.

"I have been so alone," he whispered. "I thought that God had turned away from me and then He blessed me with this gift. You are a blessing to me, dear Eliza. You are the promise of a future that I had thought never possible."

He turned her away from him then slid closer, pulling her buttocks up against his groin and settling her back tightly against his chest. He wrapped one arm across her waist and the other rested against her breasts. She felt his heart thudding against her back and his breath on her cheek.

"Could I be any happier?" she wondered and felt the swaying of the ship rocking them. She closed her eyes and drifted away.

She awoke as he moved. He was getting up. She looked over her shoulder and watched him get out of bed and slip the robe over his nakedness.

He smiled at her. "I want to get back before Ariel is awake," he whispered and kissed her softly and left quickly.

He thought he had entered the bedchamber silently, but, as he turned to go into the dressing room, he heard, "I am not asleep, Judah. You need not sneak in."

Ariel raised himself onto his elbows and glared at Nieto from under his tousled hair. "How dare you think to satisfy your lust with my sister? To use her as a whore until we reach port?"

Nieto stared in shock. "You are mistaken, Ariel, and your words insult your sister. Elizabeth is still a maiden. We were together tonight but it was not consummated. I would not dishonor her by taking advantage. I will do right by her and ask your father for permission to court her honorably."

Ariel smirked. "Honorably? Judah, you think me a fool? You are naked under my robe. Is it the Spanish way to lay naked in bed with a virgin and call it honorable? Was she naked as well? Do you put your hands on her and in her? Did you taste her private places? How honorable was that? You have compromised her severely."

Nieto stood still, waiting to tamp down his rising emotion. I will not respond in anger, he thought. That would be too dangerous. Instead he said quietly, "If she is compromised, Ariel, it will be because you choose to tell others. You alone have the power to ruin her. No one else knows. You are her brother—nay, more, you are her twin brother. Surely you do not wish to harm her. If you do so, I will marry her quickly. It is what Eliza and I both wish and so you will only make it earlier than we dare hope."

"Eliza? It is Lady Elizabeth to you, doctor. Marry her? You? Who are you, Nieto? I know what you are—a torturer and a murderer. And as you yourself told me, you are a man with no home, no fortune, no family. Marry my sister, the daughter of an earl? You aim too high for your rank in life, my man. My father will never permit it. It would bring shame to our family to have her so connected."

Nieto's anger had now become too hot to restrain. "Shame to your family? Who is your family, Ariel? My forebears were known as distinguished scholars in the Holy Land and the Ottoman Empire when your father's were still wearing animal pelts and living in caves. Your mother's family has greater distinction than your father's and even they are beneath my own. Your mother's people were money lenders and tax collectors for the Spanish kings, despised by all. Check your family history before you dare belittle mine."

Ariel sat up, his voice quavering with fury, "And what shall I tell my father about your own avowed history? About the times you lay with men as with women? You told me yourself that it was so."

"You forget, Ariel. You shared your own secret with me as well. Shall we expose each other for vengeance?"

Ariel stood up from his bed and walked closer to Nieto. His breath was coming faster, his fists were clenched. But the look on his face had changed from anger to hurt. "How could you do this to me?"

Nieto was taken aback. "To you?" he asked bewildered. "What did I do to you?"

"I told you everything about myself. I thought you cared for me. I thought you felt close to me. I thought to be as close to you as Elizabeth—perhaps even closer. You told me that I reminded you of your brother—that I understood you well because we had so much in common—music, our secrets, even our work side by side today on this ship."

Nieto thought quickly. But I thought it was Parker … not me. Was it me all along? How can I disarm Ariel so he does no harm to Elizabeth? Must I now protect her from her own twin brother?

He grabbed Ariel by the shoulders. "Oh, Ariel, I do not want to hurt you. I misunderstood. Oh, dear boy, I do love you too. How could I not? You who remind me of so much that is precious—my brother and his sweetness, his kindness."

Ariel swayed for a second then stepped even closer. He looked up at Nieto from under his thick lashes and Nieto saw that smoldering look once again. Oh dear God, how do I navigate through this?

Ariel put his hands on Nieto's face and stroked his cheeks. "Let me see you, Judah. Let me see all of you." He pulled on the robe's sash and it opened. He spread the front apart and took a deep breath. "You are beautiful, Judah. So golden, so lean." He rubbed his hands down Nieto's chest. "These scars—they are your stories. Tell me your stories, Judah." He looked up into Nieto's face. "Let me be part of your life too. You mean so much to both Elizabeth and me—both of us in love with you. I can share—I have learned to share with my twin all these years, but you must save some of your love for me." Then he kissed Nieto with a desperate passion that alarmed the doctor with its potential to turn destructive.

Nieto wrapped his arms around the younger man, thinking quickly. He whispered softly, "Ariel, let us just lie together to sleep. It would be comforting, would it not?"

Ariel looked at him suspiciously but nodded slowly. He took his nightshirt off then returned to his bed, holding the blanket up, making space there for the doctor. Nieto slipped in with the robe still wrapped around him. Ariel tugged at it until it fell off Nieto's shoulders. He moved closer to the doctor and placed his head on his chest and softly stroked the golden skin.

Nieto touched Ariel's hair—so like Elizabeth's in color and texture. Of course, they were twins after all, alike in so many ways, he thought. Did their closeness mean they shared the same desires? Or was this just the loneliness of a young man, away from home for the first time, facing new choices in his life? Did Ariel even know what he wanted? If he didn't know yet, was he just reaching out for what Elizabeth wanted?

There must be a way through this, Nieto thought. I will think of one. I must.

The doctor lay still for hours, hearing the soft sounds of Ariel sleeping, the younger man's hands holding tightly to his body. Try as he might, Judah could find only one safe path—the familiar solitary one away from the possibility of happiness and joy. All the other paths seemed fraught with danger to himself, to someone he cared for or to the person he loved.

When the sky turned bright as morning overtook dawn, Nieto rose, dressed and left while all the others were still sleeping. He walked towards the cabin shared by Parker and Jose.

As he approached, he heard the familiar sound of Jose yelling in angry and loud broken English and Parker's laughing responses. Despite being friends, the two men thrived on endless confrontations and competitions.

When he entered, he found the little Spaniard standing bare-chested, the black wiry hair on his face and his chest almost crackling with fury. Meanwhile the Englishman was placidly shaving, smiling at his image in the small looking-glass hanging opposite the door over the washstand.

"Halloo, the doctor is here, Jose, just in time. He can now confirm that what I have been telling you is true." Parker caught Nieto's eye in his reflection in the mirror and winked.

Jose turned to Nieto, sputtering, "This Anglo arse claims that Spanish farts smell worse than all others in Europe. He says that it is because we eat all the wrong foods like beans and garlic and vegetables and smelly cheeses and bad wine. And then it is because we are too…too emotional," he nearly shrieked in anger.

Parker was wiping the last bit of lather off, checking his handsome face on each side for missed whiskers, while adding with a grin, "And all that emotion tightens your bowels and your arse so that the farts build up like a parade of ships at a blockade, with the odor aging like cheese and growing ever stronger until, at the last, the farts break through and explode, felling all who are within the reach of the smell. Now if the allies could line up enough Spaniards and train them to fire off together at a signal, we would have a terrifying new weapon at our command. So tell him, Judah, that I have been telling him the medically true facts."

There was no response from the doctor, so Parker slowly turned around to check on him. Nieto was standing still with a stunned look on his face before he mumbled, "Parker, I need to speak with you. Come outside."

As they left the cabin, Jose yelled, "It isn't true, is it, Judah? The Anglo dog was just making a joke—a stupid weak joke – just the type made by pale lily-livered Anglos."

Nieto threw back over his shoulder, "Diet, yes, contributes to the frequency, smell and noise level of farts. However, I can attest that the English diet of boiled foods and ale can create equally odorous results when the Anglos 'break wind' as they so delicately prefer to call it."

"That's right! You see, you see! Your farts do not smell of English roses, you Anglo...." The rest of the tirade was muffled as Parker slammed the door behind him, chuckling heartedly until he once again saw his friend's face.

"Farts, Robbie? You stirred up the Spaniard's rage on the subject of farts?" Nieto shook his head in disbelief.

"I had to get my revenge, Judah, for a sleepless night listening to the little señor's snores, belches and yes, his farts. Besides, he is just so wonderful a target—ready to have his fuse lit over any insult. But all of this is beside the point. You have that look again—like you are weighed down by the world. Whose burden are you bearing now?"

"I need you to resume your guard of the twins."

The Englishman looked surprised. "I thought that you and Elizabeth needed private time...but perhaps that is the problem," he added thoughtfully. "Too much time alone together?"

"The problem is not Elizabeth, Robbie. Well, not entirely. It is Ariel. Ariel now is making threats...no, not exactly threats perhaps. More like appeals…for my time…for my attention. He thinks I am taking Elizabeth away from him."

Parker smiled wistfully at Nieto, "You did not see it, Judah."

"See what, Robbie? Whatever it was, no, I did not see it. Tell me what you know about Ariel. I need to be sure to close the door firmly on things that can never be."

"The boy is in love with you. First he was enamored of the Baron but later, after the ball, he became fixed on you. Throughout our journey, when you were near, he could not take his eyes away. Did you not notice that he was determined to share his private thoughts only with you and in turn, try to learn yours? I sought to distract him because I knew that he would find you closed off to him. But I am not even sure he wants you that way—in a physical way."

Parker smiled at Nieto's surprise. He added, "What I thought, in my own vanity, was flirtation towards me was really Ariel's attempt to use me to keep closer to you. He knows the feeling between you and Elizabeth and it is causing his awkward overtures. Perhaps it is jealousy for an intimacy his twin has with you that he fantasizes could be his as well."

"I will need to put a stop to that but I do not want to be cruel to him."

"Oh, Judah, as much as you wish to be kind, he will suffer for it. You will spurn the gift of his affection and that cannot ever be done without pain." Parker's brown eyes filled with sadness as he continued, "But it must be done thoroughly. To leave him hoping for a future that can never be would be unjust and much more painful in the long run."

"So you will go back to their stateroom to guard and attend to them?"

"You understand what you are asking? I will distract Ariel but in doing so, it might mean…well, you must realize where it can lead."

"You are a decent, kind man, Robbie. If he must learn the truth of his passions or explore his choices, at least he will do so with someone who will treat him with dignity and affection and keep him safe."

"Meanwhile you and Elizabeth?"

"It would be better if we were not too often alone. I fear that perhaps it would become too dangerous for her and too difficult for me. She is young and cannot see the risks to her if we go too far. I am older and I see more clearly the barriers we will face. I must be prudent for both of us."

Then Nieto turned away to stare out at the vast lonely distance of the ocean.

Twenty-Eight

The day they finally arrived in Gibraltar was brilliant with all the beauty of fine Mediterranean weather . The sunshine sparkled on the water and a pure blue sky arched above. The Rock loomed ahead, signaling their approach to the peninsula.

The twins stood on the deck and watched the crew performing their duties, pulling the ship ever closer to the wharf. While Ariel searched the crowds on the shore to see who was there to greet them, Elizabeth kept her gaze on the men on the Ruby Goddess as they worked to bring the ship to its berth.

She was not watching the work the men were doing in the carefully choreographed performance of skilled seamen. She was looking for Nieto. They had had only fleeting minutes alone for days now—only brief moments to hold each other for a few whispers and quick kisses. He was always the one to break away and always the one to refuse to set another time for them to be alone.

Now, in the last few hours, she had not seen him at all. It was as if he had become more and more absent as they approached ever closer to their destination. She feared what this might mean now that they were actually docking in the west harbor of the British-controlled territory.

At the same time, Ariel seemed to be filled with increasing energy and enthusiasm. Each day he had spent hours with Parker and with other members of the crew, learning about the work aboard a ship and participating more himself as time went on. Now he crowed with delight.

"The Baron, Eliza! He is over there by the gazebo on the pier."

The Baron's tall figure stood over the others around him. Formally and immaculately garbed as always, he scanned the decks of the ship with his hand shading his eyes. When he saw them, he raised his hat in greeting. Even from their distance, they could see the flash of his white teeth against his darker skin. The twins waved back.

Parker appeared at the exact right moment to hand them up into the Baron's carriage. When Elizabeth asked about Nieto, Parker pretended not to hear her question. Instead he stood back as the Baron's carriage pulled away. Then he too disappeared from their view into the crowds along the pier.

The coach headed towards the Admiralty House in the Governor's District where the Earl waited to see them for the first time in three years. When the Baron saw their nervousness, he reassured them. "Your father is nervous as well. He is worried that you have changed so much that he will not recognize you."

Elizabeth responded, clenching her hands in her lap, "We are not as we were before—as he remembers us. So much has happened to us both that he knows little about."

"He knows more than you imagine," the Baron said. "Many people have kept him informed. Every packet of official documents included a letter from the Countess or Lord Embry with a description of what was going on in your lives. The Earl was always desperate to know about you both."

The white structure of the Admiralty House loomed before them with the royal and naval standards fluttering against the blue skies. The Baron escorted the twins up the broad stairs as several pairs of guards saluted. They walked across the wide foyer, realizing it had been long since they had experienced the status and power of their father in his elevated position "in His Majesty's service."

The door opened into the main chamber. Suddenly, he was there, standing and waiting for them with his arms open, a broad smile across his face and the sunlight streaming through the tall windows glinting on his coppery hair. They ran into his arms and the Baron closed the door behind them, wishing them joy in this private time together.

For a long while, they did not speak—all of them hugging and weeping in each other's arms—looking into faces that had changed over the years. Elizabeth saw new lines around her father's eyes and deeper furrows in his cheeks. Ariel saw gray hairs among the copper ones and wondered if his father had grown shorter in the years that passed.

In turn, the Earl looked at his children with great wonder and loving admiration. Elizabeth was a woman now, a petite beautiful woman with a definite air of confidence about her, so much like her mother. And Ariel was transformed. He had always been part of a matched pair with his sister, but now he was different—taller and broader and darker-skinned from the sun with a firmer, more masculine handshake. The Earl clasped each child's face in his hands and kissed them, thinking how wonderful they each were now in their own way.

When they had all calmed, the Earl sat with them in a corner where they could be comfortable on couches and chairs. The twins described the adventures of the last few weeks— the pleasures, the horrors, and their concerns. He heard over and over the names of the men he had entrusted with their care—the Baron, Mr. Nieto, Parker and even the Spaniard, Jose. He was relieved that his trust in these men had been confirmed.

Tea was served as they continued to talk. He learned about the birthday ball from their viewpoints and the painful disclosures that revealed the truths under society's polite façade. He sighed with deep regret that he had not been there to protect them, but, with great satisfaction, he heard how they had managed to overcome each challenge, with the help of Viscount Embry, the Countess and their new guardians, especially Nieto.

Finally they exhausted the euphoria of the reunion. He ushered them to the door where footmen waited to take them up to their bedchambers. "It is time for you both to rest and then prepare for dinner. We have much to celebrate this evening—your safe arrival and the conclusion of a difficult few weeks. I have invited your special friends tonight in recognition of the protection and assistance they have offered to my most precious children and the completion of some complex missions."

Later, Elizabeth sat before the mirror in her room, edgy with tension. She recalled her father's word, "conclusion of a difficult few weeks" and "the completion of some complex missions." In great distress, she realized that now there would be no reason for Nieto to stay near. He had accomplished everything that he had been asked to do. He had obtained evidence that was used to break up a spy ring. He had protected her family and home and delivered her safely to her father.

What excuse could be offered to keep him here? She understood his life was built on secrecy and she feared to lose him to that dark world again. She was determined that would not happen. There would be only one reason for him to stay and her father must be convinced to make it possible.

She left her bedchamber and asked the butler where her father was. He directed her to the Earl's private sitting room. She knocked on the door. The Earl's valet opened it and ushered her in to speak privately with her father.

Twenty-Nine

Elizabeth and Ariel joined the Earl a few hours later in the formal receiving room where they waited for their dinner guests to arrive. As the clock struck seven, the butler announced, opening the door with a flourish, "The Baron von Tedesco and his party."

The Baron entered, exuding the authority and power of an ambassador of the Hapsburg Emperor. He bowed formally towards the Earl who bowed in response. Ariel greeted the Baron with a formal bow as well while Elizabeth curtseyed.

All the men of the Baron's party had followed him in. Robert Parker appeared before the twins for the first time in his naval uniform, his tall frame dramatic in white trousers, blue jacket with gold buttons and his Lieutenant Commander stripes.

Mr. Nieto entered next, carrying his surgical kit. Elizabeth felt her throat tighten as she was struck once again by his exotic good looks and his natural dignity. He was dressed in black trousers, with a deep blue evening jacket over a black waistcoat and a white shirt and cravat that made his olive skin glow golden in contrast. The well-tailored jacket emphasized his lean frame and its color highlighted the intense blue of his eyes. His dark brown hair had been expertly trimmed. But when he bowed to her, his eyes held a formal almost remote gaze.

Elizabeth felt her heart miss a beat. Was it possible that they were already growing apart? No, it must only be the formality of the setting and her father's presence next to her.

Jose followed. The tough little Spaniard was dressed in his native style, with black trousers, white shirt and a wide colorful sash around his waist, from which hung a dress sword. His presence exuded a refined pride the twins had not seen in him before.

And then there was a final surprise for all the Whartons as the last of the Baron's men entered a few seconds later. Samuel Wharton, Viscount Embry, walked steadily and proudly erect with both hands free.

The Earl stood astonished as his firstborn son, the very image of his younger self, approached, appearing whole once again. Elizabeth watched pride bloom on her father's face—lighting up his countenance with joy. With her hard-earned maturity, she acknowledged for the first time that Embry indeed held a special place in their father's heart.

To her surprise, she did not resent it. There was promise of immortality for the father in the handsome son who would inherit his title and position in the world. It was a solid connection that loyalty to the Baron could never weaken. The special place of the first born son also carried high expectations that would weigh heavily on her brother's shoulders. Ariel and she would not bear such burdens. They would have more freedom to define their own lives. In that lay her hopes for the future.

The twins were wearing their pocket watches and had brought Embry's old trick cane and their mother's prayer book and bible as their father had requested. The Earl lovingly fingered the books and placed them on the reception table which had been covered with a black velvet cloth.

Next he admired the watches as the twins took them off and showed him the inscriptions and the etched designs. He placed the watches on the table next to the books. Finally he held the cane and smiled at Embry. "I am so glad this is not needed anymore." He laid the cane on the table as well. The twins looked at each other, mystified at the display on the table.

Without a word, Nieto sat down with his kit, lit the lamp and positioned Ariel's watch in front of him. He took a surgical pick and tweezers and applied them to the back of the watch. With a few deft turns of his wrist, the back popped loose. He removed a small golden disk on which sat smaller concentric wheels.

Ariel leaned over to look at the object more closely. "It seems very much like an astrolabe, like the ones I saw aboard ship but in miniature. Whatever is it for?"

Nieto's hands stilled. He looked at Ariel, his blue eyes wide with surprise. "You do not know?"

Ariel shook his head.

He looked at Elizabeth, gazing at her with the same question in his eyes. She shook her head as well.

Embry leaned over Nieto, clapping his hands on the seated man's shoulders. "It is more beautiful than I imagined. So small and yet so precisely designed. A masterful accomplishment!"

Nieto did not comment. He placed Elizabeth's watch in front of him and repeated the process. He laid the second golden disk next to the first. Elizabeth moved closer to see the beautiful item.

Nieto looked at her, his jaws tightly clenched. "You did not know that you carried this inside your watch?"

She shook her head. For a moment, Nieto's hands were again lying still on the table. He stared down at the object he had just extracted from Elizabeth's watch.

The Viscount moved the jewel-topped cane closer to Nieto, indicating by that movement that the doctor was to continue his work. Using his pick, Nieto silently caught a tiny catch that opened the top of the cane under the jeweled crest. But that catch did not release the sword. Instead, a third disk was placed besides the first two.

Next Nieto turned to the Countess' ivory-covered Bible. He opened it and slid a scalpel along the edge of the linen lining on the inside of the back cover. Elizabeth gasped. The prayer book was a cherished belonging of her mother. She watched in dismay and then in wonder as he pried the cover away delicately as if it was a layer of skin on a patient. He removed a fourth disk. He operated on the prayer book with the same results.

Ariel stepped close again, peering down at the five glittering golden wheels in the center of the black cloth. He repeated his question, "What are they?"

Nieto gazed deliberately first at the Earl then at the Baron. His face had assumed the dead look of a mask. Elizabeth felt her chest tighten with fear. Something was rapidly changing in the room's atmosphere and dread was making her shiver as the doctor started to speak in a monotone.

"Yes, Ariel, you are correct. They are very like astrolabes—but they are even more wondrous, due to your brother's clever mind. The wheels can be spun based on a formula and then, when you turn them over, like this, the alphabetic code is revealed." Nieto turned one over and showed Ariel the two alphabets lined up on the circles. "If both the sender and the receiver know the formula that is used, they will be using the same code. The ingenuity of this is that the formulas can change every day. As long as both parties use the same numbers, the wheels can set a different code every time a message is sent.

"These wheels are what the murderers were sent to find. Not knowing the new design, they still called them clocks. These are what the young people on the boat were murdered for. These caused the attack at Belinda's home. You were carrying them with you all the time. You were the perfect couriers—totally unaware of them so you could never reveal their secret."

Ariel stood still as he began to understand the strategy. He looked at his older brother.

Embry responded calmly, "Ariel, you knew that Sherburne and Bonner had made the old codes useless to us. We had to get a new system designed and delivered quickly to our network on the Continent. We did not want either of you to know so you could act totally naturally. We believed that in your ignorance lay safety."

"Safety?" Ariel pronounced the word slowly, staring at his brother but no longer seeing anything in this time and place. "But if we had been found out, how safe would we have been, Embry? You did not see what happened to those poor people who were thought to be us. Those people had not known anything about these…these things and so they were butchered. I saw them, Embry—I saw the blood and the bodies."

Nieto stood up suddenly, his frame shaking with anger and his fists clenched. "Yes, Embry, the coding wheels were kept safe. As Ariel said, you did not see what the murderers did in their attempt to find these. They tortured and killed innocents to get at these! You did not see the horror of the crimes they committed and you do not know the crimes I committed to keep these damned things safe. If my decoy plan had not worked, if just one person had discovered the real twins, Elizabeth and Ariel would have been butchered with no chance to save their lives by turning these over. They could not have bargained for their survival. It would have been their bodies that were slashed and hacked to pieces in the stateroom. They would have died after being tortured, not even knowing why.

"We never discussed the strategy among ourselves, because I was always concerned about who might overhear. I had no idea that you had hidden this information from your own brother and sister. I had assumed they knew the plan. Far from keeping them safe, you put them in terrible danger! And you made me a tool in that deceit."

The Earl spoke up, "Mr. Nieto, you are being too harsh and you are frightening my children." He turned to the twins whose faces revealed their growing understanding of their past danger. "Elizabeth, Ariel, we did none of this cavalierly. The Baron and I conferred. The Baron sent his best men to be your guardians. Parker, Nieto and their colleagues protected you and the proof is in front of you—you are safe and the coding wheels are safe. Because you did not know, you could behave normally and in that also was your protection. With these coding wheels, many other lives will be saved as we win against Bonaparte."

Nieto turned to the Earl, his blue eyes glittering with rage. "I do not understand you, Sir. You believe yourself to be a loving father? You are standing there justifying sending your own children into harm's way, ignorant of the risk, entrusting their safety to men you hardly knew. You moved them and us around like chess pieces on a board and you and the Baron the chess masters playing the game."

Ariel asked, his voice shaking with disbelief, "Maman? Did she know about this?"

The Earl cleared his throat before responding. "She agreed, after thinking it over carefully, after the Baron and Embry had discussed this with her. We all agreed that keeping you both in ignorance was the safest path. We considered…."

Nieto interrupted, a breach of courtesy to the Earl, "I know, Sir, what happens when people are ignorant of the real danger they are in. They take no precautions and walk right up to it, smiling as they go. They die horrible deaths with no way to save themselves. How dare you, Sir, how dare you do this to others and how awful that you do this to your own children? And how dare you make me a party to it?"

The Earl now turned to Nieto, his eyes cold with anger and his lips whitened with tension. "Sir, you forget yourself and your place. I will forgive you this time, Mr. Nieto, because of your good service to my family and to the Crown. Baron, remove your man until his calm is restored."

The Baron put his hands on Nieto's shoulders. "Come, Judah, calm yourself. Come with me. I have some people who wish to speak with you. I am sure you will become calmer after you get a chance to meet with them."

He turned Nieto towards the door. Nieto shook the Baron's hands off his shoulders. He approached the door with the Austrian trailing behind him.

It opened to reveal two women—a small older woman and a young woman of about twenty with soft brown hair and piercing blue eyes. The doctor's head jerked back as if he had been slapped.

The Baron grasped Nieto's shoulders to hold him still. He then whispered a few words to the two women and ushered them into the reception room. They glanced fearfully at the people clustered around the table in the center of the room but the Baron directed them to a corner where chairs were arranged in a small conversational circle. The two women faced Nieto while the Baron left them together, returning to join the Whartons at the other end of the room.

Elizabeth could not take her eyes away from the small group in the corner. The older woman stroked Nieto's face and hair and kissed him on both cheeks murmuring in a soft accent in a foreign tongue. Nieto kept shaking his head. When she kissed him on the forehead, he finally reached out to clasp her tightly to his chest.

"Eema, ha eema shaylee, mother, my dear mother," he crooned and swayed with her in his arms as she cried softly.

The younger woman approached his side and clung to his arm, kissing his cheek and resting her own cheek against his shoulder. She kept touching his face in wonder. Elizabeth turned to the Baron with a questioning look on her face that demanded an answer.

He said, "His mother and sister. It has been more than ten years since they have seen him. No words have been exchanged in all that time."

Ariel looked at the tableau in the corner of the room. "His father?"

The Baron shook his head, "His father is not to know that this meeting has occurred. His father has declared him dead to the community. His mother and sister will never be able to speak of this meeting."

Nieto guided his mother to a seat and knelt in front of her stroking her hands. His sister sat on the floor next to him, unwilling to remove her hands from his arm.

Ariel watched the older woman brushing Nieto's hair away from his forehead as if he was a small boy. He recalled his mother doing the same for him and he felt his eyes water. He was seeing the depth of the losses in Nieto's life.

Ariel looked up at his father, standing next to him. The Earl was also watching the tableau in the corner with tears in his eyes. Ariel reached out and grabbed his father's hand and held it tightly. He saw that Elizabeth had done the same. He took a deep breath, thinking, "Nothing is worth an anger that would divide me from my family."

The small group continued to talk quietly, oblivious to the others who cast furtive glances in their direction, drawn as if to a magnet by the longing and desperate affection expressed by the three people. After a few minutes more, the Baron walked back to them and leaned over to whisper.

The mother looked up startled and rose, as did the sister. Nieto rose as well and with an arm around each woman walked them out of the room. The Baron watched them descend the stairs to the grand doors of the Admiralty House before he turned back into the reception room.

He picked up the five golden wheels delicately, saying, "The couriers are ready to leave, Earl. I shall hand these over so they are in our confederates' hands as soon as possible."

The Earl asked, "Do they know the protocol to use them?"

The Baron smiled, "It is quite simple. It is based on the luach, the Hebrew calendar. The coders and the interpreters need to know the Hebrew date that matches the English date in the first line. So the users of these coding wheels will need to consult a knowledgeable Hebrew. It is a clever refinement that Embry thought of to bring Jewish and military leaders together."

A few minutes later, when the butler entered to announce dinner, Nieto had not yet returned. Parker discovered the doctor on a terrace looking down on the streets and houses leading to the harbor. He saw two small figures walking slowly down the terraced steps, looking back every so often to wave. Nieto waved back then finally turned away. He placed his hands on the balustrade, bending over, hiding his face.

Parker touched him on the shoulder. Nieto did not respond but Parker heard a choking gasp. The sailor said, "The Baron meant well, Judah. He thought you would wish to see your mother and your sister."

Nieto looked at Parker, his blue eyes glittering with anger. "You think this was a kindness? No, Robbie," he shook his head, "this was a reminder. He never asked me my wishes. He never asked if I would want to see them now and here, in this place where his and the Earl's power is manifest. Isaac Tedesco knows me well. He knew that when I discovered that he and the Earl had conspired to hide the truth from the twins and from me that I would be angry at his duplicity.

"He wanted to remind me of his power, that he can control my mother's and my sister's happiness and lives as well as my own. He has their safety in his hands and so he can control me. This was not a kindness, Robbie. This was a threat."

Parker gasped in shock. "Surely not, Judah. The Baron is not deliberately cruel. That is not the man I know and follow."

Nieto shook his head again. "The Baron is not cruel without a purpose but he is as driven to attain his goals as I am to attain mine. He does none of this for his personal gain or pleasure. But make no mistake—that does not make him less dangerous. He will control and use all around him to achieve his ends. Even if those ends are noble, his power can be cruel. Take care, Robbie. When he knows your weaknesses, when he has all your secrets in his grasp, he will use them to force you to obey his every order."

For the moment, Parker was stilled by the thought. I will not think about this now, he thought, pushing back his fear. Instead he said, "Come, Judah, it is time for dinner. We are to celebrate the success of this mission."

Nieto stared at him stonily. "I cannot celebrate here tonight with the Earl. I cannot sit at his table. I cannot look on a man who placed his own children in such danger. Not his firstborn son, you notice—no, the Viscount is too valuable and perhaps too much like himself. And I will not dine with the Baron who just threatened me with his power over my family. I will find others to be with—others who do not ask me to obey without question and to torture and kill for them while they stand back keeping their own hands clean." He looked down towards the harbor town. "I will go there to find ways to dull the pain and to wall off the horror."

When Parker returned without Nieto and made some excuse about the doctor suffering from a headache, Elizabeth turned a desperate face to her father. The Earl clenched his jaw before smiling carefully at his guests.

Ariel watched the exchange between his father and his sister and suddenly understood that there was an agreement between them concerning Nieto. He felt a surge of jealousy that he tried to hide by being busy with his food.

But Parker was watching him carefully, noticing the flush creeping under the tan on the younger man's face. "Judah is ensnared every way he turns. This cannot end well."

Thirty

At the dinner table, the Baron kept the conversation moving by prodding Jose to share some of his adventures. The Earl accepted with good grace the coarse language and wild stories knowing that the Spaniard meant to distract the listeners from the missing man. At his orders the doctor's chair had been removed but the Earl saw the twins' gaze drawn towards the empty spot as if by a magnetic force.

The Spaniard only once brought the hilarity to a halt when he began to tell of an adventure in which Nieto was a featured player. The awkward silence that greeted the first mention of the doctor's name warned him away from the topic so he quickly went on to another story. As the meal wound down, Jose came up with a grand idea. He banged his palm against the table as the inspiration hit him.

"I know a way we can celebrate the end of our mission in splendid style. My friend Moises' sister is to be married on Thursday so he is hosting a groom's party tonight. Come, let us share their joy." He looked at the Earl, the Baron, Embry and Ariel and grinned, his very white teeth showing brightly against his swarthy skin and dark beard. "You, fine sirs, would add a refined air to the event, if you dare to come."

Embry asked, surprised, "Without formal invitations?"

The Baron laughed out loud, "There are no formal invitations to a traditional groom's party among the Sephardim—the Spanish Jews. Everyone invites their friends and cousins who in turn invite their friends and cousins. By the time it begins, there are very few people present who actually know the groom. But all are welcomed because it is a way to build the groom's settlement. Everything will cost something towards the good cause. If you have never been to a groom's party, you must go. It is one of those rare occasions when all the social rules are turned on their heads. Be prepared for uproarious and silly games. Formal evening attire and decorum are strictly forbidden!"

He turned encouragingly to the Earl. The Earl smiled broadly but shook his head, raising his hands in protest. "I fear that such an occasion is beyond my endurance, old man that I have become. Besides, I have some business to attend to this evening. But Embry and Ariel, please go with the Baron. It should be greatly amusing."

Embry looked at Ariel who had seemed unusually quiet during dinner. Perhaps such an evening would be a welcome distraction for them all. Uproarious and silly games seemed a possible antidote to the gloom that hovered over the table. The Viscount nodded at the Baron."We will come!"

Elizabeth tossed her head in disdain, "I assume women are not invited."

The Baron chuckled, "Definitely men only at the groom's party! I assure you would find little amusing in the games and jokes that will make up the evening."

When the Baron's carriage pulled up at a public house near the harbor, the sounds of laughter and singing were heard as soon as the men descended onto the street.

"Just follow my example and enjoy yourselves," the Baron said as he led the way towards the front door where a rotund man greeted them, the bowl in his lap already half-filled with coins.

"Good evening, gentlemen," he said jovially. "A shekel for the groom is the entrance fee."

Following the Baron's example, they each threw a crown into the bowl. The attendant hefted his tankard, motioning them through to the front room. "Remember to drink to the groom's health," he called after them. "Remember to drink often to the groom's good health." He laughed.

The noise level in the front room was near deafening as men moved around, greeting old friends and new acquaintances with hail-fellow-well-met slaps on the back and raised goblets and tankards. There was clearly no dress code—rude workingmen's clothing jostled silk shirts that brushed up against gypsy tunics. Embry and the Baron towered over most of the men so many eyes turned toward them when they entered.

Jose ran up. "You came. That is wonderful. Moises will be pleased to meet you." He turned and yelled into the throng. "Moises, you ox, here are some gentlemen who are eager to see if you are as ugly as they were told."

The onlookers jeered and parted to reveal the most imposing man Ariel had ever seen. Moises, their host, was indeed an ox of a man. Not as tall as Embry, but extraordinarily muscled. His head was shaved bald and there were tattoos climbing up his neck—a neck as thick as most men's thighs. Gold hoops glinted from his ears and his face was adorned with a nose flattened from being on the receiving end of many fists.

But he approached with his arms outstretched and a wide grin lighting his face that revealed several gold teeth glittering in the lamplight. "Welcome, welcome, dear sirs. Ignore the buzzing of this Spanish flea," he waved his hand as if to swat Jose away. "For tonight, we are all friends here and all equals. We aim to have fun and to make sure my sister Josefina starts her life with a good settlement from that poor sod who has promised to marry her this week."

Jose was turning around, looking through the crowd, as he laughed. "Ho, ho. Moises finally is getting Josefina married off. It is indeed time to celebrate. These here are friends with Nieto." He called out to the group. "Have you see him yet?"

"Judah, oh yes," Moises grinned and slapped the smaller man on the back, nearly sending him off his feet. "He is in the card room back there, fleecing the poor souls who think to best him at cards." He shook his head in mock sadness. "They never learn. But," he said with a twinkle back in his eyes, "he has pledged the winnings to the groom so it is all in a good cause."

The Baron laughed, "Lead us on to the card room. Let us see the contest."

The card room was packed with filled tables. But there was a crowd around the center table as men stood around watching the play. Nieto was seated there with three men. The doctor was wearing a loose linen shirt opened to the middle of his chest and a gold hoop dangled from one of his ears. There was a half-empty bottle and a small glass by his elbow and a pile of gold coins in front of him. He looked up, nodding briefly at them but he did not smile in recognition and, when he saw the Baron, his eyes narrowed in anger.

The Baron deliberately ignored him, whispering to Embry and Ariel. "They are playing a local gambling game with a short deck. Each player gets three cards and three are exposed in the center. Players can call for up to two more cards and two new cards are placed in the center. All the new cards and all cards in the center are face up. Based on what is revealed and the betting of the players, one tries to figure out who might have the highest hand. The crowd can bet on the winner as well based on what they see and hear."

While the cards were being dealt, Nieto poured himself a glass from the bottle and gulped it down. The Baron whispered, "Nieto can hold more liquor than anyone else I've met. It has a delayed effect but, when it comes, it hits him hard. But even when drinking that vile grappa, he is a devil at cards. Some say, only partly in jest, that he can see through the cards themselves since he seems to know everyone else's hand."

The three facedown cards were dealt out and the players picked up the corners to see what they had. They checked the cards in the center then the dealer asked Nieto, who was the man to his left, "More?"

Nieto shook his head 'no.' The crowd murmured—a sign of a very strong hand. The next man was asked and he signaled 'no' as well. The third player looked at his cards again and signaled he wanted two more as did the remaining player. The dealer dealt two to the center of the table and the crowd craned their necks to see over the players' heads.

Nieto smiled at the other players and pushed a pile of coins to the center. He leaned to his left, grinning into the next player's face. "Your turn, Alonzo."

The betting moved quickly. Two players opted out quickly. The one player who remained matched Nieto's bet and raised it aggressively. Nieto smiled coolly as he matched the bet then swept more coins into the center.

The opposing player matched the stack then called Nieto to show his hand. The doctor exposed two tens and the Queen of Hearts, the wild card. The other player cursed as he revealed the two eights in his hand that melded with his exposed additional eight. The crowd hooted while onlookers settled their side bets.

When the three other players signaled they were leaving the table, the Baron pushed Embry and himself forward. The Baron sat down across from Nieto, Embry took a side chair and Ariel began to move to the empty fourth chair.

Nieto grabbed his sleeve. "Pull up a chair and learn from the master. Let someone else lose their money to me tonight." He caught Ariel looking at his earring. "Like it, little one," he said winking at Ariel.

"When did you get it? You did not wear one before."

"Ah, but in London I was a drunk and a thief in service to the very proper Viscount Embry. Now I am back with the pirates and the smugglers so I need to blend in once again. That is how I live—changing as I must. I do not even recall when I first wore one."

Parker appeared, also wearing a gold hoop, to take the fourth seat, having heard the end of the comment. He added, "I got mine honestly, Ariel, in the Navy when I crossed the Equator for the first time. Judah, you were too drunk to remember. It was a night like this when Moises decided to induct you into his Brotherhood. The ceremony included drinking some vile brew and then Moises came at you waving a sail needle. When you awoke the next morning, you were thus adorned."

Nieto looked at him, squinting to focus then said to the onlookers, "Who invited this goy?"

Jose laughed, "You did, Judah. The grappa has stewed your brain so you forget what you do."

The game resumed. Embry, with his alert logical mind, proved to be a good match against Nieto who kept drinking steadily from the bottle. It was soon clear to all that Nieto cared only about beating the Baron and making rude comments on his losses.

The Baron took his repeated defeats calmly. He finally asked, "Judah, how can you drink that vile poison? It will burn a hole in your stomach soon."

Nieto cackled as he looked at the corners of the three cards in front of him. He made sure that Ariel could see them as well. He winked at the younger man. "It has been medically proven," he lectured in a suddenly serious tone, "that grappa is as healthy as breast milk… and a lot easier to get into a bottle."

The men standing around the table laughed. Nieto offered Ariel a sip. "Taste it. Tell them the truth. As good as breast milk."

Ariel sipped and felt liquid fire slide down his throat. He gasped. Nieto raised an eyebrow at him then downed the rest of the glass in one gulp, showing no reaction.

"Show-off," Parker hissed.

"If you want, dear Robbie, we could have a drinking contest next," Nieto challenged him.

Parker shook his head, "This goy is no fool, Judah. I like better odds than drinking against you—especially if you insist on that vile stuff."

"Patrone!" Nieto yelled. "This man casts aspersions on your brew. Bring me another bottle so I can prove him wrong."

Moises appeared with a fresh bottle and tipped the dregs of the first into Nieto's glass. He planted a resounding kiss on Nieto's brown curls and patted his cheek. "I like the look of all that gold on the table. My sister will live like a rich lady!"

It was Nieto's turn to bet. He pushed his whole pile of coins to the center of the table then winked again at Ariel. "There! Now they are confused. Is my hand that good that I dare everything? Or—am I tired of playing so I no longer care? Or perhaps the grappa has stewed my wits?" He downed yet another glass.

The other men threw in their cards. The hand that Nieto revealed was very weak. He had indeed tricked them all into losing. Nieto called Moises back and swept the money off the table into the bag the big man held out.

"Gentlemen," Nieto rose and bowed slowly with great dignity, "I am done with cards this evening. It is time for music." He pulled Ariel to his feet and laid an arm across his shoulder, carrying the new bottle in his other hand. "Come, little one, you will see how we Sephardim dance and sing."

The Baron and Embry rose to follow them, wondering what new vice Judah would be introducing to Ariel. Parker trailed them all.

The rear room of the inn had been set up with tables around the perimeter on three sides and an open space in the center and along the fourth side. A trio of musicians was playing music while two lines of men danced with their arms linked, challenging each other to ever more intricate steps as the crowd roared its approval.

The Baron leaned over to Embry and Ariel. "The crowd calls out requests and offers sums of money to convince the men they name to perform. If a performer refuses, he pays double the payment to the groom's fund. If he agrees, the nominator pays into the groom's fund. Either way, the groom's fund gains."

When the dance ended, there was a pause as the next act was nominated. The master of ceremonies encouraged the crowd. Was there a singer they wanted to hear? Was there a juggler or joke teller among them? What should the next act be?

They heard Jose's voice. "Judah will sing the 'good widow' song for two crowns." Cheers went up.

Nieto raised his hand, "Nay, I, the distinguished Doctor Judah Halevi Nieto, will not sing for a mere two crowns. I'd rather pay the four crown penalty and drink instead." He waved the bottle. The men around the room laughed.

Moises yelled, "Judah will sing the good widow song for eight crowns." Nieto shook his head, still refusing.

The Baron said with authority, his voice carrying with little effort to the corners of the room, "Judah will sing the good widow song for twenty crowns." The crowd applauded the princely sum.

Judah stared at the Baron in anger as if he would refuse the offer yet again. However, he hesitated. The price was perhaps too steep for him to pay the penalty or maybe he considered the benefit to the poor groom.

Whatever the reason, Nieto gave Ariel his bottle to hold then bowed in mock homage to the Baron. He motioned to the band to begin to play. After the few measures of introduction, he launched into a song in Spanish. There was a chorus line to be sung by the audience that ended with a suggestive hip thrust from the singer. The crowd sang louder and louder as each verse ended in the chorus and Nieto's hip thrusts, shimmies and hand jerks got more and more explicit.

Ariel, fascinated by the act, asked, "What does it mean?"

The Baron laughed as he leaned toward the Wharton brothers. "Oh, I think you know by the actions if not the words. The details do not matter, but the good widow is very, very good to all the men in the village as the singer demonstrates. The rest of the verses describe the ways she is good. Trust me. She has many, many ways of being very, very good."

Ariel looked at Nieto who without shame was performing a vivid sex pantomime for the crowd swishing his hips, stroking his body from chest to groin and finally winding up in a fat bearded man's lap, where he did a suggestive grind. He planted a resounding kiss on the man's lips and, in return, the fat man ran his hands up and down Nieto's chest, pretending to fondle him. The onlookers roared, throwing money at the two men.

When the song ended, Nieto bowed dramatically to the audience then bowed again to the stout man who had played along with him. Moises ordered his men to pick up all the coins rolling around the floor. With a wide grin glittering with his gold teeth, he hefted the bag, showing the crowd how heavy it was growing.

Meanwhile Nieto had gone over to the musicians to ask the guitarist for his instrument. With a great bow, the musician ceremoniously placed the guitar in the doctor's hands. Nieto sat down and began to strum.

Embry remarked, "I never thought to see the reticent Mr. Nieto performing such tricks for a crowd."

The Baron nodded, "He is only this way at events like this. Here he is protected enough and perhaps drunk enough to be unguarded. It is fortunate that he has these times. Otherwise I wonder how he could survive the strain of what he does.

"But understand there is an unwritten rule observed by those here. We never tell Nieto what he did on one of these evenings. He would be mortified if you ever mentioned the performance you just witnessed. When the poisonous grappa finally catches up with him, he will black out and this evening will be totally erased—God willing."

Ariel asked, "How can this whole room of people be trusted not to tell a tale like that?"

The Baron responded, "These are his friends and, even more, many in this crowd owe much to Judah personally. Others know what he does for their people so they are loyal to him and will protect him. Some here work directly with him. He is well loved and he is one of their nokmim—their avengers."

"He is indeed the center of attention," Embry remarked.

The Baron agreed, "This is his world now. He was born to a family of scholars and great rabbis. But he is shunned by that world because of his determination to avenge the wrongs done to the community with his own hands rather than to pray for divine intervention. He lives now with these men—the poorer Hebrew workmen, shop owners, pirates and smugglers—all living on the fringes of the community. Except Parker of course. When he is near him, he becomes Nieto's guardian. The men here call him Nieto's 'Shabbat goy,' permitted to do what Nieto cannot do for himself."

They stopped talking as sweet music rose from the center of the room where the doctor was bent over the guitar. The crowd quieted as the spell of the melody penetrated their boozy haze and reached their hearts. The music went on and on, growing more intricate by the measure.

Ariel listened with great appreciation. He was awed by the doctor's skill to effortlessly draw such complex melodies from his instrument. All those lonely nights spent thinking about music and how to transpose it from one instrument to another—all in his head. How strong he must be to keep his personal anguish hidden until it could be released it through music or drink or both, as now.

When the piece came to an abrupt end, there was a pause before the crowd erupted into applause. Nieto took a deep breath as he returned to the present time and place. He ceremoniously handed the instrument back to its owner. The musician bowed in return in honor of the doctor's artistry.

Nieto startled them all as he suddenly turned toward the Baron, saying loudly with a hard look, "Now that was worth another twenty crowns, Isaac. Pay up!" The use of the Baron's name and the harsh demand were deliberate insults—ones even the rough men in this crowd understood.

The Baron chose to not rise to the challenge. Instead, he called back to Nieto, "Indeed, yes!" as Moises pushed his way back to the table to allow the Baron to throw his coins into the bag. The big man then turned to the crowd, demanding, "All you sons of whores were also blessed to hear that piece from the great Judah Halevi. Pay up now or you will be sorry for it later!" Coins were being dropped into the bag from right and left.

Jose jumped up on his seat and announced a challenge dance. "I challenge Judah to beat me and my team."

Nieto signaled that he accepted the challenge. Jose produced a coin and tossed it. Nieto called, "Heads!"

Jose shouted with glee. "Tails—aha, I pick Moises for my team."

The big man walked into the center of the room.

Nieto pointed at Moises and Jose. "Oh ho, what do we have here? A Spanish flea and a big ox—an awkward love match, don't you all agree?" He spun around and pointed a finger at the Baron. "Isaac Tedesco for my team!"

The Baron took a calming breath. Again, Nieto was trying to goad him into an angry response by breaching the rules of etiquette. To give himself a pause to tamp down his reaction, the Baron slowly and dramatically took off his jacket and carefully untied his cravat, then rolled up his sleeves as he walked to the center of the room. The crowd applauded his willingness to join their games.

Jose yelled out to another big man in the crowd who entered the ring with loud cheers from the onlookers. Nieto looked over the crowd thoughtfully, almost choosing different people then shaking his head before considering the next man.

Finally, with a grin, he pointed to Parker. "The goy," he yelled.

Parker rose and saluted the crowd on his way to join the Baron. Jose completed his team with Alonzo, a wiry looking small man.

Nieto once again considered his options. "Ariel Wharton, my little friend."

Both the Baron and Parker tried to argue against this choice, but Nieto waved them away. Ariel eagerly went to join the group. He whispered to the Baron, "Now that I am part of this, what are the rules?"

The Baron whispered back, "The team with the last man standing wins. We dance together with our arms around each other's shoulders. We try to break the other team's chain without breaking our own by running into them or jumping or leaning on their arms. Once the chain is broken, it cannot be rejoined so each man becomes an easier target. You cannot stop moving during the dance."

Nieto grouped his team into a huddle. He whispered in a conspiratorial tone adorned with some slurred words, "We have speed and wits. Ariel, you will lead and run under their arms. Let Parker and the Baron charge against them."

Parker rolled his eyes, "Judah, you will not take down Moises. He is a stone wall."

Nieto was defiant. "Are you giving up before we even start? He is a slow-moving ox. We are lean and agile. We are clever so we will prevail."

The music started as the opposing chains of men lined up against each other. The crowd was already placing bets on the outcome. Nieto urged Ariel, "Faster, faster. When I say 'now' run under Jose's and Alonzo's arms."

The lines of dancers were moving around, looking for an opportunity to surprise the other side. Ariel led his chain into faster steps and when Nieto yelled "Now," he hunched down and ran between Alonzo and Jose, easily fitting under their arms. Nieto followed him in a half-crouch, as did Parker. The Baron however stayed erect and threw his weight against the linked arms. Alonzo's arm flew off Jose's shoulder and he started back-peddling in an attempt to stay upright. He fell on his rear to the delight of the crowd. Nieto clapped Ariel on the back in congratulations and shook the Baron's hand, his anger forgotten for the moment.

The music began again and the chains reformed. Moises snarled at Nieto, "You will need a doctor, Doctor, when this is over."

The chains kept circling each other until, with a roar, Moises headed directly for Ariel. In a panic, Ariel started to step backward. Nieto pulled on his arm and motioned with his head, "Forward and through." Ariel dove under Moises' arm and Nieto and Parker followed him. The Baron however was too tall and Moises managed to smack into him, driving the Austrian down.

The room grew silent for a split second until the Baron regained his feet, dusted himself off and shrugged to the crowd. They cheered his good-natured defeat as he headed back to his table to rejoin Embry who was watching, filled with tension, as his brother danced around the opposing chain.

Nieto's team started moving faster and faster, forcing Moises and his partners to keep spinning around backwards. Suddenly Nieto yelled "now" and Parker led a charge at Jose. The smaller man held on as long as he could but the difference in size between him and his nearest team member made it too hard. He went down with a thud. Cheers went up from the onlookers but the teams were seriously focused and did not stop.

Again, Moises led his team in a charge directly towards Ariel who lost his footing, clearly intimidated as the huge man bore down on him. The crowd cheered as Ariel got back to his feet. Nieto clapped him on his back as he left the floor and turned to watch the end of the contest.

Two men remained on each side. Moises' partner was large as well and the crowd realized that the outcome was pretty much determined. However, Nieto would not concede. He kept leading Parker in hopeless charges towards Moises' side. The inevitable finally happened when Moises charged directly at Parker forcing the tall but lighter man backwards until he lost his grip on Nieto's shoulder and tripped. Moises roared with pleasure, eying his single remaining opponent.

Parker stood up, bowed to the onlookers and walked to the edge of the ring to stand with Ariel to watch Nieto's inevitable defeat. He could tell that at long last the liquor was affecting Nieto's agility. The blue-eyed man was slower now as if he needed to think about where to place his feet. Moises and his partner kept dancing around Nieto forcing him to keep moving backwards.

In a split second change, Nieto turned in the opposite direction until he was behind Moises. He leapt onto the huge man's back with his arms tight around his neck and his legs wrapped around his waist. Caught off-guard, Moises dropped his arm from his partner's shoulder throwing him off-balance and sending him down.

The crowd burst into applause, chanting Nieto's name. Moises spun around trying to loosen Nieto's grip. Nieto raised a hand in victory, "I have not yet touched the ground. There are no rules against riding the ox."

The crowd laughed but stopped abruptly when Nieto's head swayed and his arms lost their grip. Moises stood still as Nieto gently slid off into a heap on the floor.

The Baron whispered, "At last, Judah's evening is coming to an end."

Parker and Moises raised Nieto to his feet. When the crowd cheered as the doctor wobbled into a standing position, Nieto seemed to become aware of his surroundings once again, nodding at his friends. He found his grappa bottle and, leaning on Parker, worked his way back to the Baron's table. A chair appeared just in time as one of the men at the neighboring table pushed it towards the doctor. He sank into it and took a swig from the bottle.

Parker placed a fresh glass on the table. "Judah, slow down. Here is a glass," he whispered.

Nieto looked up, bleary amusement on his face. "Why slow down? It defeats my aim to reach the blessed darkness. Isn't that the purpose?" He filled the glass then pushed it towards Ariel. "Here, little one, you need this to forget as well."

Embry pulled the glass away from his brother.

Nieto looked at the Viscount, "You delude yourself that you can protect your brother from evil. He is too good for this world. It will claim him some day."

His eyes were glazed and reddened—the pupils so large that the irises seemed black. He looked around the table at the Baron and Parker, and returned his gaze to Ariel as if he had just remembered something he needed to say. "Drink to forget, even if only for a few hours. It wipes the terrible sights from your mind. It helps you forget what you have done. You can forget what you yearn for and can never have. It erases your dreams.

"Isn't that the purpose of drinking, Baron, so that you cannot see your dreams anymore? And it kills your hopes. My child, you need a drink, don't you? To not think about the blood and the death and the pain and those innocents who died in your place. To forget that you might never have what you really want—peace, love, hope."

He waved the bottle towards Ariel who drew back as the liquor threatened to spill out. Parker's hands grabbed Nieto's shoulders. The doctor pushed Parker away. "Am I not right, Isaac? Why aren't you drinking like me? How can you stand your thoughts and your memories? Do not the dead haunt your dreams as well?

"Oh, I forget. You never see the work you order others to do. You never sink your hands into the warm blood of those whom you ordered to be tortured and to be killed. You are spared the feel of it, the smell of it, the horror of it."

Parker whispered to the Baron, "I will order your carriage."

The Baron nodded. "Get Moises to help. We should go."

"Go? Go where?" Nieto jerked his head up. He had been sliding towards the table, pulled down by the tide of intoxication. "I do not want to go anywhere. I want to stay here with my friends—the people who know about my dreams. Or maybe I can go home?

"Ah, but I remember. My father will not see me." He turned to Embry, "Did you know my father has sat Shiva for me? He sat in mourning for seven days telling people that his eldest son was dead to him and he said Kaddish for me. How does one bear that? Tell me how to bear it. Tell me please." He laid his head upon his folded arms and closed his eyes.

Embry reached over to put his hand on the doctor's soft curls. "How horrible for you, Judah," he whispered.

Ariel sat still, fighting the tears burning in his throat. These then were the burdens that Nieto had warned him of.

Suddenly, Ariel felt rather than heard that someone else had approached the table. He looked up to see a very tall man dressed all in black standing at the Baron's side. He was pale and thin with longish black hair that had a surprising streak of white running through it. His hawk-like look was accentuated by his coal-black eyes, arched eyebrows and narrow hooked nose. Another big man with white-blond hair and hard pale blue eyes was standing behind him.

The Baron rose and shook the hand of the stranger in black. "Ezekiel," he said. "You are here? In Gibraltar? But why?"

"Isaac," the stranger replied, ignoring the questions. "No need to introduce me to these men. I will not be staying long."

At that moment, Parker returned and spotted the stranger. "Ezekiel," he said angrily, "couldn't you wait even a few days before you pounce on him?"

Ezekiel briefly glanced at Parker then looked back at the Baron, continuing as if there had been no interruption but answering the question as if the Baron had been the one to ask it. "Wait? For what should I wait? For more of this?" He looked around the room and his black glare forced the men at the nearest tables to quiet down. "Stupid games and obscene jokes? Drinking until you sink into oblivion? To vomit and piss yourselves like dumb animals or worse, like the others, the goyim." He turned back to the Baron, "Arrange for Judah to meet with me tomorrow night at eight o'clock at your hotel."

"No," Parker yelled. "No, it is too soon."

Ezekiel did not take his unblinking stare from the Baron, "That Engländer goy should not be there. It is not business for him—an outsider. I wish to speak with Judah Halevi."

At his name, Judah had raised his head and stared up at the tall man standing above him. A look of almost childlike wonder crossed the doctor's face. "Ezekiel, it is you here in this place? In Gibraltar? So far from your home? You have come for me. I hadn't dared hope. Will you help me bear the pain?"

The man placed a pale, long-fingered hand on Judah's shoulder. "Yes, my brother, I will help. We need to talk when this poison is out of your body so you can think again. Tomorrow night? Are you willing?"

"No, Judah," Parker said, "it is too soon."

Nieto looked from Parker to the Baron then back at the man called Ezekiel whose hand still rested on his shoulder. "Yes, tomorrow night, my brother. I will be ready to listen."

Ezekiel nodded slowly, then staring once again at the Baron, scorn curling his lips, said loudly so that his voice carried throughout the room, "You all urge him to indulge in this evil by applauding his tricks and laughing at his stumbles. Perhaps you believe yourselves kind because you think it wipes out his thoughts and his memories and gives him some relief. Perhaps you think to have more power over him by letting him sink into the pit then giving him your hand to climb out. But you do terrible harm to him by encouraging him along this way. He is traveling a dangerous road with no good end to it."

He turned and drifted into the crowd, his blond companion following silently behind him. As they moved, men hushed and parted to let them pass.

The Baron turned to Embry, "They do not let a day go by. They know that we will be done by Thursday and they will take Nieto that day."

Ariel's head spun around. "Take him? Where?"

The Baron explained, "I call on Nieto when I need him. All his other activities are guided by the leaders of the Nokmim. Some call them the Justice Seekers, others the Avengers. The officials call them criminals. His first loyalties are to them. They summon Judah as soon as he is finished with our work. Ezekiel is one of their chief emissaries."

"Who are the leaders?" Embry asked.

"I do not know them," the Baron said. "Perhaps they are among those here tonight who are nokmim themselves. How he knew to find Judah here in Gibraltar," the Baron shrugged, "I have no idea. We can only hope to give the allies a network as secret and as swift as that of the nokmim. I never know when the Hawk, as Ezekiel is called, will appear to take Judah back.

"I must not know too much about them because I must protect my diplomatic work. You should not know about them either, Lord Embry. Their activities are never approved by any community or government agency—'officially,' although many call on them when needed. You get my meaning?"

Parker approached the table with Moises trailing behind him. "Your carriage is ready, Baron," Parker said coldly as he grabbed Nieto under one arm and Moises lifted him by the other. "We'll take Judah out now."

"It is easier if I do it by myself," the Ox said. He hefted Nieto onto his back and grabbed his arms to hold him in place. The doctor looked like a rag doll draped over the huge man's back.

When they reached the Baron's carriage, Moises and Parker maneuvered Nieto onto the seat next to the Viennese. The doctor suddenly jerked awake—his body stiff and his eyes trying to focus.

The Baron said softly, "Shush, Judah, no more battles tonight."

The doctor slumped as if he had deflated, gradually sinking towards the Baron. His head fell against the tall man's chest then slid to his lap. The Baron looked bemused and patted Nieto on the arm.

Parker leaned in and saw what had happened. He rearranged the sleeping man's body."I'll ride with the driver," Parker said, a hard edge still in his voice. "I need fresh air."

The carriage took off. The Baron looked at Embry and Ariel sitting across from him. "Remember we forget all we saw tonight. Judah will be humiliated if he knew he had let his guard down so. Tomorrow he will be in great physical pain but we want to spare him the agony of embarrassment."

Ariel looked at the Baron. "He told me it was a terrible burden to live his life. I am beginning to understand."

The Baron nodded at the serious young man. "What I do for justice is done in drawing rooms, ballrooms and embassies. It is clean and very, very polite. Nieto and his colleagues do it in the dark with blood on their hands. He is sent secretly by others in the community to do what they cannot. And then they will publicly denounce his actions and exclude him from their midst.

"He is angry at me now. He believes the Earl and I were wrong in withholding the truth from you and your sister. We have disagreed on our methods before. He will overcome his anger because he believes in our greater cause and he allows nothing to stand in the way of our goals."

"Parker is angry at you as well," Ariel said.

"Ah, yes. Parker. He is bound to me by orders of the Admiralty. He knows that when Judah leaves, he cannot follow because his duty is to me and because the Nokmim will not allow outsiders in. He is angry that I did not fight to keep Judah longer with us." He shrugged. "He refuses to understand that I have few options where Judah's loyalties lie."

They had reached the Baron's hotel. The hotel footman came out and Parker and he together lifted Nieto from the Baron's lap. They were able to half-walk, half-drag him into the building. The Baron climbed down from the carriage, turning back to the Wharton brothers.

"It was a very good night," he said, assuming a more cheerful tone, leaning back into the carriage. "We raised money for a needy young groom and you had a chance to see that we can be boisterous with the best. And," he smiled tightly, "we gave Nieto some time to find release from the tension in his life. The driver will take you back to the Admiralty House. I wish you a peaceful good night."

Thirty-One

When the Baron entered his suite, he was greeted by his butler, Mr. Graves. "Mr. Nieto is in the guest room. A bath is being drawn for him. And Mr. Parker, shall he attend the doctor?"

The Baron responded, "Yes, the couch in the dressing room will serve. He will not want to leave Nieto unattended tonight considering the doctor's condition."

Graves smiled in understanding. This was not the first time the doctor had been cared for by the Baron and Parker after a night of drinking and more. Tonight at least, there was no blood to clean off the man or his clothing.

"Graves, there is a bottle of fine oil in my dressing room for after bathing. Bring it to the guest room. It is time for the doctor to be pampered a bit."

When the Baron entered the guest room, he found Parker undressing the unconscious man who was sprawled on the bed. "I can send my man to do that," the Baron offered.

"Nay," Parker responded. "I have done this before. I think he is aware enough to help. Right, Judah?"

The sleeping man raised his head, "Wha…?" and let it fall back.

Parker grinned at the Baron. "See, almost normal."

A footman entered with a small vial of amber liquid. The Baron offered it to Parker, "This is sandilo oil that I picked up on my trip to Russia. It is very good after a bath—very soothing. It might prove comforting to Judah."

Parker nodded while he continued his work, stripping off Nieto's boots followed by his stockings and then his trousers. The Baron said good night, leaving Parker alone with the doctor.

The trip in and out of the tub was actually harder than Parker had admitted but he wanted to be alone with Nieto. The doctor drifted in and out of awareness but Parker managed to get him from the tub to the bed where now he lay sleeping, face down on the sheets, with a towel draped over his lower body.

Parker uncorked the oil flask and smelled the exotic woody aroma. He thought for a moment then stripped off his own clothes and went back to the bathing room. The water in the tub was lukewarm but still clean enough for him to wash off the smoky and boozy smell of the groom's party.

He returned to the bedroom with a towel wrapped around him. Taking the flask of oil, he climbed onto the bed. He straddled the sleeping man then poured some oil in his hands. After rubbing his hands together to warm the oil, he began to massage Nieto's neck and shoulders. He re-oiled his palms then worked in long stokes down the doctor's lean back. He crawled lower in the bed, pulled both towels away and oiled his palms once again.

This time he stroked Nieto's buttocks, slowly and caressingly, then down the thighs and calves admiring the long muscles and the soft brown hair. There was a long scar on Nieto's right thigh. Parker stroked it gently, hesitated, then he leaned down and kissed the scar.

He waited to see if there was a reaction. Nieto sighed quietly. Parker got off the bed and gently rolled Nieto onto his back. The doctor stirred in his sleep but Parker waited patiently for him to quiet down. He had been patient for months already so he could go slowly now.

Once again he poured oil into his palms and rubbed them together to warm it. He climbed back onto the bed, again straddling the doctor's body. He started stroking Nieto's shoulders and neck then down the long lean arms and across the chest, paying careful attention to each scar. He remembered some of their stories—the fights that Nieto would instigate to work out his guilt in rage and the times he would take a scalpel to himself, perhaps as a punishment for the crimes he believed he committed. Nieto had never explained his actions to his friend.

Parker ran his fingers through the curly brown tendrils on the sleeping man's chest and the path they made down to his groin. He looked behind him. There was a slowly-rising erection. He smiled, pleased that Nieto was peaceful enough to become aroused in his sleep. He prayed that meant that his friend's dreams were free of horrors.

He lightly stroked the sleeping man's face, running his fingers from the center of the forehead, around the hairline and down to his jaw. He felt the stubble on Nieto's cheek and brought his face closer to smell his scent mixed with the oil's aroma. Then he kissed the doctor with a tenderness filled with all his many months of desire.

He held his breath while he waited for a reaction. When there was none, he put his hands on Nieto's chest. Daring a more urgent touch, he stroked the brown nipples then he bent his head and sucked one between his lips.

Hands gripped his hair. Nieto's head was raised off the pillow and his eyes stared at him but his gaze was unfocused.

Parker put his head closer to Nieto's and whispered. "Let me love you, Judah. You deserve it and it hurts no one. Let me love you. Better than a whore you pay. I do this with love."

Nieto stared at him for a long time then his eyes closed and his head dropped back on the pillow. His fingers loosened in Parker's hair and Parker took each hand down, kissing its palm and laying it by the man's side. He moved back to the nipples and teased them with his lips, feeling Nieto's rising cock pushing against him as he sank lower down the man's torso.

He placed a line of kisses down the path of hair leading to Nieto's groin. Finally he turned and ran his oiled hands up and down the swollen organ, marveling at the velvety quality of the skin covering the hard muscular core. A sudden gasp made him stop again.

Nieto's eyes were open. This time, they were focused.

"Let me, Judah. Better me—a friend—than a poxy whore."

Nieto's head was raised and his hands were gripping Parker's hips. Parker waited for the push that would throw him off the bed. Nieto shook his head, as if to clear his vision.

Parker begged softly, "Let me love you."

Nieto's head dropped back to the pillow and his long strong fingers tightened on Parker's hips. He felt Nieto's thumbs gripping him. He did not feel a push, but rather a steady hold. Then he heard the words he had dreaded.

"No, Robbie, no. A friend, you say, but you desire more from me. I cannot be that to you. Do not force the burden of your love on me."

Parker caught his breath. He had hoped to finally satisfy the longing held back for months. It was too hard to give up now that he had made his desires so evident. He tried again.

He crawled up to the head of the bed and put his hands on either side of the doctor's face. He kissed him a second time. While he met no resistance, there was no response either. He saw the sad look in his friend's eyes and it tore at his heart.

"Oh, Judah," he whispered. " I just wanted to show you love. I do not ask for anything in return."

He ached with the pain in Nieto's voice as the doctor asked, "Is it really love or is it possession? I have been lost and alone but I will not find any peace here. Every which way I turn, they each call it love but I fear each has a trap that will hold me until I am destroyed. I will lose the little pride I have left in being myself."

They? Who were they? "Judah, it is only me, Robbie Parker. No one else is here now. I know it is not your way but it is my way to show love. I want nothing in return. I just want to show you love. Do not be afraid to accept it as it is offered."

Judah turned his head away but did not respond. It was over. Judah might endure his attentions just because he did not want to hurt him. But Parker knew to go further would be to impose on the man and, as Judah had feared, to make a burden of the love he offered.

He slid off to lay behind the doctor. "Judah, may I just stay with you then? I want to hold you. No more than that, I promise. Just comfort between close friends or dear brothers."

There was no sound until he heard the quiet mutter, "Yes, Robbie. For tonight, like brothers."

Parker slid his arm around Nieto's waist and pulled him closer, so that the other man's buttocks rested against his groin and his chin rested against the soft curls on the doctor's head. The Englishman tried hard but one sigh did escape his control. It was filled with his disappointment and his resignation.

Thirty-Two

Parker awoke to the soft sound of the door opening. The morning light from the windows in the sitting room illuminated the bedchamber. He lifted his head and saw the Baron, already impeccably dressed, looking at the two men lying naked in a tight embrace. Parker stared over the sleeping doctor into the Baron's eyes, instinctively lifting his arm from Nieto's waist as if to hide the evidence.

No, he thought, letting his arm drop back into place. That will change nothing. I am naked in bed with my arms around Judah Nieto. He will think the worse.

After the Baron closed the door, Parker got up and dressed. He knew Judah would suffer with terrible headaches and violent nausea. He always did after a binge. Today, it might be worse because of his feelings of guilt in rebuking his friend's wishes. The man who could coldly torture those whom he judged evil tormented himself when he caused pain to those he cared for. Parker sighed as he recognized that Judah never felt free from feeling guilty over either act. Yes, today, at least, he would take care of the doctor for a change.

When Parker entered the sitting room, the Baron slapped down the paper he was pretending to read. His face was frozen in an imperious glare as he ordered his employee to sit.

Parker hesitated. "I need to get the headache tisane ready for Judah. He will be in great pain when he awakes."

"Graves can see to the doctor," the Baron said coldly. "Sit down. We need to talk. Even you can see that is necessary."

Parker sat down. He tried to look steadily and calmly at the Baron. He thought, I will not let him make me ashamed.

The Baron leaned toward Parker, bringing the power of his gaze closer. "I will not judge if Judah found comfort with you. But I believe that he was not aware of what was happening—drunk as he was—and you took advantage of that to act on your wishes. If he did not wish for your … your attentions, he will be even more guilt-stricken when he recalls what happened. You know the risk that places him in. His recklessness grows when he is feeling guilt over his actions."

Parker replayed the events in the bedchamber in his mind. He finally responded, carefully and slowly, "Baron, I know what I wanted but when he said 'no,' I stopped. I gave him comfort as a brother might. Nothing more. For one night, someone held him and cared for him and asked for nothing in return—did not order him to kill or torture or disguise who he is. I do not presume it means more than that to him. He might not even remember that I held him as he slept. I will not mention it ever again and I trust you will not either."

The Baron kept his eyes on Parker, "Do not be a fool, Robbie. This has forever changed your relationship with Judah. I am concerned that it might have implications we cannot foresee. Perhaps the time has come for you to report back to the Admiralty for a new assignment."

Parker raised his chin. To make it clear to the Baron that he was willing to fight back hard, for the first time, he deliberately broke protocol. "Isaac, do you really believe that I did harm to Judah? Or are you worried that he found comfort by relying on someone other than you? If Judah no longer wants me with him, I'll accept it, but I will not go just because you fear losing your control over him."

The Baron sat still. Parker felt the very air in the room crackle with danger. "Robbie, it is unwise to try to bait me. Make no mistake about my power. You will not have a choice in the matter, Lieutenant Commander. You are bound by the orders given to you by your superiors. You have sworn loyalty to serve your King—that is, until you become known to be unfit for that service." He paused so that the silence weighed his words with his threat. "Know this as well. I need Judah far more than I need you. I will not let your infatuation bring harm to him or to our endeavors. You took advantage of his intoxication to satisfy your own hunger. What you did was despicable. You cannot yet know the harm you have done."

So finally, the Baron had made his threat, as Judah said he would. Sensing that all might be already lost, Parker decided to strike back. "Do not tell me about doing Judah harm. I know the stories behind the scars on that man's body. You, Isaac, make decisions about strategies and attacks and you send him off on your genteelly-titled 'endeavors' to do bloody work.

"When did you ever get blood on your hands, Isaac? Is finding justice for your people just a sport to you?" he said with a mocking tone. "You send the best of your men out to do your bidding as just another move in some diplomatic game. I have stood by his side as he used his surgeon's skills to torture men into confessing and then to execute them for their crimes. He is shunned by his father and lost to his community and tormented by what he has done. And you accuse *me* of harming him!"

There was silence again as the two men glared at each other. Parker got up, for once not waiting for the aristocrat to dismiss him. "I need to get Judah some headache tea. He will be in terrible pain this morning."

When he returned to the bedroom with the tea, he found Nieto already up, sitting naked on the couch in the dressing room, his head in his hands and his elbows resting on his knees. His eyes were closed and he was groaning.

Parker tried to hand him the steaming cup. "Sip, Judah. It is what a very fine doctor orders for headaches," he cajoled.

Nieto shook his head, waving the cup away.

Parker knelt by his feet to offer the cup again. "You must. It will help."

Nieto raised his head. His face was tight against the pain. "Why, Robbie? Why did you?"

"Why did I do what, Judah? Why did I touch you? Why did I kiss you? Why did I offer you what I thought might be some release in a safe way? Because I love you and you were alone and I wanted to offer comfort. Did I change you? Harm you? Hurt you? No, you cannot believe that. You are not such a simple man not to understand that I am still what I have always been and that you are still what you were. Now sip the tea. We need never talk of it again."

Parker turned his back because he feared to see rejection on Nieto's face. He began pulling clothes out of the doctor's luggage. Nieto sipped the tea. The ticking of the clock on the mantle in the bed chamber could be heard clearly in the silence between the two men.

Nieto said quietly, "Robbie, I do not wish to hurt you. However, it must be clear between us. I am not that way—the way you might want me to be—but I understand the kindness that was meant and I thank you for your care. In the way of a brother, I love you, if that could be enough for you."

Parker stood still for a moment, still facing away from Nieto. "It must be enough for me, Judah, so I accept it. Sip the damned tea. Then you will put on this nightshirt and get back into bed until you recover completely."

Parker helped Nieto into bed and pulled the covers up. As he was about to extinguish the lone candle whose light Nieto could barely endure, the doctor reached out for the oil flask still standing on the table. He inhaled the exotic aroma.

"Oh yes," he murmured as he lay back on the pillow. "I remember this. It was the one Isaac used…."

Parker felt icy fingers curl around his heart. "Isaac, Judah?" he asked.

The doctor turned away on his side, already drifting back into sleep, "Oh, yes, Isaac, when he comforted me."

"How comforted?" Parker tried not to ask but he was seized with an anger fueled by jealousy.

"Like a father. He rubbed my back and held me when the terrors came," Judah said in a very quiet voice. "Like my father would if he still loved me." The quiet voice gave way to heavy sighing followed by the regular breathing of sleep.

Parker sat in the chair by the bedside, watching Nieto in sleep. Gradually he drifted off himself, with his head falling against the back of the chair, until he heard the sound of weeping. Leaning over the bed, he watched the tears running down Nieto's face as he twisted the covers in his sleep.

Parker stripped off his trousers and shirt and slid into the bed, wrapping his arms around the doctor. He held the weeping man to his chest and, gently rocking him, crooned soothing words, thinking of the fatherless boy in Belinda's arms. There is so much sadness in the world, he thought. We must take joy and comfort when we can.

"No, Robbie," Judah mumbled, pulling away.

"Sssh, 'tis comfort, nothing more. Like Isaac did. Like a close relative, as you said. Let me be like a brother to you. Sleep, Judah," he whispered and felt the doctor relax again in his arms.

Nieto slept until the first bout of violent nausea convulsed his body. Parker held his head over the basin then wiped his face with a damp cloth.

"Rinse your mouth," he ordered as he brushed Nieto's curls back from his forehead. Nieto spat the water into the basin and lay back exhausted.

The second bout an hour later was more violent. Nieto retched over the basin until bile burned his throat. Parker again cleaned his face and helped him lay back in bed.

Nieto grimaced, "Shoot me if I do this ever again."

Parker smiled. The weak joke meant that Judah was returning to himself. There would be another time he was sure when Judah would feel the need to black out the pain and grief, but now, as he recovered, he would feel his usual remorse.

Nieto spoke from the bed, looking up at the ceiling. "Ezekiel was there last night. That was good—that was very good," he stated.

Parker responded carefully, not seeing any good himself in the tall man's sudden appearance, "Yes. He will be here in a few hours. He does not wait long to call on you."

"He needs me. He needs me to go with him. It must be something urgent so I will leave sooner than I thought."

"And Elizabeth, Judah? Are you so willing to leave her so soon?"

There was no answer from the doctor, but Parker saw the pain on his face. Perhaps this was the way to counter Ezekiel's attraction. So he added, "Think of all that might be possible with Elizabeth if you can stay to settle things. All you ever dreamed of—a wife, a family, a home, time to do good works. "

"Yes, it was a good dream." Nieto's voice was weighed down with despair.

Parker moved from the chair to sit on the edge of the bed. He urged, "You have the right to say no, Judah. Ezekiel will permit you to say no. It cannot always be you. There are other nokmim. The Baron can make sure that Ezekiel accedes to your wishes. Ezekiel needs the Baron's wealth for his plans, too, so he will listen."

Nieto responded quietly. "Yes, but Ezekiel knows me well. I will want to go with him. He is with me each step, by my side, as a brother should be, so I will go with him."

"Tell him then I must go with you. I must be with you step by step, as you say," Parker pleaded. "Do not leave me behind, worrying about who will be by your side. Let me be your brother too, facing the danger with you."

"You know you cannot. We alone must seek vengeance for our people. It is important that the goyim know we will not be victims anymore and that our retribution is to be feared."

"Then make me a Jew."

Nieto laughed. What a crazy thing to ask.

"Don't laugh at me, Judah. Make me a Jew. I know it is possible. I've been asking."

Judah sat up in bed, slowly as his head pounded with every movement he made. "You do not know what you are saying, Robbie. It is not simple. You will be marked forever. You will never be able to hide the truth."

Parker nodded, "I know. Jose explained it in all its grim detail and Moises offered to do it himself." He flashed Nieto a half-grin.

Nieto shot back, "The Ox would butcher you."

"That is why I am asking a fine surgeon to do it."

Nieto shook his head. "It is not only the knife, Robbie. It is the faith. You must learn. We have a long history and a complex theology. You will assume all our burdens. You will bring derision and scorn down on yourself from the greater community. You will lose your family."

Parker interrupted, "I lost my family years ago. My mother is dead and my father will not accept me as I am. I have lived among your people for years. I have watched and listened. I have even kept notes. You have seen my notebooks."

Nieto was surprised. For years, he had seen Parker scribbling in small notebooks that he seemed to always have in his pocket. He had assumed that the man was writing down observations that he planned to report back to his commander. "Those notes were about the faith? Not information for the Baron?"

The Englishman nodded, a shy smile on his face. "I wanted to learn. There is so much to know. You all do things so naturally that you probably are not aware of them. You say 'God willing' whenever you plan to meet in the future and 'the Holy God of Abraham' when you swear and you say prayers for everything, for washing hands, eating bread, drinking wine, so even ordinary days are special...."

He continued with some urgency, "You talk about a history of suffering and torment. But I see the pride you and the Baron have in all your people have done. I see the feeling of mission. You say you must complete creation and balance the world. You share that vision among you. There is allegiance to your community. When you travel, you find people to welcome you—who are part of the same brotherhood. I want that too. I want a people who need me and who welcome me. I am as lonely as you are. I want to belong with you and your people."

Nieto answered sternly, "It is more than cutting off a piece of skin. There are blessings and a ritual immersion. A religious court needs to believe in your sincerity. You must consider this further. You will join a covenant and the mark will be forever there. You can never hide what you are."

Parker responded, "I want to share this burden, Judah. In Vienna, when we first met, you told me I was a 'ger'—an honored stranger in your community. So was Ruth, the woman who became the ancestor of the great King David. Your friend, Rav Menachem, told me that story. He said it was a teaching that those who entered the covenant by choice were to be fully accepted into the community."

"Yes, but Robbie," Nieto hesitated but it must be said, "your preferences…your affections are not acceptable to the religious. Many will spurn you as an abomination because of the teaching in Leviticus so, despite everything you do, you will not be accepted by them. Ezekiel and his men...well, they are rigid about such things. He might not ever trust you despite the sign on your body. So if you are doing this to join us, beware!"

"So you are telling me that many Hebrews will despise me as much as most Christians do? I do not care about those nameless others, Judah, if you accept me as a brother." At the doctor's nod, Parker continued. "Then let me become a brother in all things. Make me a Jew. Do not make me seek a stranger for this. Jose told me that fathers often do it for their sons. Do it for the man you honor by calling him a brother."

Nieto fell back into the bed. "Let me think—I need to think about this." He put his arm over his eyes and lay still. He would have appeared to be sleeping except for the other hand that kept plucking at the cover.

After a few more minutes, Parker leaned over again. He couldn't wait. His tension made him force the issue. "The time for Ezekiel's arrival is fast approaching. Do this for me now."

Nieto sat up. "Do what, Parker?"

"Judah, do not mock me. You know what we have been discussing," Parker said, his irritation rising with his tension.

"You must say it, Robbie. You must say it to me and repeat it to witnesses. What is it that you want me to do?"

"I want you to make me a Jew."

Nieto got out of bed and went to the door. He called Graves, the Baron's butler. "I need to send a footman to the harbor town with a message."

"Very good, Mr. Nieto. Write the message and I will see that it is done."

Nieto grabbed a writing sheet and pen from the desk in the bed chamber and wrote the note in Hebrew. He folded it and on the front he lettered the name and address in English. He handed the note to Graves, who read the address and blinked twice. That was all the reaction the well-trained butler would permit himself to show.

Thirty-Three

Within moments of Graves' departure with Nieto's note, the door flew open with such violence that it slammed against the wall. The Baron stood there, quivering with rage. "How dare you do this, Judah? Order my servants on dangerous errands without my permission? And this," he held up the note, now opened and crumbled, "this is madness."

"Ah, I thought to keep it secret until it was done but I see you place spies within your very household."

"Do not try to distract me from the issue. You must still be muddled from all that drink. You cannot seriously think of performing this sacrilege."

"What sacrilege, Baron? Now I am indeed muddled."

"Your plan to make this Sodomite a Jew!" his hand quivered as he pointed to Parker, whose face went white.

Nieto on the other hand became very calm. "Do not—I warn you—do not ever say that again. If you wish to see me ever again, you will apologize. Robbie is a brother to me—closer to me than any other person—even you, Baron, and you will never say such a thing about him or to him."

"Not saying it does not change the truth of it. No matter how much you might wish it, it will never be right. You have no authority to do this. He will never be accepted as a Jew. You must realize that."

"I know that being born a Jew did not protect me from being shunned and no longer accepted. So how can it be worse for him? Send for Rav Natan, as I asked. Let him decide."

"Rav Natan! You are making a mockery of a sacred ritual. Rav Natan is a known derelict. You send for a man who no longer can perform the ritual because he has destroyed his nerves with alcohol and you will use him as the authority for this? I see you promised him a bottle of fine wine as payment—my fine wine, I assume."

"Send for him, Isaac, or you shall never see me again. I swear it."

The Baron stared then shrugged bitterly. He left the room, cursing under his breath. A few minutes later, a footman was dispatched with the note for the Rav who, Judah knew, would have already started drinking in a notorious bar in the harbor district.

The Baron returned, intending to resume his arguments but instead he found Judah ready to give him orders. The doctor switched to Ladino, the medieval Spanish-Hebrew language spoken among the Sephardim, those Jews whose roots went back to Iberia. He wanted to spare Parker from more of the Baron's curses and arguments.

"Now, Isaac, please ask your servants to bring me a basin, several pitchers of hot water, a bar of brown lye soap, some goblets, linen towels and," Nieto added with a smile, "two bottles of your finest wine."

"I will not stay here to watch this," the Baron responded in the same language, turning to stalk out of the room.

"Nay, Isaac, you must stay. I will need a Bet Din, a tribunal of three Jewish men, for this to be kosher." The Baron shook his head. "You will do this as payment for my future services, Isaac. And just think, after tonight, you will have a fine Jew who can mingle among the blond peoples of northern Europe and blend in, unlike you or me. Think how useful he will be!"

The Baron stood still, the look on his face indicating that this new possibility was suddenly intriguing.

Nieto turned to Parker, who had been pale and silent through the rapid verbal barrage between the other two men. "Have you changed your mind, Robbie?" he asked in English.

Parker shook his head but said, only half jesting, "Moises would have been done already."

The Baron stared in disbelief, responding in English as well. "This is ludicrous. From the drunken Rav Natan to the smuggler Moises the Ox. You are both mad."

Nieto looked down at his bare feet and legs, "And I—still in my nightshirt. This does indeed seem mad."

He went into the dressing room. The Baron and Parker stood like boxers waiting for the next bell.

Parker broke the silence, "When did you find out where my desires lay? A good while ago, I would guess, considering how many men you have to spy for you but even still you thought me useful. So why am I am now no longer wanted or needed? I am the same as I was. Is it because now Judah has told you he values me as a brother?"

The Baron shook his head, "I am not jealous of you, Robbie. You do not have the power to threaten my influence over Judah. I pity you for the desperation that is driving you to this. Did you wake up this morning and think, 'I know how to stay closer to Judah. I will have my foreskin trimmed off and be a Jew and then I will be able to trail him into the nokmim. Ezekiel will permit that if the Baron does not let me stay with Judah in his service.'

"Robbie, you have no idea how rigid Ezekiel and his men are about those who flaunt biblical teachings. He distains even me and my family because we live according to these modern times, rather than as if we were still in the land of Canaan."

Parker answered, "You think me insincere? You cannot comprehend that someone might want to belong to your people? Have you spent so much time among the aristocrats of Europe that you no longer value what has been yours by birth?"

"You miscomprehend, Robbie. I value what I am so highly that I am shocked that you think it would be simple to enter the covenant and belong with us. I understand that it will never be right.

"There are generations of belonging and believing that are part of Judah's body and soul as they are of mine. You will never have that. We share a history—yes, of grief, but also of bringing important truths to the world. You have none of that.

"You will always be the ger—the stranger—living among us, even following our laws, perhaps knowing them even better than most of us but it will have been learned by rote. You will never feel what we feel, share what we share. You will never belong. You will be more alone than ever."

They were interrupted by Graves supervising the footmen bringing in the supplies Nieto had ordered. When they left, before the Baron could resume his arguments, the door was flung open again.

The fat bearded man who had shared a smacking kiss with the dancing Nieto the night before entered followed by Graves who was attempting to halt his progress forward. The big man shook him off as a horse shakes off the flies that plague him.

"Baron," the fat man's voice boomed, "Rav Natan DaSilva is here at your service. I came quickly in that lovely coach of yours. I understand that we will celebrate the covenant." He looked around the once-spacious chamber that seemed to have shrunk in size now that he had entered. "Where is the babe? And the father I will instruct?"

Nieto emerged from the dressing room, clad in broadcloth trousers and a loose linen shirt with the sleeves rolled up. "Rav Natan, I am glad you made haste. We have important work today. We are to make a new Jew."

Rav Natan combed his fingers through his black beard, asking again. "And where is the babe we will consecrate?"

Nieto pointed to Parker. Rav Natan's eyebrows rose. "Your Shabbat goy? My, my—but Judah Halevi, I have not been able to perform myself for many a year. I thought you had another mohel here or even the father to do the cutting while I pronounced the blessings. My skill is not what it was. Too much fruit of the vine, I confess."

Nieto put his hands on the bigger man's shoulders. He looked into the fat man's bloodshot eyes. "Rav Natan, you will pray and I will operate. Together we will manage. I have sawed off legs and arms injured in battle and sewed up chests and heads opened by explosives. I am sure I can safely trim off some unnecessary tissue. Let me prepare first then you will lead us."

Nieto quickly stripped the covers off the bed and placed layers of toweling over the sheets. He took surgical instruments out of his bag then plunged them into the basin to which he added hot water and a sliver of brown lye soap. He gestured to the Rav.

"Begin, sir," he invited.

"I do not believe this," the Baron muttered. "This is not right. This is not right."

The fat man ignored him, turning to Parker directly, "My son, before you stands a Bet Din, the tribunal of three Jewish men. Yes, I count three here—myself, the distinguished Baron Isaac and the brilliant Doctor Judah Halevi. We will make a judgment on this request. First, tell us what you wish."

"I wish to be a Jew."

"And what do you understand that to mean?"

"I will become part of your people and share your future. I will learn your teachings and your beliefs. I will belong to you and with you."

"How will this be done, my son?"

"Judah will trim my cock so I look like a Jew."

The Baron snorted in derision.

Rav Natan ignored the interruption. "Well, yes, that is the gist of it. But more properly, Judah Halevi will circumcise you according to the covenant between Abraham Ha Rishon,

Abraham the First Jew, and Adonai, Our Lord. You understand that this covenant cannot be undone and you will no longer be a gentile. It is a covenant you make with Adonai and the People Israel. You understand all this."

The Baron began to argue once again. "You cannot do this, Judah. Forgive me, Rav Natan, you seem a good man, but you cannot turn this…this sinner into a Jew. What you plan to do is improper and dangerous."

Rav Natan finally turned to the Baron, his hands folded over his big belly. "So, Baron, the Jews where you come from all have pure souls, do they? They piss wine and shit gold nuggets, I assume. Hmm, where I live, there are good Jews who are learned men and kind men, and there are also smugglers, murderers, dissemblers and thieves among us. Even in high places there are Jews who build schools and orphanages and others—who call themselves Jews—who are fornicators and embezzlers. And there are even some who shun their own sons who seek justice for those who have been abused…."

"Rav Natan," Nieto put his hand on the fat man's shoulders again, "we are moving beyond the point. Pray continue the ritual. Ask again." Nieto then turned to the basin of hot water and started to scrub his arms and hands with the hot soapy liquid.

Rav Natan continued after stroking his beard again and turning back to Parker. "My, my—where were we? Oh, you realize that, by entering the covenant, you will leave your people and, according to them, be condemned to burn in hell for eternity. You will live in countries where you have no rights, where you cannot own land, where you are not permitted to enter certain trades and, oh, yes, you will be given the special privilege of paying extra Jew taxes to the kings and emperors for the honor of living in their ghettoes. And of course, every few generations you will have the extra special privilege of being thrown out to wander and start over somewhere else. You understand this?"

"My God, with such a picture, how could anyone not want to be a Jew? But yes, I still want to become a Jew."

"Tell me again why you wish to become a Jew."

Parker sighed with despair and looked around the room, "I do not know what else to say, Rav Natan. I have thought and thought about this. I have written down questions and studied the answers.

"Do you think me a simple child? I do not do this as a game or an adventure. I have lived among your people and I understand the hardships. There is something that calls to me. Perhaps it is the need to be close to others because there is so much out there that hates us…you. Perhaps it is because I need to follow Judah…I do not know anywhere else that I belong as much as with him and with his people. It is where I want to be."

Rav Natan gazed at Parker, "You wish to become a Jew to follow Judah Halevi? Every Jew must follow the Holy Laws given to us—not a person, but the Holy Word of God Himself. Tell me again, why you wish this? I need to understand you."

Parker was shaking his head. "No, not Judah alone. I wish to join because I wish to belong. I have traveled with the Baron from Vienna to England to Italy and now here. In each place I felt at home with the community…always different but yet so much the same, like relatives who gather and quickly become family again after years apart. I want to belong to your people. Let me belong."

Rav Natan looked at the Baron and at Nieto. "Three times he has made the same request. He has spoken with the words of the blessed Ruth, the ancestor of David Ha Melech—David the King—'let your people be my people.' I am convinced. And you, Judah Halevi?"

"I am convinced."

"And you, Baron?"

The Baron looked at Parker then at Nieto. He conceded, "I will accept this."

Rav Natan then turned to Nieto, "Doctor, I can supervise but you must do the cutting. First let me inspect the knife. It cannot be nicked or bent."

Nieto held the scalpel up to the fat man's face. He nodded in approval. The Rav turned to Parker, holding up a sheet, "We will turn away so that, young man, you can take off your clothes and lie down on the bed. Pull that sheet up over you for modesty." Parker complied as the Rav pulled a small book from his pocket then asked, "It is perhaps time to pour some wine for the blessing." He smacked his lips at the thought. "I will begin with the blessings. I need to know the name you will have in the House of Israel."

Parker now on the bed with the sheet covering him looked at Nieto in confusion.

Nieto said distinctly, "He will be known in the House of Israel as Aaron."

The Baron looked shocked, but the Rav nodded sagely, "He will be Aaron ben Abraham Ha Rishon—as all converts, the son of Abraham our father, the first Jew." The Rav chanted the prayers in loud emphatic Hebrew stressing certain words with a finger pointed to the Heavens or at Parker.

Nieto responded automatically in Hebrew as he set up the instruments on the bed beside Parker. Parker casted a nervous eye at the blades and needles displayed in a shiny row. The reality of the surgery was being laid out, one knife at a time. The Baron stood against the door, a distinct gleam of sweat on his brow as well as Nieto readied the instruments.

Finally Rav Natan approached the far side of the bed opposite Nieto and waited while the doctor spoke softly to the patient. "Robbie, I will give you what I can to deaden some of the pain but this is not an operating room and I am not well prepared. I will be quick and you will not be aware for much of the time. But you will be in pain for some days. And you will be sore for several weeks. Are you still sure?"

Parker nodded, "I want this."

Nieto put some drops of white liquid into a small glass of water. "Drink this," he lifted Parker's head. "It is bitter but it acts quickly."

Parker took one mouthful and gagged. Nieto pinched his nose so the liquid went down. He forced two more gulps down the patient's throat and watched as his eyes closed and his head lolled. He drew the sheet up Parker's legs.

"My my," the Rav remarked. "A young stallion we have here. Mmm—mmm, a fine addition to the community." Nieto put some light green liquid on a cloth and rubbed it on the surgical area.

"What is that, my son?" Rav Natan asked curiously.

"A distillation of snake venom that dulls sensation and cleanses the area. I used it in Alexandria during surgery."

"Mmm, so clever, the sons of Ishmael," the Rav remarked. "A new world is created each day, Praised be He."

With the Rav looking on, making suggestions and comments of approval, Nieto finished the operation. He sutured the edges left by the removal of the foreskin and looked up.

"A work of art," the Rav declared, clapping his hands together.

"Bandage?" Nieto asked.

"For the little pissers, I did not advocate a bandage but, for this colt, perhaps a light bandage until tomorrow and then none. What will you do to avoid arousal for the next few weeks? That can hurt like the devil and even split the stitches. I could send over my mother-in-law. One look at her and even that athletic pecker would not move for weeks."

Nieto stared at the Rav then began to chuckle. He looked over his shoulder to find the Baron shaking his head, trying to hide a grin. "Oh, give up, Isaac. It is too hard to stay angry for long." Nieto turned back to Rav Natan, "Perhaps some valerian to keep him drowsy."

"Or fine wine?" The Rav looked longingly at the wine bottle. "It is now time to toast the newest member of our people."

Nieto smiled, "I shall pour for you, Rav Natan, and ask one more favor. I will need to leave the room for a time. Can you stay to watch over Aaron? There is more wine. If he begins to feel uncomfortable, give him another sip of the white liquid. If that does not calm him, you must come get me. I will be in the sitting room."

"For you, Yehudah Halevi, I will gladly sit with your new brother, toast his health with the Baron's fine wine and read some psalms to wish him a speedy recovery."

There was a knock on the door. The Baron leaned over to open it. Graves announced that Ezekiel had arrived. The Baron looked at Nieto.

"I will be there in a few minutes. Can you ask your man to clean up the sheets and take the basin? I must clean my instruments. Ezekiel will need to wait."

Nieto entered the sitting room a half hour later. It was clear that Ezekiel was annoyed by his tardiness. He was pacing with his hands clasped behind him—hunched over, looking more like a vulture today than a hawk. The blond man with the icy blue eyes stood stonily erect near the door. He nodded coolly at the doctor and waited for the discussion to begin.

"Ezekiel, you are very prompt, as always. And I see that Klaus is with you as always," Nieto remarked, nodding his greeting at the big blond man.

"You have kept us waiting," Ezekiel responded. "It is dangerous for us to wait overlong."

"I apologize, my brother. I needed to take care of a patient. I remind you that I am a doctor. I have a sacred duty to treat those who need my services."

"And the Engländer goy is not here?" Ezekiel asked.

"No, there is no English gentile here," Nieto answered.

Ezekiel eyed him coldly as he considered this. He apparently decided to accept it on face value and indicated that they should all sit on the sofas near the fireplace. Nieto sat down next to the Baron and Ezekiel sat opposite with his blond henchman by his side.

"Ezekiel, you have come with a problem for which you need my help," Nieto pushed the discussion forward.

Ezekiel hunched over so his black eyes were close and level with Nieto's. "I have come to tell you a sad story. Six weeks ago, in a small village near Munich, some Hebrew boys were studying with their teacher, a young rabbi, in their little school house. Suddenly, four masked horsemen approached the building. Following them was a crowd of men and women screaming and pleading with the horsemen to halt their evil plan. But they would not be deterred.

"Two of the horsemen dismounted and barricaded the doors of the school. Another man on horseback broke the window with a staff and then tossed in a torch. The parents watched, wailing and begging but prevented from rescuing their sons by the hooded men armed with torches, swords and axes. Several parents were terribly injured and one died in their attempts to get past the murderers to rescue their children.

"Seven boys and their teacher were burned to death in the fire. When the masked men finally left and the parents could put out the flames, one child, an eighth boy, was found, barely alive, saved by the young rabbi who had lain over him, trying to shield him from the blaze. The boy was able to identify one man by his voice and by something he heard him say. Then that boy, the last witness, died. The man he identified as the leader of the attackers is a local official in Munich."

Nieto moved his gaze away from Ezekiel's eyes and looked past him, over his shoulder, not seeing the sitting room but the little village school in flames. "And?" he asked.

"Klaus here," Ezekiel nodded towards the blond man, "lived in the community for a month. To look at him, you would never believe he is a Jew, would you? Look at those blue eyes and that blond hair. He was able to identify the man mentioned by the child and the three others who were part of the band. It was not very hard. When goyim drink, they boast of the number of Yids they have killed. Interestingly, among them, the killers have eight sons. See how exactly Hashem balances the scales of justice."

"I will do no harm to children," Nieto said sharply.

"I am not suggesting that we visit the sins of the fathers on their children—even though they will someday no doubt proudly follow in their fathers' footsteps. We will all pray for a miracle that will change their hearts," Ezekiel chuckled without humor. It was a ghastly sound. "While we wait for that miracle, we will teach them to fear what happens to those who attack our people. So now we will avenge the eight Jewish children by punishing the four evil-doers who burned them to death."

"Klaus seems more than capable to mete out the harsh justice you seek."

Ezekiel looked fondly at the blond man. "Yes, it was all I could do to keep him from doing so immediately." He turned back to Nieto, "But, as you know, the Gadol insists we abide by our traditions. Two witnesses who saw the crime must be found and must point out the murderers and name their deeds. Then we can sentence them according to the laws of the House of Israel."

"And you need me to...." Nieto wanted to hear exactly what he would be doing. He knew that Ezekiel never hesitated to tell the truth.

"Use your fine skills and your sharp knives to convince them to confess their crimes. They must point out each other because they alone are the remaining witnesses. We will handle the rest."

Nieto looked at his hands with the long graceful fingers that could save lives and charm music from a wooden instrument and create a brother from a friend. He knew he would do this. He would use his skills to make those men give the evidence Ezekiel sought to make their deaths just punishment. He would do this to give the grieving parents a sense that they could find justice in their world, even though he knew it would never bring them peace. He would do this to warn others that they will face punishment for wronging his people. He had sworn to take on this sacred responsibility and through it he had been permitted to draw close to Ezekiel.

It was next to Ezekiel that Nieto felt that the world was in balance. Evil doers were punished for the suffering they caused. With Ezekiel standing by his side as his brother, the tall man's hand on his shoulder, the terrors slunk back into their dark places and gave him some peace. With Ezekiel, Nieto felt himself anchored to a community willing to accept and honor him as he now was.

He sighed his resignation. "You know me well, Ezekiel. You know I will do this. I ask one favor. I must leave Friday morning, not Thursday night. I have some things to do that will require more time."

Klaus responded angrily, "There is nothing you need to do that is as important as getting justice for those children."

"Sha, Klaus," Ezekiel soothed. "Judah will explain so we can understand."

The Baron spoke up, "I need Judah to come with me to an important meeting that will take place tomorrow night. He will be able to leave the next morning."

Ezekiel responded coldly, "An event with aristocrats no doubt who will debate if they should let the Jews stay in their ghettoes or if they should tax them more or maybe if they should throw them out of the markets so the Christian merchants can make more money. Or perhaps," he continued in a quieter tone, "my brother, you have personal affairs that might need to be settled, one way or another?" His black eyes peered with some sympathy at Nieto, who as always wondered just how the man knew so much of what went on in his life.

"Perhaps one of those might be the truth," the Baron responded, "but, if you want my support for your purposes, you will accommodate me in this." Ezekiel and the Baron exchanged cold looks.

Finally, Nieto added quietly, "I need the time, my brother, as you said, to settle personal affairs."

At that, Ezekiel turned his black stare back to Nieto but it had softened. Yes, he agreed, Nieto should have the time he needed to settle his personal affairs. He would leave on Friday morning to travel to a meeting point where he would join up with Klaus and his men and continue on towards Munich. Ezekiel would be waiting for him in Munich. The timetable settled, the two nokmim got up and left quickly.

Nieto turned to the Baron. "What is the important meeting tomorrow night that I must attend with you?"

"I have no idea, Judah, but I saw that you needed a reason to stay longer. Is it Robbie that you are worried about?"

"That and I need time to say good-bye to…the twins. I cannot just disappear. Can you arrange for us to meet? Here or there? It does not matter to me. I must close some doors firmly."

The Baron asked quietly, "Is it over with Elizabeth, Judah?"

Nieto winced as if in pain and looked away, "Isaac, how can it be otherwise? I had some hopes of a future there but I see now it is not possible. Ezekiel's story reminded me that I cannot live in Elizabeth's world and I cannot ask her to live in mine. I must close the doors on such foolish hopes. I see no other way.

"But it is Ariel too. I am trying to warn Ariel off a dangerous path. He thinks his future lies in working with you. You already have Embry. That is enough for one family."

"Judah, you cannot choose everyone's path for them. Your father could not choose yours. You of all of us knows there is something that calls us to travel where we must and make the choices we need to make."

Nieto smiled but there was no mirth to it. "If you believe that, Isaac, if you really believe that, then you must acknowledge that something called Robbie to travel his path and he has made a choice he needed to make. While I am gone, you must see that he is cared for. I will ask Rav Natan to study with him. I will leave Graves the name of a Jewish physician. You must also support him on his path if you meant what you have said. You must do it for me. I cannot be worrying about him while I am in Munich."

The Baron put both hands on Nieto's shoulders and gazed deeply into his eyes, "I will make that promise, Judah. Robbie will be safe here. I still have some suspicion that his motivation was not pure, but I will do this for you. I recognize that you have some deeper understanding about the struggle to find one's place in the world. You chose to diverge from the path set out for you at birth. I never faced such a challenge being content to stay on the course set for me. You have taught me much about the courage to make difficult choices."

"Don't say that, Isaac. You of all people know the truth. There has been more defiance and stubbornness to my choices than courage. I do not want others to follow me. Each must, as you said, find his own path. I choose to believe that Robbie's step was for the best of reasons. For that, we must honor him."

The Baron shook his head. "You are not willing to recognize the good you do or the courage you have. That is the real shame." He tightened his hands on Nieto's shoulders. "Honor that part of yourself as much as you curse the dark deeds you perform. Go. See to Robbie."

The doctor left the sitting room to attend to his patient. The Baron sat in thought for a few minutes then went to his desk. He wrote rapidly then called Graves. He handed the sealed note to the butler. "Have this delivered to the Earl of Aylesford at the Admiralty House. Ask the messenger to wait for the answer."

Thirty-Four

Nieto found Rav Natan snoring in the chair with his head back and mouth open. The Book of Psalms was resting opened face down on top of the fat man's high belly and the two wine bottles stood empty on the table.

Parker was sleeping lightly, his eyelids fluttering with each breath. Nieto placed his fingers on his neck, counted his pulse then felt his forehead. A strong pulse—no sign of shock. He lifted the blanket and checked—no active bleeding. He was pleased with his patient's progress.

He gently shook the Rav awake. "Rav Natan," he whispered. The big man's eyes opened and he smiled at Nieto, putting his hands around the younger man's face.

The Rav whispered back, "Judah Halevi, my son, your brother Aaron seems fine. He made not a peep all the while."

"Rav, I have to leave for some time—a few weeks, a month, maybe more. I want you to teach Aaron as long as the Baron remains here. I will pay for your time when I return."

"Judah Halevi, it will be a mitzvah to my credit to learn with your new brother. Do not diminish it by paying me for it. Some coins for charity would be kind of you. And perhaps a bottle of wine for the scholars to share every now and then would be appreciated," he winked then lumbered to his feet.

The Baron opened the door. "Rav Natan, my carriage will take you wherever you wish. You are welcome to come to teach Robbie—Aaron, I mean—once he is well enough."

The Rav kissed Nieto on his cheeks then placed a hand on his head. "May the Lord bless you and keep you, Judah Halevi, and may you continue to do good for your people."

When the door closed and Nieto was alone with his patient, he went over to check once again. Parker's eyes were now open. He smiled wanly when Nieto approached.

"How are you, Robbie?" Nieto asked.

"I am happy," he answered. "I feel completed. Funny, isn't it? There is less of me here and yet, I feel more whole."

"Is there pain?"

"Oh that. Yes, there is pain. A throbbing soreness but I have had worse," he yawned.

"Wait until you have to piss before you decide you have had worse," Nieto grinned at him.

"When do you leave?"

"Not today and not tomorrow. I will be here to watch over you. I want you to go to sleep again. It is best that you lie still for a few more hours." He lifted Parker's head to the cup of laudanum solution.

Parker shook his head and raised a hand indicating he wanted a moment. He groaned softly as he moved to put his head down, disturbing his lower body's position.

"Before I drink that concoction, tell me about my name."

Nieto began, "Yes, names are important in our tradition. You are Aaron for my brother. As you heard, you are ben Abraham—a son of Abraham. Since you have no Jewish father, you are considered the son of the first Jew—the first one who performed the brit milah—ritual circumcision on himself as a sign of the covenant between him and his descendants and God."

"I heard that tale from Moises. The Ox said that Abraham was ninety years old at the time. And the great miracle was he got up soon after and was able to run to greet the messengers from God. A true miracle considering the pain I am feeling." Both men chuckled at the image. Then Parker continued, "But I saw the Baron's face when my name was given. He was shocked."

"He recognized that I had broken a tradition by having you blessed with that name. It is not the Spanish way to name after the dead. We give the honor to a living person. And he is concerned that I am trying to replace my brother and knows that will never be possible. But I did not want Aaron's name to vanish from memory. You will help his memory live on if anything happens to me. That was important to me.

"But," Nieto continued, "this was definitely not a traditional conversion in any sense. If you wished to marry into an observant family, they would want some documentation of your conversion which of course we do not have."

Nieto stopped when Parker smiled. Ah yes, marriage would not be an issue.

"In any case, no one in the religious community would accept a conversion supervised by Rav Natan. They do not respect him anymore. And in fact we omitted a few requirements. We usually expect a person to spend much time in thought and learning before taking such a step. The brit is the visible evidence. It is a big step to be willing to brand oneself and is usually the last step, not the first. But I believed you when you said you had been thinking on this for a long while." He paused, "I did what I did because I too wanted you to belong with me in the only way that would be possible—for me."

Parker nodded then sighed quietly. At first, Nieto thought that his friend was disappointed that he had again made the boundary between them clear. Then he laid a hand on Parker's head. The patient was running a slight fever. Not unheard of after surgery but it would need to be watched.

"Tell me about your name," Parker said, yawning again.

"I was named at birth Yehudah Halevi ben Mordecai Halevi. I was named after my grandfather, Yehudah, a great scholar, and of course I am the son of Mordecai, another great scholar. Neither of them would acknowledge our connection now. I am Halevi for our ancestors—it means 'the Levite.' We claim to be descendants of the Tribe of Levi who were chosen to work within the Holy Temple. "

Nieto now insisted that Parker drink the laudanum mixture. Then he said, "I need to get some willow bark tea for your fever."

When he returned, he had the tea in one hand and the Baron's guitar in the other. "Let the tea cool a bit. In the meantime, I thought it was time for you to begin your learning. I can play some traditional melodies if you wish."

As the Baron passed the room later, he heard the soft sounds of the guitar and Nieto's voice. *"Hineh ma tov u'ma-nayim, Shevet akh-im gam ya-chad."* He recognized the verses from Psalm 133, "Behold, how good and how pleasant it is for brethren to dwell together in unity."

He opened the door. "How is the patient?"

Nieto kept strumming softly, singing his answer to the song's melody, "He is sleeping. A bit feverish but that is quite normal."

The Baron thought for a moment, "I apologize, Judah. I understand better now why you permitted this."

Nieto stopped strumming and waited to see if Parker stirred from sleep. When he didn't, he responded to the Baron, "Your apology shows you are an honorable man, Isaac. That is why I come when you send for me. Beneath our differences, there is a trust that allows us to continue on the same path. And that is why I can leave Robbie in your care, knowing that you will do right for him—for his sake as well as for mine."

The Baron nodded. "I have sent a message to the Earl requesting a chance for us to dine together tomorrow night and to have some discussions with him on matters that have transpired recently. I think it likely that we will be invited to the Admiralty House. Will that do?"

Nieto nodded and resumed strumming. He began to sing softly again.

A few hours later, he heard the patient moan. He went over the bedside and found the brown eyes staring at him worriedly. "Judah," Parker said grimly, "I need to piss and I am greatly fearful."

Nieto smiled back, "Aye, Robbie, it will burn but it will get better."

The doctor brought the pisspot over and helped the patient up enough to manage. Parker yowled through clenched teeth, "Holy Mother of God! I am on fire."

Nieto cleaned and dried him then helped him to lie down again, remarking with a grin, "When Rav Natan is here, remind him to teach you proper curses for a Jew. Your vocabulary needs to convert as well."

"Not funny," Parker moaned, settling back on the pillows.

As he straightened the covers, Nieto said, "Tomorrow morning, you will get up, sit in that chair for a few hours and take some steps. It will speed your recovery to move more. Also you will need to keep drinking fluids so you will keep pissing. That will also help you recover."

"You are ordering me to piss more? You are indeed a fine torturer. I think that you might be enjoying this a bit too much, doctor. Are you paying me back for tricks I pulled on you in the past?"

Nieto became serious. "Robbie, you asked for this—persistently to me and to a Bet Din. Are you now regretting it?"

"Nay, no regrets. I complain because I know it keeps you close by."

Nieto leaned closer. "Robbie, I need to ask you something."

Parker turned his head on the pillow, raising his eyebrows.

"I will be saying good-bye to the Whartons tomorrow night. The Baron is arranging it. I need to know how it now stands with Ariel."

"Ariel and me?" He paused. Nieto nodded. "Or Ariel and you?" Nieto nodded again. "Well, we have become good friends—friends who can enjoy each other in safety and in agreement that it is nothing more than an amusing way to spend a few hours. He is young, Judah, and still exploring. I think he is not quite sure which direction he might choose or perhaps, as with some men, he might enjoy many paths in his life.

"But you? He still admires you as much as ever and does not know… how to navigate through that dangerous channel between admiration and desire." Parker smiled gently, reflecting on how difficult such a journey was. "It is not easy to sail the narrows between such rocks. But the truth is that you will not be able to spare him the pain of your departure, Judah, despite what you might wish."

Thirty-Five

The Baron received an invitation to dinner for himself and Nieto for the next evening at eight. There was an additional request that they arrive early for separate meetings with the Earl. Nieto welcomed the chance to hand over to both the Earl and the Baron all the pertinent information he had gathered on the Bonner spy ring and the several attempts to steal the new coding rings. He needed to wrap up his various responsibilities before he left for Munich.

To prepare, Nieto spent the morning writing his reports and confirming his notes with Parker. And as he had predicted, Parker was finding the intake of fluids easing the pain of relieving himself and he was able to sit up for a few hours before the throbbing made him seek his bed again. Later in the day, Nieto prodded him to walk a few steps.

His involvement with his patient and with his reports did not distract him from his thoughts of Elizabeth. He kept reminding himself that their plans had been dreams and now they needed to face reality. Together they had spun a fantasy of a future they could share and today, he had to tear it down. But all day, he felt weighed down with grief.

The Baron and Nieto set off for the Admiralty House at six o'clock. After they were ushered into the Earl's office, Nieto presented his report to the Earl, indicating where the gaps in the information still existed and suggesting how they might find the man with the crossed eye who had given the orders to the Italians. He added his own belief that, although the man had told the Italians he was English, they had discerned an accent making at least one of them believe the man was also Italian. This made the connection to a Florentine aristocrat more likely.

The Earl listened intently but made few comments and asked no questions. Suddenly he interrupted Nieto, saying he wished to speak with the Baron alone.

Nieto objected. "My lord, the Baron was not present at these events so, if you have questions, they should be directed to me."

The Earl repeated his request firmly, "I understand that, Mr. Nieto. I wish to speak with the Baron about other matters which require immediate decisions. Please wait outside, sir."

Nieto paced back and forth in the anteroom. Something was shifting among the Earl, the Baron and himself. He had been the Baron's advisor on working with the Earl and, more recently, with his son, the Viscount. Now he was being excluded as the aristocrats seemed to be realigning their relationships.

Perhaps their differences over the tactics involving the twins had indeed created a deep rift between the Baron and himself. And being followed so soon by their conflict over the sincerity of Robbie's conversion had perhaps further deepened the schism. Or quite possibly, the allegiances that bound the upper classes together against those outside their circle were being reasserted. He was, after all, a man without a title, without power, or wealth—all the prerequisites for respect in their world.

A door opened and Ariel appeared. He smiled at Nieto as he approached. "Judah, how are you? The last time I saw you was days ago at the groom's party. I hope you did not suffer from all your drinking and carousing."

Nieto's eyes narrowed. "I remember the headaches from the grappa but tell me more about my carousing."

Ariel, realizing his error, hid his mistake with a laugh and a shrug. "Oh, nothing more than some dancing and gambling which you did very well despite your drinking."

Nieto was relieved. "I worry during such an evening that I might have offended someone or been an embarrassment."

"It was nothing like that, "Ariel said, putting his hands on the doctor's shoulders and smiling at him. Nieto stepped back causing the young man's hands to fall.

"Ariel, I must tell you that I will be leaving tomorrow and will be gone for several weeks. You will probably be returned to London by then so tonight will be a good-bye dinner—good-bye perhaps for a long time."

Ariel shook his head, his smile undiminished, "Away, Nieto, for a long time? I do not think that. There is much to hold you among us—your future with Elizabeth…and our special friendship. If you must go, you will not be gone for long. You will come back to us so we can go on. Do not fear. You will see."

The door to the Earl's study opened and the Baron stepped out. "Good evening, Sir Ariel. I am sorry to interrupt but I must ask Mr. Nieto to return to the Earl now."

Ariel smiled again, gesturing with a flourish towards the open door as if urging the doctor to enter. At Ariel's smiling confidence, Nieto felt a chill go down his spine.

The Earl was standing by a window, looking towards the setting sun. He turned to Nieto and, with a smile, ushered him to the alcove where, just a few days before, Nieto had met with his mother and sister.

As they sat, the Earl began to speak, still smiling at the doctor. "Mr. Nieto, I must say that I have been very impressed by you. I know we differed on the strategies used to transport the coding wheels safely out of England. Despite our disagreement on that point, I know you to be an honorable man. Lord Embry, Lady Elizabeth and Sir Ariel are all in accord as to your wisdom, your bravery, your courage and your kindness. This has been confirmed as well by the Baron."

Nieto did not move. He continued to gaze at the Earl, his piercing blue eyes wary. He kept thinking about Ariel's confident smile.

"First, I would like to speak with you about our family's recent history so you understand how we must navigate through potentially difficult waters.

"You are of course aware that the Countess and I were raised in different faiths. I, in fact, had no real faith. We were proper Church of England as befitted our station. It was expected in our traditional roles as lords of the manor—part of our social position, what was required of us but nothing taken too seriously nowadays.

"However, the Countess had strong ties to her faith. When she decided to be my wife, she was not welcomed into my family. However, I was an only son and the earldom's estates were entailed to the male line. My family had to accept my marriage although they made their distaste clear.

"I was so angered by their refusal to welcome my wife that I did not care if the schism was ever bridged over. I did not object when the Countess raised the children in her faith. It appeared to me the height of hypocrisy to insist that the next generation carry on the masquerade of religiosity to bow to society's prejudices. And we truly believed that by the time the children considered marriage, society would be more accepting. That disastrous birthday ball proved that we were naïve.

"As the world is now, as unfair as it seems, our sons will have easier paths than our daughter. Embry can marry almost anyone he chooses. He will be an Earl and inherit great wealth. There are many families in English society that would welcome an alliance with him, regardless of his faith. He can of course also choose among the great Hebrew families of our country or of the Continent since he has the power to raise one of their daughters in rank and yet not have her lose connections to her community.

"Ariel is similarly situated. He will be wealthy, a Viscount and likely have no difficulty finding a suitable mate."

The Earl chuckled with confidence. "After all, I know that the Baron has four younger sisters who will need husbands."

Then the Earl became somber."My concern must be for Lady Elizabeth. She will inherit wealth as well but, in her case, her wealth could put her in peril. The Countess and I fear that men will seek her hand to have access to her fortune. Common law will give her husband control not only of her estate but also her children and their upbringing. So we are determined that she marry someone whom she respects and loves and who in turn loves her so wholeheartedly that he will protect her and her children. I had assumed that such a man would be her equal, of course, with his own wealth and titles and a leadership position in his or our community. A man such as that would marry her for the quality of her person, not needing her dowry at all.

"However, she has made her wishes clear to me and they concern you, Mr. Nieto. In brief, she asked me to give you permission to seek her hand in marriage. I expressed my concern to her about your path in life. I showed her how that path would make it impossible for her and her children to live in society, to move with freedom among others of their class and even to visit with her brothers and their families, openly, without fear. Her children would suffer, prevented by the secrecy and danger surrounding your work to take up the lives that would be their birthrights.

"I told her that I would discuss my concerns with the Baron. With his suggestions we have come to some stratagems that will allow me to wholeheartedly encourage your suit."

Nieto sat very still. His hands were curled into tight fists as he continued to stare into the Earl's face. Finally he asked, "And the 'stratagems' that you and the Baron have come to… that will make me an appropriate suitor?"

"I detect distaste in your tone, Mr. Nieto. I suggest you hear me out before reacting. We will come to a mutual understanding." The Earl smiled confidently again. Judah thought, Ariel's smile was just like that—so confident, so self-assured.

"Pray, go on, Earl. I am eager to learn my future."

The Earl now spoke with authority of a powerful man, "It is quite simple, Mr. Nieto. The Baron and I still need your talents on behalf of the Crown and the allies. Your other activities must cease—those that you do with those vigilantes. While you are involved in such universally deplored activities, you put my daughter and my future grandchildren at great risk.

"In return for your cessation of those other activities, I will set you up in a surgical practice of your own in London and the Baron will provide research facilities in his teaching hospital in Vienna. You and your family will have homes in each city. You will have legitimate reasons to travel back and forth and thus you can be available to us when we need your assistance.

"Of course, most of the time you will be free to focus on medical matters in your specialty. The Viscount has already benefited from your skill and it is his and my wish that others soon benefit from your continued research. You can be a contributor to medical advancement, a leader of your community, and, when needed, an aide to us in our efforts to make Europe safer for all, including for your own people. Perhaps you might even receive a title of your own one day for your service to the Crown."

The Earl sat back, smiling, watching the emotions cross Nieto's face as the stunned man considered his good fortune.

"And, in return, I get Elizabeth as bride and, with her, access to all her fortune," the doctor finally stated with a coolness that put the Earl back on his guard.

"Mr. Nieto, this would not have been discussed except that Lady Elizabeth," the Earl emphasized her title," made her wishes known to me and said they were your wishes as well."

"Yes, Earl, she was correct. I cannot conceive of marrying anyone but Eliza," Nieto responded. " She is beautiful, kind, intelligent, spirited, and brave. In my wildest dreams, I never imagined that a woman as wonderful as Eliza would consider me for a husband."

The Earl hesitated. The use of the familiar name irked him but then he nodded, deciding to overlook the impropriety.

Nieto continued, "However, I do not recognize the man you describe who fits so neatly into your plans. You wish to cut me down in size to fit into a costume tailored for some other man—a man willing to give over his freedom to perform a part in a drama that you will direct. He may be a surgeon, he may invent some tools that can alleviate pain and he may become a leading citizen. And when you need his help, he must do as he is ordered.

"Does Eliza accept this plan as you have presented it to me?"

The Earl nodded, "This has been discussed with her and she understands that your agreement is the condition for my approval of your suit."

"Tell me, Earl Aylesford, in all honesty, did Eliza make any objection? Tell me truly how she came to accept this solution to the problem that I present to you. Did she throw the cutlery across the table? Did she stand and argue with you, her eyes blazing with fury?" Nieto's eyes stared into the distance and his lips trembled into a small smile of remembrance.

As the Earl watched the doctor's expression, his own composure faltered for a moment. A shadow of unease passed over the aristocrat's features as he recognized the gentle expression on the doctor's face. He recalled facing his own father to argue for his choice of his bride. He had thought his father cruel and bigoted. How easy it had been to think that then. But now facing the man who seemed to love his daughter as sincerely as he had loved the daughter of the banker Da Costa, he could only think that this handsome blue-eyed man lived a life so far outside the norms of society that his daughter would be in great danger. He was now fighting, as a father should, for his own daughter's happiness and safety by making these demands.

Then he thought, if this man really loved Eliza....So the Earl tamped down his sympathy to say firmly, "Lady Elizabeth heard my thoughts on this subject and recognized the truth of what I described. You, Mr. Nieto, must change your life and your commitments to permit her and her children to live the way they should in the world they will inherit. She accepts that condition now and I must hear that you do as well."

Nieto heard in the seasoned diplomat's carefully chosen words that the battle had already been waged and lost before he had arrived this evening. He still asked calmly as if the outcome was yet to be determined, "Yesterday I was told a terrible story about children burned to death because they were Hebrews. I was asked to help their families get justice. Would the man you would accept as a son-in-law be permitted to help them?"

"The Baron has assured me that there are others who can take up the cause for vengeance."

"And if everyone decides that someone else will take up the cause instead of them? Doesn't that mean that possibly no one will do anything? It is never easy for anyone to fight back."

Nieto shook his head slowly, "Earl, I have lost much of what I loved when I chose my path but I could always claim that the cause was so important that it gave meaning to my life. If I give up what I believe is the right thing to do for the very wonderful life you will permit me to share with Elizabeth, all my previous deeds are meaningless. They were only what I did until someone made me a better offer. It leaves me with nothing of my own—no family, no past, no accomplishments, no purpose other than to obey you and the Baron."

"Mr. Nieto, Judah, if I may, how did you ever think to marry my daughter? Or any other gentleman's daughter? What type of life could you provide for her? Surely you would not wish her to live as you must—hidden from view, away from family and friends, fearing retribution for your deeds. You are a brilliant man. You must have realized that your life had to become more open, more regular, more acceptable to society in order to permit your wife and your children to live full lives in safety."

Nieto sat very still and, while he still faced the Earl, his eyes were fixed again on that distant space past the aristocrat's shoulder. When he brought his gaze back to the man in front of him, the doctor's face had tightened with grief. "Yes, of course, you are correct. I had allowed myself to succumb to a fantasy that even I knew was not possible. I had dreamt that my love for Elizabeth had changed the world as it had changed me—that somehow in that new world, I could have everything I wanted—love, family and good works. When we were together, we were both able to believe in that dream.

" Now your words have awakened me to the real world once again. Elizabeth and her children should never have to live in my world. Either the world must change or I must change. And, as you well know, unreasoning hatred and terrible injustice have not yet metamorphosed into understanding and fairness to make of this world a Garden of Eden. So the only solution is that I become something other than what I am—that I solve the problem of being Judah Halevi Nieto as you suggest.

"You believe that your offer would permit your daughter to be happy and for me to have a comfortable life as a rich and respected man honored by your society. In your world, money and titles wield great influence. You can demand that people change and live according to your commands.

"However, Earl, I cannot obey your orders and become other than what I am. I have gone through too much pain and despair to find my own path. To give up the causes that make my life worth anything at all would make me hate myself for all I have ever done and what I have become. I could not be a loving husband for your daughter. Instead she would be married to a very angry and disappointed man who had no power or dignity other than what you allowed him to have. She would not have me. She would have someone you created for her." Nieto repeated in a wondering tone, "Yes, your power would create an image of a man who had no real power to do anything. An empty bauble, not a thing of value."

The Earl looked at him in amazement. "Judah, pray think on what you are saying. This has been a shock. Take time. Think of the great opportunities I offer. You will have a family again—a wife, a mother, brothers, a place in society. I believe that you feel affection for the Countess and my sons. I know they care a great deal for you. Ariel has told me that he would welcome you as a brother. You need never be alone again."

Nieto stood first, a clear break in protocol but the Earl said nothing and rose to face him. "Oh yes, I can join your family. You believe that will fill the chasm left by the loss of my own as if my history and my people were nothing and could be easily replaced. How shallow do you believe me to be? Or is it that you cannot conceive that anyone might find this offer offensive and demeaning?

"You would hold me as if I was a child—a coddled child—but still a child—not a man. It has always been the way of those in your class to believe that your wishes should command those of us living outside your gates. It is the sad truth of history that you and your peers have long had the power to force others to obey, to convince us that we must be grateful to be noticed and supremely thankful to serve you.

"And once again, you use your own child, your daughter, Elizabeth, to further another plan. You would trap me using her as the lure. You would own me and my talents and my dreams and my ideals. What type of husband could I be? What type of father to my children?

"I must leave now. I feel the power of your bribe, your offer to fulfill my dreams. I fear my resistance will weaken."

Without pausing to be excused by the Earl, Nieto left the room. The Baron was waiting outside. One look at the doctor's face told him that nothing had gone as planned. Nieto walked past him, down the staircase and out of the Admiralty House.

He did not return. When the Earl described to the Baron what he believed happened, the Austrian asked to be excused. He feared what Nieto might do. As he was leaving, he saw Elizabeth waiting for him in the antechamber. Ariel was standing at the door leading to the dining room.

Elizabeth's face was bloodless and she spoke in barely a whisper, "He has gone…gone without saying anything to me? How could he be that cruel?"

The Baron looked at her with pity, "My dear Lady Elizabeth, I saw his face—it was if he had been hollowed out and left empty. He had no words. I must find him. I fear for him."

Tears started to run down the young woman's face and Ariel went to put his arms around his sister. He looked at the Baron with his own eyes glazed with tears—the twins sharing their grief again as they had shared so much in their lives.

When the Baron arrived at his suite, he found shock and despair there as well. Robbie stood in the sitting room, wringing his hands. "Isaac, what happened? Judah came, took all his things and left. He said nothing. He left only this note for you."

The Baron took the folded note and opened it to a message written in Nieto's elegant precise Hebrew. He translated it out loud as he read, "'If I am not for myself, who will be for me? If I am not for others, what am I? And if not now, when?' It is from Rabbi Hillel, a great teacher. Judah is telling us that he must stay on the path he has set for himself because that path defines his purpose in life."

"He is gone?"

The Baron stared at the note, thinking out loud," I must find Ezekiel. Judah will go to Ezekiel to tell him he is free."

"Free? How free? I thought he and Elizabeth…? That is over?"

The Baron nodded then added, "He went without saying anything to Elizabeth or Ariel."

"Nor to me," Parker muttered, turning back into the guest room.

The Baron sent messengers to the places in the harbor where he suspected nokmim or people who knew them might be. He knew if any nokim heard the Baron was asking for Ezekiel, the news would be delivered somehow. It was midnight when a message was slipped under the front door of the suite after the knocker was rapped loudly. It contained one phrase, "In one hour."

Promptly an hour later, there was another rap on the door. Ezekiel stood there, this time accompanied by Nieto, looking drawn but very much in control.

The Baron ushered them both into the sitting room. He asked Graves to see if Parker could join them. As soon as he entered, Parker noticed that Nieto was dressed all in black, just like Ezekiel. The doctor was also holding a wide-brimmed black hat just like the tall man's one. Parker thought, with a shock, Ezekiel must hide his tell-tale white streak in his dark hair and Judah must hide his brilliant blue eyes. They will be hunted men soon—after Munich. They will need to blend into the dark shadows for many weeks. And, he realized with despair, I will not be anywhere near to help him.

No one said a word until Parker sat with the Baron, facing Ezekiel and Nieto. The diplomat began, "Judah, I am so sorry. The Earl thought only to keep his daughter safe. He did not mean to diminish what you have done but to offer you a way to live with honor and to welcome you into his family."

Nieto shook his head, "Not this Judah Halevi Nieto, who sits before you now. What he actually said was if I became less who I am and more what he wanted, he would welcome that newly-created man into his family.

"It was a blessing that he said it. I have learned much about myself in the past few hours. I am the sum of what I have done and what I feel compelled to do. I have a family now—whose members live as I do and believe what I believe, who accept the same responsibility—to balance the scales of justice for their people. Those few men who now have all the power must be challenged when they do not use it righteously and must be punished when they use it for evil. How can I then live my life according to the commands of those in power?

"I cannot do that and live as a man. Elizabeth should not be bound to such a false image of a man."

Parker started to say something but stopped. He looked at Ezekiel. The black eyes gazed back at him with a curious expression as if the man was not sure how to classify the "Engländer" now. Ezekiel said quietly, "I am told to call you Aaron, a brother to Yehudah Halevi. I have been asked not to call you 'goy' anymore. Speak now, Aaron ben Avraham."

"Judah, it is not like you to leave without saying good-bye to people you care about. Did you not want to speak with Elizabeth?"

Nieto gazed at Parker with sadness, "A closing soliloquy as the curtain comes down? That happens in the theatre but not in life. What could I say? Eliza, your father offered you to me if I was willing to become less than myself, if I was willing to become his pawn... and yours, Isaac." There was no animosity when he turned to the Baron, just resignation.

Nieto returned his gaze to Parker, "And then I would have to say that, despite my love for her, I could not destroy myself. If I did, she would have someone who looked like me but was dead inside. So I chose my survival over a life with her because I could not live like that without going mad."

"And me, Judah? Are you leaving me behind as well?"

Nieto smiled at Parker. "Nay, Robbie, I am here because you are the one person I could not leave without saying good-bye—for now. You cannot come yet. You are not yet recovered and the men I go with are not ready to accept you. I will work for that day. When it comes, God willing, you will be allowed to follow me if you still wish it. That is so, is it not, Ezekiel?"

Ezekiel continued to study Parker while he said frankly, "I make no promises, Aaron ben Avraham. You must learn our ways while I watch and consider if you can join us. I must be convinced that you entered the Covenant with the sincere wish to join our people—all our people, not just one of them, and that you are willing to live according to our teachings." And then a small ironic smile emerged on his thin face. "Aye, you must learn to live as one of us and I must come to believe in you because Judah Halevi wishes both his brothers with him on our righteous 'endeavors.'"

He offered his thin hand with the long fingers. When Parker shook Ezekiel's hand, he was surprised to find it strong and warm.

Nieto turned to the Baron. "Isaac, what you do has value for our people. I will come when I can—when Ezekiel can free me from our 'endeavors' to help you with yours." The genteel term "endeavors" had become an ironic joke among these men to hide the bloody reality of their deeds.

The Baron held out his hand to Judah. When the younger man took it, the Baron clasped it between both of his. "May the Lord keep you safe, Yehudah Halevi, and grant you the blessing of peace."

When the two men left the suite, Parker went to the window hoping to catch a last glimpse of the friend who had honored him as a brother. But nothing was visible except the gloom of the dark night into which Judah Halevi had already disappeared.

Epilogue

Embry stood by the railing on the Ruby Goddess with Elizabeth at his side, her thin arm curled around his. Ariel had left them, off renewing his friendships with Georgie and the other crew men. Elizabeth gazed at the massive shape of the Rock of Gibraltar, retreating slowly into the distance as the sails caught the wind and the ship gained speed.

The Viscount looked at his sister's profile—still lovely but so changed. There was a new maturity that overpowered the joys and enthusiasms of her younger self. He sighed with sadness. It was the transformation from child to adult with all the awareness of the pain life could hold. He pressed her arm against his body, clasping her hand in his other hand.

"I think I am beginning to understand, Samuel," she said without looking at him. "It wasn't that he did not love me as much as I thought. It was that he could not see how to be selfish enough to abandon all he believes in. I had thought that there would be no difficulties. Unlike Maman and Papa, we were of the same faith and traditions so we would not need to confront those divisions within our family. But the way we express those beliefs are so different—that was the chasm between us. It could be ignored for a while but it would always be there—waiting for one or the other of us to fall in and disappear. He understood that. I am just beginning to comprehend it."

Embry nodded. "I said a while ago that Judah was one of the few men I respect. And though he caused you much pain, I know him well enough to recognize that this was a great sacrifice for him. He did something that few men would do. He gave up the dearest thing in the world to him because he feels he has a purpose that transcends his own desires."

Elizabeth finally looked at her brother. "So he is to be a martyred saint to his people?" Her voice was bitter.

"No—not a saint for sure. It was a courageous act but there was much fear in it as well. Judah feared that his life would become meaningless—that he would be lost to everything he was in the past and that he would be powerless to act freely in the future. In that, he was right. He was asked to become part of a society that would expect him to play a scripted role. I know well the golden shackles of that world. In doing that, he feared he would no longer be the man you fell in love with and he did not want that for you or for himself."

Her lips trembled. "But it was wrong of him not to give me that choice. He made a choice for himself. He never spoke to me so we could have come to an understanding—perhaps a way to go on together. Or a promise to wait until things became clearer."

Embry sighed. "I think that was his greatest fear—that if he faced you, he would falter and surrender. You have great power over him. So he avoided the possibility."

There was a pause then she said, her chin lifted, looking more like the defiant girl she had been just a few weeks ago, "I am very angry at Papa. I thought he would understand and be more willing to help us. He and Maman—they fell in love even though they came from different worlds and faced much opposition. Why was Papa so unbending in his terms? Surely, he has been more willing to negotiate with foreign diplomats."

Embry smiled, knowing she could not see him, staring as she was again at the Rock in the distance. "Ah, Eliza, you are his princess—not a wizened foreign diplomat. His heart was entwined in the discussion. He could not bear the thought of the danger you and your children would face if you lived Judah's life. So he demanded that Judah join our world.

"Our parents, despite their different faiths, lived in the same world. They were both raised in great wealth and with an understanding that they were to be paragons in their communities. It has ever been their expectation that we—their children—would lead in the same way. Judah walked away from that role in his world and has lived a hidden life with much danger. The Earl could not accept that for you."

Elizabeth faced him again, her cheeks flushed with shame. "I am really angriest at myself, Samuel. I did not fight hard enough for him. I did not confront Papa the way I have confronted you so often—to force you to give me what I wanted if not by the righteousness of my argument then by sheer persistence. I was frightened that I would win. I was afraid what my victory might have meant. The truth was I did not want to give up everything I have to go with him into his dark dangerous world. Did I not love Judah enough to make that choice? Am I a spoiled, selfish child still? Or a coward?"

"Not a coward, Elizabeth, and not a selfish child. You are honest. Honesty has always been one of your finest qualities and I have admired you for it.

"Most people have years to think through their choices—even choices not as difficult as yours were. You are just eighteen and have been forced to learn much about the outside world in a very short time. It is a dark and dangerous world. Judah is…well, he and I are of an age where we have spent more time thinking about the path we choose to travel."

"Will I ever see him again, Samuel?"

"I am not sure he would permit that to happen—at least not in the near term. I will be in contact with him from time to time in the future. He is still one of the men the Baron relies on and we will be working together—on some of those mechanical things you call my 'toys' if not on larger endeavors. I will make sure you know he is well, if you wish. And if you permit, I will let him know how you fare."

Elizabeth wiped away the tear that was making its way down her cheek. "I thought that he was my beshert—the other half of my soul, yet I let him go. But I cannot conceive of going on without him. The hole in my heart is so great."

Embry took a small wrapped object from his pocket. "The Baron said Judah wanted you to get this when the ship had left Gibraltar."

Elizabeth regarded the silk packet that her brother held out to her. She made a mewling sound but no motion to reach for it. Quietly, Embry unwrapped it for her.

Nestled in the silk was a gold chain from which hung a single red stone encircled with pearls. It was a simple ornament, one that a man of limited means might give to a woman he loved.

Embry murmured, "'A woman of valor…is valued above rubies,' so it is said in the Book of Proverbs. Judah wanted you to know how much he values you. I believe he also wanted to call on your valiant nature to overcome your grief."

More tears slowly slid down Elizabeth's face as she took the necklace from Embry's hand. She clutched it tightly to her lips but said nothing.

Embry leaned over and kissed her head. "Time, Elizabeth, is a great healer. You will find your own path in life. As Judah often reminded me, you can only write one page at a time in the book of your life. You cannot turn back to change what you wrote before and we all will ultimately read the same final chapter. So you can only do what appears right to you each day. I pray you both find peace along the way."

Brother and sister stood side by side, arms linked, watching the Rock grow smaller and smaller as their distance from it increased. Even when it had descended out of sight beneath the horizon, Elizabeth stared in the same direction. She knew the Rock was still there. Nothing would move it and it will take millennia for it to change in any significant way.

Learn how it all began…

You Shall Know Our Names

by

Ezekiel Nieto Benzion

The First Tale from the Judah Halevi Journals

Soon after his ninetieth birthday, the "Lion of Labor," Reuben Nieto Benzion, handed his grandson, Ezekiel, his most cherished possessions—the 200-year-old journals of the doctor, Judah Halevi Nieto, preserved by his family in the "old country" because they honored the man who wrote them. Reuben Benzion ordered his grandson to tell him "the stories Judah wanted us to know. Let me know the names of these great men in our family before I die. Write down their tales for future generations to understand who they were and what their legacy is."

Learn what the Halevi journals revealed and what they veiled behind clues, puzzles and vague names and dates. Discover how the blue-eyed Spanish doctor fought his way past his own grief to dedicate himself to confronting oppression and hatred. Find out how the mysterious man called the Hawk transformed the doctor's life—rescuing him from his old terrors to lead him into new battles.

And the tales continue...
Coming in Summer 2014

Claims of Family

The Third Tale from the Judah Halevi Journals

The doors of The Riding Club in Vienna open to only a few men, all of them powerful, privileged and wealthy, all of them men who prefer the company and love of other men. It is a world of secret passions that Darius, its master, manipulates with great skill. He uses the secrets he collects to guarantee the safety of the Club's members and the men who "entertain" them there.

Darius has his own secrets. He loves the mysterious Italian, Nance, who, performing as Miss Nancy, viciously attacks the powerful men of the Empire. Now Darius holds the key to Nance's fondest dream. Can he keep the news secret so that Nance remains close to him and safe from harm?

Others want the truth to come out to right the wrongs done to innocent people. Darius finds himself facing powerful men determined to use Nance to reach their own ends.

Darius needs help to protect all he loves. He is advised to go to the man known as the Hawk for help. But the Hawk will not help men whose lives and loves are "abominations" and Darius will not demean himself to beg him to do so. The Baron von Tedesco, working within the official channels, and Judah Halevi Nieto, working in the shadows, convince these two powerful men that by becoming allies they might win against the forces that oppress both their peoples.

Made in the USA
Charleston, SC
20 May 2014